Living Promises
Amy Lane

Dreamspinner Press

Published by
Dreamspinner Press
4760 Preston Road
Suite 244-149
Frisco, TX 75034
http://www.dreamspinnerpress.com/

Living Promises

Cover Art by Paul Richmond http://www.paulrichmondstudio.com

ISBN: 978-1-61372-046-2

Printed in the United States of America
First Edition
July, 2011

eBook edition available
eBook ISBN: 978-1-61372-047-9

Readers love *Amy Lane*

http://www.dreamspinnerpress.com

To survivors and researchers and doctors and sufferers and people who have succumbed and people who live with hope and people who volunteer their time and people who pray for all of the above.

Prologue

Collin: Beware of Reckless Driving

WHEN Collin Waters was five years old, he was sitting in the backseat of his parents' Ford Taurus while his father drove, singing loudly to REM's "Losing My Religion." He was playing with his trucks, which he very much enjoyed, even though he would rather take them apart and put them back together than play "freeway." Dad had asked—very politely too—that Collin not take things apart in the back of the car. Since Dad was a big man with a deep voice who tried very hard not to yell, even when Collin dumped cereal over the floor and forgot to do his reading and let out his big sister's rat on complete accident and used his mom's favorite DVDs for rocket-launch pads and dressed the cat up in his engineer's outfit so he'd have someone to play with, well, Collin tried to do what he said.

Collin adored his dad.

Right now, that off-key rumble of "Losing My Religion" was comforting. If Dad was singing, he was in a good mood, and since today was snack day and Collin was very sure the cookies in his backpack would be a success, Collin could respect a good mood. Dad would sing, and then Collin would go to school and his mom's awesome cookies would make this a very good day.

Then Dad's singing was interrupted by Dad's voice, fractured and uncertain. "Oh… oh God…."

The car swerved, and then swerved again, and Collin was thrown against the door, and he began to cry.

"Daddy? Daddy? *Daddy!*"

But his dad was slumped over the steering wheel, his beefy shoulders canted sideways and his eyes closed, and the car was bumping, thumping over the dividers and over a sidewalk and *wham!* into a pole, and Collin's head hurt from smacking on the seat in front of him, and his shoulder hurt from the seatbelt, and his daddy wasn't answering, and his backpack was on the ground, and his cookies were all mashed and....

By the time the paramedics got there, he was swinging his feet against the bottom of his seat, screaming, "Daddy! Daddy, wake up! Daddy! Daddy, wake up!" with irritating regularity.

But as he figured out later, when he was older, Grayson Waters had just suffered a massive fatal coronary and would never, ever wake up.

Collin's mother did all right then. It was hard—Collin and his four older sisters never doubted, even once, that the love of Natalie Waters's life was her big, bluff mechanic husband with the receding blond buzz cut and blunt fingers and the off-key voice that could sing children's songs with a surprisingly comic lilt. But Natalie had started her own business, and everybody pitched in, waited tables, manned the grills, or helped clean up, and they always had enough to eat and they always had a place—the same place, the tiny-for-a-family-of-seven house in Levee Oaks—and they always knew they were loved.

But something in Collin seemed to have rattled out of his ears as the unmanned car had thumped across the road, jumped the curb, and smacked into the telephone pole. Some vital piece of human machinery that kept dangerous impulses in check and called strongly for self-preservation was decidedly missing. It was like Collin, even at five, had seen his father die and decided that, hell, if it was going to happen at random, it might as well be encouraged and even welcomed.

Or that was his mother's explanation for the next thirteen years.

It was what she said the day he was six and a half, and she arrived at home just in time to watch him jump from the roof of the house to the roof of the garage to the neighbor's hedge, because, he said, he saw a superhero do it in a movie. That earned him a trip to the hospital, a cast and a pair of crutches, and moratorium on superhero movies for the next three years. (His older sisters never forgave him for this.)

It did not, however, fix the problem.

Neither did wrecking his bike when using the garage door as a stunt-ramp (and getting thirteen stitches and an overnight stay for suspected internal damages) when he was ten.

Nor did wrecking his bike against the *neighbor's* garage when he was twelve because, in his words, "We were out of ice cream, and Joanna wouldn't get me any."

Nor did the *several* near-expulsions for fighting in junior high and high school.

Nor did having his car, earned with his allowance for waiting tables in his mom's diner, spray-painted with *fucking fighting faggot* in his junior year, after he came out by wearing a rainbow goalie's jersey on the soccer field. His coach was especially pissed—he was the best goalie the team had ever had, and no amount of homophobia in the town's history could make the guy kick Collin off the team.

No. Collin was not one to let experience get in the way of a good idea or terrifying fearlessness. His mother often, sometimes tearfully and sometimes at the top of her lungs, told him that she was going to bury him before he was twenty-five, and he would say, nonchalantly and with no apparent regret, "You know I love you. Give me a good sendoff."

But he was not so nonchalant the day his mother and sisters came home early from the movies and found him balls-deep in Tommy Kennedy's ass, as Tommy was bent over the dryer in the garage. He was, in fact, fairly mortified—and Tommy was downright hysterical, and not with laughter.

Tommy was the best fuckbuddy in Levee Oaks High School, though, and after Crick Francis had come out and graduated two years before, Collin had a nice little stable going to pick from too. Collin heard the garage door open and saw the halo glare of the white lights and kept pumping his hips while saying, "Just shut up, Tommy, and fucking come!" Being the gentleman that he was, he nailed Tommy's prostate and gave him a reach-around. Tommy squealed and came all over his hand, and Collin grunted and poured himself into Tommy.

The car's engine turned off, and Collin hugged Tommy to his chest for a moment. "Run inside, clean up, run out the front door," he murmured. "She's gonna be pissed at me, but she's not gonna go gunning for you."

Tommy ran off, all the better to live to tell the story about a zillion times in the coming months, and Collin turned to face his mother.

The girls had squeaked in disgust and run inside, missing Tommy by moments and leaving Natalie shaking her head in pained resignation.

"Aww Jesus...." Natalie sighed and kicked at the tire of the car.

Collin, for once feeling just a tad self-conscious, grabbed a towel out of the clean laundry and wrapped it around his waist.

"Aww, Jesus, Collin," Natalie said again. "Tell me you at least used a condom?"

Collin blinked. "A condom?"

"Dammit, you took health class! You know, a condom? Syphilis, Chlamydia, HIV?"

He had taken health class, it was true. He'd slept through it, cheated on the tests, and scoffed at the just-say-no culture of fear taught in American public schools. He had not, however, been caught naked by his mother, having a piece of the local fuckbuddy tail. Maybe it was being in front of his mother, and maybe it was because eighteen was half a month away and maturity was crawling into his brain like an ant in his ear, but for some reason, a missing piece of Collin's human machinery reasserted itself in the workings of his mind.

In that moment, he felt fear.

Chapter 1

Jeff: Caution: Broken Heart Ahead

"IS THAT good, baby?" Kevin purred in Jeff's ear, his thick, dusty dark brown fingers twisting savagely at Jeff's nipples.

Jeff Beachum screamed and collapsed forward onto the pillow. *Oh. My. God.*

Jeff had never considered himself a size queen, but Kevin was hung like a bear on Viagra, as long as the guys in the stroke mags bragged about, thicker than a sixteen-ounce water bottle and—*glory-God-mother-Mary-Jesus-crap-and-fuck*—uncut, and he was ramming that monster up Jeff's ass and *gimme-hallelujah* did it feel so *goooooooooood....*

Kevin's chuckle was strained behind him, and Jeff screamed into the pillow again as Kev hit his prostate. *Fuck. Fuck, fuck, fuck, fuck, fuck, fuck, fuck, fuck!*

Jeff's cock (modestly sized, he was the first to admit) was leaking a steady stream of pre-come into the condom, and Jeff wished for the umpteenth time that he'd thought to get tested a year ago instead of six months ago. If his twelve-month window came up clear when Kevin's did, he'd consider going condom-free.

Kevin pulled back and slammed forward again, and Jeff whined, wriggling his ass and reaching to yank on his cock, because he wasn't shy in the least. Kevin had gotten tested about a week before he met Jeff, so Jeff figured they had a year before they could do it bareback, and at the moment, he didn't give a shit.

"You like that, club boy?" Kevin rasped, and Jeff whine-begged some more and wriggled his hot, tight little ass.

"Keep fucking, GI Black-Man," Jeff panted, Kevin's pet name maybe the last thing he could remember.

Two months before, Jeff had been outside Gatsby's Nick, taking a smoke break and freeing himself from the sweaty crush on the dance floor. He'd been sticky, breathless, and almost giddy. Finals were over, which meant he had one year of UC Davis med school under his belt. As he was exhaling into the hot June night, a group of jack-booted jarheads thumped by, OD green T-shirts stretched wide over massive chests, heads absurdly square with their regulation buzz cuts, fatigues as crisply pressed as starched linen shirts.

Jeff had enough smoke and air left for a low whistle, and damn him and his mouth, off-limits or not, that was what he did.

He was not prepared for the biggest guy—a six-foot-five, Panzer-built black guy—to turn around and start advancing on him. Oh shit.

Jeff did what he did best: smiled ingratiatingly and cracked wise. "No offense, GI Black-Man," he said, trying his best to look innocuous-gay and not aggressive-gay. "I was just admiring the view. Doesn't mean I'm going to go galloping in and picking the daisies, right?"

The GI's shirt was stretched wide over his chest, tight enough that his nipples made little tents in the mild night air. Those dark-skinned hands grabbed hold of Jeff's best dance shirt, one of the new microfiber kind that would stretch out, and Jeff found his back up against the rough faux-brick of the club, wondering if he still remembered how to fight after all those skirmishes with his older brother. His cigarette fell from his fingers, and Kevin's combat boot crushed it into the cement.

"Look scared." Kevin's voice sank to a smoky murmur, and Jeff didn't have to fake anything—his eyes were wide, his heart was beating, and he wasn't sure this was really happening, even a little bit at all.

"I'm not looking for trouble," he said uncertainly, and Kevin's eyes, huge and brown and expressively rimmed with thick black lashes, raked him from his shoulders to his knees, with a special appreciation for Jeff's crotch in his tighter-than-breath, hip-dropping skinny jeans.

In a voice meant to be heard by his friends, who were standing nearby and watching the two of them with great amusement, Kevin barked, "Well, you found trouble, club boy!"

Jeff cringed, because Kevin's voice was deep, and he was holding Jeff practically off the ground, and if this situation wasn't what he was starting to think it was, he was still in a whole lot of trouble. "I meant no offense," Jeff said, holding his hands up placatingly. One hand accidentally brushed the Marine's stomach, and it wasn't Jeff's imagination: Kevin shuddered, and one side of a full, chocolate-pink mouth turned up appreciatively.

"None taken," Kev murmured, sotto voice, and Jeff's breath caught again. To Kev's friends, expecting to see fear, fear was exactly what it looked like. But Kev was close enough for Jeff to feel the brush of his hip against Jeff's cock as it tightened in his jeans, and their eyes caught and lingered in what could only be described as an instant eye-fuck.

In his "outside" voice, Kevin said, "You 'bout ready to go back inside, club boy?"

"Anything you want, GI Black-Man!" Jeff was playing the game too—his voice was scared, but his eyes were all come-hither-and-fuck-me-dammit, and Kev's mouth twitched appreciatively.

"That's what I thought!" he snapped in disgust and threw Jeff back against the wall again.

Jeff cracked his head and said, "Ou-uch!" in maybe his gayest voice, rubbing his head and glaring at this new dream pick-up in reproof.

Kev let his voice drop—still loud enough for his friends, but soft enough for Jeff to know he felt bad about that. "You'll live. Just don't let me see you here again."

Jeff's heart dropped, but then Kevin's voice dropped even lower, and he added, "In about two hours. Wait for me."

"Yes, sir!" Jeff couldn't stop the unrepentant grin then, but Kevin rolled his eyes, shook his head, and turned around to go off with his Marine buddies, accepting their slaps on the back and attaboys for "keeping the little faggot in his place" as though he hadn't just promised to take that "little faggot" home and fuck him silly.

Which he had proceeded to do for the next two months.

And now, one month before he shipped out on his next tour, Jeff was savoring (and screaming for) every stroke. Even though Kevin had promised forever and for always, and maybe especially because he had, Jeff wasn't taking a single touch for granted. Especially if it was Kevin's beautiful body, deep inside Jeff's own.

"C'mon, club boy!" Kevin panted now. "C'mon… scream for me, dammit!"

"Yes, *sir*!" Jeff gasped, and then he gave his cock a particularly hard yank just as Kevin drove himself forward, grabbed Jeff around the middle, and shouted "Boo-yah!" in his ear.

There was blinding white behind the blackness in Jeff's head, and his body shook with frozen fire, and he came hotly into his condom, the come scalding the end of his cock as it pooled.

They panted, Kevin nuzzling Jeff's ear and chuckling in that bass rumble he had. "You like that, club boy?" he murmured, and Jeff shuddered in aftershock.

"I always like that, GI Black-Man," Jeff told him truthfully. Even that first night, when Jeff had topped because, as Kevin said a little shyly, not everyone was ready for the full package that first night out, Jeff had loved sex with Kevin. His hands were strong and capable and absurdly gentle, and Kev's little club boy felt cherished and protected and treasured and all of those silly things that made being in bed, touching someone's skin, the best place in the world to be.

They shifted then, preparing to separate, and Jeff felt it—a trickle of wet, down from his asshole to his ass cheek and his lower thigh. He was still stunned, wondering what the hell *that* could be, when he heard Kevin's equally stunned voice behind him.

"Fuck."

Fuck? "Fuck what?"

"The fucking condom broke."

Kevin's body slid limply out of his, the remains of the rubber still wrapped tightly around the base with the shreds of the sheath stuck to the skin around it. The rest of the limpening, black-skinned length of him was still shiny from come.

Jeff turned slightly, sitting up on his knees, and he and Kevin Turner met one another's shocked and admittedly bemused eyes. Jeff, the eternal optimist, gave a crooked grin that hid the adrenaline rush in his chest. "Well, the damned things were getting in the way anyway."

Kevin's massive hand came up and pushed Jeff's head into that ginormous sweating chest. "Don't be scared, club boy. We'll be all right."

Jeff closed his eyes then, relaxed into his lover, and just once ceded control of the world to the gods.

SIX months later, Jeff still couldn't bring himself to regret that moment, not once. Not even when his test results came back positive, not when he felt compelled to quit med school, and especially not when Kevin was shipped home to Georgia in a pine box instead of home to Jeff's arms, in the flesh.

He and Kevin had been in love. Kevin had sent letters, and he re-read them until they were in tatters, and in spite of the danger of being read, in spite of the risk of losing everything he'd worked for in the military, he had signed them, "I love you, club boy" every time.

Jeff had enough experience with sex for sex to know the difference between Kevin's touch and other "club boys" out for a quick fuck. He'd had them, given them, enjoyed them—but wouldn't be willing to die for them.

He'd spent two months of his life wishing he could have died for Kevin, because it sure as shit couldn't hurt any worse than being alive without him did.

The thought consumed him one cold, loveless day in February as he waited in the CARES clinic in midtown for his consult with Herbert Schindler, MD. Herbert had been Jeff's advisor in med school and had probably saved Jeff's life. The day Jeff had gotten his HIV test results back—the white cell count so suddenly spiked that there was no doubt in his mind that his last month with Kevin, the month after the rubber broke, had been when he'd been exposed—he'd gone to Herbert, holding his angular jaw as stoic as he could make it, and told him he'd probably have to quit med school.

Herbert had seen the devastated young man and not the tough, bitter, aged one, and had canceled his next class and taken Jeff into his office for a sit-down.

When Jeff was done with their little chat, Herbert had steered him away from quitting entirely and along the path to be a physician's assistant.

"Less pointy shit," the big, bluff, balding doctor had harrumphed. "Less chance of cross-contamination, easier to get a job. Less time in medical school too."

Even the blunt-spoken Herbert Schindler trod delicately around pointing out that, new gains in drug therapy or no, time might not be a luxury Jeff could indulge in, so that would be a factor. He didn't have to. Jeff *was* a med student. He knew the facts.

The facts were that he didn't have the insurance or the cash to keep himself alive—the drug cocktail and the viral load testing and all of that shit was expensive. For a moment he actually wondered if he would die before he had a chance to regret falling in love with Kevin Turner.

And Herbert literally saved his life.

"Here, fill this out." He threw a chunk of paperwork across the desk at Jeff, and Jeff barely managed to reassemble the mess of it and put it neatly back in the battered manila folder.

"What's this?"

"It's an application to the VA hospital to be an intern. Once you're working here, you get health insurance, regardless of prior conditions."

"But I'm only a first year med stu—"

"Which is long enough to be an intern if you're going to be a PA— and if you have a little help from your friends."

"So I'm connected?" Jeff asked, impressed with himself—and with Herbert, of course.

"My boy, consider me your benefactor," Herbert said expansively, and he had a little twinkle in his eye, so Jeff took a risk that maybe he could crack a joke.

"So, sort of like a godfather to a fairy?" He amplified his "gay," flopping his wrist and trilling, and Herbert laughed good-naturedly.

"No hitting on me," he said with a totally straight face. "My wife gets jealous."

Jeff had laughed then with complete relief. He'd enjoyed Herbert's class—had, in fact, been one of the few students to suspect that Dr. Schindler had a wicked sense of humor underneath his rather placid exterior, and it was wonderful to "play" a little with a friend. "Well, sugar, it's a good thing you told me that. You give me this much help, and my inner flirt is going to peek out."

Herbert raised an eyebrow, and Jeff flushed, and then Herbert grinned—out-and-out grinned—and said, "I think your inner flirt needs to stay in your pants where it belongs, young man. Those things tend to get into trouble when you let them off their leash. I should know. I have six kids."

Jeff had laughed for a minute, and then, just that suddenly, swallowed and looked his professor in the eye. "I don't know, Dr. Schindler. It looks like you sort of adopted me too."

Herbert Schindler's mouth turned ever so slightly. "I hope someone would do the same for one of my sons," he said softly, and Jeff had nodded with a lump in his throat. He hoped so, too, with all his heart. Anyone who did this much good in the world deserved to know his nearest and dearest were well taken care of.

He'd thought so even more two months after that, when Kevin's buddy, the only one who knew Kevin's big, gay secret, had called Jeff from a satellite phone to tell Jeff that Kevin was dead.

Jeff had shown up on Herbert's doorstep—literally, his home doorstep—at two in the morning and, after apologizing profusely, had sobbed his heart out for over an hour. He hadn't known whom else to turn to. All of his club friends had turned out to be just that—"club friends"—and as for his own family?

He'd shuddered when Herbert had suggested, delicately, that Jeff might want to have some family support. After that Herbert had simply sat on his couch as his wife brought him coffee and a pillow and cradled Jeff's head against his chest like the father he was while Jeff, funny Jeff, who was never without a smile and a quick story or a smart-assed remark, wished that AIDS happened quick, like a hand-grenade to the heart, because that would be a mercy killing. A mercy killing was, as Jeff tried miserably to joke, the only thing he could think of to live for.

Over the next couple months he learned to find other things. Small things, it was true, but they worked.

A week after Kevin's funeral, which Jeff didn't attend, since A. it was in Georgia, and Jeff couldn't afford to go and B. Kevin hadn't been out to his family, and Jeff wouldn't out him when he wasn't alive to make the decision himself, Herbert's wife had shown up with soup and a kitten.

Jeff hadn't eaten in about a week—something his current drug cocktail was making easy—but if he'd thought that exempted him from Mrs. Schindler's matzo ball soup, he was wrong.

Unlike the visit, which Herbert had warned him about, the kitten was a surprise.

The kitten was a Scottish Fold—the kind with the weird folded ears and bug-eyed faces—and it threatened to be the size of a Labrador retriever when it grew up. Mrs. Schindler had pulled the steel-gray fuzzball out of a cat carrier and sat it in Jeff's arms while she heated the soup.

Jeff had looked at the creature, which was both pitifully cute and adorably ugly, and the cat had blinked slowly back. "Mrs. Doc Herbert, I hope you don't mind if I ask you what in the hell this is?"

"It's a cat," she said, ruthlessly taking over his student efficiency apartment and setting his one pot up on the hotplate to heat up the soup. She was a squat, mid-sized woman who favored polyester pantsuits worn over wide hips and had short, dyed black hair. She also had really kind, expressive brown eyes. When Jeff had fallen asleep on her couch the night he'd found out about Kevin, he'd woken up covered in a blanket with a box of tissues and two ibuprofen on the coffee table, and a cat purring on his hip with enough force to vibrate the windows.

He liked cats. In fact, he liked this one, but, "They're not allowed in this dump," he had to tell her, a little wistfully. The kitten had taken up a determined purring on his chest, and he found that, although his heart still felt empty, the purring was warming the empty place.

Mrs. Doc Herbert had shrugged. "So find another place. Your internship is paid—you're no longer a starving student, and you are almost officially a grown-up. Get a house—"

"I hate yard work."

She shrugged. "Get a condo with a pool, then. Just make sure it takes pets."

Jeff looked at the purring thing on his chest again. It seemed like an awfully small deal for which to turn his life upside down. Then he looked around his apartment. Kevin had practically lived here those three months before he'd shipped out. Jeff had kept one of his long-sleeved dress shirts in his closet, and Kevin had slipped a couple of OD green T-shirts in his drawer the day he'd left. They'd taken pictures in that last week, stealing the camera from each other to get candid photos, and finally, one of the two of them, taken from the length of Kev's long arm as they'd lain in bed. Jeff had had the picture developed and framed before Kevin had shipped out and had given Kev a wallet-sized one. The picture—Kev grinning wickedly into the camera, Jeff peeking shyly (a surprise, for Jeff) out at the lens from Kevin's cheek—sat next to his bed.

He didn't want to leave this apartment. Kevin was here.

His eyes watered up then, and he wrapped his hands around the kitten in preparation to give it back, and then Mrs. Doc Herbert read his mind and wrapped her fingers around his.

"Baby, you have to find a reason to eat. A reason to wake up and take your meds, and throw up, and take them again. You have to find a reason to go to work, and then go to school, and then go home again. The reasons are out there—and you're tougher than you act, so I know you'll find them. But right now, this is your reason."

The kitten, feeling the possibility of having to leave, dug in its claws and meowed imperiously. Jeff swallowed and looked apologetically at the little fuzzball. "No offense," he told it, "but you're not much of a reason."

The kitten sniffed at him and shrugged, then dug in, as if to say, "Take it or leave it, asshole. You're the one contemplating annihilation by apathy." Or maybe that was just his conscience speaking. The gay man's trill was a little bit similar.

Jeff frowned at the creature again. "Please tell me it's a boy," he said.

Mrs. Schindler rolled her eyes. "Oh please, Jeff. Like I'd even *try* to get a girl in your bed."

Jeff choke-snorted, and the kitten grumbled—an honest-to-God grumble—and dug in a little deeper with his claws, and Mrs. Schindler served up the matzo ball soup. Before she left, Jeff got the recipe, because sometimes, when the drug "therapy" got too bad, it was the only thing he could keep down.

That was how he made it. Six months after diagnosis, there he was, waiting for a consult with Herbert as his favorite doc did his one day a week at the CARES clinic in midtown Sacramento, and wandering restively around the lobby. There was a big bay window looking out into a not hideous (but not bum-free either) neighborhood at midtown, but the day was gray and cheerless, and Jeff was experiencing a sudden case of the fidgets.

He'd been told to counsel some of his patients with hand or arm problems to take up knitting, and he'd taken it up himself, to see what muscle groups it affected. He found himself missing his knitting—he honestly thought he might become one of those obnoxious gay men who brought their knitting in public, just to keep him from the feeling that the clock was ticking at odd hours of the day with nothing to fill the time.

On his third pass around the room with a stop at the water cooler, he found he had company.

It was a kid—barely legal, but pretty. He had a strong jaw, a faintly crooked nose, probably from fights, and dark blond hair, combed smooth and long on either side of his face to that strong jaw. His eyes were mostly light brown, with gold flecks and surprisingly dark lashes.

He walked like an alpha dog, all shoulders, and Jeff thought that if he'd met this kid clubbing six or seven years ago, he probably would have gone out in back with him to take it against the wall, because *Jesus*, this kid was a stunner.

And he walked like he owned the world, and that had always turned Jeff's key. The rainbow bracelet around his bony, still-growing wrist was especially attractive.

Jeff shook off that moment of attraction, feeling like a dirty old perv, and looked a little deeper, because as much as he walked like he owned the world, the kid's eyes kept darting, in spite of his best intentions, and he must have swallowed about a thousand times since he'd stood up to keep pace with Jeff in their little trot around the room.

Jeff sighed. He liked to think of himself as a selfish bastard, really, but given the kindness he'd gotten—not only from Dr. Schindler, but from the entire staff of the VA hospital, who had accepted him like he hadn't been a charity case of everybody's favorite doc—he sort of felt like he owed it to the world to change his approach to life a little.

Besides, he was discovering, as he worked his internship in physical therapy, that he liked helping people. He enjoyed it. He was still a selfish bastard, but he selfishly got off on helping people, and that carried over, even into the CARES lobby when you were waiting to see how your HIV drug therapy was working.

He got the kid a paper cup of water and said, "Kid, you wanna come outside? I know it's cold, but I'm falling asleep in here."

The kid's relief had color, taste, and smell. He looked up at the still-pretty, middle-aged woman sitting in the middle, reading a cooking magazine like it was homework, and said, "Mom, I'm gonna step outside, 'kay? It'll be another fifteen minutes, right?"

The woman pursed her lips. "Collin, we can't be late for this...."

The kid closed his eyes and nodded. "Five minutes, Mom. I swear. Just... just...." He swallowed again. "Just let me get some air, 'kay?"

The woman nodded. "That's fine, baby. Just don't run away." She said it like it was a real possibility.

Collin grimaced and walked back to her, kissing her on the cheek and showing honest affection. Jeff couldn't help it—he heard what the boy said. "I've put you through enough, Mom. I just want some air, I promise."

They got outside, and Jeff figured he'd take a couple of chances. This kid had five minutes to get his head together, and he obviously wanted Jeff's help.

"Are you as gay as you look?" the kid asked, and Jeff had to laugh. He thought *he* could be tactless.

"Is there any way to be *not* as gay as I look?" he asked, honestly curious, and the kid laughed a little himself. Jeff was wearing jeans— tight, tight jeans, because he didn't have any other kind, and if he had to do an hour of sit-ups a morning, he was going to keep fitting into those damned skinny jeans no matter *what* the drug cocktail did to his body. He was wearing a V-necked, faux-cashmere sweater in turquoise blue and bright, shiny leather loafers with pretty tassels, because he *liked* them, dammit, and he was gay, and gayness had its privileges.

The kid laughed and pulled out a pack of cigarettes as they got to the outside wall. Jeff almost pointed out that the no smoking ban extended around the perimeter of the building and then figured that it was, perhaps, the last thing the kid needed to hear. Besides, Jeff promised himself one a day, and it looked like he'd get his early this day.

"These are bad for you," he pointed out gently, taking the second to last one from the pack. Camel, unfiltered. He shook his head. Figured. This would have to be two days worth of smoke—he hoped the kid made this good.

Collin grunted, took the last one, and crumpled the empty pack in his hand. "I know. I told my mom I'd smoke one a day, you know? That way I could keep my will to live."

Collin held out a lighter, and Jeff puffed appreciatively and then stepped back and leaned against the wall. Collin lit his own and Jeff sighed again, exhaling smoke. Ah... unfiltered nicotine. It was like eating real chocolate mousse when you'd been eating the kind that was actually non-fat yogurt for a couple of months.

"I know what you mean," he said, enjoying the rush. "Sometimes, it's the little shit that gets you out of bed in the morning."

The kid nodded. "You know, last month, I had to tell everyone I'd ever slept with or kissed or given head to or gotten a blow-job from that I was positive and they needed to get tested. I ran away first."

Jeff caught his breath with the simplicity of that. Who wouldn't want to run away before he had to do that? "What made you come back?"

Collin took a deep drag of his cigarette, his cheeks hollowing and his high cheekbones standing out in relief. He looked suddenly old in that moment, old and hard and dangerous, and Jeff thought that if he'd never met Kevin, this kid would have rung his bell but good, dirty-old-man shame or no.

"My mom. All the shit I put her through? Man, if she could hug me and call me her boy after all of that…." He shook his head. "If she could do that, the least I could do is ball the fuck up, right?"

Jeff nodded. He liked this kid. Brave, responsible—but with that core of bad boy that had made Kevin's wicked eyes in that jarhead uniform oh-so-irresistible. But Jeff's raw and bleeding heartstrings weren't what was at issue here.

"How was it?" Jeff asked softly. That was really what the kid had wanted to talk about, wasn't it? Why else pick an obviously gay man to confide in?

"It sucked," Collin whispered, shaky on the exhale this time. "We were all so tight, yanno? All the queer kids, fucking each other silly because we could. It… we just felt invincible. Like, we were only fucking each other, so where were we going to get AIDS, right?"

Jeff didn't correct the fact that it was HIV in this stage and not AIDS. When you were what, seventeen? Eighteen? Whatever—you weren't going to appreciate the difference, and you sure as hell weren't going to appreciate the lecture.

"How bad?" Jeff asked softly.

Collin shrugged and looked away. "Well, none of them are talking to me now—you know. Like *I* was the only one fucking around, right? And only two of, like, ten got tested, and they're positive, and their parents just… just took them out of school before graduation, like they were plutonium or something. And no one mentioned a thing—not a single fucking thing. It's like it doesn't exist." Collin shook his head, clearly bewildered. "I mean, *fuck*. Some of those guys weren't out—they have *girlfriends*, and the girls are just walking around, not knowing that the guy giving it to them might be HIV because he felt like getting frisky in the bathroom or behind the gym after a dance or what-the-fuck-ever. And I just...."

Jeff turned his head, and Collin made eye contact. "I'm just so fucking lonely, you know? My dad died when I was a kid, and my mom... she busted her ass so we could have a good life, and I just pissed it all away, and I don't want to even talk to her about it... about any of it... because I already put her through enough...."

Ah, damn. The kid had thought he was tough, hadn't he? He had—and now he was fighting to be tough, not to cry, to keep his chin square, and Jeff thought if he was any more goddamned tough, he'd blow apart like a pane of damaged glass. Collin sucked hard on his butt one more time and then ground it out under his waffle-stomper in the weed-filled fine gravel on the side of the brick building.

He took a few more breaths and then said, apologetically, "That's the end of the smoke, right? Time's up?"

Jeff followed suit with his own cigarette, although it was only half gone. "C'mere, baby," he said softly, and opened his arms, and suddenly he had an armload of terrified teenager.

"You listen to me," he whispered fiercely. "You talk to your mom, because she wants to know. She won't be able to help, but you'll feel better, okay? Just fucking talk to her. She drove you to the goddamned clinic and is making you take this like a man—she'll get it." Collin's arms tightened convulsively around his shoulders, and Jeff could sense a strangled full-body sob. "You're one lucky kid, you know that? You got your mom. You got family. You be grateful to them, and you let them help you, you hear me?"

Collin nodded, and that pointy chin dug once into Jeff's shoulder, and then they could both hear his pocket buzz. His mom, Jeff thought, probably texting him because his appointment was up.

Collin backed away, and Jeff missed his warmth against the chill of the day almost immediately. "Thanks," he said, wiping his face with the back of his hand. "I mean, just some random stranger, dumping all over you...."

Jeff waved a hand. "No worries, baby. Go on in, your mom's gonna freak, 'kay?"

Collin nodded once, awkwardly, and backed up before hurrying away. Jeff watched him go, feeling his chest tighten and an absurd quiver to his chin. Oh, God. He wanted more than anything to call his mama and tell her everything.

But even if he did, it wouldn't solve a thing. He leaned his hands on his thighs and squatted heavily in the February fog, trying to get his bearings and shoulder the load he'd been given. He had a condo that he loved, with a gym and a pool, and a shit load of houseplants and a gi-fucking-normous cat named Constantine who insisted that if Jeff were not there to give him luvvies, the world *would* fall apart. He had a dinner a month with the Herbert Schindlers, and patients who had started leaving him thank-you cards, and a promising profession doing something it looked like he might love very-much-a-lot. He had a promising white cell count and a low-dose drug cocktail instead of a high-dose one, and if he had to do an extra zillion and a half sit-ups to keep his girlish figure, well, so-the-fuck-be-it.

He was doing fine, thank you.

But still, that didn't keep him from wishing with all his heart on days like this, and not for things like a cup of hot chocolate either. So he let himself wish, telling himself he was a fool, because wishes—especially *his* wishes—were the kind that wouldn't come true. The permission didn't help: as much as he wished he could go back in time and get a condom that wouldn't break, or warn Kevin about the ambush in the road, or even warn himself not to take a smoke break on a muggy June night, he couldn't help but add one more wish in the wishing star hat before he straightened up and swished like a man into the clinic for his consult.

It wasn't wrong to wish for one more glimpse of that absurdly beautiful, heartbroken kid who walked like he owned the world, was it?

Chapter 2

Jeff: My Baby Sent Me a Letter

FIVE years later, Jeff still didn't regret falling in love with Kevin Turner—but he still hadn't told his mother about him, either. He'd told her about the HIV, but he wasn't even sure if his father knew.

He called his mother every Monday, 8 a.m., like clockwork, and he had since his father had kicked him out of the house shortly after he'd started college and come out to his parents. (Herbert had once asked him how much of a shock could it have been to Jeff's father, and Jeff had shrugged, his expressive, angular body making the move dramatic. He wasn't sure either, but a surprise it apparently had been.)

The problem with his mother went beyond the fact that Jeff hadn't lived at home for ten years and beyond the fact that he was gay. It even went beyond the fact that Jeff had to actually *bribe* his mother's nurse to let him speak to her, since his father had told the nursing home not to accept his calls.

The problem went directly to why she was in a nursing home at age sixty-two to begin with, and it had started not long after Jeff went to school.

"Jeffy?" His mother always sounded so breezy and confident, much like she had when he'd been a kid and she'd been the most popular soccer mom in Coloma, with the best goodies and the house full of neighbor kids because their house was the best, that's why.

"Hey, Mom!" Jeff made his voice match hers and waited to see where mom was on the space/time continuum this week.

"How are the kitties?" Lillian Beachum asked, and Jeff blew out a sigh of relief. She was apparently pretty close to current. Sometimes she wasn't always in the right year, and he would have to remind her that he was no longer in med school, and that his career goals had changed, and sometimes, he would even have to remind her that he was gay, and he wasn't going to be looking for a nice girl to settle down with. Lillian would always laugh then (as Archie, her husband, had not) and say, "You know, Jeffy, you think your father and I would have figured that out, right?"

But not today. Today, she asked him how he was feeling and if the doctors were sure he was going to be okay, and then she asked him about Constantine, the big sloth, and today, she even remembered Katherine the Great, the Maine Coon cat that his friend Shane had given him for his birthday this year, only about a month late because Shane had been recovering from broken ribs (big dumbfuck ex-cop) and hadn't been able to get Jeff what he'd had in mind all along. Jeff had tried to protest that he didn't need another cat-mountain in his condo, but Shane knew his cats. This one was large, even as a kitten, drooled a lot, and went completely limp as soon as you picked it up. It was even calico, and all that long calico hair was just so *pretty*, and Jeff had been charmed immediately.

"Katy and Con are fine, Mama," Jeff told her now. "Katy still hasn't stopped drooling when she sleeps—it's just so sad! She lays there with her head sideways and her tongue lolling out! I mean, if I'd wanted a cat who did that, I would have bought a boxer, right?"

Mama laughed, and Jeff counted that as a score for his side. Anytime Lillian Beachum laughed, that was one for the angels.

And then the angels wept.

"So, Jeff, when are you going to visit me? I don't see anyone anymore! Your father was here this weekend, but Barry's always so busy with his job, and I haven't seen you since... well, I can't remember when!"

Jeff took a careful breath in and out of his nose. "I'll try to make some time next week, Mama," he lied. He would—if his father wasn't standing guard over her like a pit bull, afraid he was going to spread the gay. Like gay was any worse than Alzheimer's, right?

"Are you still worried about your father?" she asked innocuously. "Oh, honey, he'll get over it. You can't be as proud as he was of you and think a little thing like who you kiss is going to get in the way!"

Except he had. Jeff's father had let a little thing like that get in the way. And then he'd gotten in the way of Jeff and his entire family. Jeff's older brother, his mother, aunts, uncles, cousins—he'd been part of a collective in Coloma, dammit! He'd been surrounded by Beachums and Porters and Martels and Beauforts, and then, the summer before his freshman year in school, before his *free ride* thanks to a swim-team scholarship and top-notch grades, Jeff thought he'd tell his family, the closest, inner core of his family, who he really was.

And he'd lost all of them, inner family, outer family, just plain *family*, forever. His mother's phone calls had started getting vague about six months after that. Not long into Jeff's junior year in college, he'd had to do some quick talking around nurses who had been coming to take care of her. One of them had taken pity on him and arranged the talks he had now.

And some days Mom remembered that her youngest wasn't invited home, and some days she didn't.

"Well, Mom, as long as you know that I wish I was kissing you on the cheek right now, okay? Now give the phone to Becky—I want to get a picture of you."

He did this every so often—and he sent Becky one of himself. Sometimes his mother was stunned at how old he looked. Sometimes she remembered that he was in his thirties. Either way, he made prints of the pictures he got back and kept a progression of his mother, almost as if he'd been allowed to visit her for the last eleven, twelve years.

"Bye, sweetheart," his mother's voice quavered over the phone. "I love you."

"Bye, Mama," he said back, locking that steel cage around his heart so it wouldn't break. "I love you too."

His mother looked like she always did in her picture: her needlepoint in her hands, her hair—black once, like his, but all gray now—brushed back into a ponytail, and her face, lined and serene, beaming into the camera. Leave it to his mother to go old and crazy in the sweet, saintly grandmother way. If she'd gone crazy in the raving-old-bat way, Jeff might have had an easier time pretending that he had no family, none at all.

It hurt, but it was an old pain, and the rest of his day was promising, so he dislodged Katherine the Great-Big-Fat-Drooling-Shedding-Fur-Monkey from his chest and then Constantine-the-Comatose from his lap, where one of his legs had gone a bit numb. Con flopped over to his side, one gray paw curled against his massive chest and the other stretched out, almost above his head, and glared balefully at Jeff. Kat glomped on top of Con, and the two began a contest to see who could groom the other one best. Jeff sighed and then smiled at them, because they were absolute darlings, and he adored them both. Then he stood, brushing the stray cat hairs from his red satin dressing gown, and padded down the hall in his fleece-lined leather clogs to get dressed.

He paused at his room and pumped some man-sturizer/hand-sanitizer onto his hands from a bottle on the dresser, then pulled his pressed white coat with the three-quarter sleeves out of the closet along with his natty black slacks with the slick, shiny leather shoes. He put on something dressy underneath—a crisp poly/wool button-up shirt with a mandarin collar and pink-and-black vertical stripes—and took out his lined belted leather jacket to keep him warm in the November chill. He considered the outfit and then smiled softly and went to the rack of scarves he'd brought out in late October.

He liked scarves—he had silk/cashmere blends, angora, sturdy wool—but he picked one from his "scarf of honor" peg. All three scarves on the peg were hand-knitted. The first one was in a simple garter stitch, in handsome eggplant, that went on forever. Jeff's best friend, Crick, had a sister who liked to knit; she'd made that for him last autumn, and it was one of his prized possessions. Shane had a scarf from Benny as well, but Shane, the big furry traitor, had given his scarf to his snotty little boyfriend Mikhail. If Jeff hadn't adored Mikhail almost as much as he adored Katy and Con, he wouldn't have let Shane live that down, but since Mikhail had worn the thing damned near into June that summer, Jeff figured he'd let it slide.

The other scarf on his rack had been knitted by Crick himself. Crick had taken up knitting on Jeff's advice for physical therapy on his hand and arm, injured in battle when Crick was serving in Iraq. Crick's knitting was painful, stitch-by-fucking-stitch knitting, and while Deacon had gotten his first effort, Jeff had gotten his second, in forest green, and he wouldn't trade it for the world.

The last one, Jeff had knitted. He usually knit for charity or for friends or the people at work, but this one, he'd knitted for himself.

Jeff was really good at it. This was a complicated braid cable, in a handsome space-dyed wool/silk blend of subtle navy and charcoal with a hint of green every so often in the mix. He fingered the wool, liking the texture under his skin, and then sighed. So pretty—but it didn't go with his shirt.

He picked the eggplant one that Benny had knit him instead, even though she wouldn't be there to see it. God, he missed Benny—everyone at The Pulpit, Deacon and Crick's home, did. But Benny was down in SoCal, getting her education, and Deacon and Crick were here, being family to the rest of their odd assortment of people, and Jeff would have to settle for an evening after work, knitting with Benny's family, instead.

He was looking forward to it. Hell, he was *dressing up* for it. That would have to be enough.

Work was fun—some of his favorite patients were on the roster for that day, and he loved a good, chatting patient with fun stories to tell.

Marjorie Bell was one of those. She was a big woman, far bigger than was healthy, with a face that refused to line, even in middle age. She had short, blonde-gray hair and a wide freckled face, and a neck that hadn't recovered from a car accident about five years before.

She taught high school, now that her husband had retired from the Navy, and her stories about her students made Jeff laugh until he needed to pee. He always scheduled an extra fifteen minutes to her sessions just to talk with her, and she always used it. Today was no different.

"Okay," she was saying this day, as Jeff applied his magic heated sonic wand of love to the tissue at the base of her skull, "so we've just covered Lord Byron, and how the guy slept with anyone and everyone, male and female, and was driven out of England for totally boinking his half-sister, Augusta. That's out of the way, we've got fifteen minutes to go, so I decide to launch into my 'Don't get knocked up during Winter Ball' spiel, right? I mean, it happens every year. You see these kids with the six-month baby-bump walking the stage at graduation, and you're like, 'Really? Winter Ball? You couldn't have fit a couple of rubbers in your teeny-tiny little handbag with your cell phone or something?'. So in the middle of this, a girl comes in from the office—she just got to school and doesn't know what we're talking about—and she says, 'Okay, so what're we doing?'."

Margie let out a low moan of relief at that moment, because Jeff took the heat massager to just—that—spot on her neck, and Jeff kept it there for a minute until her whole body shuddered with tension relief and she could continue her story.

"So what did you say?" Jeff prompted, and she laughed a little and arched into the sonic vibrator for another knot in her painfully twisted neck.

"I told her we were talking about how not to get knocked up during Winter Ball, and she says, 'Don't worry about me! I'm going with my cousin!'."

Jeff couldn't help it. He had to pull the sonic wand away so he could laugh. "Ohmigod! That's hilarious! What happened?"

Margie stretched, the motions graceful and svelte, almost like Constantine's stretching, and at odds a little with her size. "Well, the whole class totally broke up, and then this one guy, who was lost on the whole Byron thing anyway, suddenly breaks out with, 'Man, and make sure your condom's fresh! Those things go bad after a year!', and there was only five minutes of class after that—like I was going to get *that* class back!"

Jeff snorted softly, still laughing. "Oh, honey, that's priceless!"

Margie laughed with him and then swiveled around on her little "victim's stool," as she called it, and rolled her eyes. "Yeah—let's see if I can keep my job after that gets to the parents, though!"

Jeff frowned and took the little K-Y covered baggie off the end of the wand, then wiped the rest of the glide gel off of Margie's neck. "How do you mean?"

Margie's shrug was resigned. "People get awfully het up when you talk about sex, you know?"

Jeff rolled his eyes back. "Well, they get pretty homoed up about it when you talk about gay sex, so I guess that's about right!"

It was Margie's turn to laugh, and she did so with gratifying heartiness. God, he loved to make someone bust up. He collected stories in his head all day, witticisms, catty remarks, anything he could think about. It was like his drug, the one thing he could do that would make himself feel better, and he indulged in his emotional crack as much as possible. He thanked the gods for folks like Margie, who just handed it out for free by the truckload. They pretty much kept him sane.

Margie grabbed her 4X T-shirt and threw it over her head, over her lunchroom-lady bra, and turned comfortably around to Jeff, who was making notations on her chart.

"You're doing about the same, Margie," he said, trying not to nag, "but you know what would really make this whole PT thing take off?"

Margie rolled her eyes. "Yeah, yeah, Doctor Jeff. If I lost the extra human hanging around my neck—I figured."

Jeff smiled at her softly. Weight problems sucked. He knew it. It was one thing for him to spend hours at the gym or to measure his calories with a scale and a calculator—he had the time. But Margie? Margie still had three kids in school. Her time after work was a maddening whirlwind of soccer fields, dance studios, and Aca-Deca meetings. Margie was lucky if she could order McDonald's and remember not to get the extra-large fries.

"Well, darling, you know I worry. Who else is going to keep me apprised on the doings of the depraved youth of America, right?"

Margie grinned and waggled her blonde eyebrows wickedly, then turned away and started to pack up her purse with a rather studied air. "Um, that reminds me, Dr. Jeff—I won't be making my appointment for next week. I'll be back the week after."

"Yeah?" Jeff cocked his head. "What's doin'?"

Margie shrugged and kept her back turned. She mumbled something that sounded like "ohw paedgent mercury." Jeff blinked and asked her to repeat it, and on the fourth try, he was able to make out the words "outpatient surgery."

Jeff stared at her blankly. "For what?"

Margie still wouldn't look at him. The sides of the walls—which he'd decorated with seascapes and kittens, and the floor and the ceiling—*those* she looked at. Finally she looked at him, her shoulders hunched defensively, and her chin quivering alarmingly.

"C'mon, honey—what's doin'?" he asked, as gently as he could.

"No big deal," Margie said, trying to keep her jaw stoic. "Just, you know, a Lap-band. The stomach-stapling thing, right?"

Jeff blinked, not sure where the verklempt woman came in with the everyday procedure. "Isn't that a good thing, sweetheart?"

Margie shrugged again and looked away. "You know, doll, it's just embarrassing. You want to lose it all by yourself. It's... it's humiliating to find yourself in this... this emotional vortex, and you can't pull your way out of it, you know?" She shook her head and shrugged and tried to wave away the tears, and Jeff had a sudden memory of Crick's voice on the phone.

He'd been slouched on the couch with Constantine on his lap, and wondering—without framing the thought, mind you—if maybe Constantine wouldn't be happier with the Mr. and Mrs. Doc Herberts forever. His favorite show, CSI, had just gone to reruns, and, dammit, his last cigarette had made him throw up, and so had his last cookie and his last hamburger and his last anything-the-fuck-else that made life worth living and his little personal pharmaceutical/biology experiment worth the potential outcome.

And to make matters worse, a group of teenage boys had practically run over him on skateboards as he'd left the supermarket that day, calling him an "old faggot" as they did.

Now the "faggot" part he could have lived with—but the "old?" That was just too fucking much.

And then the phone rang, and he didn't recognize the number, and then when he picked it up....

"So, hey. This is Crick, the poor bastard you tortured the other day, you remember?"

Holy shit. The gangly kid with the motor mouth and the horrific injuries and the smoking hot boyfriend and not a trace of self-pity. The one he'd talked to for the whole session, and whom he had thought about—not even in a sexual way—for the next two days. The kid had been fun. He'd been funny. He'd been one of the best things about Jeff's week.

"Yeah, sweetcakes, how could I forget?"

"So, um, Deacon's busy, I'm still a walking liability, and, um... hey. Do you want to go shopping or something? God, Deacon can't shop for shit, and I feel so damned slow when it's Benny and the baby. You think?"

Jeff had almost cried. "Oh babydoll, I think you're gonna regret that. Do you know how many malls I can haul your gimpy ass around? What did you want to look for?"

Yeah. Jeff knew about emotional vortices, didn't he?

Jeff didn't care if Margie weighed at least twice as much as he did—she was a sweetie, and every week, she made him laugh. He opened his arms and waggled his fingers, and she stepped awkwardly into his best fairy-Jeff-father hug.

"We all need help sometimes," he said softly, and was gratified when her hug went from awkward to earnest.

"Yeah, well, I guess if you're twice the woman, you need twice the help," she muttered, and he hugged her tighter before he let her go.

"I'll make your appointment for two weeks from now. I expect miracles, Margie—don't disappoint me!"

Margie grimaced. "You *are* a miracle, my darling boy. Let's just hope I don't have some bizarrely shaped, anti-band stomach or that my fat hasn't developed intelligence and a will to take over the world."

Jeff laughed some more, because he couldn't help it. "If it does take over the world, could it make it so diet dessert doesn't taste like shit? I'm *dying* for chocolate mousse something, and it is not my week to indulge!"

Now it was Margie's turn to look at him softly. "Well, you let me know when it's your week, and I'll have a bite of that, right?"

A flush stole over Jeff's features. Margie was smart—he'd seen her eyeing the double-glove layer he used when treating patients, and she knew him well enough to inquire after his health when his "vitamin" doses got too hard to hold down. He may not have told her his big HIV secret, but she had probably guessed.

"It's a deal," he said quietly, and she smiled warmly back. She left then, in a flurry of receipts and pens and lotion samplers from her gigantic purse, but their conversation seemed to echo in Jeff's head for the rest of the workday.

He was just finishing his charting when the phone in his little office rang, and his words to Margie about needing help practically exploded in his head.

"Is this Jeff Beachum?"

Jeff recognized the voice, even if the name was unfamiliar—he pronounced it "Bow-shaam," and this guy pronounced it "Beech-ump." Jeff had only heard one other person call him that, in that same hesitant, crisp, military way, and that had been on pretty much the worst day of his life.

"Lieutenant Lucas Blaine," Jeff said, his mouth drying up, turning to sand, and then exhaling powder. "I remember you."

"Yeah, uhm...." There was a pause, and Jeff imagined some jarhead fidgeting with a cell phone, wearing fatigues and a grimly bashful look. Lucas had called Jeff to tell him about Kevin, and even then, Jeff couldn't have picked him out of a crowd. They hadn't spoken since.

"See, the thing is," Lucas continued after about a quarter of a century, "Kevin sent you a letter. You know... a 'coming home' letter? The kind we're supposed to have sent home if we're coming home in a box?"

Jeff actually felt his head *swim*—like the backstroke and everything. He'd hoped for a letter, after Lucas's call, but he hadn't expected one. Kevin had made it more than clear that his parents would rather he died a Marine than live a faggot.

Jeff had told him at the time that he'd rather have him live, period, and Kevin had laughed like it was a given.

"I didn't know that," Jeff said now, from way under the water in the crazy pool where Lucas had just dumped him. "What happened to it?"

Lucas sighed. "It got sent home in a packet with his letter to his parents—I was supposed to get to it, but I forgot about it that day. I was...." He sounded impatient with himself. "I'm sorry, Mr. Beech-ump, but I was wounded that day too."

Twenty-five-year-old Jeff might not have given a fuck. Thirty-one-year-old Jeff found that he did. "I'm sorry about that, Lucas. I didn't know."

"It's my fault," Lucas muttered again. "I'm sorry. It's my goddamned fault. I didn't mean to let Kevin down. And...." His sigh was so gusty that it actually echoed in the earpiece. "Kevin trusted me. He trusted me with who he was, and he trusted me with you, and I really let him down, and I didn't mean to, and now shit is just way fucked up...."

This big, tough jarhead sounded like he was going to fall apart, and after five years as PA Jeff Beachum, Jeff found he couldn't let that happen. "Now come on, babydoll—it can't be that bad. You and me, we're still breathing, so nothing's happened that we can't take back, has it?"

"That's what I'm trying to tell you. Something *has* happened, and it's awful, and I can't fix it."

Jeff tried to pull his head out of the crazy end of the what-the-fuck pool and ask a question that would help him figure out what was going on. "Lucas, what in the fuck are you talking about?"

Another one of those feedback-inducing sighs. "Kevin's got a little brother——"

"The youngest one? Martin? He's, what? Fifteen now?"

"Fourteen. And curious. And he wanted to see his brother's letter, because I guess it freaked his parents the fuck out. So he goes searching for Mom's scrapbook, which she shoved up in the attic, and he found not one letter, but two. And the other had your address on the inside. I don't know if you still live there, Mr. Beech-ump, but he grabbed all his lawn-mowing money and hopped on a fucking bus. He's on his way to see you."

Little black dots started swimming in front of Jeff's eyes.

"Mr. Beech-ump? Mr. Beech-ump?"

Jeff sucked in a great lungful of air, and the spots swam faster. Spots swimming in the crazy pool, right? Swimming crazy spots, doing the backstroke in what-the-fuck-inated water....

"Mr. Beech-ump? Mr. Beech-ump? Are you there?"

Another lungful of air, and the crazy spots stopped doing the backstroke and started to fade from his vision.

"Honey doll," he said, wondering how strong his voice could actually be, "all things considered, I think it's best that you call me Jeff."

DEACON and Crick listened to the whole story that night, while Jeff practically sat in their laps and poured it out.

He was supposed to be going over to knit with Crick and Amy, (one of Deacon's closest friends from high school) watch some television, and play with Parry Angel, who was missing her mama now that Benny had gone away to school and needed her fairy-Jeff-father to make up the slack. That last was a guess on Jeff's part, but since Crick's family at The Pulpit had managed to replace the Beachums and Beauforts and Masons and Porters and what-all that Jeff hadn't had since his dad had kicked him out of the family, Jeff was going to take his every chance to be a fairy-Jeff-father. God, he missed playing with kids—they were the world's best source of laughter, and Parry Angel would sit and giggle at the faces he made at her until his chest filled and he felt like he ruled the world.

Anyway, Jeff was supposed to go over for a quiet evening with friends, but he'd taken one look at Deacon, Crick's husband, and found that his chin started to quiver and his face started to crumple, and the next thing he knew, he was coming unglued in Deacon's rock-steady arms. Suddenly Amy had Parry and her own daughter, Lila, in Crick and Deacon's bedroom, watching a Disney movie on their television, and Jeff was doing a reprise from his time on the couch with Mr. Doc Herbert five years ago.

Except this time, he had Deacon (who looked just as befuddled as Doc Herbert to have a grown man falling apart on him) on one side, and Crick on the other, patting his back awkwardly with all the heart in the world.

He did not cry all night. In fact, when he looked at the clock, he'd hardly cried for ten minutes, and yes, he did linger for a moment on Deacon's hard chest.

Then he sat up abruptly and frowned. "You've lost weight again, haven't you?"

Deacon sat back and glowered—and then, characteristically, blushed. "I swear to Christ, Jeff, if you had that whole fucking meltdown just to feel me up, I'll beat the shit out of you."

Jeff sniffled and wiped his cheek with the back of his hand. "As if!" Behind him, he could almost feel Deacon and Crick exchange some disgruntled glances, and then Deacon stretched out his arm and Jeff leaned on his hard—and too lean—chest again.

"I've never seen you come unglued," Deacon mused, and Jeff gave a little purr.

"We're even," he said, and then corrected himself. "Okay. You're up one. Now, you have officially seen me come unglued."

"It wasn't pretty."

Jeff sniffed with a little bit of disdain. "I hate you, you know."

"If you *really* hated him, you'd stop *groping* him!" Crick had clearly had enough, but Jeff wasn't frightened off. For one thing, as far as Deacon was concerned, Jeff had as much sexuality as Benny. For another, well… he hadn't snuggled into another man's chest for a *long* time. Even if it was completely platonic (and nothing was stirring all points south, so Jeff was reassured), it was really, really wonderful.

"What are you going to do?" Deacon asked, and Jeff snuck a peek at him from under dark lashes. God, Crick's man was gorgeous. Oval face, square hairline, small nose, firm, not-quite-pointed chin, and the most amazing green eyes—if it weren't for the fact that Deacon couldn't even see the sun when Crick smiled, Jeff liked to think he might have stood a chance.

But then Jeff couldn't have leaned on the two of them when his world was falling apart. He'd learned a long time ago that lovers were the first to go.

"I have no idea," Jeff mumbled now, soaking in the comfort. "As far as I know, Lucas Blaine is coming out to meet the kid. They know each other—Lucas was Kevin's best friend growing up. Then I told Lucas to call me and we'd meet somewhere." Jeff shuddered, feeling that horrible, oily nausea that came from knowing someone who should love him was going to rip up his insides like Con liked to rip up couch pillows.

"Do you want to meet here?" Deacon asked, and Amy's voice popped over the couch, along with a *beee-yooo-tiful* eighteen-month-old baby.

"That would be a horrible idea. Uncle Jeff, give Lila a hug and a kiss, because she's going down in the porta-crib right now before she makes us all batshit, okay?"

Jeff swung the baby over his head and into his lap, and Deacon used that opportunity to disentangle himself. The move was none-too-soon: as soon as he was done, two and a half years of sturdy toddler tumbled into Deacon's lap and started making demands.

"Sing!" Parry Angel demanded. Amy had done her hair after her bath, and it perched in a curly brown ponytail that bobbed when she shook her head. "Sing!"

Deacon bounced her on his knee, making her giggle, and tried to be stern. "C'mon, Angel, you know you've got to ask nice for that!"

Two big blue eyes with a fringe of lashes almost as thick and dark as Jeff's own batted up at Deacon, and they all had to laugh.

"Pweeeeaaazzzee?" she asked winsomely, and Deacon Parish Winters was, as always, helpless before his namesake.

"Yeah, Angel. C'mon." He pulled the little girl up to his waist, and then Lila gave Jeff a sloppy kiss on the mouth and scrambled up after her favorite playmate, not to be left behind. Deacon laughingly scooped them both up, blowing bubbles on their necks and negotiating the narrow hallway easily as he took them to Parry's room, the better to lay them down and sing them to sleep. Jeff sort of wished he could go in there and listen himself—Deacon's singing voice was wonderful, but unless he was putting Parry Angel down, no one got to hear it.

Amy, tiny, vital Amy, had, in the meantime, scrambled over the couch and practically into Jeff's lap.

"Hey!" Jeff protested, but Amy just giggled, wiggled her little bottom between him and Crick and said, with much the same imperiousness as her daughter, if truth be known, "Hug. Need hug now!"

So Jeff got to hold her, and something shuddered out of his body that he hadn't been able to let go of when he'd been sobbing on Deacon, and he thought that Deacon's ex-girlfriend (and best friend's wife) was a very, very wise woman.

"Hello, Precious," Jeff muttered. God, he missed Benny. Parry Angel's equally tiny mother would have done this for him too—and probably sooner, because she had *no* sense of propriety either.

"Hello, Jeffy. You gonna live?"

Jeff whimpered. He wasn't proud. "Reluctantly."

Amy didn't laugh. Instead, she went straight to the heart of the matter, her voice coming from between the hollow of Jeff's arms and chest. "You change that to 'with enthusiasm' immediately, you understand?" She pulled back and glared at him and met eyes with Crick. Jeff's own expression was amused, but to his surprise, Crick's was not.

Crick's brown eyes, his best feature in what was really an angular, barely pretty face, were intent on Jeff, and Jeff shifted uncomfortably. "Oh, sugar—I do *everything* enthusiastically, right? Even fall apart like a big gay baby!"

He tried a giggle on the two of them, and they didn't seem to be buying it.

"This is gonna suck worse than a vacuum cleaner to the balls," Crick said, his customary tact, diplomacy, and word-smithing fully apparent. "Amy's right—it shouldn't be here. If this kid's family is as freaked out about the gay thing as you say they are, this will be like, enemy camp to him or something. Meet him somewhere close, because the family is going to want to be close by, but make it public. Make him feel safe, okay?"

At that moment Andrew came in, looking at the couch with long-suffering eyes. Andrew was Deacon's hired man and another member of the family. Crick had saved his life, if not his leg, when they'd been overseas, and Andrew had found himself on Deacon's door after his discharge. At this point, the family wouldn't let him go if he tried to leave.

"I'm sleeping on the Barcalounger again tonight, aren't I?" he asked, trying to seem put-upon, and Jeff grinned at him tiredly.

"Well, since I can't convert you, big guy, and you're not big on the group snuggle, I'm thinking you should at least settle there for the short term."

Andrew's big, dark hand came out and ruffled Jeff's hair, in spite of the careful layering of hair-care products that Jeff used to keep it from cowlicking like a herd of heifers with dry-mouth. "Okay, but since the girls are in bed, can we watch something grown-up?"

Jeff perked up. "How about *Sense and Sensibility*?"

"Yes!" Amy crowed, practically bouncing in his lap with excitement. She picked up the remote on the coffee table and started scrolling through the Netflix queue on the television screen. "Jon hates it, I could never convert Benny to Jane Austen, and I'm *dying* to see it again."

Crick stood up so fast the couch almost tilted. "I'm going to go listen to Deacon sing," he muttered.

"For two hours?" Jeff managed to twinkle at him, and Crick rolled his eyes.

"At least until the hot guy courting Kate Winslet shows up," Crick replied dryly, and Amy tittered.

"I take it you've tried to convert Crick," Jeff said dryly, and Amy snuggled back in his arms. Her husband, Jon, was planning to pick her and the baby up in about an hour, but Jeff supposed that one of the plusses of having a gay ex-boyfriend—and a whole lot of gay friends period—was that a girl was never short a snuggle buddy. Jeff could live with that tonight, even if it meant no knitting was going to get done, period, the end.

FIFTEEN minutes later, Deacon and Crick came out of the girls' bedroom. Deacon heaved a mighty sigh and then settled down on one of the stuffed chairs to watch. Crick huffed, Deacon rolled his eyes and came to the couch to sit with him, and Jeff had to smile. Deacon would re-set the stars in their course for Crick. Changing his seat was not such a big deal. They all continued to watch, Jeff and Amy in complete absorption, until Deacon sighed again, made Crick give him the remote, and then paused the movie.

"The diner," Deacon said into the silence.

"The one next to the gas station?" Jeff wasn't surprised—Deacon and Crick ate breakfast there on occasion. It was a pretty decent place for a small-town greasy spoon.

"Yeah. It's near The Pulpit, you can take a few people but not too many, and it's public. You and this kid sit down, have a civilized meal, and see what he wants. All you gotta do is decide who you want."

Jeff gnawed at his lower lip and thought. "Crick," he said, because the guy was his GBFF, "and Kimmy."

"Hey!" Amy protested, and Jeff looked at her and shrugged.

"Kimmy and Shane are going through that whole how-to-be-a-counselor program, sugar. I'd ask Shane, but I think that's one too many big, white, gay men at the table."

"White?" Andrew asked. Although nearby Natomas was fairly diverse, in Levee Oaks, any skin color beyond a deep tan was very much in the minority.

"Yeah," Jeff said absently, wishing he could turn on the movie and disappear. "Kevin was black... what?" He looked up at all of them, Andrew included, because they were looking a little big-eyed. "I'm the white theatre kid—I'm *supposed* to be gay. Kevin was definitely a surprise."

"I should say so!" Andrew muttered, nodding. And then, as though everyone was looking at him with judiciously pursed lips, he grimaced and rolled his eyes. "Where'd you say this kid's from?"

"Georgia," Jeff said, wondering why he'd asked.

Andrew shook his head. "Oh my God... someday, you're going to have to let me know how you managed to seduce a Georgia boy—that's just not done!" And then, before Jeff could shake his head and say that Kevin pretty much had him at "Come fuck me!" Andrew went on. "And I really should be there, Jeff. This is a whole new thing here—something I don't know if you're ready to deal with. Race in California is not easy. Race in the South is a whole new world for California boys, you hear me?"

Jeff nodded his head, vaguely aware that he didn't understand at all. "So you'll be there?" he asked, grateful for the support anyway.

Suddenly Andrew sucked air in through his teeth. "When?"

"Two o'clock, day after tomorrow. Lucas's going to meet him at the bus station and bring him."

Now Deacon was making that sound too. "Go ahead," Deacon murmured. "I'll be fine."

"I can't," Andrew snapped back. "That stallion's a monster! I'm not leaving you alone, not...." Andrew trailed off, and Jeff wondered briefly why, before Deacon started talking again.

"No, I'll be fine!"

"Forget about it, Deacon!" Crick and Drew both snapped, and Deacon flushed.

"I take it someone's got to get laid instead?" Jeff asked, hoping his acid humor could even out some of the rough emotion he heard staticking up the room.

"Yeah," Deacon told him, and Jeff didn't miss the look he was shooting Crick. "Lucy Star. There's an outfit from down south that *really* wants one of her last babies, but their stallion isn't dummy trained."

Jeff huffed and looked mournfully at the frozen screen. "Could we clarify for those of us who think horses are only pretty if they've got half-naked men on them?"

Deacon's gentle chuckle was enough to soothe Jeff's ruffled feathers. "Usually, stallions are trained to fuck a pretend horse—a dummy horse. He comes into a jar, we ship the jar off to someone, and some mare gets lucky without getting the shit beat out of her during hot horse sex. This one isn't—and if we're not there to manage him, Lucy could get seriously hurt."

Jeff blinked at him. "Haven't horses been having sex without our help for thousands of years?"

"Yeah, but it hasn't been a lot of fun for the mares. Lucy's a friend—Ambush doesn't have to buy her dinner, but I want to make sure that fucker doesn't hurt her, either."

"It's a two-man job," Andrew said, and this time Jeff understood. Crick was a good man with horses, and his injuries were becoming less and less of a liability, but with something like this, Andrew's prosthetic leg would be less of a problem than Crick's crippled hand and arm.

"Well then, you have to do it!" Jeff said, inwardly wishing he wasn't such a nice guy.

"I'll be okay by myself," Deacon said, and Crick said, "Deacon…." with a sort of threatening undertone, and Jeff pulled himself out of his own misery long enough to realize that there was something going on between them that only they were privy to. He looked at Amy, but she shrugged, and together they listened to Andrew and Crick do some sort of subtle emotional blackmail to get Deacon to accept that Andrew couldn't help Jeff this time, he had to stay on the ranch and help Deacon.

So it was resolved then, Jeff thought, feeling a little better about it all. He had Deacon press play on the remote and got to watch his comfort movie in peace.

Chapter 3

Collin: A View to a Crushing

"WHY don't you ask him yourself?" the short man with the curly blond hair asked irritably. Irritation seemed to be the guy's principal emotion, Collin thought as he bustled around the tables in his mother's diner. He got to keep his insurance policy—the one currently keeping him alive—if he worked as her employee once a week. He didn't mind; he owned the garage next door, so it was simply a matter of putting Josh, his one employee, in charge for a day and running over to help Mom during the rush.

"Because he's *your* boyfriend," Jeff said with a shrug. "He's the miracle worker with cars—I just drive the damned things!"

Oh yes, Collin remembered Jeff.

Jeff had come into his mom's diner once in a while over the past year, and every time Collin had wondered, *"Do I say anything? Would he remember me? The guy damned near saved my life—shouldn't I thank him or something?"*

So after that first "spotting" about a year before, he had sort of stalked the guy whenever he came in. Today, for instance. Collin had been doing accounts in the garage when suddenly he'd looked up and seen the Mini Cooper parked in front of the diner. Abracadabra, hey-presto, whoopie! Collin's coveralls were stripped off, his apron thrown on, Josh was told he was alone in the garage, and Collin was suddenly the world's greatest son/busboy.

A nice lady held out her glass for more water, and Collin almost shot her a dirty glance. Dammit, how was he supposed to listen in on Jeff's personal conversation if he was in back getting a pitcher of water?

He remembered himself at the last minute. If nothing else, serving a clientele and owning his own business had taught him how not to be a complete asshole to the innocent and unsuspecting. He just kicked his ass into gear a little quicker so he could listen in on the pretty, narrow-faced, pointed-chinned, brown-eyed, dark-haired sweetheart of a bottom who was trying to cajole his buddy to have his boyfriend work on the Mini Cooper.

When he came back, a pretty woman with a waist-length braid of brown hair and (holy shit and ohmigod the legendary) Crick Francis, whom Collin remembered from high school, had joined them. The two of them, along with Jeff-the-sweetheart, had pulled out their knitting, and Collin tried not to roll his eyes. Omigod—was there anything more precious than a couple of boys knitting with their glitch-bitch? Of course, the little blond diva seemed the more possessive of the brown-haired woman—maybe he didn't like sharing.

"You are making me something, cow-woman, or that is just pretend and make-believe, like your sex life?"

"I'm making you a gag, Mickey, so I can fucking knit in peace."

Collin bussed the table across from them and tried not to smile. (He was lucky, there really had been work for him to do, or he would have just hung out, looking creepy.) Oh, he liked her. She reminded him of his oldest sister, Joanna. Joanna liked that word too—and didn't hesitate to use it.

"You want to knit in peace, go hide in the bathroom." Mickey shrugged. He had a charming Russian accent, but Collin wasn't nearly as interested in him as he was in Jeff.

Jeff looked tired. His angular shoulders were slumped over the table, and he followed the conversation around him with a weary smile, but he still managed a little bit of theatrics for that last comment. "That's just… just *ewwwww*!" He waved his hands in disgust, and Mickey rolled his eyes.

"You do not live with her. She reads in there, she does homework and pets the cats. Maybe if she actually knit in there, she would finally *finish my fucking sweater*!" He said this last with emphasis, and Collin had to actually stop and stare. He'd seen people knit sometimes, and he'd seen them flip the bird, but never in his life had he seen a woman knit *and* flip the bird at the same time.

"You're just jealous because I knit my brother's first," the woman said smugly, that middle finger still extended, and Jeff looked at her in admiration.

"You made a sweater for *Shane*? Kimmy-love, you're a wonder. He's like, a man-mountain—you must knit like the wind!" Jeff's hands were busy, but his elbows danced in repressed drama. *God*, he was fun to watch.

"Seriously, Kim—I'm totally impressed." In high school, Crick had been flamboyant and hard to miss. Maybe it was the company—Jeff was, without a doubt, the gayest thing Levee Oaks had seen since the forties, and the little Russian diva wasn't far behind—or maybe it was the painful-looking scarring on his arm and hand, as well as his now-famous tour of duty in the mid-east, but something about Crick had mellowed, become subtle and quiet and a little bit dangerous since Collin had idolized the guy as a lower-classman. Looking at him now, through adult eyes, Collin could see that he was plainly pretty, for a male, with high cheekbones and big, liquid brown eyes. There was a peace to him now that had been missing in school. Collin could totally relate.

Kimmy was smiling smugly, blushing a little with the praise. "I cheated. I used worsted yarn."

"But not chunky—" Jeff still sounded like this was a good thing, until Mikhail interrupted.

"Yes, but she made it *brown!*"

"Shane looks awesome in brown!" Crick defended, surprised, and Collin had to smile. Yup, still a little bit of total-gay-man left in Crick.

Mikhail sniffed and rolled his eyes. "Shane looks good in everything. I just wish you people could see him in something besides brown."

Jeff and Kimmy met eyes, and Kimmy's middle finger lowered. Collin, watching, started to like Jeff's friends *very* much, and was just thinking about moving over to their table and starting up a conversation, even though all he had was something completely brilliant like, "Uhm, knitting is cool!" His half-realized notion was interrupted, though, by the bell above the door and an unlikely pair of men walking through.

The older one was in his mid-twenties, blond-brown hair hanging down to his shoulders, brown eyes, and an enviable tan. The teenager next to him was almost as tall as he was—nearly six feet if he was an inch. He was black, with what looked to be one of those trendy hair-buzzes with something funky carved into the tight, black, short-cut curls. The kid was gangly and intense, with shoulders that threatened to become truly alarming when he matured and an upper lip that was curled up in hostility; he was looking for something to hit. Collin was a little concerned when Jeff looked up at his friends and gave a "girding the ol' loins" sigh that Collin's mom probably heard from in the kitchen.

"There's my cue, guys," he said softly, and Kimmy's hand came out and squeezed his arm gently.

"Remember, we're here for you, baby."

Jeff kissed her cheek and then walked forward, his hands tucked defensively into the pockets of his zip-up sweatshirt with the AEROPOSTALE logo on it. He pulled his hands out, though, and straightened his shoulders when he got to the older man, extending a hand in greeting.

"Lucas, it's so good to meet you." He gave a little chin-nod to the man's hair. "I wasn't aware that you'd left the service—I hope civilian life is treating you well."

Lucas extended his own hand, and then, to everyone's surprise, pulled Jeff in for one of those macho man-hugs, the kind with the fist-thump on the back. Jeff looked stunned, but he returned the fist-thump a little awkwardly, and when he straightened up, he looked decidedly more relaxed.

Lucas was looking a little abashed but determined. "Kevin was my best friend," he said gruffly. "I… you know. His whole life, he was lost and looking for someone and a place to be safe. When we shipped out, he told me that he'd found a home. I… I was really happy for him. I'm just glad he found you before… you know."

Jeff's smile was crooked, like it hadn't set right after an old break. He looked up then to the young man, who was fidgeting uncomfortably. "Martin?"

A pair of angry, dark eyes looked out at him, and Jeff tried a winning smile that got him precisely bupkiss.

"How about we sit down over here?" Jeff asked, pointing to the table next to where he'd been sitting. "My friends are over here at this table—Mikhail, Kimmy, Crick, this is Martin Turner."

Kimmy was the one who stood and smiled warmly. "Hi, Martin. It's so good to meet you." Martin's eyes widened, and he automatically smiled. Kimmy was a pretty woman, and she had a sort of warmth that would appeal to a kid who looked far away from home.

"Hi, ma'am," the kid said softly, and Collin heard some deep south in there. *Jesus, Jeff—where did this kid come from?* "Why would you be here?"

Again, that warm smile. "I'm getting a degree in counseling, and Jeff thought you might need a friend who... who wasn't quite so different from you, you know?"

Martin pursed his lips and looked at her doubtfully. "Well, lady, it's not like you're black."

Jeff rolled his eyes and sighed, as though they'd thought of this. "We had a straight black man for just that reason," he said peevishly, "but apparently he had to see a man about a horse."

The kid whipped his head around to look at him sharply. "Are you joking, asshole, because I don't take to being messed with!"

Jeff shook his head, seemingly oblivious to the kid's anger. "I *wish*! Andrew's a great guy too—you'd like him. But he works on a horse ranch near here, and he absolutely couldn't be spared. You'll probably meet him later if you want, but in the meantime, wouldn't you like something to eat? I mean...." Jeff grimaced, and Collin, who had heard him speak, wondered what he was fighting not to say. Was it "honey" or "sweetstuff" or "baby"? *You can call me "honey" anytime you want!* But the thought was interrupted by Jeff making another painful attempt to talk like a straight man. "Martin, wouldn't you like a good meal? This place is like home-cooked, and if nothing else, you've come a long way. Let me sit down with you and buy you some food."

The kid grimaced, and Collin wondered how long it had been since he'd eaten well. He looked rumpled—his oversized jeans were wrinkled, and his gigantic T-shirt was creased and stained, as was his big, hooded sweatshirt with cartoon characters in gangsta poses all over it. Underneath all those clothes, that tall, gangly kid must have weighed one-fifty, soaking wet.

Collin could practically hear the kid's stomach growling from where he stood.

Twenty minutes later, Collin was bringing out plates of food. A naked baked potato and salad for Jeff; chicken-fried-steak, home-fried potatoes, bacon-butter-beans, and French onion soup for the kid. The conversation at the table still appeared strained, and even that ground to a halt when the food arrived.

Collin brought coffee and a light lunch to the table with Jeff's friends, and he noticed that Lucas, the guy who'd brought the kid, had sat right down and made himself at home. He smiled a lot at Kimmy, and she gave him guarded glances back. Collin, after all his years waiting tables, started filling in the blanks. He liked making up stories about customers, just like he enjoyed taking cars apart and putting them together like big, greasy, irritating puzzles. Customers were unpredictable; cars were, for the most part, totally and completely rational, and together, they made an enjoyable living for a guy who hadn't thought he'd be around this long.

"So, how did you meet Jeff?" Lucas was asking, and Kimmy smiled a little bitterly.

"If I told you I didn't remember, would you believe me?" she asked, and Mikhail and Crick both snorted into their coffee.

"I'd believe you didn't remember a fucking thing about that day, cow-woman," Mikhail said acidly. "Or I would if you hadn't been coming onto the poor man like a heifer in season."

Kimmy grimaced. "It wasn't my fault," she said, blushing, and then she looked up at Lucas and blushed some more. "Oh God. Trust me. You don't want to know that story. Let's stick to you, young'un. How long are you out here for?"

But Lucas wasn't going to be dissuaded that easily. "I'm not that young," he said quickly, and Kimmy raised her eyebrows.

"Twenty... four? Five?"

"Seven," Lucas supplied. "And you are... twenty-nine?"

"Thirty-two," Kim told him, looking a little miffed. She'd been hoping he'd be younger, Collin thought shrewdly, refilling her coffee and trying to be invisible. It was like his own little stage play, and he got to be an extra that nobody knew about. Unfortunately, the damned lead player wasn't doing anything to keep his attention!

"You didn't answer the question," supporting-player-Kimmy said now. "How long are you out for?"

Supporting-player-Lucas shrugged his impressive shoulders under his denim jacket and T-shirt, and Collin thought wistfully that it was a shame the guy was obviously straight. Not that he'd be interested *now*, not with Jeff at the next table, but once upon a time, he might have liked to hit that.

Lucas sighed. "Well, as long as I want to, I guess. I was living with my folks when Martin's folks called up and told me that Martin had run away. I can hang here as long as it's friendly and as long as he needs me."

Kimmy's aloof expression thawed, probably against her will, Collin was willing to wager. "That's nice. My brother and I are opening a shelter for runaways—not every kid on the planet has someone who will look out for him, you know?"

Collin had heard of the place—Promise House. A house on a vacant property had already been renovated over the summer, and the eyesore acreage cleared and made livable. It had four spots open, four filled, a couple of employees, and Kimmy and her brother were close to being credentialed in counseling to make the place work completely. Collin had no idea where the little diva with the curly hair fit into this plan, but he thought that maybe it would be "moral support" for Kimmy's brother.

Hey, that guy could have supported Collin through high school, and Collin would have had no complaints.

But once again, that guy was not Jeff.

And Jeff was, finally, opening his mouth to take center stage.

"Uhm, Martin?"

"Mmmphh?" Omigod! Was that kid *still* eating?

"I understand...." His voice was shaking. Jeff took a deep breath to steady it and a naked sort of pain crossed his face. Collin realized his own hands were shaking. This man had been his hero for five years and his stalker-crush for one of them, and Collin had never realized how much pain he'd been in, not even a little. "I understand you have a letter for me?"

Martin sent him a look of deadly hostility and then grunted. Reluctantly he stuck his hand into the pocket of his sweatshirt and pulled out an envelope that looked dusty and old.

Jeff nodded as though this weren't the most important thing in the world and reached out to take the paper.

The kid's hand clenched on it, and the look he sent Jeff was decidedly unfriendly. "My brother wasn't a fucking fag," he said, his own voice shaking.

Jeff closed his eyes and swallowed. "Your brother was one of the best men I've ever known. Can I read my letter now?"

Unsatisfied but obviously unable to come up with another retort, the kid let go of the letter and shoveled in another bite of fried steak, potatoes, and gravy.

There were only two tables left in the diner after the rush, one of them belonging to Jeff's friends and the other belonging to Jeff. Collin didn't feel self-conscious in the least about watching Jeff read the letter in his shaking hands, because *everybody* in the restaurant was watching him read the letter, even the kid, who, as Jeff started to wipe his eyes unobtrusively with the backs of his hands, actually stopped eating.

"Oh God," he said when he got to the end. "Oh Kevin... Jesus. No...." Suddenly he looked up at Lucas, his face twisted with pain.

"Did you know?" he asked, and Lucas looked away.

"I guessed," he said. "I... awww... fuckitall...." Suddenly Lucas was wiping his eyes too. "Goddammit, Kevin. Godfuckingdammit!"

"Is it true?" Martin asked, and he looked from one man to the other. "Did my brother kill himself? Did you give him AIDS, you assfucker, so he had to kill himself?"

The kid came out of his seat and across the table, and Collin acted on instinct, grabbing him around the middle and crashing to the ground in a full tackle. The kid's chair went shooting across the room into Lucas, and there was a sudden silence after the clatter, broken by the kid shouting, "Get off me, motherfucker, just get the fuck *off me!*" He swung his elbow back and it connected solidly with Collin's nose, and for a moment, all Collin could focus on were stars and stars and the fact that, *oh fuck*, he was pouring blood down his shirt.

Collin stood quickly, holding his head back and looking from the corner of his eye for a napkin dispenser, and the kid scrambled up in a tangle of knees and elbows and reached in to help. Collin held out a hand and called, "Mo—mmmm! We neeb cween-ub oub hewr, stat!"

He heard his mother shout, and then the kid looked around at all of the stunned faces, Jeff's included.

Collin knew the exact moment the kid decided to flee—Collin had probably had the same expression on his own face when he couldn't face the mess he'd made too.

"Awwww, fuck this shit!" And Martin was gone, crashing out into the concrete-colored afternoon, leaving complete chaos in his wake. For a moment, the door swung open, and they could hear him pounding down the pavement in his Converse sneakers, dodging out of the way of cars as they came.

"I'll get him!" Lucas called, and Kimmy was out the door behind him.

Crick said, "Aww, fuck—someone's got to tell law enforcement he hasn't done anything. In this town they'll have his ass just for being black!" And then he and Mikhail went sprinting out the door, leaving their knitting behind them.

Jeff stood for a second and watched the herd of people disappear in search of one lost, confused kid, and then cocked his head a little as Collin staunched the blood from his nose. Calmly and collectedly, Jeff pulled a pair of purple steri-gloves from his back pocket—or out of his ass, for all Collin knew—and grabbed another handful of napkins and the pitcher of ice water from the other vacant table. Before Collin knew it, the sweetheart of his big-alpha dreams was telling him very competently to tilt his head and sit down, dammit, sit down!

Collin's mother came bustling in with a mop and a pair of rubber gloves that were standard practice when cleaning and gave a little *tsk*.

"It's not his fault," Jeff said with a hard swallow. "He was trying to keep the peace." Jeff sent him a rather huffy eye-roll, though. "I *can* take a punch, Collin. I may be flaming, but I'm not fragile!" He pronounced it "frag-*aisle!*" with a little trill on the end, and Collin wished his nose would stop bleeding (damned cocktail—he was pretty sure there was something in this go-around that was messing with his coagulation, because he'd had a hangnail the week before that had barely healed) so he could smolder at the guy and make him blush. But no, here was Collin, god of sex, with his nose in the air, trying to keep his mother from getting too close while he HIVed all over the place.

Oh holy shit and wait just a cotton-fucking-minute.

"You rebeber be?"

Jeff's shook his head and rolled those expressive brown eyes again. "Wow, boyfriend, you're quick! You keep picking up speed and next time, maybe you won't let the terrified teenager bolt out the door!"

"He bwoke by noze!" Collin protested, feeling as though he really were not being seen at his best here.

Jeff huffed and softly manipulated Collin's tender tissue. It hurt—it hurt like a sonovabitch, and the cool, impersonal touch was just that— cool and not sweaty or blushy or hot or any of the things that Collin had dreamed about. Jeff was holding himself back, too, so that their faces weren't that close, and he was looking Collin in the nose and not the eyes—ouch! Collin winced, because dammit, that hurt!

"Yeah, sweet thing, I know it hurts, but I don't think it's broken. An ice pack, a change of a shirt, and you'll be ready for date night, right?"

Ah-ha! An opening. "You buyin'?" Collin tried to make his eyebrow waggle as grown-up as he was feeling these days, but Jeff actually had the *nerve* to tousle his hair.

"Oh, baby, you *are* precious. Can't you see I'm waiting for a backlog of emotional luggage to clear customs? Dinner plans are *so* not in my future. Here, Ms. Collin's Mom, let me get that, okay?" Carefully, Jeff took the ice pack away from Natalie, who looked at her son with wide eyes and a bemused smile.

Collin found himself batting Jeff's hands away and taking the ice pack, putting it firmly against the bridge of his nose. "Sit, Momb, I beed to go change." He had to—you just didn't wander around in a bloody shirt when you were infected, now did you? "Web be cwean ub, firtht, 'kay?"

Jeff patted his shoulder and sighed. "I'll clean up, big guy. You were trying to do the knight in shining armor bit, the least you could let the gay-man-in-distress do is pick up the wreckage."

Collin tried to protest, but Jeff waved him off, his eyes getting wearier as he did so. "Go, Galahad, go. I need something to do while I wait for them anyway."

Collin trotted across the field/parking space to his garage next door, where he had a big sink with stiff scrub brushes and lots of industrial strength hand-cleaner, as well as a couple of changes of clothes. For a minute, he was reassured—the smells of hot engine oil and concrete were home to him, and his manhood reasserted itself. A pat on the head? Like a little kid? Oh *hell* no! Jeff, the guy Collin had been thinking about (stalking) for the last year was finally talking to him—there was no *way* he was going to let it go at that!

Josh was underneath the hood of a much-abused family minivan as Collin ran in, and still underneath it as he ran out. The car was on the hydraulic lift just far enough for Josh to lie underneath and his feet were sticking out. Collin skidded to a halt, though, as he was trotting through the practically pristine garage bay, and turned around to say something.

"Christ on a cracker, Joshua, how long does it take to replace a fucking blower in the A/C unit?"

Joshua startled, because Collin heard his head thump on something, and something else clattered down through the car's engine to bang on the concrete below. "Goddammit, Boss, do you think the blower's the only fucking thing wrong on this piece of shit? The blower's done, but they've paid for an hour, and I'd like to see this thing vaguely improved by the time they get it back, that okay with you?"

Collin grinned. Joshua was like a national treasure or something. Fully straight, a grandfather of four, Joshua had been bored to tears in retirement from a job in middle management until he'd seen Collin open the garage. Apparently, cars had always been Joshua's secret passion. He'd hung around constantly as Collin had set up, offering advice, giving orders, and even hauling stock and setting up equipment, until Collin had finally said, "Goddammit, old man, if you want a job, you're going to have to wait for me to get some fucking customers!"

Joshua had looked around the garage appreciatively. "Customers I think you'll get, but if you don't mind, I'd prefer they do their fucking someplace else."

"I can't pay you squat!"

"Don't want squat. Give me some fucking cash when you can afford it, and we'll be just goddamned fine."

Collin had started out paying him minimum wage, cutting the check apologetically and feeling like shit when he calculated the taxes. Now, though, he paid Joshua a full mechanic's salary, which Joshua used to take his wife on cruises and spoil his grandchildren rotten. Underneath the hood of that family crap-mobile was the grizzled-headed, potty-mouthed, god-fucking-damned salt of the fucking earth.

The first time Collin had flirted with a man in Joshua's presence, the old man had raised his eyebrows. Collin had looked at him challengingly. "You got a problem with that, old man?"

"Got a problem with your pick-up lines, asshole. You couldn't pick up a picnic basket with that bullshit. Just because you're pretty doesn't mean men are going to swoon at your feet, you know. Men got better sense than that!"

Collin had laughed. "And women?"

Joshua had harrumphed and repositioned his red ball cap on his bird's nest of iron-gray hair. "Women humor us into thinking we're worth something. You probably got the right idea, hotshot. You go after men, at least they know we're all frauds with a pecker, so you're on a level playing field. Now go away. I want to finish this tune-up so I can go home and be fooled by my wife some more."

Collin had left that day, but not before realizing that he may grow to love this old man with most of his cynical black heart.

Today, Joshua would work on this car until he liked its chances of running for a while before it came back. If they'd had other cars waiting, he would have done them first and then gotten back to the minivan in the interim, but they didn't, and the old man just liked working on cars. Collin got the feeling that the garage was the same for him as it was for Collin: refuge, sanctuary, and home.

And he could swear like a trucker there, and nobody would think twice about it. Collin was pretty sure that was a plus in the old man's book too.

But right now, Joshua's extensive four-letter vocabulary was not what Collin wanted to hear about. Right now, he wanted to hear about Jeff and what had made him look a thousand years sad.

When he got back to the diner, coming in from the door closest to the street, none of Jeff's friends had returned, but the mess had been cleaned up, the table had been set right, and all of the dishes had been bussed to the kitchen. The other table sat vacant, the knitting still on it, but most of the cups had been taken away and the leftovers neatly boxed. Collin made a frustrated sound, wondering, because Jeff's little blue Mini Cooper was still out in the front, but Jeff was nowhere to be found.

"Mom…?"

Natalie looked around the corner, her dyed red hair pulled back into a fuzzy ponytail and her lightly lined oval of a face still serene and dear. "He's out back, sneaking a cigarette. Turn down the libido for this one, okay, Collin? Whatever that little scene was all about, I think he just got a solid kick to the balls."

"Mom, I've loved this guy for five years—believe me, I'm not gonna rush things now!"

"Loved?"

Collin didn't want to deal with his mother's shock or her questions or any of the crap he knew she could throw his way, so he just sprinted through the restaurant to exit out the back door. Sure enough, the sweet smell of desperate tobacco was there to remind him that he hadn't had his "daily" cigarette in about a week.

He tried to slow down as he took his first step, so as not to startle his quarry now that it had finally gone to ground, but Jeff, it appeared, was beyond being startled.

He was leaning back against the brick wall, one foot propped up behind him, staring into space as he deliberately inhaled and slowly exhaled into the grayness of high-clouded November.

"Get all changed and bag your clothes, Skippy?"

Collin bit back a scream of frustration. Old men, young men, he'd surely bagged his share, but none of them had made him feel like a little kid with such a few short words.

"You find your runaway homophobic teenager?" he asked, hoping his voice was back to normal. The ice pack had helped, and a few Motrin had relieved the swelling, so that, at least, didn't suck.

Jeff sighed and inhaled again, blowing out a thin stream of smoke in silence. "Nope, not yet. I'm hoping Kimmy and Lucas find him first—they're less likely to freak him out."

Collin nodded, and decided to go for the fifty-thousand dollar question with the bonus set of steak knives and the new dinette set. "So, um, who's Kevin?"

Jeff looked at him sideways. "You have to know me better to know who Kevin is," he said flatly, and Collin fought back a snarl.

"Well, you know who I am, right?"

Jeff's shoulders curled a little, and that insouciant, *the worst has happened and I'm still alive* posture lost some of its spine. "Yeah," he said softly, looking at Collin from underneath dark lashes. "I remember. I'm glad to see you stuck around."

Collin warmed himself in that soft, almost shy look. "You really saved my life that day, you know?"

Jeff shrugged, and his spine straightened. "You saved your own, kid. I just gave you an ear."

Sudden shaft of brilliance. "Everyone needs an ear, Jeff. Even you." Ooh... Collin, who usually scrubbed people raw with his Brillo personality, was damned proud of that one.

Jeff flicked the cigarette to the ground glumly. "You think I haven't told everyone chasing down my problem?" he asked, and there was no sign of a trill, no sign of the flamboyant flirt that Collin had seen coming into his mother's restaurant for the last year. There was just a tired man who seemed to be a little lost.

"Yeah, but you haven't told them what was in that letter that made that kid run."

Jeff sucked in a hard breath and wiped his eyes with the heel of his hand. He grimaced and reached into his pocket for a small bottle of extra-spiffy hand sanitizer.

Collin wrinkled his nose. "Holy God—I can smell that shit from here. What in the hell is *that*?"

Jeff sent him an affronted look. "White Citrus, from Bath and Body Works. Jeez, kid, not everyone gets off on grease-cutter and dish soap."

Collin rolled his eyes. "Excuse the fuck out of me if I try to keep the 'man' in 'gay man', okay? Now are you going to tell me or not?"

Jeff's pocket buzzed, and he pulled his phone out and sighed. "Fuck. The kid's dis-a-fucking-peared. Goddammit. I gotta call Shane. He'll have some buddies who can look for him." Jeff turned around to go inside, and Collin wanted to smack his head against the brick wall. He had him. He *had him*, right here, and he couldn't seem to get any closer than he had been in five years.

"Jeff!" he called, right as Jeff grabbed the swinging glass door. Jeff looked up, and Collin took a risk.

"Last time we did this, you gave me a hug that saved my life. Um, can I return the favor?"

The look on Jeff's face was... almost peaceful. It was like hugs were his language, and he finally had a chance to communicate. He barely bothered to roll his eyes as he opened his arms and gave the little wrist-flipping gesture to get Collin to come closer.

Collin was eye-level, and that obviously surprised Jeff, but Collin wasn't going to wait around for Jeff to be surprised. In one step, Collin was inside those long, angular arms, wrapping his bulky biceps around Jeff's shoulders and holding him with hard, purposeful security.

Jeff looked surprised for a moment, and then he must have seen Collin's intent as he moved his face closer, holding his hand to the back of Jeff's head as he barreled in for a kiss.

Chapter 4

Jeff: Fractured Fairy Tale

So. Not. Fair.

Yeah, Jeff remembered him. The angular cheekbones, the square jaw, those things had filled out, and so had his chest, and his arms were truly amazing. The dark blond hair was parted in the middle and hung to sweep his jaw line. Most of the time Jeff had seen him, it had been pulled back behind his ears in a half-ponytail, but not today. The long hair made him look young, and tough, and... oh, damn, the kind of kid that Jeff would have gone for in a heartbeat a half a million years ago.

Up close, his eyes were... amazing. They were an average color—brown, like Jeff's, but they also had flecks of gold and flecks of green, and these dark brown lashes, and that bad-boy's lean mouth was drawn up in a scowl, and he was holding Jeff in a way that... oh, God.... Jeff could hardly remember being held like this.

The last person to do it had been Kevin.

For a moment, the weight of Kevin's brother, of the letter sitting in his pocket like a piece of cannon-shot, of Jeff's careful little bubble of hedonism, was supported in those wide-fingered bony hands, and Jeff felt almost young as those arms wrapped around his shoulders, even as the one hand cupped the back of his head and angled him for a kiss.

His mouth opened under Collin's lean-lipped twist of triumph, and Collin's tongue swept into his mouth. Ahhh... ahhh, God....

He must have whimpered, melted, something, because in about two seconds, Collin had his back pressed against the wall, his shoulders pinned, and was ravaging his mouth like Patton ravaged the Philippines,

only with less khaki and more—oh Christ, more tongue. Five years...
could he really have survived for *five years* without being kissed?
Without being held? Without smelling sweat and feeling stubble against
his chin?

Collin *growled*. There was no other word for it—a warm,
possessive rumble came up from his chest, and he ground his hips up
against Jeff and, oh, God....

Shit—wasn't he in the middle of something?

Pulling away and ducking under Collin's arm was easy, because
Collin wasn't expecting it—and horribly difficult, because Jeff didn't
want to do it.

"You're a sweet boy," he said, but he was panting so it probably
didn't sound as condescending as he was trying for. He tried again.
"You're a sweet boy, Collin, but I've got some shit to do right now!"

And with that, he managed to trot through the door of the restaurant
and flee out the other side.

KIMMY and Mikhail were waiting for him in the front of the restaurant.
They had apparently rounded up all of the stuff at the table while Jeff
was lapsing into emotional maelstrom, and were ready to go.

"Did we pay up?" Jeff asked, hoping they'd left a hell of a tip after
all of that.

Crick's car was still parked outside, so Mikhail cast a sour look at
Kimmy and then, as the shortest, climbed into the back of the Mini
Cooper, saying, "Yes, and moose-woman here left half a fortune in cash.
I hope that boy's cow-eyes were worth it, heifer—that money would
have paid my rent back in the old country."

"The boy wasn't making cow-eyes at *me*, Mikhail. Besides, I
thought your ass paid your rent in the old country!" Kimmy shot back,
and Jeff grimaced. She and Mikhail really must have loved each other
for her to go there. Mikhail wasn't exactly ashamed of his past, but he
didn't usually let it be used as target practice, either.

"Okay, it would have paid *your* rent. I would have lived in a
fucking palace, how's that? And I was talking Lucas, making the cow-
eyes. The other one was obviously aimed at... what does he want?"

Because Jeff had just turned the key as everyone belted in, and now Collin was hustling out with three twenties in his hand.

"You overpaid," he was saying darkly as Jeff buzzed down the window, and Jeff sent Kimmy an annoyed look. Kimmy shrugged.

"It's not like *you* were giving him any love!" she snapped, and like a sudden storm in a clear sky, Jeff felt a full on blush take over his body.

"Kimmy was trying to make up for your trouble," Jeff muttered, scowling, and she smiled sweetly. Since she never did anything sweetly, Jeff suppressed the urge to flip her off.

"Did you mention that *you're* the one that cleaned up?" Collin thundered, doing the offended pride thing, and Jeff tried very hard to look at him with his "this is only a kid" glasses, but they didn't seem to be working. When he looked at the kid from the corner of his eye, when he wasn't expecting a terrified boy, Collin ended up bearing a striking resemblance to Deacon.

"I didn't mention jack, I didn't know she overpaid, and, dammit, give the tip to your mother, who's a lovely woman, if your manly pride is too tender. Now I'm sorry to tell you to piss off, babydoll, but piss off!"

"The kid vaulted an iron fence," Kimmy said helpfully before Jeff could peel off in an embarrassment-fueled snit. "Lucas kept after him, but he lost the kid at the storage place by the levee after I came back to get reinforcements."

Jeff turned and glared at her. "How in the hell do you know that?"

Kimmy had a sweet little oval of a face, the kind of loveliness that could get away with the worst sort of language and the most irritable looks because she had a warm heart and her brother's warm brown eyes and was stunningly attractive.

"We exchanged cell phones, fuckhead. Now make nice with the cute boy-king and let's roll!"

Jeff fought back a scream and turned around to glare at Collin. "Did you have anything else to add, because we're a little busy here!"

Collin scowled back at him. "You going to be at The Pulpit later? Because I know where it is, and I can catch up with you there!"

He couldn't help it—a groan escaped. "It was a kiss, sweet thing, not a declaration of love," he muttered, and because he hadn't taken the car out of neutral or taken the parking brake off, he didn't kill them all when he thudded his forehead against the steering wheel.

But the window was still open, and Collin leaned down into the car and placed that warm, demanding hand on his shoulder, then lowered his head so that his lips brushed Jeff's ear and that longish, bad-boy hair tickled Jeff's jaw.

"It was a declaration of intention, and we both know it," he said on a growl, and Jeff closed his eyes against the idea. Then Collin looked up at Kimmy and Mikhail. "I'll be there at six—will he be there?"

"Oh *fuck* yeah!" Kimmy said, sounding delighted, and Jeff shot her a betrayed look.

"Heifer!"

Collin's throaty laughter was still inside the car, and Jeff's chin was being grasped in strong fingers that smelled a little like engine grease and a lot like industrial hand cleaner, and then Collin gave him a hard, marking, kiss goodbye before backing up and out of Jeff's tiny car and personal space.

"I'll be there!" he promised direly before turning back toward the diner.

Jeff leaned his head against the steering wheel again, with his eyes closed, and listened to his engine idle in the shocked silence.

"I don't suppose either of you missed that?" he asked after a moment. He risked turning his head and saw that both Kimmy and Mikhail were eyeing him with almost twin expressions of titillated mischief. He turned his head back to looking at his knees under the steering wheel.

"Are you shitting me?" Kimmy asked. "Best show I've had all year. What in the fuck was that about?"

"He thinks he's got a crush on me," Jeff said weakly, straightening up and releasing the emergency break. "I'm going to have to set him straight."

"What an appalling thought," Mikhail said appreciatively. Kimmy shot him an outraged look, and the little Russian held out his hands. "No, cow-woman, I am not thinking of straying on your brother. It's just good to know that such a one plays for our team. And I think Jeff is full of shit—why would you want to turn that offer away?"

"Where are we going, Kimmy?"

"To go get Crick and Lucas. Crick drove us here, but he's got the keys." She looked behind her and grimaced. Both men were pretty damned tall, and there was no *way* they'd fit in the back of the Cooper comfortably. "Or maybe just to go help them look. Or figure out how to get everyone to their cars. Or… fuck, I don't know, it's a clusterfucking transportation nightmare, and we're the only ones not walking. Either way, about two miles down—they're near the levee road."

Jeff swore. Crick put on a good front, but his body wasn't ready for quite that long a run, not if he had to turn around and come back. "One of you is going to have to get out and stay with Lucas after we get his keys," he muttered. "Crick's going to need to come back with us."

"Cow-woman will do it," Mikhail said with a slight sneer. "He was making cow *eyes* at her, just like you were trying not to make with the garage/bus boy, and I think it's time one of you got laid."

"I think it should be Jeff," Kimmy said promptly. "My ex-drug-abuser is still visible in my rearview. How long has it been, Jeff? You're starting to give off maiden auntie vibrations here!"

Jeff sighed and wished he could pull over and run away. Deacon knew the answer to this one, because Deacon could identify. Deacon would have happily gone without sex for the rest of his life if Crick hadn't come back from Iraq. Crick knew the answer, because he and Deacon didn't keep secrets, but Crick, (showing surprising tact, for Crick) hadn't actually said a whole lot about it. But now, because Jeff had no emotional defenses whatsoever at the moment, his clean little secret was about to escape. "Not since Kevin," he muttered, and an appalled silence blanketed the car.

"Holy God," Mikhail said reverently. "I thought your virginity grew back after that long."

"Yeah?" Kimmy asked with interest. "When's that happen?"

"Longer than six months," Mikhail snapped.

"Bitch."

"Heifer. And I'd say about two years," Mikhail said decisively. "Because that's how long it was for your brother when we met, and I have never met a more innocent man."

Kimmy snorted. "That's just Shaney. His whole brain is stuck on permanent virginity."

"Not anymore," Mikhail said with some considerable pride. "But we are talking about Jeff. How in the fuck do you go for five years without fucking?"

Jeff *really* didn't want to talk about this anymore. In fact, he didn't want to talk about *anything* anymore. Mostly, he wanted to go home, take a nice long bubble bath, and curl up with Con and Katy and watch a comfort movie and eat chocolate. Even if his stomach hadn't been doing well this go-round, maybe it was time for chocolate to become his friend once again. But the silence was holding in the car, and Kimmy and Mikhail were both expecting an answer, and both of them were being damned decent about tracking his problem all over Levee Oaks.

"A large collection of the world's finest sex toys," he told them honestly. "And lots of flavored lube. Kimmy, love, do I turn here, or are we driving off the levee into the river?"

Because, you know, that sounded like an option too.

IT TOOK some car shuffling to get Lucas and Crick situated, and in the end, the kid was still nowhere to be found. Shane, the big, hairy, Hoover ex-cop had tipped off his old partner, Calvin, to keep a lookout for Martin.

"I told him he's lost, he's hungry, and he's pissed off, but that he's not a bad kid. Calvin will keep his head, but let's hope he's not the only one."

Jeff sighed and flopped back on the couch at The Pulpit, and Shane gave a sympathetic grimace. Crick was outside, apprising Deacon and probably helping the big, horny horse get laid, because God knew that seemed to be a twelve-person job, and Lucas was out there too. (Seriously, how many grown men did that really need?) Kimmy was in the back bedroom with Parry Angel, because the little girl had been so happy to have another girl in the house that she'd needed to play dolls immediately, and Jeff, Shane, and Mikhail were in the living room, strategically trying not to mention that dinner needed to be started, and it was usually the idle who ended up lending a hand.

"Thank you," Jeff said quietly now to Shane. He couldn't seem to summon his usual cattiness, and he could tell Shane was bothered when his expressive brown eyes got big and confused.

"Thank you? That's it? Thank you?" Shane shook his head decisively. "Mmmno. Not gonna fly. You gonna tell us what made this kid go apeshit or what? Because all reports say he knew you and his brother were tight when he walked into the restaurant. What in the hell was in that letter, Jeff?"

Jeff glowered. "I don't want to talk about it," he muttered, and was disheartened when Shane turned pleasantly to Mikhail and said, "Mickey, could you do me a favor and start dinner? Jeff and I have some history here, okay?"

Mikhail rolled his eyes. "If you were not naked, it was not history worth writing down."

"Mickey, please?"

Mikhail stood up and smacked Shane's cheek lightly. "It is a good thing you are cute, you big, stupid cop, or I would cook the same thing for you that you tried to poison me with last week."

Shane grimaced, and Jeff grinned. By all reports, Shane could fuck up a microwave burrito. Then Jeff remembered exactly who had said that, and his heart fell again. He looked dispiritedly around the little room with its ugly, comfortable couches and bowl of flowers above the television, and didn't see hide nor hair of cheap yarn or construction paper or really dirty paperback romances.

"Christ, I miss Benny," he said into the silence, and Shane sighed too.

"God, so do I. She's coming for Thanksgiving, you know."

Jeff perked up. "Really? The whole week? Because I'm telling you, as much as I love Crick, that girl sure did make the spirit of this place, you know?"

Shane nodded, something in his expression guarded enough to make Jeff want more information. "What?"

A shrug. "I don't know. I... just heard her talking to Deacon, and Deacon talking back... something about the tone of their voices. I don't think she's doing well. And you know Deacon—he wants her to come home, but he doesn't want to say so, because heaven forbid he should ask for anything because *he* wants it, but he doesn't want to get in the way of her education, and... you know."

Jeff nodded. "Yeah. A big alpha-male morass of suppressed needs. Honey, I've heard the song, I know the tune, I can sing the words in my sleep."

"Yeah," Shane said with a suppressed twinkle, "but you're the only man I've ever met who trills the high notes in a baritone."

Jeff couldn't help it. He giggled and looked at the brown-haired, brown-eyed, man-mountain of a cop with true appreciation. The year before, Shane might have thought up that line, but he wouldn't have had the balls to say it. After a year of finding Mikhail—and quitting the force to do something he was truly more suited for—Shane was a little more relaxed and a lot less awkward.

And he seemed to care for Jeff like a brother in their little unconventional family, and it didn't look like he was going anywhere until he got an answer.

Sure enough, his next words were sober and quiet, and Jeff thought about what a wonderful thing it was that he was going to try to be a youth counselor, because even the most hardened juvenile delinquent would have to think twice before getting in the face of that much massive patience.

"I know you're going to tell Deacon, Jeff, but why not give me a dry run, okay? I mean, if I fuck it up, you can whine to Deacon about me, and that, at least, will make you feel better."

Jeff looked at him helplessly. Jesus, the guy's only flaw was that he thought he was a fuck-up, when really he was about the world's nicest human being. And Jeff, the master of the high-gay catty epithet, had really not let him live in peace since they'd met more than a year and a half ago during dinner at The Pulpit.

"You're not going to fuck this up," he said, keeping his voice soft. Really, what was the big secret? It had happened years ago, right? And Jeff had lived just fine not knowing the particulars. Nothing had changed, really, right?

Shane shrugged, and they heard a bout of swearing—in Russian—from the kitchen. "He doesn't know he does that," Shane said softly, the little grooves in his cheeks deepening. "He likes to think he only speaks Russian when he's doing it on purpose, but when he's not thinking about it... it just slips out."

Jeff smiled in spite of himself. Mikhail was a complicated, irritating little man, and Shane was a patient, soothing, simple one. Seeing two people work together like that was both inspiring and depressing. Right now, it felt like family, and maybe that was what Jeff needed to get this off his chest.

"Kevin...." Jeff's throat closed, and he swallowed hard. "You've got to understand. He was so proud of being in the military. He... he wanted to be someone his little brothers and sisters could look up to. He wanted to be the first person in his family to go to college when his second tour was over. He...." Oh God. How long had it been since he'd talked about Kevin? "He was just so damned proud, you know?"

Shane smiled. "Was he as proud as Deacon?" he asked, and Jeff had to laugh.

"Yeah," he said softly. "Almost exactly as proud as Deacon. Apparently, it's what killed him."

"How?"

Jeff looked away. "You see, he'd gotten tested for HIV before he left, but it hadn't shown up yet. When my numbers spiked, I wrote him—it was five years ago, the whole digital thing wasn't as big in the military as it is now. If he popped positive for HIV, he would have gotten sent back home. It probably wouldn't have been a discharge—lots of ways to get it, right?—but he would have had to explain to his family, and that might have meant coming out, and then... all that pride...."

"Where does it go, right?"

"Yeah."

Jeff took a deep breath and tried to say this right. "See, when he was killed, all Lucas knew was that they were hunkering down behind a burned-out tank, surrounded by enemy fire, and waiting for a helicopter to come bail them out. The copter wasn't more than ten minutes out—they didn't have long to wait. There was a structure nearby—something a little more solid than the tank, something that would give them a better chance. Suddenly, Kevin turned to Lucas and said, 'Here, I've got a plan. Give me a sec, and then you guys run for shelter.'."

Shane hissed air through his teeth, and Jeff looked at him appreciatively. Naïve, yes, but nobody ever said the big guy was dumb.

"I...." Oh God. For all his crying on Deacon the other night, he'd thought he remembered the real taste of pain. "His letter...."

I'm sorry, club boy. I had this whole picket fence set-up lined up in my head for us when I got back from my tour. When I was ready, I thought I'd be strong enough to tell the world. But I'm not ready, and I'm not strong enough, and don't think I don't know that I gave you this problem, and if I have to face you sick because I made you that way, I might as well put the gun to my head myself.

As it is, I think I'll let the enemy do the honors.

Shane did the unexpected thing then. He reached over and grabbed Jeff's hand.

Jeff clung to it. "They teach you this in counseling school?" he asked, keeping his caustic edge intact.

"Yup. I'm getting an A." Another big, wide hand came up and covered Jeff's other hand.

"Good to be an extra credit project, big guy."

"Well, you're high maintenance enough. I'm just glad to get something out of it."

That right there straightened Jeff's spine, and he ripped his hands reluctantly from Shane's. "High *maintenance!*" he shrieked. "*I'm* high maintenance? May I remind you of last year? Do I have to? Because, I'm telling you, by the end of that fucking week, I was going to stab you myself!"

Shane chuckled dryly and stood as another round of clattering and incensed Russian swearing emanated from the kitchen. "I'm gonna go help him before he rearranges their kitchen. Benny would never forgive us." And with that, he ruffled Jeff's hair, mindless of all the hair products Jeff used to hold it in place.

Well, he could, Jeff scowled, smoothing his hair back. Big dumb ex-cop mountain just let his curl like a blackberry bush; it was no surprise he had no respect for anyone else's 'do. He was just about to go check himself in the mirror when it occurred to him: damn Shane and his patience, he'd actually imbued Jeff with the teeniest bit of serenity.

Christ, boyfriend was *good!*

And then there was the sound of a strange car coming up the drive, one with a big monster, macho, big-dick engine, and Jeff had a moment to panic.

Oh God. Whatever the hell that was, it sounded like something Collin would drive.

"Oh shit! Is that a fucking Camaro?"

The kitchen overlooked the driveway, and Shane's delight practically rattled the walls. "Would ya look at that, Mickey! It's a goddamned Chevy Camaro—man, I bet it's been modified too!"

"I take it that's a car?" Mikhail's skepticism took some of the thunder out of the air.

Jeff didn't stick around to hear the reply.

Sure enough, as he walked out of the house to lean against the porch rail, he could see it. The big-dick car was a brilliant, candy-apple red, with some sort of whoopty-dick-hickey sticking out of the hood to make it look even more masculine and intrusive, and Jeff couldn't help a sniff of disdain. Ostentatious much? Really? He never would have guessed.

Jeff looked beyond where Collin was parking in the fading twilight to see where Deacon, Crick, and Andrew were, and if they were setting up to come inside soon. He couldn't help this either—one of the principle things that had attracted him to Crick's life at The Pulpit was the family table, and Jeff needed that security like nobody's business.

And he would have given his left furry nut not to face that kid who had nearly managed to kiss him silly. Unfortunately, there didn't seem to be a collection service for that—just Collin, getting purposefully out of the car.

"You found your runaway yet?" Collin asked as Jeff leaned against the porch rail.

"Nope. Black teenager loose in Levee Oaks. I'd alert the media, but they'd discover this little nest of gays and try to smoke us out like wasps." Jeff wiggled his fingers to indicate both smoke and wasps, and Collin's mouth quirked up.

"You gonna invite me in?" Collin's boots made hollow thumps coming up the wooden porch steps, and Jeff shook his head.

"Not my place, kid. Wait 'til Deacon comes back from inseminating his horse, and he'll invite you in."

Collin's lean, hard-edged mouth curled up in a grin. "Inseminating his horse? Man, I heard the guy had balls of solid rock, but I had no idea!"

Jeff flushed. Oh for sweet Christ's sake, of all the fucking things... dammit, that was a joke *he* should have made! "Grow up!" he admonished, and Collin rolled his eyes. "What are you doing here?"

Instead of leaning on the railing next to Jeff, Collin came up behind him and leaned against him instead. "I told you, princess," he growled, "we've got some unfinished business to tend to."

Jeff shoved himself backward, his head connecting hard with Collin's jaw, but he didn't care. "Really? You're going to come on to me today... for *real*?" He was dumbfounded. No fucking discretion. This kid had no *fucking* discretion, no clue about people, and no *fucking* sense.

As evidenced by the completely blank look on his face. "What's wrong with today?"

"What's wrong with today? What's wrong with today?" Jeff was vaguely aware that he was stomping his foot and waving his hands and that all of his carefully Shane-earned serenity had just jumped off the porch and into the manure pile on the other side of the barn. He couldn't make himself give a shit—even a horse-sized one.

"Babydoll, have you not noticed that I'm still dealing with the mess made by my dead boyfriend? Because if ever there's a day *not* to hit on someone, that would be it! Maybe we've noticed that, hello, I'm just sort of dangling from the sanity building, kicking and screaming, and then you want to come along and step on my fingers?"

"Hang in there, baby, there's a reason for that—"

But Jeff wasn't going to let him finish. "Why in the fuck would I want to kiss a guy who can't read a goddamned mood, that's what I want to know!"

He was not prepared for Collin's hands on his shirtfront, or Collin's solid, rangy body backing him up against the wall of the house. Suddenly, they were face to face again, and his hands were hanging helplessly at his sides, and Collin was glaring at him with exasperation.

"Maybe because you need someone today, you ever think of that? Maybe I'm just trying to be there for you like you were for me! Jesus, try and support a guy!"

"I've got plenty of support!" Jeff snapped, damned grateful for it. "I'm not alone in the universe, Collin. The sentiment is appreciated but—"

Collin cut him off. "I'm not talking family, genius, I'm talking bigger than that!"

Jeff smirked, because their groins were touching, and Collin had an obvious package, and wasn't it just like the kid to try to bring *that* into it. "My, my—aren't we humble!"

"And I'm not talking about that any more than you were talking jock strap as support!" Collin snapped, and Jeff had to reluctantly smirk again in appreciation. At least the kid was quick on the uptake, and that was nice, and then he got mad all over again because, dammit, the kid shouldn't even *be* there. Jeff was going to have dinner with his family and wait for news about Martin and be *safe*, dammit, and *protected* and *loved* and all that shit that family gave you and Jeff had craved for so damned long!

"Look, Skippy," Jeff said through clenched teeth, forcibly unclenching Collin's hands from his Aeropostale sweatshirt, "your help is appreciated, but really? We got it covered. You want to stay for dinner, I'll have Deacon give you the invite, but I'm good, got it?"

Collin's jaw clenched and his eyes narrowed, and what was left was not a child's expression at all. "You really are something else, aren't you? Man, you may have your little family all happy about how well you're doing, but I've been watching you for a *year*, and I can tell you all that it's bullshit! You feeling like crap and calling me 'Skippy' ain't gonna make it any fucking better!"

"Well random busboy fucking isn't going to do it either, Skippy!" Jeff snapped, and now that strong-jawed face showed absolute fury, and Jeff resisted the urge to clap his hand over his runaway mouth like a little kid.

He wouldn't have had the chance, because Collin's mouth came down *hard* on his, all teeth and frustration and bruising anger and passion—oh Christ, he tasted edgy and dangerous and….

Jeff put two hands on his chest and shoved.

"I'm not interested in being assaulted," he panted, turning sideways and backing up toward the porch. "Now go down and wait by the car, and I'll go get Deacon."

Collin wiped his (puffy, bruised) mouth with the back of his hand and gave a gritty smile. "What's the matter, Jeffy? What are you afraid of?"

"Know-it-all-kids fucking with my peace," Jeff snarled, surprised by his own candor for a moment.

Collin nodded like that was what he thought. "Look, man, don't think I haven't learned something watching you. You play a good clown, you know that? You laugh, you tell funny stories, you give *swell* advice. But I saw your eyes when you read that letter, and if these people can't see that you're ripped open and bleeding to death, well, that's because they don't care enough about the man to see past all the gay—*fuck!*"

Because that, right there, was when the red curtain went up in front of Jeff's eyes, and his fist connected solidly with Collin's jaw.

Chapter 5

Collin: Sweet and Sour Jawbreakers

COLLIN was standing right at the porch rail, and he almost went ass-over-teakettle over the edge. He didn't, though—he bounced back from a crouch, and his fist, still pretty quick from being voted "most likely to fight on a dime" of his class at Levee Oaks, came back out and caught Jeff square on his own jaw, and Jeff stumbled down the stairs, landed on his knees, and came up spitting like a cat.

And jumping like one.

Collin found himself being pummeled by some solid fists and one furious man who seemed to forget his jokes and his trilling voice and his front to the world in an effort to hammer Collin into the cold, solid ground. Collin took a couple of swings—he didn't want to hurt the guy, but *dayum*, that fist connected to his nose again, and this time he heard a crunch and knew it was broke, and he had to stop this bullshit *somehow*.

Jeff swung again, and Collin grabbed his fist, using his momentum to swing around and haul Jeff's arm up behind his back. Jeff just had time to squeal, "Let *go-oooooo* douchebag motherfucker!" when they were both hit by a blast of freezing water from a hosepipe attached to the barn.

Jeff screamed like a bird, and Collin swore like a sailor, and still that relentless blast of water kept at them until they were both on the ground, holding their hands over their heads to keep the nasty, stinging pellets out of their eyes and mouths.

Abruptly the water was shut off, and what was left was a pleasant bass voice calling out, "Jesus, Crick, goddammit, I told you to turn it off!"

"Oops!" Crick sounded completely unrepentant, and Collin squinted past the water running in his eyes to glower at his erstwhile hero. Crick saw the look and rolled his own eyes, fumbling with the lever for the hosepipe with his bad hand and saying, "Don't look so pissed off, Sparky—you want to come over to our place and start shit, you gotta be prepared to be hosed!"

"Oh, ha ha!" Jeff snapped. "And what about me?" He wiped his hands carefully across his red eyes, and blinked rapidly—all that shit he put in his hair must have run into them.

The guy giving the orders harrumphed. "I'd place money on you being the one to throw the first punch."

Collin snorted painfully, sputtering blood everywhere, and Jeff reached behind his shoulder and smacked him on the back of the head. "See if you get that dinner invite now!" he smirked, at the same time that pleasantly deep voice said, "Andrew, could you go fetch me the first aid kit and disposable sani-gloves I keep in the tack room? We're gonna need a pair for me and one for Crick, okay?"

Collin's nose was pouring blood, and he looked sideways at Jeff and saw that the guy he'd come to seduce had a split lower lip and a cut on his eyebrow. Fan-bloody-tastic. Jesus, Collin could *swear* he was better at the whole pick-up thing than this. Maybe he needed to run his technique by Joshua for some polishing.

"I'b thowwy fow da twouble," he said, feeling foolish—again.

Deacon—it *had* to be the legendary Deacon Winters, town hero and good boy, until he'd come out as the love of Crick Francis' life—gave a mild smile. "You know, if you'd wanted a dinner invite, all you had to do was ask."

Jeff huffed behind him. "You're letting him *eat* here?"

"Letting him? Hell, Jeff, I'll spring to pay for your first date. Any asshole who can get under *your* skin is gonna be someone to keep around!"

Collin couldn't help it. He was muddy, wet, and almost as cold as Jeff (whose pouty lips seemed to be tinged a little blue from being wet in the November twilight.) His nose felt like it had exploded with prejudice, and there was blood pouring down his face, but still, Collin felt a smile stretching across his bruised lips.

Apparently, he was in.

In a minute, though, the smile was gone. Deacon was hovering over him, his hands cased in the purple steri-gloves, checking to see if the explosion of pain on the front of his face needed to be set.

"Yup, you got yourself a break, kid."

"Gollin."

"'Kay, Collin, we've got two choices here." Deacon sounded faintly out of breath, and Collin wondered if he'd had to run when the fight broke out. "We can either let this sit, and you'll bleed all night, and it'll hurt like a sonovabitch, or we can realign it right now. The pain'll make you puke, but it'll be over and done with and you can get on with your life."

"Option B," Crick said. He was over with Jeff, cleaning up the cuts on his face, and for a minute, Collin was blindly jealous. Damn—all he'd wanted was a soft moment from the guy, and he'd gotten decked. Crick, who apparently had Deacon to come home to, got to spend time staring soulfully into Jeff's eyes. Well, Collin had to concede, except for the fact that Crick was busy casting surreptitious looks of worry at Deacon. Collin blinked and tried to focus his eyes on the guy to see if he was sending any messages back when two strong hands—one with a slightly crooked thumb—set up on either side of his nose.

"Wai'!" Collin sputtered, aware that Crick had chosen option B but that it might not necessarily have been *his* first choice, but Deacon was nothing if not fast and efficient.

Deacon said, "I'm gonna count to three, right?" And then he said "One, two—"

And Collin's entire face crunched, exploded, and trickled out his eyeballs.

"*What in the fuck happened to three*?!!" His vision was black, and he felt a powerful need to void his lunch, right there between his knees.

"Three's the scary number. We don't linger on three."

Deep breaths, deep breaths, deep breaths... holy shit! He could breathe!

Collin squinted up into Deacon's face in the lavender darkness as Deacon held an insta-ice cold pack to his nose. "Thanks," he muttered, meaning it both sarcastically and sincerely.

"Any time. As long as you don't spook the horses." Deacon put Collin's hand on the ice pack and got heavily to his feet. "Okay, you two. Into the mudroom. It's colder than an ice-monkey's third nut out here. Crick and I will get you some clothes." Deacon looked up then and addressed what Collin realized was a porch full of people—the little blond diva and the pretty woman from the diner, a big, burly guy with dark, curly hair carrying a blue-eyed toddler, and a mid-sized black guy who was in the process of taking said toddler into his arms for a warm hug.

"Alright, everyone, show's over. Does Crick need to start dinner?"

"We're covered, Deacon," said the really big guy. "Mikhail cooked."

It wasn't Collin's imagination—everybody let out a big sigh of relief.

"We're much obliged, Mikhail. Let's get these guys washed up, and we can sit down."

Which was how he managed to get naked with Jeff. Granted, they were both huddling in the mudroom at The Pulpit, each wrapped in a big towel and a horse blanket, but, well, yeah, they were both naked.

Jeff was beautiful. He must have used a tanning booth or something—not to extreme, because that would have been dangerous—but his skin was pale gold all over. And he was quite fit, too, because for all its angular lines, his body had obviously been worked on. They were gym muscles, meant to be pretty, and they worked. His waist was long, but not as long as his legs, and Collin had gotten a glimpse of pert, taut ass as Jeff had wrapped a towel around his waist before retreating sulkily to a corner with his blanket. That was okay. Collin could still see some rangy, muscular chest and get a glimpse of pretty rose nipples, and all in all, Collin was enchanted.

He was even more enchanted when he realized that the guy had been checking him out under lowered, sculpted eyebrows.

He couldn't help the smirk that stretched his face, and Jeff couldn't help noticing it.

"Don't get all excited, Ramjet, I never said you weren't pretty," Jeff snapped, and Collin's smirk became a full-fledged grin.

"I was prettier before you broke my nose!" he said, but he said it happily, because while it still hurt and his eyes still watered, it had gotten him an invite to dinner, and it was so totally worth it.

"Yeah, well, I'm sorry about that," Jeff muttered. With a sigh, he held up his manicure to check, and the glower he sent Collin should have shriveled pubic hairs if Collin had any shame at all, but he was pretty sure he was past that. "Mostly because I just had that done, dammit! My stylist will never forgive me!"

"Oh, princess, you have other assets, believe me." Collin made sure his gaze lingered on the exposed patches of Jeff's chest and his trim stomach and the faint trail of dark hair that disappeared underneath the SpongeBob SquarePants beach towel.

Jeff rolled his eyes. "For the last time. Shut. The fuck. Up. You and me, Skippy? It ain't happening, you hear?" Jeff sighed, and some of his 'tude leached out of his spine, and he was left, a tired man, slouched in front of a beat-to-shit top-loading washing machine. "Man, and you know what? In all of this weird funky bullshit you brought, we *still* haven't heard from Kevin's little brother."

"What freaked him out so bad?" Collin asked, and maybe by now he'd earned the right to know, or maybe Jeff was just tired and worried, because the tired man stayed.

"His brother stepped in front of enemy fire so he didn't have to get shipped home with HIV," Jeff said quietly. "His parents knew, I guess, but Martin just found out. So, you know. He just sat on a bus for a week so I could tell him it wasn't true—his brother wasn't gay, and he wasn't...." Jeff's voice broke, and his hand made fluttery motions, and then he was just still. He turned his head and looked outside the mudroom window into darkness that looked like a dropped velvet stage veil. "He wouldn't rather die than come home to me."

"That's not true." Oh God. Now Collin really *did* feel like a first class heel. Jeff had been right—he'd totally stepped in some serious shit, and Collin knew why he hadn't wanted anyone without emotional backstage passes to venture near.

But Collin knew a little bit about harboring a sad little man behind the big happy curtain, and he knew that sometimes, that sad little man just needed to be held.

"Where you going, Skippy?" Jeff asked, backing up so hard his ass must have been bruised by the washer by now. "I didn't tell you to get all up in my schnozz, you know!"

"It's a very nice schnozz," Collin soothed, "but that's not why I'm here." And here he was. Six inches away from the sweetheart of his dreams—and not planning to even cop a feel.

"Yeah?" And there was a thread of need in Jeff's voice that Collin couldn't have turned down or betrayed if he'd tried.

"Yeah."

It was awkward at first. Jeff held his body stiff, and Collin tended to engulf anything he was near, but they managed. Eventually, Jeff was flush against him, his head tender on Collin's shoulder, and Collin relaxed his chest enough to be soft and to yield, and there they were. Holding each other in the mudroom at The Pulpit, and Collin shivered with how sweetly that taut body fit against his. Nice... so very, very nice.

Then Jeff relaxed just that last fraction of his body, and Collin gave a soft sigh and held him just a little tighter, and it ceased to be just nice and became amazing.

"Ewww." Crick's voice behind them made Jeff jump, but Collin managed to stay exactly where he was, keeping Jeff pushed up against him. "If I'd known you two were going to be making out, I would have let you eat naked!"

Collin maintained his self-possession—for one thing, just giving someone a hug didn't qualify as being busted in the least. "Thanks," he said over his shoulder. "We'll be dressed in a sec."

"Yeah, whatever. Just don't make too much noise or Parry's gonna come in and see what her uncle Jeffy's doing during the spin cycle, 'kay, Sparky?" And with that, Crick was gone, and Jeff was making a show of moving up and out of Collin's arms. He was smirking even as he put his hand across his eyes.

"Crick...." Jeff shook his head. "Sorry, man. Crick's just Crick." Jeff tried to pull away some more, but Collin's arms grew hard around his shoulders.

"That's okay," Collin murmured, inexorably. Jeff must have been truly needy, because he allowed himself to be held some more. "I'm sorry, you know."

"For what?" Jeff's voice rumbled against his chest.

"For whatever I said to make you sock me in the nose."

Jeff sighed and tried one more time to pull away. Collin didn't let him. There they were, at détente, when Jeff said, "This family is everything to me, you understand?"

Collin heard him—really heard him—and said, "Got it."

With that, Jeff straightened finally, saying, "I'm getting a crick in my neck, Sparky—you do know I'm as tall as you, right?"

And there they were, face to face, and Collin directed a very level look directly into Jeff's brown eyes. "Yeah, Jeff. I do."

Jeff flushed and looked away, making a show out of going to the stack of clothes that Crick had left. "Oh, Jeebus!" he mock swore. "Crick, really?" He shook his head, dropped the blanket from his shoulders, and pulled up a flannel shirt and pair of wranglers.

"What's wrong with flannel?" Collin asked curiously. "Flannel and jeans are warm and sturdy."

Jeff's glare was decidedly sour. "Warm and sturdy is warm and sturdy. Armani is fan*tabulous!*"

Collin felt his lips curve into what even he knew was a besotted smile. "You do know that you make a gay pride parade look like a KKK rally, don't you?"

Jeff smirked again. "You get extra points if you get the guy in the super-spiffy white PJs to blow you, right?"

Collin laughed outright then, and Jeff shook his head, letting out a sigh that sounded like it had held up the world.

"Collin?"

"Yeah?"

"I'm sorry I was such a shit. I mean... I wanted you gone, I won't lie, but I try not to be mean, you know? I was cruel. I...." He sighed and tilted his head back toward an imaginary rain. "I should have taken you seriously from the get go. You deserved that, okay?"

Oh wow. It was like Christmas, but better, because he was about to see Jeff's ass.

"Okay," he conceded, trying not to sound like a little kid. Jeff probably didn't notice anyway. He was too busy trying to fit his skinny ass into another man's boxers and figure out the intricacies of an honest-to-God button fly.

DINNER at The Pulpit was a lot like dinner at his mother's house, except with more swearing. The people eating there were like family—maybe even tighter, because while Collin adored his oldest sister, he could have lived without his uptight, prissy youngest sister, Paige, and Charlene, the one just older than Paige, pissed *everybody* off on a systematic, malicious basis, but they were stuck with her. In contrast, the people at this table had picked each other. Yeah, there was some clashing of personalities (Jeff's snotty little diva friend could have really rubbed everyone raw if he didn't try so hard to be nice to them) but mostly, he got the feeling that what locked them there and made them help with dishes after dinner and offer to get dessert and fetch each other sodas from the fridge in the mudroom was that they *liked* each other, and they *chose* to be family together.

Jeff gazed at them all like he'd lay down in traffic for any one of them any time they asked.

What made Collin start to warm to the folks there was that none of them looked like they'd ask. But they'd offer to do the same thing for Jeff.

"So," said Mikhail (aka "snotty little diva") "Jeff, what are you going to do with this boy if you find him?"

Jeff stopped, a forkful of some sort of wonderful casserole on the way to his mouth. "Do with him?" he said blankly, and Mikhail rolled his eyes.

"And this, this is what happens when you live alone. You have no idea how to care for anything but your own pussies."

There was a rather stunned silence at the table, and Mikhail slowly turned red. "Cats," he said belatedly. "Pussycats."

Kimmy, of all people, started cracking up, throwing half a dinner roll at Mikhail and crowing when he ducked. "Oh. My. God. We need to bring that kid *here*—there are *way* too many gay men in this room if you forget the second half of that word!"

"Pussycat!" Parry Angel clapped from her little high chair. "Pussycat, pussycat, pussycat!"

"You like the kitty cats, Angel?" Deacon asked indulgently from next to the high chair. The little girl grinned at the man who had seemed so intimidating to Collin just a half an hour ago.

"I want a kitty, Deacon!" Parry said with starry eyes, and Deacon just shook his head.

"We've got horses, Angel."

"I'd take care of it," Crick said suddenly, and Deacon looked at him, surprised.

"You want a cat?"

"They're supposed to be good for your blood pressure," Crick said earnestly, and to Collin's surprise, Deacon scowled. Crick returned the look blandly and looked out at the rest of the table, asking Mikhail to pass the milk in what was obviously pretense.

Deacon let out a sigh and shook his head and then turned fondly back to the little girl. "If Crick's willing to deal with the kitty poop, Angel, I don't see why not." He cast a quick look at the big guy with the curly hair. "Shane, does your contact at the SPCA have any likely victims?"

Shane grinned at Parry Angel, who grinned back. "Always. Yeah, we can find someone for her. Probably half-grown, because it needs to be big enough to defend itself. Can you deal with some scratches, Angel? Kitties get rough!"

"Kitty!" Parry obviously didn't hear anything past the achievement of what seemed to be her fondest dream, and Collin had to laugh.

"My sisters' kids are veterans of kitty wars," he said into the chuckles around the table. "They'll take all sorts of abuse, as long as it starts with whiskers and a tail!"

"How many sisters do you have, Collin?" Deacon asked in that deep voice of his.

"Four. Joanna, Gina, Charlene, and Paige." He wasn't aware how expressive his voice was until he heard grunts of suppressed laughter around the table.

"So, uhm, tell us how you really feel about them," the young black man—Andrew, right?—said from Parry Angel's other side.

Collin didn't have the grace to flush. "I think Joanna and Gina are awesome, but if Charlene had been drowned at birth, Paige might have turned out halfway tolerable, why?"

The table burst out into raucous laughter, and Kimmy turned to her brother, crowing, "Now where was this guy when we were kids?"

Shane's lean mouth turned up at one corner. "Don't look at me—you're the one he would have drowned at birth."

Mikhail stuck his tongue out at her to emphasize the point, and Kimmy laughed even harder.

"So you own the garage by the diner?" Deacon asked, and the table settled down, and Collin had to keep his eyes from popping. He recognized this. This is what his mother had done to every boy his sisters had ever brought home—right down to Charlene's ex-husband, whom his mother had pronounced a money-grasping asshole. (Collin had also observed that he'd spent some time staring at Collin's ass, but he'd said it to Gina, and so Gina had been the only one to give him the secret high-five when the fucker had run off with his male personal assistant and Charlene's investments from her job as a financial broker. Charlene had spent the last two years blaming Collin just for being gay, and Collin was not appreciative.)

"Uhm, yeah," he said, knowing he was being put on the spot as a potential suitor for their favorite "brother," Jeff. "I'm good at cars, took the classes—and I suck with authority. My own business seemed the way to go."

Everyone at the table nodded, like they totally got that, and he figured that the only soul at the table in a traditional vocation was Jeff himself, so maybe they could forgive him for not being a banker or something.

"Business good?" Deacon asked between mouthfuls.

"Oh yeah—it doesn't hurt that my one employee would work for free if I let him."

"Joshua Spencer?" Deacon asked, and Collin realized that the guy was grilling him using as few words as possible. He wanted to whistle. This man was *good*. And cute. God—*so* cute. Collin would have bottomed to be nailed by *that*, but he got the feeling that injured or not, Crick would kick his ass through several states if he even suggested it, so he didn't.

Collin took a bite to fortify himself and nodded. "Yeah. Man, I *love* that guy. He's like a full helping of roast-beef awesome. When he realized I was using computers and shit to do my diagnostics, he started taking the classes to learn how to use the equipment online—and I hadn't even hired him yet. He just wanted to know how it worked. He talks to cars like they're people, and he talks to people like they're not stupid. If he hadn't wandered into the garage when he did, I would have been just another fuck-up with a failed business, that's for damned sure."

"He didn't wander in," Crick muttered. "That was Deacon's doing."

Collin almost dropped his fork. "I'm sorry?"

"He's full of shit," Deacon said, suddenly so red that his nose and ears almost glowed. There was something not quite healthy about that glow, and Collin looked at Jeff to see if he noticed. Jeff had his head cocked toward Crick, though, and didn't seem to.

"No, remember? It was right before Jon and Amy's wedding. You were talking to Patrick about the new business opening up? You told him that you wished the kid opening the place had someone like you had Patrick, and Patrick said that he knew a guy who was itching to get out of the house. You were the one who suggested it—I was there!"

Collin looked at the house patriarch with fascination. He hadn't stopped blushing, and he couldn't seem to find his tongue. "Patrick's a good man," Deacon mumbled. "I couldn't have made this place work if he hadn't been there those first years."

"Who's Patrick?" Collin asked, and Deacon shot his partner a miserable look when Crick didn't answer.

"He was my father's best friend," Deacon said, taking a deep breath, like it was difficult to fill his chest with the thought. "If he hadn't been here when Crick was off in Iraq, The Pulpit never would have made it. And by the time he was ready to retire, Andrew was here and saved our lives all over again."

"I know it," Andrew said with mock arrogance. "I really am a gift from God."

Deacon shot the young man a grateful look, and some of that terminal blush faded. "And you're humble too," he said dryly.

Andrew shot him a grin that told Collin that maybe Andrew had needed The Pulpit as much as Deacon had needed Andrew.

"Well, I'm grateful," Collin told them frankly. "Not for you, Andrew, but you seem very nice." He waited for the smart-ass to fade for a minute. "Joshua is pretty awesome—it was solid of you to think of me."

Deacon shrugged. "Small businesses need to stick together."

"And of course, Levee Oaks could always use some more gay!" Collin popped back nicely.

He was gratified to see Deacon crack up, even if all he said was, "That too," with a rather conservative lift of his eyebrows.

As the dinner progressed, Collin started to see how the whole table could be gathered there to make this one man happy. Everything from buying a baby a kitten to a casual helping hand for a stranger—Deacon Winters was actively and quietly making the world a better place through simple kindness.

It was something Collin, who'd had to work long and hard to conquer his own basic self-centeredness, had no choice but to admire.

Dinner ended in a clatter of banter, and Collin found himself side-by-side with Jeff as they did dishes.

"How'd we pull clean-up?" he asked, trying to get Jeff to smile. He'd been quiet and preoccupied through much of the last of the meal.

"We weren't around for prep," Jeff answered automatically. "How fucking hard is it to find one lousy teenager? Seriously? This town is the size of a condom machine—man, two quarters, a twist of a knob, that kid should have fallen into our laps by now!"

Collin had to laugh. "You have cats," he said, pulling the topic from the clear blue something—anything to distract the poor guy.

"This is important because…?" Jeff paused in the act of drying a dish to stack it in the cupboard, one hand extended dramatically with the towel.

"Just making conversation. The little guy, Mickey…."

"Mikhail."

"Didn't his boyfriend call him 'Mickey'?"

"Do you want that man-mountain to kick your teeth in?" Jeff's expression was totally serious.

"Not particularly."

"Then you'd better call him Mikhail."

"Okay, Mikhail. Whatever. He said you had pussies. I'm going to take a flying leap in logic and assume that's the only kind of pussy to get past your front door."

Jeff's expression fought between fondness and indignation. But it had truly been a shit-kicker of a day for him—Collin could tell by the way he shook himself, like a long-limbed puppy, and settled on fondness.

"Yeah, I've got two cats, Con and Katy. They're...." Jeff's wide, expressive mouth curved into a grimace of absolute infatuation. "They were both gifts. It's like people went out of their way to give me pets that were so huge, moving would need a writ from the wildlife foundation. Con doesn't just sit on you, he sits on you, around you, and over you. And you'd better bring your breathing mask if you want to pet Katy. If I brushed her every day I could probably spin enough yarn to knit a sweater."

"Are you feeding her the right kind of food?" Shane asked anxiously as he came into the kitchen with the casserole dish for Collin to wash. Jeff's expression changed from animation to exasperation to a sort of kind indulgence.

"Yes, man-mountain, I'm feeding her the anti-hairball shit you bought me. Con too. That's not going to change the fact that she's a big hairy beast who weighs over twenty pounds and whose ancestors were probably domesticated for their wool!"

A slow grin split Shane's broad, handsome, placid face. "Best birthday gift *ever*," he pronounced, and Jeff rolled his eyes.

"Maybe," he grudged, but Shane wasn't fooled.

"Hey, Mickey!" he called. "I told you a cat was better than a gift card to Forever 21!"

Mikhail's voice drifted in from the living room. "For him, maybe. That's because he's already bought out the whole store!"

Collin looked at Jeff from under hooded eyes. "You do like your pretty clothes, don't you?"

He was rewarded, and handsomely so, when Jeff blushed. His complexion under the tan was unexpectedly fair, and the blush swept up his cheekbones. A couple of freckles and a tiny mole that Collin had never noticed appeared on the side of his cheek.

Jeff floundered for words for a second, and Collin was about to make a classic move—the patented "quick-kiss," in which he took advantage of that downturned face and Jeff's uncertainty and touched lips just long enough to make him think of later—when Shane hollered from the front room.

"Jeff! Calvin just buzzed me. They've got Martin in custody, man—we've got to go get him quick, or he's going to have to spend a night in lockup!"

Aw, fuck.

"Aw, fuck!" Jeff turned around and trotted out of the room, shouting, "Goddammit! Does anyone have any fucking shoes?"

Clear as day, a small, piping voice echoed, "Fucking shoes!" and then Deacon's soft baritone, with, "Goddammit, Jeff, canya try not to teach her that word when Crick failed?"

"Fucking shoes!" Parry Angel sang. "Fucking shoes, fucking shoes, fucking shoes!"

Deacon's voice rumbled softly, but Collin was too busy cracking up to hear how he handled the little girl's new vocabulary word. He pulled himself together and dried off his hands, wandering into the living room in time to watch Deacon organizing the troops, the unrepentant little girl bouncing on his lap.

"Andrew, you up for this?"

"Got nowhere else to be, sir!"

Deacon rolled his eyes. "Crick...."

"Yessir! Stop calling him 'sir', Andrew!"

"Nossir!"

"Jesus!" Deacon swore, and then looked down at Parry Angel, who beamed up at him.

"Who's Jeebus?"

"Someone who's not going with Jeff. Kimmy—did you call Lucas?"

"No, Deacon—but I'll have him meet us there."

"Good. Jeff, you've got Andrew, Kimmy, and who else?"

Jeff sighed and rolled his eyes. "Shane, of course."

"Hey!" Crick protested, and Jeff shook his head.

"Really, Crick, this kid has a temper worse than yours. You two in the same room together is a bad idea, okay? Besides—Shane can pass. He's not going to freak Martin out, okay?"

"Shane can pass?" Crick muttered indignantly. "Shane can *pass*? I spent two years in the fu—rickin' United States Army in the height of Don't Ask, Don't Tell, and *Shane's* the one who can pass?"

One entire side of Jeff's face crinkled up in disgust. "Don't get your lacy panties in a wad, Lieutenant Princess. If the Army couldn't figure it out, that's *their* bad. Besides. Shane's friend is the one who's going to spring the kid, and I'm not bringing the whole fam-fu-rickin'-damily, right?"

Crick sighed. "Right. Right. I just hate...."

"Being left behind," Jeff finished sympathetically. "Well, sorry, Buttercup, but the rest of us have to go."

And that was it. He was just going to walk out the front door and leave Collin there, in a stranger's house, to say goodbye. Shit! Or he would have, if Shane hadn't looked up at his little diva and grimaced.

"Hey, Collin—I hate to squander your ride on him, because he doesn't know sh—quat about cars, but could you take Mickey home?"

"I can walk, big man. It's no big deal," Mikhail said indulgently, but Collin saw an opportunity to pump the little dude for information, and he wasn't going to let it slide.

"No, no, that's okay," he said, as casual as a stalker in a park. "I'll take you. I live nearby, it's no big deal."

He didn't miss Jeff's grimace, and he couldn't refrain from a wicked eyebrow raise to show that he realized exactly how much information he could mine from the cocky little man, and that he planned to fully take advantage of it.

But Jeff had other fires to tend, and Collin wasn't offended in the least when the object of his desire gave a wicked huff and stalked out of the house, yelling at Kimmy that she'd better ride with him because he didn't know where in the fu-rick the fu-ricking police station was.

Chapter 6

Jeff: The Ex-Cop and the Cop-out

JEFF was unrepentantly glad about leaving Collin behind as he and Kimmy peeled out of The Pulpit in a spatter of mud and gravel.

"Turn right here—it's near the courthouse on the main drag, but about a block behind."

Jeff grunted, grateful that Kimmy was one hundred percent common sense, and then the wretched woman blew that whole line of thought.

"He's really cute, you know," she said tentatively, and Jeff looked at her sideways in the early November dark.

"So's Lucas." Even Jeff, for all his self-absorption, hadn't missed the way Kimmy had shied off of Lucas's obvious interest.

"Lucas's a little young for me," she said, and he didn't miss the grim warning in her voice. He'd been there when her ex-dickhead had shoved her face in a bowl of cocaine for spite, and he'd helped talk her down until he was sure her brain wouldn't just blow a gasket and bleed out her nose. Yeah, Kimmy had some mileage on her and some rough road under her feet, but that didn't mean she should write off all that sweet attention as something she didn't deserve.

"So's Collin," he said quietly, and he felt her squeeze on his shoulder.

"Honey, I've seen young—that kid's not young."

Jeff wanted to close his eyes and curl up with his cats so badly. "Yeah, well, neither am I."

"Oh, Jeffy—you can't say that." Kimmy laughed, and it sounded tired but natural. "You're about exactly my age, you little shit. You can't tell me that the over-thirties don't get a happy ever after—that's just no fucking fair!"

Jeff managed a laugh. "For you, Kimmy, I'll hold out a little hope," he said, meaning it.

"Hold it out for both of us, Jeff." Kim's voice dropped, and without the caustic humor, she sounded vulnerable. "He's obviously serious, or he wouldn't have made you throw a punch to get rid of him, right?"

"Oh God." Jeff hadn't even thought about it. He had bruises along his ribs and on his jaw from where Collin had gotten his own blows in, but until Kimmy said it, he hadn't even really connected the fight to his own fist. "God—I swear I haven't decked a guy since…." Now he had to laugh. "Since your dumb-shit brother!"

Kimmy laughed delightedly. "Shaney? What the hell did he do?"

Jeff thought about it and shivered. "He didn't tell us, you know? About almost getting killed down in LA. And then he told me, and he was working as a cop up here, and I just…." Jeff didn't want to think about it, but given that he'd just gotten in his second fight in a year, he figured he probably should.

"You know, I love the big hairy mammoth like a brother, right? It just pissed me off. You get used to someone hanging out at the dinner table and think, 'He's as solid as a rock. I don't have to worry about *him* disappearing from my life!' right? So it turned out that he was taking that risk, and… I don't know, there he was, on his ass, looking shocked as hell."

Kimmy's laugh was soft and throaty. "God, I wish I'd thought of that. Of course, I'm sure he wanted to come drag me home by the hair around that time, too, so I wouldn't have had any ground to stand on to throw that punch, you know?"

Jeff nodded and made an accepting little sound as he shifted the car and made a hard right toward the courthouse. "You and Shane are good people." Because she was a girl, he could say this to her, whereas he would have made her brother work for it. "Maybe give Lucas the time of day the next time he asks, you think, sugar?"

"Backatcha," Kimmy said. "And however this falls out, you may want to stop by Collin's garage and tell him thank you for giving a shit, right?" Jeff took a turn and swore when the steering got picky, and

Kimmy chuckled. "Or at least ask for him to look under your car, since now we know why you'd rather have Shane do it instead."

Jeff fought off a whimper. For someone who professed to be a self-centered bitch, Kimmy was exceptionally perceptive. "Yeah, yeah. Kid. Time of day. Maybe. Can we, I don't know, focus on the troubled teenager here?"

"I thought we were," Kimmy said sweetly.

"He's in his twenties!" Jeff defended, feeling put upon.

"Wasn't talking about him, darling. But never mind—we're here—turn right in there."

Lucas was already in front of the squat, yellow police station, a denim jacket on over his hooded sweatshirt, and Jeff couldn't help but notice his blush when Kim told him thank you for meeting them. Well, good for Kimmy. Somebody might be able to leave her baggage at the station, and wouldn't that be nice?

The jail was small and sterile, tucked down a hallway around the corner from the entryway. It was used for small-time offenders, drunken in public, shoplifting, and waiting-for-someone-to-take-you-home-and-pay-your-fine type fuck-ups. After Shane had led them around the corner and went to confer with his old partner on the little Levee Oaks force, Jeff couldn't help feel that for all his freakish height and teenaged defiance, Martin looked more than a little small and a little lost huddled on the cot at the end of the small room.

"Oh, Jesus, what do you want?" the kid snarled, and Jeff tried hard to hold on to his fading sympathy.

"I want to make sure Kevin's little brother doesn't end up sleeping on the streets," Jeff said baldly. "Hope you don't mind, but that makes me feel like shit, and I hate feeling like shit, so here I am."

"So this is all about you?" The kid's expressive eyes were narrowed with contempt, and Jeff let it roll off his back.

"You bet. I've spent six years trying to get over your brother, and you come barreling in here with all your hatred and your judgment and rip that wound open with a fucking chainsaw, and you think I'm going to give a *damn* about you? Show me someone to like—or hell, even respect—and I'll make this about you, is that a deal, little man?"

Or maybe not so much with the rolling off. Jeff hadn't even felt that resurgence of anger, that snapping disconnect between the funny man who didn't take shit seriously and the fucker with the temper who used to throw a fist before he thought.

But maybe some raw emotion was called for, because Martin's tightly folded arms relaxed, and he backed up slightly, as though intimidated by Jeff's gay self.

"What do you mean, 'getting over him'?"

Oh Jesus. "Kid, your brother was the love of my goddamned life! Do you think I just... I don't know, got news that he was dead and went out and hit the clubs?"

"Well we sure didn't see you at the funeral!"

Jeff closed his eyes and swallowed, trying so very hard not to show this one, trying so very hard to keep his gaping chest wound closed so his heart wouldn't fall out. "Really, Martin? You really think I would have been a big hit there at the funeral? Your folks were already grieving. How excited would they have been to have me show up, so they didn't even have that?"

Martin glared at him for a minute, and then his shoulders slumped. "You didn't miss much," he muttered. "Apparently, all that nice shit people said about him was a lie."

"Shut up!" Jeff hissed. "You *shut up.* Your brother was one of the best men I've ever known—"

"Yeah, but he wasn't good enough to come home, was he?"

"You think he was going to get a hero's welcome if he came home?" Jeff snapped. "They may have repealed Don't Ask, Don't Tell, like, this *morning,* but six years ago? He would have gotten a dishonorable discharge, and he would have been sent home with a terminal disease and no health insurance. Six years ago, his entire career—everything he'd worked for, everything he'd done to make you proud—all of it would have been shit on. Flushed down the fucking toilet. And your folks still wouldn't have talked to him, and all he had was me. And... you know, he was afraid I'd get sick too." Jeff's breath caught as he remembered that letter. *If I have to watch you get sick, I might as well put a gun to my head.* God. Fucking Kevin. Jesus.

"Have you?" the kid asked, brutally curious.

"No, but only because I've got the killer health insurance." Jeff thought about Doc Herbert, and Crick and Deacon. "And good friends who take care of me," he added, grateful for his blessings as he hadn't been in a long time.

"So what's that like?" the kid asked, again with the no-holds-barred curiosity. "I mean, you know, the AIDS thing?"

Jeff blinked. Had he thought about this question—*really* thought about it—since Collin had asked him five and a half years ago?

Probably not.

Easy to bitch about the symptoms and the drug regimen and the small shit. Easy to make it funny in your own head, and not once, not ever, own up to the big, black fog mass boiling in the center of your chest. Easy not to think about it and just deal with it, because thinking about it took you to that place where someone else's mother had to come in and feed you and give you something else breathing to take care of, because everyone knew you were just one sleep away from cashing it in and giving it up.

Kevin had it easy, the sonuvabitch. Kevin had high-octane explosives and ammo when he found out.

Jeff swallowed and looked at Martin and thought, *This is Kevin's brother. Kevin died because he was afraid of it. He needs to know the truth.*

"Wouldn't know," he said, his voice flat. Fuck this. Fuck this kid, fuck this situation, and fuck this shitty question. "It's not the AIDs thing right now—it's still the HIV thing. But it's scary as shit. It's waking up every fucking day and saying, 'I've got to take these pills at these times and deal with the fact that they make me feel like crap, because the alternative's worse.'. It's wondering if what you're eating is going to make you puke, or going to make you bloat, or if your hair is going to start to fall out, or if your liver's going to fail—and still going to work and doing your job. It's...."

Jeff swallowed, suddenly thinking about Collin on that long-ago day, and the confident young man who had followed him to a friend's to make sure he was going to be all right. "It's a hard way to grow up fast," he said after a pause, and for the first time, he saw Martin's expression soften, just a little.

"I... I'm sorry," he muttered. "I'm being an asshole."

Jeff twisted his mouth. "Can't argue there." God, he was ready to change the subject. "Uhm, kid—my friend is working on bailing you out of here. You planning on going back to your folks anytime soon or what?"

"They won't even say his name," Martin mumbled, and Jeff pretended that didn't hurt a lot.

"Look, we can scare you up some place to stay...."

That softness went away. "I'm not gonna have to live with a fuckin' fag, am I?"

"You shame your mama, boy!" Andrew snapped, rounding the corner just in time to hear Martin lose his human personality again.

Andrew's presence was like some sort of magic zinging charge in the air, and Martin's face both became more animated and relaxed a little. "I'm sorry," he said, automatically contrite. "I just...." He scowled at Jeff. "I'm not my brother!"

"And you're nowhere near my age!" Jeff retorted acidly. "And you weren't going to sleep on my couch anyway."

"He wasn't?" Andrew asked, surprised, and Jeff flushed. He'd actually been planning on his guest room, but the kid had just been so *hostile.* Jeff remembered that he was supposed to be the emotional adult here and blushed even more. "I was sort of, you know... doesn't Promise House have a bed?"

"Yeah," Kimmy said, right behind Andrew. "Thank you for asking." She sent him a dry look, and he stuck out his tongue in annoyance. "Which teenager is going to sleep on it?" she asked in return, and Jeff took a deep breath because she was right.

"Martin, would you like to stay with Kimmy in Promise House? It's sort of a place for kids without a place to stay, right?"

Martin's eyes narrowed. "Just Kimmy?"

"There are a couple of kids there now. Everyone has his own room, you have to share a shower, there are two employees who are damned nice people, and my brother and I take turns staying in the counselor's room for now. He doesn't live far away, though. He's in and out most of the day."

Martin's scowl faded, and he cocked his head to hear what she had to say. *Kevin used to do that,* Jeff thought, his heart suddenly adrift. For the first time in years, he let himself miss Kevin. He expected his heart to open up into a big heaving vortex and swallow him whole, but it didn't. It ached fiercely, gave one big throb that stopped his breath, and resumed its normal beat, a little sadder and slower than before. Jeff struggled to breathe again like a living human being on earth and not a dying one on

Mars, and Martin completely ignored him to consider what Kimmy had just said.

"You won't call my folks?" he asked suspiciously, and Kimmy shook her head.

"We'll suggest that *you* do, but calling your parents isn't our job. Keeping you safe while you're an unsupervised minor, *that* is our job. You'll be expected to choose some sort of work at the place—we've got some light construction, some animal care, some groundskeeping or some crafts-for-cash you can choose from, and you'll be expected to abide by house rules—"

"I'm polite," Martin said. He must have caught Jeff's rolled eyes, because he added, "Most of the time," rather sheepishly under his breath.

Jeff remembered himself at fourteen. God, he'd been the evil side of snarky—he'd laughed at anyone over twenty-five, finding fault with everything from their weight to their posture to their music. He'd been absolutely sure that all of the bullshit that adults let themselves get sucked into would *never* happen to him.

He found his patience again, and a moment to regret fobbing Martin off on his friends, but Martin and Kimmy were on a roll by then, coming to terms with no sex, no drugs, no disrespect, no stealing, no music after ten o'clock, no fighting, no smoking....

Jeff tried not to wrinkle his nose. God, being a kid sucked. He backed off for a moment and let Kimmy work, because girlfriend was good.

"Jeff, you're not off the hook, you know," Kimmy said, just as he was immersed in a vision of himself, a shower, the kitties, and that long-promised chocolate.

"Hmm-what?"

Kimmy put her hands on her hips and her feet in the third position (because twenty-seven years of dance did not just disappear, especially not when she was still dancing the fair circuit with Mikhail when they had time) and raised an eyebrow.

"You're *in loco parentis*, sweetcheeks. You have to come in for counseling with our little man here twice a week until he finds himself another place to bunk."

"I *what?*" That was both of them, Jeff *and* Martin, and if Jeff had been a violent man or, well, a violent man toward *women*, he would have bitch-slapped that woman to the other side of the fucking moon for her smirk alone.

"It's written into the charter for the place, Jeff. It's how we get away with setting up a place that lets kids run away from home. We gotta try to talk them back there. Since Martin's folks are on the other side of the fu-rickin' country—"

"He's not two," Jeff snapped at the same time Martin said, "I'm not four!" and Kimmy's smirk grew deeper, wider, and popped a couple of dimples.

"See? You two have a lot in common already. Seriously, Jeffy— you don't want your little man here to be shipped back off to bum-fuck, Missouri—"

"Oh *now* you can swear in front of me!" the kid snapped, and this time, Jeff was a half-beat behind *him* with, "He's from Georgia, sweetheart!"

Andrew snorted loudly, and Kimmy kept on talking. "So that's the deal. Martin, you sign a contract, we keep you and put you to work, and you and Jeff get locked in a room with a counselor twice a week, and when you're ready to go home, we'll get you there."

"Are *you* going to be my counselor, pretty lady?" Martin tried a cheesy smile, then, and a soulful look from those deep brown eyes.

"Not if you come onto me, you little perv. You keep that shit up, and it's going to be my brother!"

"As long as he's straight!" Martin hit back, and everyone else in the room snorted.

"Oh you wish!" Kimmy rolled her eyes.

"Hey!" Shane said, walking in with Calvin and wearing all his good nature on the outside. "I can pass!"

"I can vouch for that," said Calvin, using the keys on the electric lock by the door. "And he can take a hell of a beating and give it back, too, so don't think the whole 'dancer boyfriend' makes him weak."

Martin stood there, mouth a little open, as the locked, barred door unclicked and swung partway open. "You were a *cop*?"

Shane shrugged his massive shoulders. "Yes, I was."

"Did they make you quit because you're gay?"

Calvin rolled his eyes. "Like that stopped him. No, young man, he quit because he's the clumsiest motherfucker I've ever met, and we all wanted him to live!"

"I got *knifed*!" Shane protested indignantly, and Calvin looked at Martin and shook his head.

"And he got his ribs bruised, and he got knocked down, and beaten and—"

"This conversation is no longer funny," Kimmy said soberly, and it was Jeff's turn to snort.

"Jesus, Kim, you're telling me. Are we good to go?"

Kim nodded, then looked at Martin and sighed. "Kid, did you bring any clothes or anything? Man, I don't know how long you spent on that bus, but you're *rank.*"

Martin looked down at himself and for the first time started to fidget like he was embarrassed. "Uhm, no," he muttered. "Sort of just, yanno, ran to the bus station and bought the ticket."

Lucas had come in with Shane and Calvin—Jeff had the feeling he'd paid some sort of fine. "I got your clothes from your mom's, Martin. Uhm, they're in my car. I can follow you guys over."

Martin looked at him like a stricken little kid. "Uhm, how many of my clothes?" he asked with meaning.

Lucas looked away. "Most of 'em," he said, the soft Georgia in his voice low and strong with embarrassment.

Jeff looked at the kid, then looked at Lucas, and his heart sank. *Oh shit.*

"Lucas, can we talk a minute?" he said, and Martin glared at them both. Jeff didn't give a shit.

"We'll be outside, playing clowns in a car," Kim said with a sigh. "Jeff, I think you're going to need to take Andrew home—is that okay?"

"Does he have to go?" Martin said quickly, and Andrew met Kimmy's eyes with a grimace.

"I can stay the night on the couch, if you like," Andrew said, but it was clear he was pretty reluctant.

"It's a good couch," Shane said coaxingly, and Andrew shook his head.

"C'mon," Drew said, something clearly weighing on him. "Man, I know you worked here, Shane, but I really hate this place."

Calvin grimaced at them all good-naturedly. "I'm not fond of it either," he said, and the whole group of them moved out toward the front and the parking lot, leaving Jeff there with a very pretty man with long hair, brown eyes, and an unhappy expression.

"Did they really kick him out?" Jeff asked quietly.

Lucas couldn't even look at him. "I don't know what to tell you. Kevin was my best friend, you know? I keep telling myself that he had to come from somewhere. When we were kids, his mom had the best house on the block—always cookies, always iced tea with lemon, always good movies to watch, yanno?"

Jeff had to swallow. "I had one like that," he muttered, wanting his bubble back. It had been a great bubble, double-reinforced denial, layers and layers of clear don't-think-about-it shellacked over the über-strong sound waves of the psychic scream that had ripped his chest six years ago, but that the bubble had never allowed the world to really hear. The scream hadn't gotten out yet, but ever since Lucas had called, the bubble had grown too thin to protect him, too worn to keep the pain out, too fractured to give the world that glossy, blushy glow anymore.

"Had?" Lucas turned to look at him, and Jeff's throat was almost too tight to swallow.

"I… uhm… haven't been home in a while," he said, and Lucas nodded as if something made sense. "So, Martin?"

"His folks gave him an ultimatum, I guess. They said Kevin was dead, and they weren't going to talk about it, and if he wanted to find out more about his brother, he'd be dead to them too."

The walls were cinderblock, painted pale yellow. Maybe it was supposed to be like sunshine, or maybe it was supposed to hide the dirt, but suddenly Jeff had a vision of pounding his head against one just to see what his blood would look like when it spattered.

"We'll take care of him," Jeff said, making it a promise. "Me and Deacon's people—we'll take care of him. No worries."

Lucas nodded and then let his worry show through. "Look—would y'all mind if I stuck around? I've got…." He laughed a little, without humor. "I've got, *literally*, nothing going. I quit the Marines, got a nowhere job—and God, it wasn't until I drove out here that I realized how much I didn't want to go back to Georgia. I mean, I can get a little apartment here, whatever. Find a job. I've got some money saved. It's just that kid—he was like my little brother too. And…." Lucas's voice got tight, and Jeff wondered if he gave this big straight man a hug, would they be able to ever stop clinging to each other. "I really miss Kevin," he managed to finish, and Jeff had no idea what kind of Marine Lucas had been, but Jeff figured he scored points for bravery right about there.

"This is a good place," Jeff said after a moment. "If you don't mind all the gay, I'll give you Deacon's number. Between Deacon and Shane, I'm sure we've got a line on a job for you. They always need help, you know?" Jeff thought about how much they could have used Andrew at the diner that day and thought maybe that was an understatement. "Anyway, here. Let's go outside, and I'll give you Deacon's number, and you follow Kimmy and Shane home and talk to them about it. Make sure Martin knows you're hanging out for him. I've got a guest room you can use for a bit, but it's not as close as it could be—you're welcome, though." Hell, he'd been ready to offer it to Martin, right?

But Lucas shook his head. "I've got a little motel room for the night, but I 'preciate it. Thank you. Seriously, thank you. Your people seem real nice—and Andrew's from Georgia, so that'll be almost homey, right?"

Jeff smiled and, as usual, opened his mouth to chew on his toes. "And he's straight—that ought to count for something."

Lucas didn't smile, and his eyes were soft as Jeff had ever seen a grown man's. "I was never like that, you know," he said quietly. "Because Kevin, he was like... since we were babies, he was my friend. It didn't matter if he was black, and later, it didn't matter if he was gay. He took better care of me than my own family. I just... God. If I can do right by him, I might be worth something after all, you see?"

Jeff nodded. He wanted to hear that story. More than almost anything, he wanted to hear that story. But first, he *needed* to get his bony white ass home.

Eventually, it was all settled. Everyone was going to Deacon's or Shane's and hunkering down for the night. Everyone but Jeff, who was just going to his own pin-neat condo, with his kitties and his first-edition prints and his big-screen television and his quiet and a box of Kleenex and a big bottle of Motrin for the headache and a copy of his favorite comfort movie—*Brokeback Mountain*, not that he'd ever let Crick know that—and his warm flannel pajamas and the vast, white, icy, aching loneliness waiting in the void left by his shattered heart.

Chapter 7

Collin: The Long and Winding Road

COLLIN had to wait three days to see Jeff again, and he worried the entire time.

His conversation with the frustrating little diva on the way home had not helped him worry one bit less.

"So…," Collin had led.

"So what?" Mikhail replied crisply, practically challenging Collin to put it into words.

"Jeff. How do you think he's doing?"

"Like shit. Why do you care?" Even in the dark Collin could see one corner of a sulky little mouth pulled up in apparent disdain. But Collin had seen Mikhail in the same room, and he knew without thinking that the two were friends. Mikhail was either just being a bitch—a possibility, Collin would give him that—or protecting his friend.

"Because I care. Jeff's a good guy. He helped me out of a bad place a while back. I just want to help return the favor."

"Jeff doesn't need any favors, returned or otherwise. Turn left here."

Collin sighed and did what the little man said. He was surprised to find himself at a cattle fence with a rather odd contraption built along top of it. The thing looked like a long wooden bench, except it was only about six inches across, and it was four feet off the ground. It led from the top of the cattle fence to the top of the porch railing. There was a little stool outside of the fence where the wooden rail connected and Collin could not figure out what in the hell it could be for.

"Look, I'm just trying to find out about him. I mean, I don't know what you saw in there, but I saw a guy who was on his last fucking nerve, you know?"

Mikhail pursed that sulky mouth and glared outside. What looked like a hundred dogs had all gathered, voices raised excitedly, tails waving in greeting, and the little man's expression grew both overwhelmed and determined.

"Yes," Mikhail said, "you should worry. I am worried. I am worried for Jeff, and I am worried for Deacon, and I am worried for my big, stupid cop—but that is because he will get hurt because he loves these people, and I cannot protect him from that."

Whoopee! An opening! "So, uhm, what can you tell me about—"

Mikhail's brows snapped together. "Collin, right?"

"Yeah."

"My big, stupid cop has the most *amazing* cock. You should see it. Circumcised, because he's American, but truly"—Mikhail held his hands apart, showing what must have been an exaggeration—"truly, truly gifted. He gives amazing blow jobs and fucks like a god."

Collin, who didn't think anything could make him blush, found that he wished Mikhail would stop talking, and that he seemed to be sweating in the November chill. "Uhm...."

"I can tell you this, you see. Because he is *my* big, stupid, hairy cop, and his secrets are *mine* to share, yes?"

"Yes," Collin managed, because now they weren't talking about sex and personal business and... shit. "Yes," he sighed, truly understanding what the little man was saying. "Yeah. I understand. I'll ask Jeff when I see him."

"Good. It is good. Jeff should have someone who can ask the personal questions. With him, it is always the joke, the funny man." Mikhail shook his head. "Even funny men need someone to hold them when they cry."

The hell of it was, he sounded like he knew.

"Thank you for the ride, Collin. And if you see my big, stupid cop, tell him that the seats were leather, the engine was a four-twenty-six V-8 and the paint job was not as 'trick' up close as it was from far away. Your pin-stripe man sucks. Goodnight."

"Hey!" Collin protested. "I was the pin-stripe"—the door slammed—"man," he finished weakly. Then he watched as, instead of moving to the latched gate to open it and squeeze through, Mikhail did a truly remarkable thing.

He trotted across the cattle guard to the little stool by the gate, hopped up, and then, putting his hands squarely on the little bench, hoisted himself up to a handstand. From the handstand, he did a graceful arch until his feet were touching the six-inch board. He straightened then and pattered down the length of the "bench" to the top of the porch rail, where he vaulted over the side to the porch, pulling his key out almost when his legs were still in the air.

He managed to slip inside the door before the dogs even figured out he was on the porch, and Collin was left, sitting in his idling car, thinking, "Huh…" for an embarrassingly long time.

So WHEN Jeff drove his car into Collin's shop for maintenance three days later, Collin was damned relieved. He'd been planning to stop by The Pulpit later that night on his way home just to beg for the guy's phone number, but this way, he wouldn't have to. Jeff had to give him a number for the paperwork, and if there was a code of garage mechanic ethics that said "thou shalt not use your client's phone number to call them up and hit on them," he had no knowledge of said document.

"So, Sparky," Jeff said, giving his trademark snarky-face as he got out of the little blue Mini Cooper, "you think you could take a look at this without violating my warranty?"

Collin nodded. He was certified with most of the dealerships—Saab, no; Mini Cooper, absolutely. But he didn't fall into Jeff's leading trap of thinking they were just odd acquaintances. If he'd picked Jeff up at a club and given it to him against a wall—yes, he could probably do that. But he'd kissed Jeff, and kisses were important, and he wasn't wasting two of his best kisses to be, "Hey, nice to see you again!"

"How's Martin?" he asked personably, and was interested to watch Jeff's normally animated face grow still and guarded.

"Spiffy," he said with a brittle smile. "Absolutely wonderful. Just saw him today, actually. He's"—beat, beat, beat—"settling in."

Oh Jesus. "He doesn't mean any of that shit personally, you know that, right?" Collin asked, flipping the hood of the car open and scanning an almost pristine engine. He started going through a leisurely check of fluids as he talked, but he wasn't expecting it to be that easy. This car was as regularly maintained as Jeff himself.

"What shit?" Jeff asked, his eyes almost blind with all the effort he was putting in to not seeing what Collin was talking about.

"Whatever shit makes you look like you swallowed a bug."

Jeff wrinkled his nose, the first spontaneous expression Collin had seen on his face since their little chat in the mudroom at The Pulpit. "That's just gross," he said with feeling. "Think of a better analogy or quit talking."

"How about we skip the analogies, and you tell me what's wrong. You look like shit." He wiped the oil dipstick off with the cloth he stuffed in his blue coveralls and moved to check the steering fluid.

"How about we skip the personal disclosure and move to the part where we fix my car!"

Goddamned stubborn man would make a bank vault look like an open-air picnic!

"I don't know—why don't you tell me what I'm looking for?"

Oh please, please, please let it be something small and stupid that makes me look like a hero, please, please, please....

Jeff put his hands on his cocked hips and blew out a breath of air. "It's not steering right," he said with a frown. "It takes some time in the morning before it's not too stiff to drive, and you can hear it making noise when you make sharp turns."

Fuck.

"Well, shit. That sounds like you're missing steering fluid—"

"But I just replaced it!" Jeff protested, and Collin grimaced.

"Yeah—I was afraid of that. If you just replaced it, that probably means it's building up in the suspension." Collin took a deep breath and prepared to oust himself from the running of alpha male for good. "This is going to take a whole new part. I can get one used, maybe from the network, if price is a problem...."

"No, no." Jeff shook his head. "I'd rather have a new part—but how long will it take?"

Collin let his deep breath out. "It's going to take me at least a week to get it in. If you want a place to have it faster, one of the bigger chain repair shops might actually have one in stock."

"And do that to a friend?" Jeff asked, his indignation making him perch, almost like a meerkat, shoulders back and hands at the chest. But his faith—and his loyalty—were touching, and Collin's own shoulders relaxed a fraction.

"'Preciate it," he grunted. "You can drive it now, right? Not comfortable, but drivable?"

Jeff nodded. "Yeah—it's been going on for a while."

"Then hold onto it for a bit. Give me a chance to go back and put out an order and see how long it's going to take. Again, I'll let you know up front, a bigger chain place could make this whole process easier—even for the installation, because they've probably done a few of these a month, and we don't get them a lot."

Again, that adorable indignation. "Yeah, but this is my *baby*. You think I'm going to leave her in the hands of someone who doesn't know her?"

Collin let his relief show in his smile this time. "Excellent. I'll go place the order and come back with a timeline."

Collin watched Jeff through the window as he waited on the phone to the parts distributor. The man was never still. His hands were always in motion, patting his car's roof, fidgeting with something inside, sorting through the stack of mail he kept in the little island between the seats. There was no "lounging back and taking it cool" for Jeff—check the name on the form—Beachum. About the only thing he didn't do was check his hair, but Collin was pretty sure that was because it had been primped enough already that day. He did, however, straighten his natty silver trench coat over his long-sleeved camel-colored sweater and make sure his shirttails were fashionably *un*tucked from his tight black slacks about six times before he pulled out his über-phone and started to press buttons on *that*. Collin was greatly cheered, even as he sat on terminal hold.

"He's cute," Joshua said, coming up behind Collin and wiping his hands on a towel. "You gonna get him a tiara for the prom?"

Collin pulled one corner of his mouth up. "Jeff would probably wear it," he muttered, wondering why the parts distributor always seemed to be made of time, especially when he was in a hurry.

Joshua watched as Jeff dusted another bit of imaginary lint off of his black trousers. "I have no doubt. You gonna take him?"

"I would if he'd go," Collin muttered, tapping his pen. "I'm just lucky he's letting me work on his car."

"What's his hang-up?"

"God, too many to count. It's what makes him so fascin—yeah, I need the power steering apparatus of a 2008 Mini Cooper, you got one of those hanging 'round handy?"

He was put on hold again and was surprised when Joshua didn't just wander back to the garage like he usually did. When Collin looked at him as though to ask why, he was surprised to find Joshua's gray eyes were looking back impatiently, waiting for his attention.

"You're not just playing with this boy, are you?"

Collin blinked. "No," he said, meaning it. "Look, Joshua—about five and a half years ago, he—"

"When you were diagnosed." The old man's voice was no-nonsense. Collin had told him about the HIV because they were forever scraping knuckles and banging elbows in their job, and he'd wanted Joshua to know that the safety protocols were no joke.

"Yeah. When I was stupid and scared and about two minutes from taking off and living on the streets instead of growing the fuck up, okay? And he took five minutes out of his day—and he must have been as scared as I was, you know?" Worse, if Collin had put things together right about Big Tragic Dead Boyfriend and when that had all gone down.

"Well, five minutes does not a winning personality make," Joshua said sagely, and Collin grunted, trying to find words for it.

"I know that. Back then, I thought he was a god."

"And what do you think of him now?" Joshua asked curiously, and Collin watched as Jeff started to bob his head in time to what was probably the clock-watching theme to Jeopardy.

"I think he's fuckin' adorable."

Joshua laughed a little. "Well, good for you. Go court him like a Trojan—"

"With a pocket full of 'em for good measure," Collin finished dryly. It had been Joshua's mantra for Collin's dating life during the past three years. While Collin was nowhere *near* as promiscuous as he had been in high school, he wasn't a monk. He was honest, up-front, and deadly careful about protection—but he'd read all that HIV literature twice for good measure, and nowhere in there was the clause about living like a monk, or a chastity pledge (and he'd been stupid enough to believe Charlene's threat that there would be), so he figured he was good.

"Mr. Waters?" came the voice on the other end of the line, and Collin was so startled he almost dropped the phone.

"Yeah?"

"About that part you ordered...."

Collin got down to business, because he was good and he was competent and he had pride in his work, but he *so* wished he always had Jeff to look at when he was dealing with the parts people. Even watching him put on his designer sunglasses and lean back against his car to play video games on his phone was a treat—Collin had always liked pretty boys and classic bottoms. He was just an old-fashioned guy that way.

When he came out of the office a few minutes later, he moved stealthily. He wanted a peek over Jeff's shoulder to see what he was playing. *A-ha!*

Jeff jumped and stared at him with big eyes, and Collin realized he'd said that out loud.

"*Angry Birds!*" Collin crowed, trying to cover for the fact that he didn't mean to scare the shit out of the guy.

"Happy Cats? Psychotic Dogs? I give," Jeff muttered, clearing the screen on his phone. "What's the subcategory, and what game are we playing?"

"*Angry Birds,*" Collin told him with a roll of his eyes. "That's the name of the video game!"

Jeff blushed, and Collin gave thanks for skin so fair you could see a dull red, even under a tan. "It's fun," he muttered, and Collin grinned.

"For my six-year-old nephew, yeah, it's a blast!"

"Did you have something you needed to tell me?" Jeff shoved his phone in the back pocket of his slacks, but Collin had some doubts that it would stay there—the slacks were pretty damned tight as it was.

"Yeah. The part will be here in a week, and in the meantime, don't go on any long trips, and don't go on any short trips with windy roads, because your steering could go all stiff and nasty"—*don't laugh at the dirty joke, don't laugh at the dirty joke*—"at any time."

Jeff smirked. "Stiff and nasty? Are you telling me my car is horny? Because I don't see a hot Lexus with a probe for its tailpipe, so I think it's going to be *sorely* disappointed."

"Dammit!" Collin snickered. "I wasn't going to go there!"

"You perv! Cars don't swing that way!" Jeff chortled, and Collin lost his manly snicker and actually dissolved into a giggle.

Jeff paused then and looked at him in surprise, and Collin's giggles faded.

"That was, uhm, the first time I've heard you sound young," Jeff said, looking embarrassed. "I keep forgetting you're—what? Twenty-three?"

Collin swallowed, cursing himself and the untimely giggle. "Twenty-four. Why does it matter? You keep calling me Sparky and reminding yourself—why does it bother you when you forget?"

Jeff flushed. "Look, I'm sorry, I've taken enough of your morning. If I'm going to drive up to Coloma today, I've got to get a move on!"

And the age thing was dropped like an egg from a high school gym roof.

"Coloma!" Collin protested. "Did you not *hear* me? I said no winding roads and no long trips! You're going to take a car with faulty steering up to *Coloma*? Jesus, are you taking stupid pills or just missing your adrenaline rush this morning?"

Jeff rubbed the back of his neck and looked up into the grayscale November sky. "Shit," he muttered. "Shit, shit, shit... no. You're right." He glared at Collin sideways before his eyes went back to their "thinking" position again. "Not that you're tactful about it, but you're right. No—it's the whole reason I stopped by in the first place. I'll get a rental car." Jeff keyed up his phone again, obviously looking for the closest one, swearing, "Fuck, fuck, fuck, fuck, fuck" the whole time.

Collin looked at Joshua over Jeff's shoulder and pointed to his watch. Joshua shrugged and made "go away" motions, and Collin was grateful. "Look, I'll take you," he said, turning around and unzipping his coveralls as he went. He had a long-sleeved T-shirt underneath, but still, the chill hit him as soon as the zipper was down. He looked up to see Jeff trotting in his wake.

"No need, Sparky!" Jeff was saying, dogging Collin's heels with his mouth set mutinously. "I'm a big boy, I know how to rent a car."

"Yeah, but I'm the boss, so I can work late tomorrow and take off today, right?"

"Yeah," Jeff snapped in exasperation, "but why do you need to?"

Collin stopped in his tracks and looked at Jeff with enough incredulity to make the other man falter. "Because I want to. Isn't that enough?"

Jeff took one of those deep, cleansing breaths that were starting to piss Collin off to no end. "I don't need anybody with me when I do this," he said, as though speaking to a child, and Collin caught his chin with enough firm pressure that pulling back would have caused a scene. It was a risk, but Collin gambled right, and Jeff stayed put, furious and still, as the two of them stood toe to toe.

"I don't even know what you're doing, Jeff, and I can tell you need someone. You need someone so bad, it's like I keep waiting for you to shatter if no one holds you. All your friends are taken, Jeffy—you may as well give me a shot. I've got pretty strong arms, I can do a whole lot of holding."

Jeff swallowed, and Collin had to rethink how very fragile Jeff's shell of self-reliance really was. "This is going to be really messy," he whispered. "I didn't even ask Crick."

"Crick doesn't want to kiss you like I do," Collin whispered back. "I think you should give me a chance to see if I'll spook."

Jeff nodded and took a dignified step back. "Are we going to drive the monster big-dick car? Because Mikhail hasn't shut up about how wonderful it all is—I think he's trying to make Shane jealous."

Collin grinned. "I think that's sort of impossible, since it's pretty obvious Mikhail would walk on fire for the guy."

"Yeah, but he's pretty hilarious when he tries, so Shane lets him." Jeff's smile was maybe the strongest thing about him.

"Yeah, we're taking the Camaro—it's out back. Park the Mini in that spot right there"—Collin pointed to the "next-up" spot in front of the office—"and grab your stuff. I'll be right there."

Jeff nodded and turned back toward his car, and Collin concentrated on going from grease monkey to dream date in record time.

He knew he succeeded when Jeff rolled his eyes as Collin walked up.

"Very cute, Sparky. Who are you trying to impress?"

"You're not enough?" Collin asked, smirking. His reward was an almost fond smile that Jeff tried to hide as he opened his side of the car and got in.

"I already said you cleaned up pretty," Jeff replied smartly, and Collin tried not to make his preening too obvious. He obviously failed.

"Stop it, Sparky—you're becoming insufferable. I'm not going to tell you what you already know, so give it up."

Collin had to laugh—Jeff could do that to a guy. He started the car and pulled away, making sure he had enough fuel to get the hell out of Levee Oaks for sixty miles or so, and then continued the conversation. "Okay, fine. So my über-man-hawtness is wasted on you. Whom did I just take a GI shower for?"

Jeff shuddered and winced, turning his head to actually look at Collin in his freshly scrubbed, freshly shaved, man-fumed, pit-stopped glory. "You did *what*? In the bay of your *garage*? *Jesus*, kid—I was asking for a ride, not a date!"

"Well I didn't know who we were meeting!" Collin protested, but secretly he was very pleased. It was worth a cold hose, a rough towel, and going commando because his briefs smelled like engine oil if Jeff thought he looked date-worthy. "Uhm, who are we meeting?"

"My mother," Jeff muttered, as though this actually hurt him to say.

"Your *mother*!" Oh shit. "We're going to meet your mother and you couldn't let me go home and put on underwear?"

"Well," Jeff snapped, "it's not like she's going to remember who in the fuck you are in ten minutes anyway!"

Oh. "Oh," Collin said gently. "Uhm, Alzheimer's?"

Jeff shrugged, and there was a silence then. Collin let it stretch out, figuring that Jeff would fill it when he was ready. Collin was right.

"It started right after I left," Jeff said with a sigh, and Collin didn't pry to see when that had been. "She has good days and bad days, and I'm not sure how much she'll remember. I'm not actually going up to see her—I'm going up so I *can* see her. They may not even let us in."

Collin tried really hard to take that in stride. Tried, but couldn't. "Why wouldn't they let us in? And who is 'they'?"

Jeff blew out a sigh, and Collin realized that this was the discussion he'd hoped to avoid by not having anyone help him. He didn't want a soul to know this—more pain to tuck under his belt and pretend didn't exist.

"'They' is my father. He cut me out of the family when I came out, but mom and I kept in touch." Collin gasped, but Jeff kept going, his voice very carefully leeched of all animation, anger, bitterness—life. "When this"—hand gestures to indicate the awfulness of age and disease—"started happening, I had to sneak around to talk to her. I've been bribing the nurse for the last couple of years, and we get our phone call once a week, but the nurse just got fired—"

"For taking bribes?"

"For taking it up the ass in the supply closet," Jeff retorted, the first bit of emotion creeping into his voice. Of course—humor. "And quite frankly, I think if you work a job like that one, you should get your own room and complimentary porn, just to take the edge off. But it doesn't matter. Becky's gone, and now I've got to go and try and beg to see my own mother."

"Is your father as stubborn as you are?" Collin asked, and almost ducked from Jeff's fulminating look. "I'm just asking! Maybe you can reason with him!"

Collin couldn't fathom a world in which his family simply turned away. It had taken him eighteen years to finally get it through his thick head, but he now realized to the soles of his feet that his father wouldn't have left him voluntarily, and certainly not while driving Collin in the back of the car. He lived in the garage apartment not because he couldn't afford a home of his own—he'd actually bought a small house. Then he'd fixed it up and sold it. His mother liked knowing where he was; it made her happy to know he was safe. He figured he'd caused her enough anxiety when he was growing up that he owed her a little bit of ego and independence to ease her mind now.

The idea that Jeff's father just... just wouldn't *want* him. It was ludicrous. Nobody did that anymore, did they?

"Is my father as stubborn as I am?" Jeff muttered. "The man has barred me from seeing my mother for over a decade, Collin. Claims I'm morally corrupt. He's the family fucking patriarch, too, so there goes my brother, my cousins, and every damned soul I grew up with. Is he as stubborn as I am? Who gives a fuck? Seriously—I don't even give a shit anymore. I just want to talk to my mom once a week, okay? It's not much—it's not dinner at The Pulpit, or the right to call up Crick and Deacon and cry on their couch. It's not buying dresses for the little girls—"

"Girls? There was only one at dinner."

"Deacon's best friend's baby, Lila. It's not spoiling the little girls rotten, and being called Uncle Jeff, or getting to plan Shane and Mikhail's wedding, or sending care packages to Crick's sister at school. It's not any of that shit, but it's the one thing left from a happy childhood, dammit, and I'm not going to roll over and go tits-up just so that bastard can take it from me, you hear?"

"Yeah," Collin said thoughtfully. "I hear." He heard a core of steel in the man's voice, that was what he heard. He heard why maybe Jeff wouldn't want to hear a thing about The Pulpit that wasn't shiny and bright, and he heard why maybe he put so much effort into keeping his funny-man mask on for a group of people who were maybe not fooled for a minute, but who loved him too much to let on otherwise.

Jeff was quiet for a minute, and he tilted his head back again, like he was trying to ease an ache in his neck.

"I've got some ibuprofen in the glove box," Collin offered helpfully, and Jeff shook his head.

"Thanks, but no. Rips up my stomach like nothing else." Jeff kept his head tilted back and his eyes closed, and Collin heard the weariness in his voice, like a lead weight hitting the bottom of an icy ocean.

What to do? What to do, what to do…. Collin wasn't great at comforting. He was pretty good at being there through the rough stuff—his last boyfriend had lost his sister in a car wreck while they were together, and Collin had hung in there through the funeral and the grieving and the pain. In the end, though, Luis had needed to move on, and Collin had been ready to let him go. So Collin could drive Jeff to this horrible family confrontation and could probably hold him up if he fell down—and that was what Collin had wanted to do from the very beginning.

But he was at sort of a loss as to what to do for a tired man with a headache and what seemed to be the world on his shoulders.

But he couldn't just do nothing.

Tentatively, he reached out and put his hand on Jeff's knee. He was surprised—and a little bit humbled—when those long, well-manicured fingers laced with his and squeezed hard.

Collin pulled his arm back, keeping Jeff's fingers laced with his, and managed to drive one-handed most of the way up Highway 50 until he had to take the exit that got them to what was, apparently, Jeff's hometown.

Chapter 8

Jeff: The Frosty Cold Tip of the Big Fucking Iceberg

JEFF wasn't sure which part of his day sucked worse: waking up to Becky's quietly remorseful phone call, the wreck of the Titanic that had been his counseling appointment with Martin, or finding that he was weak enough to let Collin take charge of his life and give him a ride to what promised to be a complete Hoover suck-fest that would vacuum what was left of his life-force out a gauge eighteen needle at mach six.

Add that to his odd conversation with Crick the night before, which had left Jeff with the vague feeling that something big and bad and out of his control was going down right in front of his eyes... well, shit. When Collin's touch, his simple, human touch, entwined with Jeff's cold, sweating, clenching fingers, Jeff thought he might very well have to hold on for forever, and even maybe longer.

He clenched Collin's hand and kept his eyes closed, and relived the dagger-most-fine points of his conversation with Kevin's little brother echoing in his head.

"Yeah, you loved my brother so goddamned much you gave him AIDS, didn't you!"

Ouch. Just fucking ouch. Jeff looked at the kid, hands on his hips, elbows out, and stopped himself from asking how Martin's parents managed not to drown him at birth. "The goddamned rubber broke, kid. Do I have to draw you a picture, or have I already strained your little squirrel brain with TMI?"

Martin's eyes grew big and round, and his skin grew sallow and white in the pink part of his lips. "That's all it takes?" *he asked, horrified.* "One broken condom?"

"Theoretically, yes," *Jeff snapped, thinking,* Please don't go there, please don't go there, please don't go there....

"Theoretically?" *Martin looked at him with incredible suspicion.*

Jeff peered around the little counseling room with misery. All he saw was a bunch of teenager art, some concert prints, a little coffee table, some cheap chairs, and Kimmy, Martin's safe person, looking back at him with incredible compassion in her eyes. Jeff looked back at her and tried to be bitchy about it, but he couldn't. Kimmy had moments like this from her own life, he was sure. Moments her judgment had been piss poor or motivated by weird, internal twistings instead of sane, rational thought. One did not have all your brother's gay friends gather together to save one from an abusive ex-boyfriend and a bowlful of non-consensual cocaine if your life-choices were all sunshine and lollipops, did one? No. If anyone knew how badly personal evisceration was going to sit with Jeff, it was probably Kimmy, but that didn't make it any easier.

God, this whole steaming pile of funky dog shit would be so much easier to bear if he could hate her.

"I don't know if it was just the once," *Jeff said quietly.* "We just ditched the whole condom thing altogether after that."

"Oh for Christ's sake!" *Kimmy snapped.*

Jeff looked at her dryly. He was much happier now that she'd done something wrong than when she was the model of emotional and professional health. "Did we skip the class on tact, Kim, or do I want to see your grade on that one?"

"Seriously," *Martin muttered, sharing an incredulous look with Kimmy.* "Even I know that's a fucked-up idea!"

Jeff sighed and scrubbed his face with his hands. How did he put it into words?

For starters, Kevin had been going off to war, and Jeff might not ever see him again. Jeff wanted his touch all over his body—it was that simple. He didn't want anything between them, not a thought, not a fear, not a rubber.

And, as bullshit starry-eyed romantic as even that had been, it didn't even compete with the other reason.

He was going into this gig HIV-free—about as pristine as he'd been when he'd lost his virginity to Troy Wilkins in the locker room after swim practice in the eleventh grade. (Troy had known what the hell he'd been doing too—he fucked like a god, and, yes, had a pocket full of rubbers, because that boy had plans. Last Jeff had heard, he had a law degree from Stanford, and good for him. He also had a wife and kids, which Jeff wasn't so sure about, but, well, to each his own.)

So if Kevin had just given him HIV with one broken rubber, Jeff didn't want to be pissed at him for it. Jeff didn't want Kevin going off to war thinking that Jeff would never forgive him for an ass full of AIDS. Jeff had been the one to ditch the protection, and Kevin, embarrassed and guilt-ridden, had gone along with him. This way, Kevin had said, it wouldn't be some dumbassed accident, it would be their own dumbassery instead.

World's worst fucking idea. Jeff had known it when he'd done it. But he'd sworn—sworn!—he'd never look back at their time together and regret a moment, or a breath, or a dumbassed decision. And he hadn't. Until now. When he had to explain to Martin the convoluted thinking of two men who were not thinking at all but feeling, heart full, into a marriage without a wedding, a life of "I do" that had come way too abruptly to "'Til death do us part."

"It's complicated," Jeff said lamely into the expectant silence, and Martin had turned away in disgust, and that, boys and girls, was the end of the goddamned session.

Clutching Collin's hand now felt like thievery. He had no intention of giving this kid the time of day, and he was a complete and total fraud.

As he surfaced from that conversation with Martin, relived his and Kevin's optimism, remembered that heady, fuck-it-all, freight-train love that had just pinned them to the tracks, he felt, deep in his bones, the weary certainty that he couldn't do that again. His heart wasn't ready for it. He was beyond that now. No love for Jeffy. It hurt too much. Jeffy was strong, Jeffy was wise, and Jeffy couldn't survive another heart shattering—he couldn't do it. The same things that made this kid *so* attractive—the big-dick car, the big-dick walk, the snarky humor, the big-dick attitude—those were the things that were risky. Those were the things that led to disaster.

Jeff needed to not give him any hope. No promises. Not even a held hand in a quiet car. (*Sort of* quiet—the damned thing had an engine that would wake James Marshall, founder of Coloma, and that guy had been dead for a century and a half!)

But even that was a lie, because Jeff couldn't seem to make himself let go of that rough-knuckled, strong-boned hand.

But he had to give the guy *something*. Jeff may be the self-acknowledged fairy-Jeff-father of gay men, but that didn't mean he didn't have a sense of honor like any other alpha male on the planet, did it?

God, give the kid some truth, one truth, one truth at all, so Collin wouldn't regret holding hands with an old 'mo who had too much emotional baggage for a summer fling, much less a long-haul winter shack-up of a relationship.

"Your age," Jeff said, as he felt Collin shift his body before he took the turn off to Highway 49. He sat up and looked around, feeling refreshed, as though he'd been napping or meditating instead of dwelling on an emotional Hoover of a morning. God, as much as the next few hours were going to suck, fall in the Gold Country was something special. The grass was green instead of brown, the oak and pine trees were a dark holly color, and the maples and mulberries were spectacular and flaming as they gave their leaf-shedding swan song.

"My what?" Collin was peering at the signs and, after a glance at his gas gauge, took the left and pulled immediately into the gas-'n-sip to fuel up. Well, a monster of a car like this would probably guzzle fuel without mercy or repentance, wouldn't it?

"Your age," Jeff said, as Collin turned the engine off. His voice sounded abnormally loud in the sudden silence.

Collin turned toward him, and as the chill of the altitude seeped past the windows, Jeff was aware that Collin's body radiated heat like some sort of high-octane furnace. God, the kid really was just like his car: muscles, heart, and a slick exterior—heaven help poor Jeffy, who hadn't gotten him some in too long a time.

"What about my age?" he asked softly.

"The problem is...." Jeff looked sideways and frontways and anywhere but at those perceptive golden eyes. "The problem is, you really grew up in a hurry, kid. And you're—Christ, you're way more grown-up than I am at this point. I'm going to keep calling you Sparky or rookie or what-the-fuck-ever, to remind myself that I've got"—he fought the urge to giggle—"baggage. Issues. God, like a luggage store, hanging out in my psyche, right? And you—you're young, and you've obviously got your shit together, and you don't need me crapping it up. I shouldn't have taken your help, okay? But I did, and I'm sorry, and I'm going to keep calling you Sparky, just so you remember that you've got other options and this whole crush thing should be something you hurdle over, or it's going to fall on your head."

"Why don't you let me decide about that?"

Jeff couldn't even look at him. "Nobody should have to wrestle my demons, Collin," he said softly. "I at least got to be young, okay?"

Collin's gentle hand on his chin forced Jeff to meet his eyes, and Jeff's heart started to beat a little bit faster when he saw the slow, smug smile on the kid's face.

"Oh, Jesus, that was a mistake!" he muttered. Whatever he'd said, it had given the boy hope. "What was it? I'm trying to scare the shit out of you, dammit—how'd I fail?"

"You called me 'Collin'." The whisper of those lean lips against Jeff's scowl was enough to close Jeff's eyes, and he even leaned forward before that terrific, radiating heat backed off, and the fingers on Jeff's chin with it.

"Can I get you a soda, Jeffy?" Collin asked, his eyes crinkled with the insufferable knowledge that yes, for half a second, Jeff had let himself want.

"Coffee, Sparky," Jeff snapped. "Grown-ups drink coffee. And I'll get my own, thank you. I've got to hit the head."

"Get me a soda, would you?" Collin called smugly as he got out of the car and ran his card through at the pump. "I prefer diet lime or lemon or something, okay?"

"Anything you want, Sparky!" Jeff called back with the kind of salute that left only the middle finger extended. He could hear Collin's strong laugh echoing off the concrete of the gas station until the door of the mini-mart closed behind him.

JEFF got him a soda the size of a kiddie pool, hoping the guy's bladder would burst on the long drive between civilization and what Jeff had always thought of as a backwoods suburb.

Coloma itself was a small tourist attraction in the middle of some damned pretty country. Among the twistings of Highway 49 were smaller roads leading up hills to tiny neighborhoods of houses on big tracts of land. Those were the kids who went to the school and the people who ran the local businesses. The touristy things were all there—local artists were showcased in a couple of stores, tea shops, little cafés, the inevitable tacky-knick-knack shop, the kind that would have a T-shirt with a finger up a nose and the saying, "I found gold at Sutter's Mill."

A block behind the tourist buildings were the business the locals used—video stores, banks, feed stores (although those had gone the tourist route lately, because not nearly as many people had large animals these days to support them), and, of course, one office in a refurbished Edwardian-era home: Beachum, Porter, and Mason, Partners at Law.

That was Jeff's father, and his father's cousins, establishing their own little patriarchy over the small tourist town like Burgermeister Meisterburger himself.

"Turn right here," Jeff muttered, pointing to an almost-invisible road behind a feed store. "Here. There's a small parking lot—you can stay with the car."

"Really?" Collin's lip curled up when he was mutinous. It was, uhm, actually really hot, and Jeff's palms had already been sweating since that intense moment in front of the gas station. Collin had grudged him some show tunes on the stereo—that, too, had been sort of endearing, especially when Collin launched into Valjean's part in the beginning of *Les Mis*. He had a surprisingly solid baritone—not as nice as Deacon's, but still solid. He swore he'd make Jeff pay by making him listen to Rise Against the entire trip back, and although Jeff protested, and loudly, he privately thought it was worth it.

"Uhm, yeah," Jeff said, trying to put a spine where his swish threatened to take over. "You—well, you know, if you go down the main drag, back the way we came, there's a really nice state park. It's got a walk along the river to the mill where they discovered gold, and a statue of James Marshall, and the story of the—"

"I grew up in California, Jeff. I know about the fucking Gold Rush, okay?"

"Yeah, well you don't need to know about this."

"Shut the fuck up and get out of the car. I'll hang around and be ambiguous gay man in the background, Jeffy, but use me while you got me."

Jeff let out a frustrated growl and then hauled himself out of the car and stalked up toward the nice, conservative entrance of the Holly Ridge Rest Home, pulling his alpaca scarf up around his neck in the November chill. Christ, it was cold up here. He should have remembered gloves, but back in Levee Oaks, it was about ten degrees warmer. Fuck. He hated the fucking cold. Would rather bake himself in the sun like a poached salmon.

He checked the lay of his scarf again and was about to move his hand up to his hair when Collin's hand, warm and strong, grabbed his.

"Don't touch the hair, Jeff. It's fine. You look great. When was the last time you saw her?"

"We might not see her now," Jeff said, hoping his voice didn't sound as mournful to Collin as it did to himself.

Collin's arm wrapped around his waist, and he lowered his head to Jeff's ear. In the reflection of the bay window they were approaching, it looked unbearably intimate, but Jeff couldn't make himself pull away.

"How long?" he asked gently.

"Twelve years," Jeff rasped, and then they were through the automatic doors, and propriety gave him an excuse to pull away from Collin before he ran away completely.

His discussion with the director of the home was short and to the point.

"We're sorry, Mr. Beachum—you realize that we're under strict orders not to let her have any contact from you, you understand?"

"We went to high school together, Clarice. Call me Jeff, and stop giving me that line of bullshit. It worked twelve years ago because I was nineteen, and I didn't know any better. She remembers me, visits from me don't upset her, and I work in the health-care profession—if my mother wants to see me, she can bloody well see me, and if she wants to accept my call, I shouldn't have to find the right nurse to bribe, I should be able to give her a cell phone of her own and talk to her."

"Well, since Rebecca doesn't work her anymore, that's hardly an option—"

Jeff wanted to smack that condescending smile right off her face. "It was only an option because it was easy, heifer! It's not easy anymore, and I have the right to see my goddamned mother!"

"Your mother has the right not to be bothered by sex deviants."

Oh Christ. Jeff knew that voice. "Oh. My. God." He didn't even turn around. "Do they have some sort of gay-sighting hotline here?" He aimed the question at Clarice and was gratified to see her squirm.

"I had the receptionist call your father when you walked up," she explained weakly, and he rolled his eyes.

"Wow, Clarice. I couldn't have figured that out without your help. It's a good goddamned thing you're here."

Clarice flushed. She'd gained a bit of weight since high school, but unlike Margie, Jeff's favorite patient, he couldn't seem to see past the hips and the coarsened skin and the graying hair and little tiny pig-like eyes to the good person inside. "He has a right to know," she said, a bit of attitude creeping into her expression, and Jeff's returning smile was unpleasant—even he knew that.

"Does he have a right to know that I've been paying part of her rent?" Jeff asked, holding a trump card and proud of it.

"What?" she asked, and behind him, he heard his father's flinty tenor echo, "What?"

"Rebecca called me last year and let me know they were raising the fees. She said that Mrs. Beachum's husband was unable to pay, and I paid the difference. I even signed a partial lease. So, Clarice, I'm footing part of the bill, you ice-cold bitch, and I have every right to see the resident I'm paying for, and I have a right to leave her a cell phone, and I have the right to make sure she's got someone to help her use it. Like I said, Becky was expedient. Becky was a way to avoid this scene right here. But I haven't seen my mother face-to-face in twelve years, so maybe it's a good thing Becky got herself some, because I think I'm sort of fucking enjoying it, you know? Now excuse me, I'm going to go visit my mother. And don't bother escorting me—I know the room number. It goes on the line next to my signature on the fucking check you cash every month."

Jeff felt a hot surge of triumph under his skin, and he didn't even fight to keep the snarl off his face as he turned on his heel to leave.

His father tried to stand in his way. "Now, Son—"

"I'm not your son anymore, remember, Mr. Beachum?"

God, he looked old. How could he look so old? His face was lined and his hair was gray and grown long. When had his father grown his hair so long? A little gel, a tie, he could have a queue like the other South Placer hippies. *God*, Jeff thought, his anger coming up hard to set the tight muscles in his mouth and his cheeks, *if only*. So much of South Placer was tolerant and accepting—and high off of some premium greenbud, he'd give them that. But not his father's little corner of the universe. Not Archie Beachum, who'd never had a liberal thought in his body, (although he'd apparently had a liberal swimmer in his boner, because Jeff was living proof.)

That lean-lipped mouth thinned. "Jeffrey," he said warningly, "now see reason."

Jeff's vision went the same color it had when he'd decked Collin. He had to fight to breathe, fight to see his father clearly—fight not to fight. "Reason?" he echoed dully. "Reason? Old man, I've got nothin' to respond to that. You...." Oh God. A thousand moments flashed behind Jeff's eyes, moments he'd kept out of the slide show for twelve years because watching them hurt too much.

"You—shit. Archie, you nursed me through strep throat when I was seven. You—you went to every swim meet I ever raced. You took me out to a steak dinner when I got my scholarship. And all of that went away one day when I came home and said I didn't love who you expected me to. All of it." Jeff's voice seemed to detach from his actual body. His mouth moved, and he wasn't sure what was going to come out of it. It was like listening to someone else talk. *That's good. Let's listen to this other person talk.* Because when that guy was talking, all this shit happened to him, and not to Jeff. Jeff was in his bubble. Jeff was going home to his cats and having dinner with Deacon and Crick on Sunday. Jeff was good.

And this other guy—God. He was saying shit that Jeff was glad *he* didn't have to remember, because *Jesus*, would that suck.

"What you were doing was unnatural," Archie intoned, and Jeff's voice was incredulous.

"*Jesus*, Archie. I wasn't going to make you watch! I wasn't even going to bring a boyfriend around, you know that? I just wanted you to know who I was. I was still your little boy. I was still Mom's youngest son. You just... just *forgot that* for twelve years? I mean, you may be a soulless old bigot, but—but I mean, Jesus, Dad. I was under the illusion that I grew up loved—"

"You were loved!" The old man's voice was breaking. That should have been sad. Jeff couldn't make himself be sad about it. He was aware—sort of—that Clarice-the-fucking-bitch-Thomas was backing up against her desk and looking greenly for some way out of this family reunion. He was much more aware that Collin was pushing himself off the wall tensely, looking for a moment, a reason, anything, to reach out and support Jeff and to help him and to be *that guy.*

Jeff didn't get *that guy.* Jeff could do just fine on his own.

"It's not love if it goes away with the snap of your fingers, asshole," Jeff said coldly. "Now I've got a right to see her, so you just go away and let me, and I'll be out of your hair."

"You're the one who left without looking back!" Archie snapped, and Jeff curled his lip.

"I think I just established that *that's* a colossal crock of crap, didn't I, Archie?"

"Well *I* didn't know that!" Jeff's father snapped. "*I* thought you walked away and never looked back!"

"I sent you cards, Dad!" That other guy—he seemed to be hurting. There were tears in his voice. Jesus, Jeff was glad he wasn't that other guy. "You, Barry, Mom. You got birthday cards, Christmas cards—you had my address, you had my phone number—you couldn't have fucking called?"

"You couldn't have either?"

"I *did*!" Jeff shouted, and there was a hand on his shoulder, hot and urgent, and he was straining against it, angry, heated, furious. That other guy's voice and Jeff's heart… they were starting to beat together to the same awful rhythm, and Jeff tried really hard to keep them separate.

"You called *her*!" Archie shouted back. "You didn't once apologize to *me*!"

"I will *not* apologize for who I am!" Oh fuck. That had hurt. His throat hurt. It felt ripped, shredded, torn, and tight. "I will *not* apologize for having my entire life ripped away when I'd bought a lie for nineteen years that I was loved!"

"*You were loved*!" Archie yelled, and Jeff shook his head, fully himself, and, goddammit, in tears like the big fucking queer-assed-'mo he'd always been.

"Emphasis on *were*, Dad, right? Because I may be loved now, but it's not you who's doing it, you know? I had to go out and get a new family—I did. I had to find an old uncle who talked me through the worst day of my life and his nice wife who gave me a reason to live. I went and found a brother who didn't give a shit if I was gay or straight but who really likes to shop with me, and his sister, who likes to knit, and a father who's younger than me but who makes sure I show up for Sunday dinner anyway. I found cousins who love me, and babies...." Jeff remembered that last time at The Pulpit and found, against every scrap of common sense, a smile from somewhere he hadn't believed in. "I taught a baby the F-word, Dad, just like my cousin's baby, except this one is going to know my name in ten years, I guarantee it. There are two little girls out there who call me Uncle Jeffy, and they love me, and I bring them dresses and I go to dance recitals and swing them around the yard, and their mothers adore me and think I'm the best babysitter ever, and you know the best part?"

He was wiping his face on the sleeve of his trench coat. Shit. He was going to get moisturizer all over it. It would probably stain. But he couldn't quite seem to stop, and he was sagging back against a big, strong, comforting body, and he didn't want to fight against that anymore, not even to get a goddamned Kleenex.

Archie just shook his head to Jeff's question, and Jeff saw without seeing that his father, the man he'd worshipped until he was nineteen and that was taken away, too, was wiping his face on the sleeve of his black trench coat as well.

"The best part, Dad, is that none of these people are going to rip that away from me because of who I am. They know who I am. They love me. They think I'm a good guy. I am a good guy. I've got a good family. But you're not in it anymore because you told me you didn't want to be. But Mom—she never told me that. So I'm going to go visit her, and take another picture of her, and maybe see her around Christmas, because I've goddamned earned the right to."

He took a deep breath then and realized that he was in the center of what was probably a really embarrassing scene. Half the staff of the retirement home was jammed in the doorway to see what the ruckus was, and Jeff—well, Jeff was blubbering like a baby.

"Now," he hissed, furious and a little embarrassed, and heartbroken, "get the fuck out of my way."

And his father, the man whose word had been law in his house growing up, the man who had ripped his blanket of security away when he hadn't quit growing quite yet, backed up and got out of his way.

Jeff shouldered his way past the onlookers, trying not to take too much pleasure when his pointy shoulders made contact with some people's arms or chests, and fought his way clear of the crowd of people who had apparently decided they'd had enough entertainment for the afternoon and weren't going to follow him. He and Collin walked in silence to the elevators, because his mother lived on the second floor, and stood there, waiting for the ding.

The silence was wearing—even that short a moment—and it was wearing. He had to say something. He was supposed to say something. Jeff always filled in the silences. It was his job.

"Jesus," he murmured as they watched the dial and felt the heat of what must have been the entire town on their backs, "she's the one with Alzheimer's, and he's the one who seems to have forgotten the entire fucking thing."

"Shut up, Jeff," Collin said gruffly, and Jeff managed to look sideways at him as the door dinged open. His face was taut, and his eyes were red, and he looked, maybe, the tiniest bit like Jeff felt, and Jeff was sorry for the kid. He'd tried to warn him—maybe not good enough, but he'd tried to tell him it wasn't worth the baggage, hadn't he? He'd tried.

God, no. He hadn't. It hadn't been enough. Whatever he'd done, it hadn't been enough, because the kid was still here, and God help him, Jeff wanted him still there, just for a few hours more.

The elevator was full—two blue-haired women in the little electric scooters and one with a walker all looked at the two of them in surprise. They both moved chivalrously to either side and smiled in tense silence as the women buzzed or hobbled out, and then moved into the elevator as though half of Coloma wasn't watching them, apparently the town's only two faggots, getting into an enclosed space together.

"Sorry about th—"

"I said shut up, Jeffy," Collin muttered, and Jeff found himself being turned roughly, without a hello or how-are-you, and engulfed in a hug that went on forever and ever and ever. The elevator moved at its snail's pace to the next floor, and still, Collin held on, and Jeff clung to him. Collin reached out and hit the close-door button twice more while little old people sat in befuddled silence, and kept Jeff snug and wonderful until the shudders of reaction stopped making it impossible to move.

JEFF'S mother had been... distracted. Surprised to see him, but distracted. She'd just seen him last week, she laughed weakly, why the long hug? Why the tense face? It was just so upsetting, Jeff, because the girl—the one she really liked, the funny one, with the bawdy sense of humor, she wasn't there. People didn't seem to realize what a complete change of routine that was when the girl wasn't there, did they?

Jeff agreed with her and nodded and made all the right noises and tried not to be too disappointed. If he'd thought about it, he would have realized that this wouldn't be a big dramatic reunion. Alzheimer's was a terrible disease—the last twelve years of his mother's life, completely gone. Hell, she was talking about Jeff's swim meet practices, and even, at one point, smiled benignly at Collin and asked him if he was on Jeff's team.

Collin had raised his eyebrows at Jeff and said that yes, yes, in fact, he *was* on Jeff's team, and Jeff shot him a droll look. *Very funny, Sparky. Team, get it? We play for the same team? Oh yes we do!*

But still, he was grateful.

The visit was short, but Jeff managed to secure an orderly and assure the young man that he had complete permission—which, he assumed, since no one had come after him and made a scene, he did. He left the cell phone charging along with explicit written instructions for when Jeff would call and how the calls were to be handled. He was grateful when it seemed to be a sure thing and even more grateful that bribes weren't involved this time. Becky had been nice, and she'd been providing for her kid, which was why Jeff hadn't minded the extra money, but this way, he was sure that his phone calls could continue even if there was a sudden change in personnel.

Jeff took his mother's face between his palms and ignored her distracted look. Instead, he concentrated of the realness of her soft, lined skin under his palms and the kind vagueness he saw in her blue-gray eyes.

"I love you, Mommy," he said quietly, not caring of Collin could hear him but not wanting to shout either. "I love you, and I'll see you around Christmas."

"Be good at school, Jeffy," his mother said gently. "Get good grades—your father's so proud of you, you know, being a doctor. Your brother always brags about you. Such a good boy." She patted his cheek and then looked off into the distance behind Jeff's ear and simply faded away. He kissed her forehead and was grateful. He'd seen Alzheimer's move a lot faster.

Thank you, God, because she still knows my name.

This time, he fumbled for Collin's hand in the elevator. He still felt like a thief, there was no denying it, but sometimes thieves stole things because they needed them to live.

He had brief words with Clarice on the way out of the door, but his father wasn't there, and Jeff was glad. He couldn't do that again, not now. Not when the memory of his mother was so raw in his mind. He and Collin got into the car and didn't speak until they hit Highway 50, and then it was because they hadn't eaten.

Collin pulled off at a strip mall in Cameron Park, and they went into the Red Robin there to eat.

Then Collin started talking, randomly it seemed, but he was funny about it. He talked about his sisters, and how he deprived them of superheroes for three years, and how none of their husbands (or ex-husbands) were good enough for them, and his nieces, whom he seemed to spoil almost as much as Jeff spoiled Parry Angel and Lila Lisa.

Jeff listened to him, distractedly at first, and then, as dinner wore down, with most of his heart. God, the kid was funny. Snarky, yes, and a smug little bastard at times, but, well, funny.

Jeff had always really loved people who could make him laugh.

He remembered that when he started talking. He remembered how much he liked to laugh, how much it meant when he could make someone else do it. He shared some of his best stories—many of them gifted to him by other people. He told about his first meeting with Crick, a boy who'd just been given a crippling disability while he was already living with a healthy dose of guilt, and how Crick hadn't let that get him down. He told Margie's story about the student with the backpack full of condoms, and Mikhail's story about living on the streets in Russia and not knowing what a "top" was, and Benny's story about having her hair-trigger big brother teach her how to drive.

He made Collin laugh—he made him laugh a *lot*. And he was happy with himself, as they drove back to Levee Oaks. He thought that he had maybe given a part of himself that he could live with.

Collin pulled back into the parking lot by Jeff's car, and the silence fell between them for the first time since they'd walked into Red Robin.

"Thank you," Jeff said quietly, looking out into the fog. Levee Oaks was the flat part of a valley, with a big ol' river cutting through it. Lowland fog in the fall and winter was a part of life. But the fog over a parking lot lit by a soda light had a peculiar, pink and melancholy property, and Jeff found his "funny" slipping away.

"You're welcome," Collin said, and Jeff blessed the fact that he didn't play all coy about asking thank-you-for-what.

Collin's big hand came up to Jeff's cheek, and Jeff resisted for a moment and then sighed. God. He'd been so weak already. What was one more moment of weakness, really?

"What are you going to do now?" Collin asked quietly, and Jeff leaned into his touch and made everything worse by cupping Collin's hand to his cheek. For a moment it wasn't about what Jeff owed the kid, it was about what he needed from the man.

"I," Jeff said, feeling the irony well up and unable to stop it, "am going to call my mother on Monday, and go see her probably a few days after Christmas."

"That's a good plan," Collin said, dryness creeping into his voice. Jesus, was Jeff so easy to read?

"It's part of it," Jeff muttered. God. Him with his big words to his father—he'd really let the ball drop, hadn't he? He'd managed to avoid thinking about Kevin's little brother all day, but he couldn't avoid it—not here in the honest quiet of the car.

"Going to clue me in on the rest?"

Jeff looked at the grim lines of Collin's face and thought that he didn't look twenty-four at all. He looked almost ageless with purpose, firm and resolved and, well, grown up.

"I'll let you know if it works," he said with a sigh. He didn't want to talk about it. Just like going to Coloma that afternoon, he was afraid words would pollute his good intentions and he'd be left with a coulda-woulda-shoulda and an empty place in his chest for the cats to purr in.

"Jeff!"

Jeff held up a forestalling hand before Collin could blow all that strong stoicism with a well-earned tantrum.

"Cool your jets. I know—you've been a stand-up guy. You have. I'm eternally grateful, and even if you don't want my gratitude, you've got it. Look…." Oh God. Deacon would never forgive him. "I'll tell you what. Sunday dinner at The Pulpit. I know, I know—I'm sure you've got some sort of family things of your own—"

"Pizza video night, first Friday of the month," Collin confirmed with a quirk to his lean mouth, and Jeff smiled. Good. Good. He liked families. He *needed* families. Collin's sounded like fun—and wouldn't that be nice.

"Okay. Sunday dinner at The Pulpit—we start cooking around three or four, eat at six, you decide when to get there. Bring whatever you want. Seriously. You like French bread, bring that. You like pie, that's your thing. No alcohol."

Collin lifted his eyebrows, and Jeff shrugged.

"No alcohol. It's a rule." He was damned if he'd tell about Deacon's alcoholism. He got permission with his stories—he was careful. He had permission to tell about Mikhail's past; Mikhail didn't give a shit. Deacon's past was Crick's secret. The family knew, but it wasn't Jeff's story.

"Do I need to call?"

Jeff shook his head. Crick was going to get a blow-by-blow—this conversation included. That was the way GBFF worked, wasn't it?

Collin nodded and Jeff said, "Good, see you then," and put his hand on the door handle, but Collin's hand on the back of his neck stopped him.

"Jeff?"

That quick. That warm hand on the back of his neck, the heat of it through his hair, the memory of it on his back in the elevator or twined with his on the way up the hill, sturdy in the small of his back… that quick, and it all came flooding back.

Jeff's skin buzzed fiery, and his stomach went cold with excitement, and he closed his eyes, because he was weak today, because he needed, and he needed so very badly, and he wasn't going to say no, wasn't going to turn away… God. He was so tired of being strong. "Yeah?" he asked huskily, his head still turned away, but leaning back into the heat of those strong fingers.

"Are you going to look at me?"

"Yeah, okay, fine." He shifted in the seat and turned around. Collin dropped his hand, and by the time he was situated, there was that pretty, lean face, up close and personal, those golden eyes dark in the diffused light, that lean mouth turned up just at the corners, and that nose—that nose with all the character, the one that had been broken more than once (and was, for that matter, still bruised from when Jeff had done it himself) was close enough to bump gently with Jeff's.

So he did.

Jeff gasped softly, and his lips parted, and he nuzzled back. Collin's mouth quirked up, and that was the last thing Jeff saw because his eyes closed, and then that mouth was on his own, and the kiss began.

It tasted... oh God. It was better than chocolate. It was... it was chicken marsala, or prime rib. It was hearty and strong and warm and filling, and Collin's tongue swept into his mouth without shame and *claimed* him. Jeff groaned and let him. It was his day, he told himself, his day to be weak. He was going to taste this kiss with everything in him, he was going to devour and accept and experience. He raised a shaking hand to Collin's shoulder and shuddered, and Collin's arms went around his shoulders and held him so tight....

So tight. Nothing bad could happen to him when he was held that tight.

The kiss ended, but Jeff kept his eyes closed until Collin's forehead bumped his.

"Was that so bad?" Collin asked, and Jeff opened his eyes and pulled back, wanting to give the kid this, because it was honest, and Collin deserved honest.

"It was everything I was afraid of," he whispered, and he rubbed his cheek against Collin's lean one to take the sting out of the words.

Collin pulled back, trying to figure out what he meant, and Jeff used his opportunity to escape. He was out of the car and heading for his slightly defective Mini Cooper before Collin could even frame a reply.

He was halfway to Shane's home for runaway teenagers before he could stop rubbing his tingling lips and remind himself that there was really no cause for optimism, none at all.

Chapter 9

Collin: Friday Night Pizza

IT WASN'T actually the first Friday night this month—two of his sisters had begged off, and his mother had some sort of business seminar, so they'd postponed it to the eleventh. That worked out well—it was a holiday, and Collin would have given Joshua the day off, but the old man was as eager as Collin to clear out their backlog and get things spiffy for Thanksgiving and Christmas. Everyone who had time off during the holidays would come in for a tune-up or a smog check, and that was their bread and butter right there.

So, lucky Collin, he got to go face his family about two days after he'd faced Jeff's. He'd dreaded it. He wondered if his officious sisters could sense the life-altering undercurrents of angst and drama just coursing under his skin.

He was somewhat reassured when he showed up with the beer (his family *always* did beer) and Joshua and his wife Elsie showed up with the salad, and all his obnoxious sister Charlene said was, "Jesus, Collin, do you always have to bring the help?"

She said it to him quietly when they were in the kitchen at Collin's mother's house, otherwise Collin would have done what he'd done when they were kids: jump on her and stick his slobbery finger in her ear until she screeched like a wounded parrot and apologized. As it was, he had the age-old comeback of, "Jesus, Charlene, could you detach your bitch for a while and deal with the fact that I love them more than I love you?"

She looked startled at that, and even a little hurt, and ask Collin if he gave a ripe shit. At that point, life-altering experience with Jeff's family or not, it was the truth.

And maybe even more so, he thought moodily, bringing Joshua a beer as his sisters squabbled over the movie and Elsie listened from the outside, clearly trying not to put a word in because she was a visitor and very much not family.

"What are you thinking, Collin?" his mom asked. "You look like you swallowed a bug."

"Not a bug," Collin muttered. "Just Charlene's attitude. Why's she got to be so mean about Joshua?"

Natalie looked grimly at her youngest daughter, dressed stylishly in tight black slacks and tall boots, with a bright scarlet silk blouse under her blazer. Everyone else was in jeans, with the exception of Joanna's youngest daughter, who was in a fairy princess dress. (Joanna had been a most definite tomboy—the fact that her youngest lived in that dress was, as her mother kept telling her, the most divine karma *ever*.)

"Yeah, well, she hasn't been laid since Mark left—what do you expect?"

Collin turned to his mother in admiration. She never ceased to amaze him. She loved them all—he'd taken over the diner for two days while his mother had talked his sister down from an emotional ledge after her husband left—but that didn't mean Natalie was going to let Charlene get away with snobbery.

"I expect her to bring her own date," Collin sulked. He was the baby; old habits were hard to break.

"I could say the same thing about you!" his mother said pointedly, and his sulk turned cagey.

"I, uhm, well, maybe." *Smooth, Collin. Awesome.*

"So, that guy at the diner...," his mother led, looking at him winningly. She had the same light brown eyes he did—she just knew how to bat them more prettily.

Collin was shocked when he felt heat run under his skin and up his cheeks.

So was his mother. "Jesus, Collin, you didn't even do that when I busted you with Tommy in the garage!"

Oh God. The blush was getting worse. Jeff didn't know about that. Jeff, who kept telling him what a grown-up he was and how much of a man he seemed, didn't know that six years ago Collin was dumb enough to get busted by his family banging Tommy with the laundry!

Natalie turned to her son with real surprise and a thoughtfulness she hadn't had, even when she'd been thinking about ripping Charlene a new one. "Collin...."

"Has he told you about his new guy?" Joshua asked, stumping over with his beer clutched reverently in his hand.

"I saw him last week in the diner," Natalie said, still looking at her son in wonder. "I had no idea they were a thing."

"We're not yet," Collin muttered, wishing it wasn't quite so warm in his mother's living room.

"Yeah, but that didn't stop them from taking a little day trip together!" Joshua cackled, and Collin cast him a despairing look. The laugh abruptly stopped. "What? You look like I just stole your best pair of jeans—what happened that day?"

Collin shook his head and looked down at his soda. No beer for him, not with his white count getting a little low. Alcohol was bad news with the HIV, there was no doubt about it, especially in cold and flu season. "It was—man, he so didn't want me there. And I don't know how he would have made it without anyone there." Collin hadn't said a word to Joshua—not in two days—about what had gone down up in Coloma. But that didn't mean it hadn't weighed heavy on his mind.

"Collin, what did you go do?"

Oh God. It wasn't his story to tell, it wasn't. But as he looked at his mom, her graying hair dyed the same red-brown it had been when he was a kid, the lines around her eyes and mouth more smiles than scowls, he was just so grateful for her. Jesus, he'd been such an unmitigated pain in the ass.

"His mom has Alzheimer's—she's in a home, right? And his dad wasn't letting him talk to her. So he'd been bribing a nurse for phone calls, and she got fired, so he had to go up there—and God, Mom. He hadn't been back for twelve years. And the whole fucking town was like jammed in the office, and they were all so horrible to him, and all he wanted to do was talk to his mom, right?"

"Collin...." Joshua had disappeared, and Natalie Waters was taking her son's heated cheeks between her hands and shushing him, pulling him into the kitchen, where they could be alone.

"That's all he wanted to do," Collin gasped when the door had closed behind them. "And he got in there, and she didn't even remember he'd been gone for twelve years. She thought I was on his swim team from high school. And she was so pretty, you know, like you, but older, and he... God, Mom. He was so wrecked. And there was that whole scene in the diner, and it sucked, and he...."

Christ. Collin was not going to cry. Not here. Not in front of his mother.

Suddenly he bent down, because he was over six feet tall and she was barely five-foot six, and he swept her up in his arms and gave her a rib-cracking hug. "God, Mom," he muttered as she hugged him back. "I'm just so glad you didn't give up on me. I mean... I'll live in the garage for the rest of my life, just so's you know I'm so grateful. 'Kay?"

Her half-frightened giggle in his ear was enough to let him know he had to get his emotions under control. "Jesus, Collin—I'm just glad you survived."

His shoulders shook, and he laughed out some of the rougher emotions rioting in his chest. "I'm glad I survived with you here," he muttered, and then set her down with a sigh. He heard his sisters out in the living room, laughing. Charlene's brittle squeal didn't fracture on his nerves the way it used to.

"How's your friend?" his mother asked him in the almost awkward silence.

"Hurting really bad," Collin told her. "Unbelievably bad. I don't know what to do for him—he's not letting me, or anyone, I think, in to help, you know?"

Natalie shook her head. "I think maybe what you've been trying to do? I know it's not easy for you." Her laugh was wise and sad. "I *really* know it's not easy for *you*, especially, Collin. Least patient kid on the planet, you were. You know we took you to be diagnosed for ADHD?"

Collin nodded his head. God, yes, he knew—just because his mom had put up with a lot didn't mean she suffered in silence.

"My point is," she said, rolling her eyes dryly, "that you've been stalking this guy like a cat. Cat isn't your style. Rhinoceros on steroids—*that's* the boy I know and allowed to live. So, you know, whatever you're doing, keep doing it. He means something to you—whoever he is, however you knew him or know him now, he *must* mean something to you."

Collin nodded mutely and tried to put together the handful of times, really, he'd been in Jeff's company and see how it added up to this compulsion to know what made the guy tick and to see that he would be okay.

It didn't. All that was left was that moment in the shop and the realization that he'd go through a hundred days like the one in Coloma just to know he had the right to watch Jeff fidget and know that no one else would see him the way Collin did.

His mother ruffled his hair. "I'm gonna leave you alone, sweetie. Bring him around sometime, okay?"

"I told him he'd have to come eventually," Collin told her with a slight smile. "I'm having dinner at The Pulpit on Sunday—he owes me one. What?"

His mother's expression was pained, and he couldn't figure out why. "Oh, Jesus, honey. Those people at The Pulpit—they're *family.* You go ahead and court this boy—"

"He's older than me!"

"But not older than Joanna," she snapped back smartly. "Anyway, go and court him, but promise me we get you on Christmas and video nights, okay?"

Collin grimaced and shook his head, turning away to look out the window over the sink, into the black darkness of a November evening without fog.

Eventually, he went back into the front room and took his place on the floor with Kelsey (the kid in the fairy princess dress) on his lap. Her little bottom felt like it was made of tree limbs and boulders, and she had elbows that could cut steak, but when he wrapped his arm around her and felt her snuggle back, it was like everything was going to be all right. She was three years old, and Joanna's other daughter, Allison, (who was sitting in Elsie's lap, much to her Auntie Charlene's disgust) had been born about three months after that dingy gray day at the Sacramento CARE clinic.

They started *Beauty and the Beast*, because the first movie was always a kids' movie, and Kelsey snuggled right into him, like he was her favoritist person ever. The *second* movie, when the short people went into Mom's guest bedroom and went to sleep, was the movie that people spilled blood over. Everyone except Collin, because watching the first movie with Kelsey and Allison and Gina's son, Gage was as close as he might ever get to fatherhood, and once he'd decided he wanted to live, and live well, he found that he *coveted* the spare moments of fatherhood that came his way.

Collin remembered Jeff's pride that he had "nieces" at The Pulpit and held Kelsey just a little bit tighter. *You and me, Jeffy. We're a lot more alike than you think.*

"What did Mom talk to you about?" Joanna whispered in his ear. She did it while she was handing him popcorn, and it took him a minute to get the plastic bowl situated before he could turn and answer.

"Courting," he whispered back, making sure Kelsey was so into the movie she didn't hear.

"You courting someone or someone courting you?"

Collin gave his favorite sister a droll look over Kelsey's head, and she laughed quietly, holding up her hands. "Okay, okay—you courting someone. That's an improvement, Collin. Me likey."

"An improvement? And improvement over *what*?"

Joanna had a wicked sense of humor—it was probably where Collin first learned to love people who could really make him laugh. "Yelling, 'Fire in the hole!' and blowing your brains through a straw?"

Collin smirked and tried not to suck the scratchy part of a popcorn kernel through his windpipe. "I enjoyed those relationships," he said with as much of a straight face as he could.

Joanna reached over his shoulder and ruffled Kelsey's hair.

"Not as much as you're going to enjoy something that lasts longer than a week and a half and gives you more of this," she said seriously, and he dropped a kiss on the straight, fine blonde hair standing static with electricity right under his nose, and nodded.

"Shhh…," he said, watching as Gaston started to lead the troops to defeat the beast of the unknown. "This is my favorite part."

But he thought about it, and thought about it carefully, for the rest of the evening. Hell, he thought about it right until he surprised the hell out of himself by showing up at The Pulpit on Sunday at four. Jeff wasn't there yet, and he was going to make himself busy in the kitchen, but he saw that Crick pretty much had it under control.

"Hey, do me a favor, would you?" Crick asked, looking... well, older, was the only way Collin could describe it.

"Yeah, sure—anything."

Crick looked at him, maybe really looked at him, for the first time since the moment he and Deacon had needed to break up a melee in their driveway with a pipe hose. "You really care about Jeff?" he asked, seriously, and Collin nodded.

"Yeah."

"Good." Crick reached in the refrigerator behind the counter and pulled out chicken and set it down, then started rooting in the cupboards for marinade. "He's going to need it. Look, Collin—here's the thing, okay?" Crick looked at the assembled ingredients and mumbled to himself for a minute, like he was trying to remember something. He stopped for a moment, gave it up, and then turned back to Collin like this was serious business. "The whole family is going to be here, everyone but my sister Benny, and she already knows, and we're going to drop sort of a bomb on the world here, yanno?"

Collin's eyes bugged out. "You're not moving, are you? Because Jeff...."

Crick smiled wearily. "Are you fucking shitting me? Do you have *any* idea what it cost us to fucking stay here? Jesus, talk about drawing the wrong fucking conclusion—I'm surprised you and I didn't bump into each other more during high school!"

Collin preened, flattered that his hero had actually noticed him. He wasn't proud of the preen, but he didn't think there was a thing on the planet he could do to stop it. "You were pretty into Deacon after...."

The preen went away, and so did any pretense to lighthearted banter. Crick's best friend—some said his first boyfriend—had died in a car crash in Crick's sophomore year. Collin had been in junior high at the time, but it was a small town.

"I was sort of into Deacon before Bobby died," Crick answered with a *very* crooked grin. "But yeah. After that, I came to live here, and The Pulpit was pretty much my life. Still is," he said with a smile, and it wasn't Collin's imagination. There was something palpably wrong with Crick's smile, with his words... hell, with *everything*.

"So," Collin said, "if you're not moving...."

Crick shook his head and concentrated very hard on chopping vegetables for the salad. Collin noticed that these people seemed to eat a lot of veggies for horse ranchers—he'd have figured Deacon for steak.

"Look, man, you'll find out soon enough, but if I tell you before I tell the family, there's going to be a massacre on our hands, okay? But the thing is—and don't take this the wrong way—but there's going to be the little girls here, and Martin—"

"Martin?" This was news.

Crick's look was eloquent and annoyed. "Goddamn Jeff for a rutting sand-fucker anyway. Jesus, what does he think is going to happen if he actually picks up the fucking phone and gives you some precious fucking information? You're going to stick your tongue down his throat via the fiber optic network? Shit!"

Collin's lips twitched as he tried very, very hard not to laugh. Crick Francis may have been older, and he may have been more worried man than fucked-up kid, but his mouth was still a thing of beauty as a functioning cesspool, now wasn't it? "I take it that Martin is coming with Jeff?" he asked neutrally, and Crick sent him a look of pity over the salad fixings.

"You take it that Jeff has found the perfect shield in case you want to try to, I don't know, give a shit about him? Yeah. Nothing crashes a fucking date like a teenager hauled in kicking and screaming by the scruff of his neck!"

Collin was forced to laugh—at the same time he was forced to agree. "He felt obligated, I guess," he said, trying to reason through the hurt. "He… family matters a lot. I guess like he felt…." God, he couldn't say it. The hurt was a lot bigger than he'd thought at first, and he couldn't seem to squash it into his chest the way Jeff had.

Crick stopped chopping vegetables, ostensibly to stretch his crippled hand. But while he was paused, his face did a complicated dance, like he was trying to make something a priority in his head when in reality, it was the last thing on his mind.

"Martin's his family, too," Crick said quietly. "If…." His eyes closed really tightly, and he seemed to change the track of what he was saying in midair. For someone who had known him when he was young, this seemed almost as impossible for him to do as Collin's mother had said that stealth was for Collin.

Crick cleared his throat and started again. "If I had died when that missile hit," he said, like this was a more comfortable thought than he'd had in mind, "if I had died, Deacon would have taken care of Benny and Parry Angel. I have no doubt in my mind. They may have been the only things keeping him on the face of the planet, but he would have stood for them. This is no different. Martin needs someone—maybe even specifically Jeff, who is the last part of his brother that Martin has left. I don't think it has anything to do with you, you know?"

Collin swiped a slice of red pepper and munched on it. "Except," he mumbled, still trying to get a lid on the hurt, "he is the perfect excuse for not getting close."

"That too," Crick agreed, and he stretched his hand again and started chopping vegetables in moody silence.

"I'm sorry," Collin said after a minute. "You said you had something for me to do?"

Crick nodded. His straight black hair was falling in his eyes, and his narrow, pretty face was taut with shit he wasn't saying. He threw his head back to shake the hair out of the way and gave Collin another one of those weary grins.

"Look, all I need is this. When we start dessert, could you, I don't know, take the girls and maybe Martin, too, if he'll go, into the other room? Jeff will tell you what it's all about, and I have no problem with that—either that, or you'll hear people anyway. But it's going to be chaos, and people are going to be mad and hurt and… and just really fucking worried, okay? Anyway, if you could just, I don't know, manage the chaos? Pick Jeff up off the floor when it's over? Man, that would help so much."

The knife started to mince a tomato savagely as he spoke, and Crick kept after it for a few moments until it was well-diced pulp, the movements so heated and angry that Collin was afraid to say anything in case he broke Crick's concentration. The knife-work stopped, and the remains of the tomato leaked sadly on the cutting board. Crick looked up from them with another one of those cardboard smiles.

"You poor baby—I imagine you're thinking this is way over your pay grade, aren't you?"

"Well," Collin said brightly, "maybe I should ask for a raise!"

Crick's smile fixed itself for a minute, and Collin could suddenly see what Deacon Winters had seen in Crick for their whole lives.

"Maybe you should get one from him without asking!" he said with a waggle to his eyebrows, and Collin laughed until they both watched Jeff's Mini Cooper pull up the driveway.

Collin watched as Jeff got out of it, with Martin mirroring his motions on the other side, and suddenly his heart gave a vicious squeeze in his chest.

Maybe he didn't have a choice in the matter. Maybe he needed to just fucking earn his keep.

Chapter *10*

Jeff: Communication Breakdown

WHEN Jeff left Collin after that disastrous visit to Coloma, he was pretty sure he was cooked and done. But that didn't stop him from jumping with both feet into another big cauldron of bubbling emotional goo.

Shane's baby, Promise House, his home for runaway teens, was on a stretch of property right next to Deacon's. Apparently, clearing out the unused acreage of star thistles and grasses also cleared it out of rattlesnakes, to Deacon's immense relief, and what was left was about six acres of horse property with a house that Shane had recently had completely rebuilt on the original foundation.

Although the house looked like a large, two-story family home— the kind that also got turned into hotels and B&Bs—Shane had also gone for practicality: the east wing was for girls, and the west wing was for boys, with a big dining room and common room in the middle, as well as a large kitchen with cabinets that locked for knives and medication. There were two smaller rooms by the common rooms for counseling and private conversations. The whole thing was decorated eclectically. The common room was bright and cheerful, the counseling rooms were pastel and soothing, and the bedrooms had white walls with a *lot* of posters.

Jeff assumed the kids were allowed to decorate their own rooms, and he was greatly cheered. His own room growing up as a kid had been covered with pictures of Matt Biondi and the entire 1992 Olympic swim team. His parents had assumed that was because he was good at the sport, and he'd assumed they'd get the idea when he put the poster for *The Phantom of the Opera* up next to the poster of the half-naked swim team. So much for assumptions. Still, those posters, and the ones of *A Chorus Line*, and Abercrombie and Fitch, and the poster for *Reality Bites* to feed his Ethan Hawke obsession—they all let him be who he wanted, even in the confines of his father, and the church, and his very, very justified fears that who he wanted to be was not what the world wanted from him at all.

Kimmy looked up from where she sat, playing a hand of cards with two girls in jeans and hooded sweatshirts. The girls looked up at him, the expression on their faces carefully neutral, and he smiled and gave a flirty little wave to prove he was absolutely not a threat even at all. Then he answered Kim's questioning look.

"Can I see Martin?" His own voice startled him, because it didn't sound like a question at all. It sounded like a politely phrased command, but even though Kimmy raised her eyebrows, she didn't seem to hold it against him.

"He's in the kitchen with Lucas," Kim said. "They're on dish detail."

Jeff let his eyes widen and his eyebrows shoot up and was rewarded by Kim's blush and the girls' titters.

"He got a job at a linen service," Kim muttered. "Apparently we're his last delivery."

"That's convenient," Jeff said blandly, and Kim's blush intensified.

"Shut up, Jeff, and go get Martin. Grab whatever conference room you want to destroy—do you want me there?"

Jeff shook his head. "When this fails spectacularly, I'd rather not have witnesses, thank you," and he took a step toward the kitchen when Kimmy stood up and put her hand on his arm.

"You look like shit, Jeffy," she said for his ears only. "If this goes south, I'm taking you into the conference room myself to see what's going on in your poor tormented little self, okay? You're not getting out of here without someone, right?"

Jeff swallowed and blinked rapidly. Jesus, you walked a girl through one of the worst moments of her life, and she thought you owed her. "Appreciated, Kimmy. I'm just being… a stubborn bastard, I guess, right?"

Kimmy kissed his cheek. "God, Jeffy—it's a good thing you're a flaming 'mo, or a girl could think you were just being macho to impress her."

Jeff rolled his eyes and made his way to the kitchen, feeling grateful.

Martin and another boy his age were wandering around the kitchen, hunting and pecking like they didn't know where to put things but were making a good faith effort to do it anyway. Lucas and an older man Jeff didn't recognize were washing and drying, and Jeff remembered that Shane and Kimmy had hired an employee—probably a couple, if he thought about it. Kimmy and Mikhail were still dancing on the weekends, and Shane was going to school for a counseling degree. They all needed to sleep, and most nights, somewhere besides the house.

But the heart of the place was Shane and Kimmy—of that, Jeff could have no doubt.

"So, you're saying just because I'm black, I play basketball!" Martin was scoffing as Jeff stood at the doorway and listened.

"Naw, man—I'm saying that just because you're black, you get *women*!" the other boy said, grinning and throwing a dishrag at Martin's head.

Martin fielded the dishtowel and twisted it tight and began to stalk his intended victim. "Are you saying a gentleman kisses and tells?" he teased back. The towel shot out with a wicked snap, and the other kid, a white boy who was too thin and had nicotine stains on his fingers and teeth, howled good-naturedly.

"Mr. Allston!

The older man rolled his eyes in Lucas's direction and cleared his throat. He must have been an ex-cop or an old shop teacher or something equally intimidating, because that one little sound made Jeff's shoulders straighten and his eyes grow wide. Martin stood the same way, dropping the towel to his side and apologizing promptly.

"I'm sorry, sir."

"Forgeddaboudit," Mr. Allston muttered amicably, and Martin scowled at the other kid before going back to putting away dishes.

God, he was a good boy. Just like Kevin, he had that sense of honor and that integrity and willingness to do right. Jeff owed him. It wasn't rational, or even sane, but it was the truth. Jeff could lie to himself and lie to the other people in his life, even Crick, even, God forbid, Collin.

"Martin," he said hesitantly into the warm, bantering clatter. "Uhm, Martin?"

The boy looked up, his relaxed, open expression hardening, becoming self-protective, even as he saw Jeff's eyes. Lucas and Mr. Allston, and the kid who'd been giving him shit, all looked up with interest and caution, and Jeff wanted to crawl under the linoleum. God, all this effort to bare his soul, and there wasn't even a hot guy or a foot rub at the end of it. He hoped Kevin was laughing his ass off up in Valhalla, because someone ought to be.

"Yeah?"

"Can we, uhm, talk for a minute? Please?" He was never going to get used to this feeling, like his chest was cracked open by rib-spreaders and he was pinned to a gurney like a grisly butterfly in God's most sadistic collection.

Martin looked him up and down for a minute, and Jeff sighed.

"Look, kid. You asked me a question this morning. I gave you a bullshit answer. Do you want a real answer, or were you just asking it to make me squirm?"

The silence in the kitchen was now electric, and Martin looked reluctantly at his new friends. "Conference room," he muttered, and Jeff let him lead the way.

When they got there, Jeff closed the door behind him and looked at Martin on the other end of the room. Neither of them made any move to sit down, and Martin's expression was as hostile as a rabid crocodile.

Crap.

"I didn't want to be mad at him," Jeff said into the silence, and Martin reacted in confusion.

"What? Who?"

"Your brother." Jeff crossed his arms in front of him. It was childish and immature, but he didn't want to feel like a dissected frog, so he didn't give a shit. "It's the reason I told him we didn't need condoms anymore, after the first one broke. See...."

He started pacing—he always did his best thinking when he was moving. It's why he'd loved dancing and swimming so much. He'd felt liberated and empowered.

"I was virus-free, Martin—I mean, religiously paranoid about the whole thing. I was a med student, right? We got the whole grisly breakdown of what HIV can do to you. I never left home without a rubber, and, honestly, my last relationship before your brother was about six months before we met. I mean... I'd had my club days, right? But med school wasn't a joke, and I was...." God, he'd been so dedicated. He'd wanted to be a doctor, and... shit. He probably could be now, couldn't he? But five, nearly six years ago, things hadn't seemed so certain, and he'd needed the health insurance a lot more than he'd needed the ambition. "I was really sure I was going to be the next... I don't know. McSteamy, or McDreamy, or McGay-me or what the hell ever. So I got tested every three months, and I had the white cell count of a virgin on an all anti-oxidant diet who ate vitamin C for dessert, you know?"

Martin was just... just looking at him. He didn't answer, but he did blink very slowly and nod a little, and Jeff swallowed and looked away from him. Who wanted to hear your brother was a man-whore? But Kevin had been honest—completely and totally honest. Gloryholes, rent-boys, he'd done his share, and he hadn't always been careful. But he had been with Jeff.

"So when the condom broke, I... I knew if I got infected, even from that one thing, it would be Kevin. And I didn't want to be mad at him for it, so I talked him into that crappy decision just so it could be me and not him. I mean...."

Jeff hadn't thought he could cry anymore. Maybe it was that stupid thing your body did, where once you had a good cry, you just couldn't stop. He hated that thing. Nothing made him feel weaker, and for a moment he stood, pressing the heels of his hands to his eyes.

"Gaaawww!" It was the only word he had. Lame and useless, but there you go. He pulled his hands away and said, "Kid, you would not believe the day I had. It was probably the worst fucking judgment on my part to come here and spill my guts on you, but... well, let's just say I was in a 'the truth shall set you free' sort of mood and leave it at that."

"Are you?" Martin said into that total non sequitur.

"Am I what?" But Jeff knew.

"Are you mad at my brother?"

Heartbeat. Well, shit. He'd said the truth would set him free, right?

"I'm furious. But not for that." His shoulders slumped. Did he really have work tomorrow? His eyes wandered to the clock hanging over the door. It was hard to tell how late it was in November—it just got dark so early. Well shit—it was hardly seven o'clock.

"What are you mad about?" Martin asked into the quiet.

"Kid...." Jeff couldn't look at him. It sounded so pathetic. "Your brother promised me a happy-ever-after. He did. I mean, I knew where he was going, and I knew it was dangerous, but...." He shook his head, looking absently at the spiffy new linoleum. It was actually a saturated pastel-purple. Mikhail or Kimmy must have picked it out—Shane would have gone for green or brown. "It didn't seem to matter. I trusted him. My family had sort of ditched me, and I'd been... so alone, through college, you know? And he said he'd get back and we'd have a house and a picket fence and... and I believed him. So even before his fucking letter...." *Fuck.* "Even before that. I was pissed. I...." His voice was breaking.

"I mean, what sort of fucking world is this, kid? They don't let you see your mother, they don't let you go to your boyfriend's funeral... and it's all so faceless. It's 'they'. There doesn't seem to be a person involved, or someone you can talk to, right, to make this shit better, it's just your whole world is controlled by 'they', and... it's just 'you'. 'You' and your cats and your memories of when you hoped for something more." He was rambling. Wandering. But he didn't seem to be able to divorce Jeffy from the pain in his chest anymore. Maybe a day like this one did that to you.

His self-distraction ended abruptly when Martin took a few hesitant steps forward. Jeff looked up, and Martin was suddenly human-distance close.

"I'm sorry about the funeral," he said quietly. "I am. You're right—'they' wouldn't have let you come. But I wish you could have seen that, at least, you know?" Martin's voice got wobbly now, and Jeff wondered if there was any way to get a karmic cleansing of this particular room. Did rooms like this one, pleasant and soothing, did they ever get so saturated with tears that the tears just came? "They...." The kid caught himself, and his shoulders were shaking, and Jeff took two steps in to see if the kid was going to repel him. When he didn't, Jeff took two more steps and put his hands on Martin's arms, hesitantly.

The kid almost fell into him, with relief maybe, at not carrying this burden alone.

"They burnt his flag," he finished on a sob. "Before I left, I asked my dad what happened to Kevin's flag, and he said he'd burnt it."

Oh Jesus. Jeff wrapped his arms around Kevin's little brother and let the kid cry on him, like maybe he hadn't cried since he'd seen his brother's memory torched and flared in ashes.

It seemed to go on forever, but Jeff didn't mind. This was Kevin's little brother, a part of Kevin, and for this moment, the kid seemed to need him. God, it felt good to be needed.

Eventually the storm eased up, and Martin backed away, sniffling, wiping his face with the back of his hands and looking away. They stood there (awkwardly) for a minute, and then Jeff shuffled his feet.

"Look, kid, do you like it here?"

Martin shrugged. "Yeah, it's all right."

"Because I don't have anything for you to do in the day, so I'd have to drop you off here in the morning or something, but… if you want… I've got a spare bedroom. It's…." Jeff smiled and remembered Collin's words from that day at The Pulpit. "It's so gay it makes a gay pride parade look like a Baptist revival, but… but it's a home. I've got two cats, and a Wii, and Netflix, and every DVD known to man, and books—"

That got Martin's attention.

"Books?"

"Yeah. Books. Thrillers, mysteries, true crime…." Jeff resisted the urge to cackle. "I've sort of got this fetish for grisly murder-mysteries. Do you like to read?"

Martin's animation deflated politely. "I'm sort of into fantasy and science fiction—*The Wheel of Time, The Hunger Games*—"

"I've got the last one," Jeff offered. "It was really good."

Martin perked up again. "Yeah?" He looked around for a minute, like he was afraid someone would hear him. "I, uhm… I mean, I like this place. I want to come back. Did you know they take you next door to let you clean up after the horses? The guy there—"

"Deacon?"

"Yeah—you know him? He's awesome! He doesn't talk, right, so he's like all mysterious and shit, but you should *see* him on the horses. It's fuck... frickin' amazing. Anyway." Martin looked around again. "The people here are nice," he said quietly. "And I was lucky. And I never said thank you, because I guess you called your people in big time to take care of me. But...." His mouth worked, and he started to bounce the way that normally active teenagers did when they would rather be moving or talking. "I... I want to spend a day shooting hoops by myself, or reading a whole book, or... just being in my own head. But they don't let you do that here. I mean, I understand why." Martin looked around again and shuddered and dropped his voice.

"That boy, Alec, the one in the kitchen?"

Jeff nodded.

"He was doing *meth* on the streets. And he's totally committed to rehab and everything, but... but... if he doesn't have something to do, like, *every second of the day*, he's thinking about drugs. And he keeps sneaking outside to smoke, and I think Kimmy and Shane let him, because they know he's trying really hard, but Mikhail came and caught him, and he just went off on a rant about how bad that shit was for you, and then Alec was in tears and...."

Martin's look was miserable. "The people here are really nice, man, but there is *way* too much drama. You know, my folks, what they did to Kevin's memory wasn't right, and I don't think I can face them, not right now, but...."

"You don't belong here," Jeff said, saving him from the embarrassment of saying it. "You're a good kid. You get good grades— Kevin was so proud of you, even in, what? The fourth grade? You have a family." Jeff stopped his chin from quivering with ruthless determination. "Even if you never talk to your parents again, you have a family, you understand? You're Kevin's family, and I can't leave you here another night, not when you don't want to stay."

Martin nodded and wiped his eyes again, then frowned. "I... you don't have a boyfriend or anything? Because... I mean, I'm still not great with it, you know? And that shit would just creep me the fuck out."

Jeff thought of the way his lips still tingled from that kiss in the car, the way Collin had been a stand-up guy for a shit-kicker of a day, and he felt his heart shrivel a little, when he hadn't realized how full it had been. "I've got a candidate for the position," Jeff said, remembering how hot Collin's eyes had been. "And I haven't... not since Kevin. But don't worry. Don't worry. I'll... he'll understand."

Martin looked relieved, and Jeff closed his eyes and begged Collin's forgiveness. Or maybe, he begged for Collin to be true to his twenty-four-year-old heart and take off for the hills—it had been a long day. He wasn't really sure where his prayers were supposed to go.

FOUR days later, he still wasn't sure, but he had decided that having a roommate wasn't so bad.

Martin was neat and courteous, although Shane cautioned Jeff not to expect that to last. "A comfortable kid is a sloppy kid. Just like grown-ups."

Jeff figured he could deal with nasty sweat socks in his living room and unwashed dishes in the sink when he came home, but so far, it hadn't happened. It helped that of the four days, Martin had spent two at the shelter for runaways, helping the other kids with their chores and enjoying going next door to The Pulpit or playing with Shane's dogs or playing videos with friends. Jeff thought that maybe having an escape valve from all of the intense unhappiness that went in to making a runaway kid helped. Martin *had* been living a happy life. His world had shifted, in the blink of an eye, and just like Jeff had, he needed time to readjust, to shift his thinking, to decide if the world was really a happy place or not.

Jeff had been lucky—he'd had the dorms, he'd had school, and he'd had the club scene and the dancing and being around people just like him who were out, proud (and, let's face it, hellaciously horny), and, on the dance floor, free. Martin was fourteen. He didn't need to go clubbing; he wasn't ready to be living in a dorm room by himself. He needed a family, and Jeff was pleased that the boy had decided Jeff would pass, at least until he was ready to go home. They'd talked about that, or rather, *not* talked about it.

"I did call my folks," Martin had said, "and they won't let me come home if I'm going to talk about Kevin. I'm not ready to go home and pretend I never had a brother."

Kevin had been fourteen years older than Martin, with three kids in between them. Jeff remembered that, Kevin talking about his little brothers and their sister and how proud he'd been. How much he thought Martin was going to be the best of all of them, maybe because Kevin himself had done most of the raising. Apparently Martin hadn't forgotten help with homework, and Kevin picking him up from school or taking him to the park. Jeff found that that pain, that pain of Kevin being gone from the world, was a little less sharp, knowing that Jeff wasn't the only one who missed him, who'd known everything that he was.

They discussed it on the way to Sunday dinner—but not before Jeff had his own little discussion in his own pointy little head.

Oh God, is Collin really going to be there? Really? How would Jeff tell him? Would he understand? Maybe they will just… date. That would be good. They would date, but no sleepovers. There. That was a plan. Jeff would run with that.

Please, please, please, Collin….

Oh Jesus, Jeff, you moron, this is the perfect excuse to push him away!

But he kisses like a fucking god. I don't want to push him away!

Yes, yes you do because—

Shut up. I don't want to talk about that. I had five minutes of happiness, and we're going to pretend the big black bird in my chest is, like, a starling. And it's dead. And thinking about love doesn't hurt. Oh God. It does. It does, it does, it does.

So what are we going to do?

We're going to date!

We. Are. So. Fucking. Stupid.

About that point in his little conversation with himself, Martin reminded Jeff about Lucas, and Jeff suggested that maybe they should invite Lucas over, or maybe ask the guy if he wanted to take Martin to the movies.

"Should I ask him to bring Kimmy?" Martin asked slyly, and Jeff grinned, holding up a clenched fist for Martin to bump. Martin did, and they had another thing to bond over—their complete willingness to mess with Kimmy's love life. Because, as Martin said, "She's a really nice lady, and I think Lucas would treat her good."

And Jeff would get to dish with her about it, and that would be win/win too.

Jeff pulled into the driveway at The Pulpit with mixed feelings, and Martin obviously had them too.

"Wait a minute—I thought you said we were having dinner with Crick!"

"Yeah," Jeff muttered absently, seeing Collin's car.

"Then why are we at Deacon's?"

Jeff pulled up next to that big-dick car and did a double take at Martin, who looked obviously puzzled. He'd been to The Pulpit on several occasions—Shane took the kids over to help Deacon with the work, and the kids liked being with the horses, and Martin had this idea of Deacon as a mystery man and horse god, and Jeff had just assumed....

Well, he knew what they said about assumptions.

"Crick is Deacon's husband—you didn't know that?"

Martin's jaw literally fell open, and of all the emotions Jeff had expected to feel this night, this particular level of irony had not been among them.

"Well, Martin, honey, you do realize that not all gay men have my fabulous sense of style, right?"

Martin scowled at him before his face lit with some evil triumph. "*That's* a stereotype! We spent two hours yesterday talking about gay people and stereotypes, man, you can't *tell* me that you talking about how being gay gives you style isn't a stereotype!"

Jeff had to laugh. God, he liked this kid. "Martin, are you good at basketball?"

Ooooh... that was tough. He was—Jeff had seen him at the shared condo basketball hoop, and he'd been good. "Yeah."

"Is that because you're black, or because you're tall and like to practice?"

Martin grinned. "Because I'm tall and like to practice."

Jeff nodded, and Martin started nodding too. "Maybe, sweetcheeks, I have a good sense of style because I'm gay, and I like to practice. The 'gay' gives me permission, that's all."

Martin shook his head and got out of the car. And then, without being asked, he pushed the front seat forward and reached into the back and got out the extremely intricate casserole that he and Jeff had spent the morning assembling and cooking. Jeff usually brought bread or dessert, but Martin had been interested in cooking, and Jeff didn't get a lot of chances to cook for more than one.

"Hey," Martin said as they were walking up the porch, "Deacon and Andrew are out in the stables—do you think I can go visit?"

Jeff shrugged. "Why not? You're here as a guest tonight, not an employee. Can you deal with Deacon's new identity?" Oooh... crucial question. Martin had idolized Kevin too.

But it seemed to take Martin by surprise. "I guess," he said thoughtfully. "I mean... it's not like... it's not like he's going to be anything other than Deacon, right?"

Jeff raised his eyebrows meaningfully.

"Jesus, just shut up!" Martin shoved the casserole at him, and Jeff took it with an "Oof!" and a ginger effort not to touch the warm glass under the insulating towel.

He balanced the dish in one arm, turned the knob on the front door, and walked practically right into Collin's arms.

He had to do some quick dodging with his hips to not end up wearing that casserole—or dumping it all over Collin's lap, either. Good thing, too, because if he'd dumped it, they might have both ended up naked in the mudroom again, and wouldn't that be a shame?

"Whoa!" Collin laughed, wrapping one arm around Jeff's waist and reaching out with the other to steady the heavy dish. "Food is our friend!"

"And not on our clothes," Jeff said breathlessly. The world stopped spinning, and he got the casserole under control, but Collin's arm was still wrapped around his waist, and Jesus, was it solid! Jeff looked up almost shyly and saw that that angel's face, with the high cheekbones and narrow cheeks and pouty lips and gold-brown eyes, was smiling at him, asking him to share the joke, and he found that, oh my God, was he blushing? He was. He was staring at this boy, silly-stupid, and *blushing.*

He cleared his throat and backed up, and Collin let him with little more than a raised eyebrow. "Good to see you, Jeffy—did you think I wouldn't show?"

Jeff shook his head. The thought honestly hadn't occurred to him. "It's good to see you too. Uhm…." Oh shit—Martin! "You may have noticed that I did something stupid since the last time we saw each other."

Collin covered it quickly, but Jeff caught the hurt that flashed across his face and cursed. No. No, this man (man!) was not going to take the suggestion of just "dating" to satisfy Martin's carefully indoctrinated homophobia, oh no he wasn't.

"I'm sorry, Collin," Jeff said quietly. "It's not… ideal, not for you and me, anyway. I…." Oh, apologies did not sit well on him, not when he was doing as much right as he possibly could. "You know, you may want to ask a boy out on a real date before you get all pissy about his prior commitments, you think?" He thrust out his chin and cocked his hips, and Collin's lips curved up reluctantly in a warm, almost breathtaking smile.

"You are awfully damned high maintenance, you know that?"

Jeff bit his lip and the shyness returned, and he looked at Collin from the corner of his eyes. "Thank you, Collin. You're a good… God, you're such a good man."

Collin's eyes widened, almost in horror. "Oh shit! I'm the nice guy? You're going to give me the nice guy speech? Dammit—I just helped Crick with dinner, and you're going to give me the blow off—"

Jeff started to laugh—it wasn't bitter or condescending or ironic, it was just laughter. "Cool your jets, Sparky. Sometimes, being a good guy really is hot, you know? It was a compliment, one that had 'and you've got a great chest!' tagged at the end."

Collin's smile was blinding, and Jeff felt the casserole wobble in his arms. Or maybe it was his heart. "I do, don't I? My chest is pretty awesome, right?"

Jeff laughed some more. "You've got the pecs of a god, Sparky. Now get out of my way, I'm going to go wow Crick with my cooking abilities, okay?"

Something darkened on Collin's face, and Jeff couldn't have even guessed what. It didn't matter. Collin stepped back—Jeff missed the heat from his arm immediately—and gestured Jeff from the living room to the kitchen with a courtier's grace. Jeff couldn't stop the rather goofy grin that took over his face, although he tried valiantly before he got into the kitchen.

Crick wasn't fooled for a minute. The expression on his face as he took the casserole from Jeff bordered on... relief?

"Have a nice conversation, Jeffy?"

"Shut up," Jeff muttered, setting the casserole on the counter. "So, you're cooking—to what do we owe the honor?"

Crick was actually their best cook, next to his sister, but Benny wasn't there. Crick had been spending more and more time outside, helping Deacon, and the cooking had fallen to the less competent when there had been family there. Once—shudder—the cooking had even fallen to Shane. Jeff remembered that moment. He'd been the one to spring for pizza when the pile of blackened quesadillas had toppled over onto the kitchen table and Deacon had broken into a surprising fit of the giggles. Crick, Jeff, Mikhail, and Andrew had skipped the giggles and gone right into squalls of laughter, and they might have just stayed there, *literally* laughing their asses off, except Parry Angel had complained piteously about being hungry.

Speaking of which....

"Where is everybody?" Jeff asked curiously.

"They're all out in the barn. We got a new yearling to break, and she's something of a showstopper. Jon and Amy took the girls out to see her, and Kimmy and Lucas went with them. Shane and Mickey aren't here yet... wait...." Crick looked up and Jeff with him, and watched Shane's monster GTO (also a big-dick car, if Jeff thought about it, but since all the engine parts were on the inside and it was painted black instead of candy-apple-red with white pinstripes, it had never occurred to him) came rumbling up the drive.

Jeff leaned forward and peered out the window. "How much do you want to bet that little bitch got laid while we were waiting for him?"

Crick chuckled. "They could have been tending the animals," he said mildly. "I won't know until I see them come in together."

Jeff looked at him sideways. "You can tell when they walk in?"

"Mikhail's all soft and dreamy after he's gotten some," Crick said, grinning. "He's like a talking star thistle, most of the time, but after he and Shane have been together, he's practically Miss Congeniality."

Jeff laughed, loving Crick very much in that moment. "Well, we can't have that," he preened. "We all know I'm the prettiest one."

Crick rolled his eyes and shook his head negative. "*Deacon's* the prettiest one—he just won't get on stage." And then Crick's face took on a shuttered look, and Jeff actually connected a couple of dots that were *not* connected to himself.

"Wait a minute. What's going on? Collin looked like he'd swallowed a bug and didn't want to share too!"

Crick's face was narrow and pretty, with big, expressive brown eyes that were *not* meant for keeping secrets. How he'd managed two years in the army had always amazed Jeff—it had been a major miracle, sort of like Crick surviving his injuries at the end of the tour. Whatever was contorting his mouth right now was painful and frightening and, most terrifying of all, *hidden*. Crick was keeping something *hidden* from him. *Crick*, who had spilled pretty much every secret he'd ever had, including how he'd lost his virginity, in half an hour of physical therapy when they'd first met, was keeping a *secret* from his best friend.

Jeff's first thought was hurt. And then he remembered—and God knew, it was tough for a guy who'd been living alone with his cats for five years—that maybe the world didn't always revolve around the problems belonging to Jeff.

"Crick, what's wrong?"

Crick swallowed. "Look, we're going to tell everyone after dinner, okay? And if I tell you first, the whole world's going to get their panties in a wad, and…." Crick shook his head. "Look, just remember, when we tell the family, that I've had this on my chest for a month, okay? And Deacon made me promise not to talk about it until we knew details, and it's been hard, and maybe you'll be pissed, but I'm going to need a friend who's not my irritating, know-it-all little sister, okay?"

Jeff nodded. He wanted to kick something. Dammit, he'd been so close to equilibrium, so close to feeling like the world might someday be safe again.

"Crick?"

Crick waved his hands and looked away, and Jeff… well, Jeff was the last person to hammer through a friend's bubble of safe emotions, wasn't he?

At that moment, Shane and Mikhail came walking in, and Crick looked up at them, almost in desperation. Shane was taking off Mikhail's coat to throw on the coat rack by the door, and Mikhail, several inches shorter than his "big stupid cop," looked sideways up at Shane, his expression unguarded and absolutely adoring.

Crick gave a little sniff, trying to get himself together, and said, "I'm not taking that bet—they've probably been fucking like monkeys for the last three hours."

Jeff laughed and bumped shoulders with his very best friend. "Hell, Kimmy was at Promise House since early this morning—I'm betting it was all day."

Crick nodded in absolute agreement and then called out, stopping Shane from taking his own jacket off. "Shane, could you go out and tell everyone to wash up? We're about good to go here!"

Mikhail walked toward them carrying two pies, one chocolate and one banana cream, that he'd reclaimed after Shane had taken his coat.

"So," Jeff said sweetly, "we're taking bets. How long were you two in bed? Three hours, or all day?"

"Fuck you, and wouldn't you like to know," Mikhail retorted without slowing down as he blew past them both to put the pies on the counter.

"Three hours," Crick said matter-of-factly. "They had to take time out for Mikhail to cook."

"All day," Mikhail snapped back. His pretty little face was insufferably smug. "I made the pies last night. So, what have you cooked in order to make my dessert look good?"

They were having broiled chicken breast with some sort of low-fat sauce, a broccoli vegetable dish that Jon and Amy had brought over, Kimmy's winter-fruit salad, French bread (brought by Collin), and, of course, Jeff's chicken casserole to fill in the blank spots. Jeff wasn't sure how it worked out—whether people just stopped by for dinner, or if it was family Sunday—but somehow, they always had a good spread. It was just The Pulpit, maybe—everyone wanted to make it good, and so it was.

Collin sat on Jeff's left at the big, battered, wooden kitchen table, and Martin sat on his right. Collin had talked engines with Shane, cats with Mikhail, smartass with Crick and Jon, and babies with Amy. He seemed to regard Deacon attentively, and generally, he fit right in.

Jeff kept trying to remind himself that he was now guardian to a kid who didn't like gay people and he had to watch himself, but he watched Martin, still regarding Deacon with some sort of awe, and hope kept growing in his belly like the proverbial watermelon plant. Oh Jesus... he had to rip that thing out by the roots, or it would leave a hole somewhere in his body where the bad things could get in!

"Jeff"—Crick leaned over his shoulder on the way to fetch more milk from the fridge—"why's Martin looking at Deacon like that?"

Jeff took a better look at Martin—he'd been listening to Collin talk about putting an engine together. Jeff had no idea what the boy was saying, but he kept using his big, battered hands to talk, and it was doing all sorts of fun shit to Jeff's libido—and tried not to laugh. Martin wasn't just looking at Deacon in awe; he was looking at the guy like he was a particularly strangely shaped puzzle piece, and Martin needed to know where to put him.

"Don't worry about him, sweetie. He's just trying to make the gay fit, that's all."

Crick snorted. "Good luck!" he muttered, before going off to get that milk, and Jeff leaned over to talk to the confused adolescent next to him.

"He's the same guy, you know."

Martin looked at him and rolled his eyes, but the gesture was lacking the usual sarcasm. It was more like a superior look of affection. "Yeah, yeah, I'm figuring that out. Give me some space, fairy-Jeff-father, I'm doing my best."

Jeff grinned. "Did you just call me...?"

"Yeah, yeah... tomorrow I'll call you something shitty and mean. There's women present today." And then he smiled at Lila Lisa, the little fair-haired angel sitting in the tot seat next to him, and batted his eyelashes. "Aren't you a little lady, oh yes you are!"

The little girl squealed happily and reached out goopy hands, and Andrew warned across the table, "Watch out, Martin, she's going right for the—"

"Ewwwww! Ick!"

"Yeah, the nappy hair. Sorry about that, my man."

Martin laughed and stood up, obviously on his way to go wash baby-goo out of his neatly buzzed and crimped 'do. (Jeff had taken him to get new designs carved into his tight black curls, and God forbid that expenditure in cash should be obscured by chicken casserole!) That was when Deacon cleared his throat meaningfully, and Jeff was programmed enough to the family dinner table to wrench his attention from his own thoughts to family patriarch.

And then Crick looked at Collin, and Collin squeezed Jeff's shoulder. "You'll have to tell me why I'm getting sent to the kiddie table," he murmured. It was the most intimate thing they'd shared since dinner started, and it pretty much soured the dinner in Jeff's stomach.

Sure enough, Collin stood up and said, "Martin, you want to get that one, and I'll get the troublemaker over there by Deacon?" He made eyes at Parry Angel, who squealed "Colly!" and waved back. "Let's go get them washed up and we can eat dessert in the front room, okay?"

Martin nodded and asked Amy permission and picked up the little girl like he had long ease picking up younger cousins and such, and Jeff's throat ached. God. God. How had he lived without this for all those years? How could Martin's family ask him to live without it now?

And then the children were gone, and Collin was herding them into the living room with the promise of banana cream pie, and the rest of the family was left, looking at Deacon.

Jon, Deacon's best friend since grade school, was sitting on Deacon's left. He was a beautiful man, golden hair, tanned skin, the face of an angel, if angels modeled underwear for Calvin Klein. He was also terribly in love with his Amy, who took Martin's seat to be closer to Jeff now that they had lost three people on their side of the table.

"What's up, Deacon? Does this have anything to do with the running?"

"What about the running?" Crick asked, his voice sharp.

"He's been going easy on us," Shane said with a shrug. "Five miles maximum, five days a week instead of seven—it's like a trip to the Bahamas, as far as Deacon's concerned!"

Crick relaxed, but it was Deacon who answered.

"Yeah. Yeah. Guys, look—I told Crick I'd say this, because I made him keep it to himself for the past month or so, and we all know how good he is at keeping a secret, right?" Crick usually sat at the other end of the table from Deacon when there was family dinner, and now, he stood up and moved to Deacon's end, pulling Parry Angel's high chair out of the way and stealing Amy's vacant seat.

He sat down heavily, not like a man who was not quite twenty-six, and took Deacon's hand with an uncharacteristic quiet. "I'll help," he said softly, and Deacon's hand tightened obviously over Crick's scarred one, and the table fell so very silent, they could hear the little girls playing in the next room.

"About six weeks ago, I fell off my horse," Deacon said into the silence. His cheeks were red, and it wasn't a... healthy color. His cheeks were red and his lips were pale, and Jeff's watermelon plant died a sickly, acid-eaten death in an instant.

"You fell off your horse?" Jon said neutrally, and Jeff could almost sense the coiling spring in Deacon's best friend.

"I did." Deacon smiled faintly. "And it was so uncharacteristic of me that Crick made me go to the doctor. And the doctor said my heart wasn't working right, and we did some tests, and then we did some more tests, and then it got harder and harder to walk across the yard, and then they told me I had to cut back on the running but that I needed to keep doing it, and then...."

He stopped and shrugged, and Crick said, "Then they stopped giving him tests and got to the point."

"Thank God for that!" Deacon joked weakly. He was left with a hurt and angry silence.

"So what is the point, Deacon?" Jon asked, and Deacon did an unexpected thing and reached out and clasped his hand too. Underneath the table, Jeff felt Amy's hand digging into his thigh, and he wrapped his arm around her shoulder tightly, because, God! This was not what he had expected.

"The point is, I've got some sort of thing... my heart is scarred. Apparently I've been having mini-attacks for quite some time, and my heart—"

"Being as stubborn as the rest of him," Crick muttered.

"Well, yeah, anyway, it started re-forging new paths over the scar tissue that has built up because the original problem wasn't fixed, and

now there needs to be surgery. They need to run a wire up inside my…
that artery in my thigh… what is that again, Jeff?"

"The femoral artery," Jeff said blankly.

"Yeah, that. They need to run it up inside my thigh and to my heart,
and then doodle about for a while, carve off the scar tissue, re-forge
some new pathways, and then put in a pacemaker for good measure. The
surgery will take a few hours, but it's not too invasive, so the recovery is
going to be about ten days to two weeks. We were going to do it right
after Benny's finals, so she can make sure our favorite angel has a good
Christmas, and that way, none of the clients will be too put out because I
won't be there for riding lessons or to break or anything like that. It's
not—"

"If you say 'not a big deal', I'm going to fucking kill you, asshole!"
Jon said tightly from Deacon's side, and Jeff looked at their clasped
hands and realized that Jon was practically breaking Deacon's fingers in
his own. "How could you not tell us!"

Crick wrapped his arm around Deacon's waist and rested his sharp
chin on Deacon's shoulder, and Deacon smiled gently at his oldest and
dearest friend, and then, one at a time, at everyone around the table. "I
wanted a name for it," he said at last. "I wanted a diagnosis. I couldn't
just come to you all and say, 'Something's wrong—let you know later!'
I… you all know how my dad went out."

Jeff swallowed. Massive fatal coronary—he was dead before he hit
the ground. Deacon had been what? Twenty-two? Twenty-three? Crick
had just turned eighteen. Either way, they had been young and orphaned,
a lot like Jeff had felt at that age, and that same monster was out to get
them now. Jeff swallowed again and nodded. Yeah. Yeah, of course.
They all knew how Parrish had gone out.

"Yeah, Deacon," Jon said. He seemed to have assumed the role of
speaker for the family, and Jeff? Jeff was so stunned, his breath so
stopped in his chest, he didn't have any way of claiming that control.

"I didn't want to do that to you, I didn't. I've been taking nitro and
pretty much being the doctor's bitch, you know? But until we got a
surgery date and a plan, I didn't want to worry you all, either."

"God, Deacon," Jon breathed, and Deacon grabbed his best friend
by the back of the head and hauled him to his chest.

"I'm going to be okay, you know that, right?" he asked, and then he looked up to where Amy sat, and Crick released his hand and stood with actual grace, kissing Deacon on the temple and getting out of the way. "I swear, Amy, I'm asking for help this time. I'm telling you—isn't that good enough?"

"You asshole," she muttered, and then she knocked over her chair in an effort to launch herself at him and he held both of them, no tears, no yelling, just quiet, in a bond that Crick seemed to understand, and that was good enough for Jeff.

He looked up as Crick plopped in the seat Collin had left, and Shane scooted over one and Mikhail sat on his lap and Andrew took *his* seat, and since Deacon was otherwise involved, they turned to Crick for answers.

"A month and a half?" was the first thing out of Jeff's mouth, followed by, "How could you not tell me in a month and a half?"

"It was subtle, at first," Andrew said softly from across the table, and Kimmy leaned in to hear him, Lucas at her side. "He'd just... fade out and then come back, gasping for breath. Or his shoulder would ache, and he couldn't figure out what he'd done to it. The falling off the horse was our first big sign—he just passed out and fell over."

Jeff's mind went back to that day two weeks ago, that horrible day when he'd gotten the call from Lucas, and he remembered wanting Andrew's help. Of course Andrew couldn't leave Deacon—not when Deacon might keel over at any given time.

"Benny knows?" he found himself asking numbly, and Andrew answered him too. Under the table he felt Crick's hand, fumbling for comfort, and that was one thing Jeff knew how to do.

"Once we got the prognosis, we called her. She was hating being away from the baby anyway—she jumped on the chance to come home and start school from here. But yeah, she knows. She's trying hard not to freak out, you know?"

Jeff squeezed his GBFF's hand. "How could you not tell me, you stupid asshole?" Well, that was comforting, right?

Crick smiled at him weakly. "Well, you've had your own plate— that made it easier, you know? But it wasn't easy." Crick looked up at the table filled with friends he and Deacon had turned into family and said, "It wasn't easy keeping it from any of you. But Deacon was right.

We had to have an answer and a plan, or it would have just been a lot of worry and speculation, and… you know. It sucks."

"Christ, does it!" Andrew swore fervently, and that seemed to break the tension a little.

"Deacon," Crick said loudly, "you about done with your little threesome over there? It's time to put the girls in the bathtub, and I want some goddamned pie, you hear?"

The family gathered. They talked softly; they tried to tell jokes to break up the tension. Eventually, Amy went to give the girls a bath and Collin and Martin came back into the kitchen, picking up on the changed vibe curiously.

"Why's everyone so quiet?" Martin asked, and Jeff looked at him, trying to find his footing.

"Deacon's going to have surgery before Christmas—we're a little worried, that's all," he said, and because Martin was fourteen, that was enough.

"He'll be fine," he said confidently. "I mean—look at him, he's healthy as a horse!" And before Jeff could contradict him or tell him that sometimes looks could be deceiving or burst his bubble any more, Collin grabbed his arm and hauled him out to the mudroom.

There was a ten-degree temperature drop from the house proper to the laundry room/mud room, and Jeff found he was shivering uncontrollably.

"You look like shit, Jeff—what happened?"

For a moment—just a moment—Jeff wanted to put his head on that broad chest and unload the way he had the week before and simply trust in Collin and what he seemed to be feeling, and to cede control of the world to the gods. And then he remembered that sometimes the gods hated you, and you never knew when that whole "ceding control" thing was going to work or going to rip your heart out and gnaw, and that was when he wrapped his arms around himself and backed away from Collin like he was a psycho axe-murderer in a horror movie.

"Sparky, I… I can't do this. I can't do this. I… I just can't."

Deacon was sick, and Jeff's family was at risk, and his heart was at risk, and his mind was black vortex and chaos, and he couldn't seem to find the light… couldn't seem to find the balance… and all he knew, all he could really fathom, was that if Collin touched him, he would fall apart.

And with that, Jeff left the cold mudroom for the freezing outside, walking blindly in the darkness for the barn, because at least there would be an animal warmth in the barn, and right now, it was the only comfort he could think of.

But he couldn't even think of that as he walked. About all he could do was stumble into the place with the big animals and the hay and picture the hurt and frustration on Collin's face as he'd pushed out, one more time, and run away.

Chapter *11*

Crick: Growing Up

"THAT went well."

Crick wrestled one-handedly with the laces on his boots. He knew he was supposed to use the injured hand, but it ached fiercely, and dammit, he was tired of shit that ached, so he just let it sit, awkward and twisted, at his side, while he tried to get undressed.

Deacon came out of the shower wearing only his boxers and still toweling his hair. He moved with unconscious grace, and Crick's heart just leapt up in his throat at such a simple thing. Deacon, getting ready for bed.

"How're Jon and Amy?" Crick asked. Of everyone there that night, Deacon's best friends through school had been the most devastated. Maybe it was because they'd known Deacon's father and remembered that pain, or because they'd nursed Deacon through detox when Crick hadn't been there, or maybe just because they'd all known each other since they were in Kindergarten together, but Jon, especially, had looked like he needed to go home and get drunk and sing old songs until his wife told him to get the fuck over it because she needed him.

"They feel like shit," Deacon said with a sigh. "I told them that this time I was telling them—you know, asking for help before I was half-dead. They said that was real fucking gentlemanly of me, but it didn't stop them from being pissed anyway." Deacon sighed. "Jon... Jon took it personally. Not the secret, right, but the sick. He just... he doesn't even want to think about it, you know?"

Crick grunted. Yeah, he knew. But think about it was about all he had been doing for the last two months. He couldn't even watch medical dramas or crime shows on television. It didn't matter if it was a serial killer or a saint being shown in full makeup on the gurney, Crick saw Deacon, and his heart stopped beating. They'd been watching a lot of sitcoms, and Deacon hated them, but he'd read sports autobiographies or something while Crick lay on him and watched, and took a little bit of comfort from escapism and the fact that Deacon couldn't possibly love him any more.

"How's your friend?" Deacon knelt down on one knee, right there in his white cotton boxers and bare chest, and started working the laces himself. Everybody was gone, Parry Angel was down for the night, and Andrew was asleep in the living room on the couch, as he had been since Benny left. He could, theoretically, move back to his little stall apartment in the barn, since the "muckrakers" that Deacon used to hire now came from Promise House, where they had a proper home and supervision, but he was family, and especially since Deacon had fallen off his horse in October, it made everybody feel better to know there was one more person in the house to keep his head and take care of Parry Angel if something went heinously wrong.

"Jeff?" Crick answered. Like there was someone else who had run away into the barn, leaving a frustrated suitor and a puzzled teenager in the house, in the middle of the chaos left by Deacon's announcement.

Deacon grunted, working at the boot. His hair was falling forward across his forehead, and Crick thought about brushing it aside. He didn't, though—that would have distracted Deacon, and sometimes, it was just nice to look at him and know that for the moment, he was whole and well and where he was supposed to be. With Crick. "Yeah, Jeff. How is he?"

"Not good."

"What'd he say?"

Crick grimaced. Jeff had never struck him as the closed-off type—not like Deacon. Deacon had really not had a problem, this last month. He'd learned to carry his nitro around, dealt calmly with the doctors, and reassured Crick on a minute-to-minute basis that he felt fine. Of course, with Deacon, unless he'd amputated a limb and was pumping blood, he'd say he felt fine, which was why this whole thing had Crick going not-so-quietly bananas around him.

But Jeff had surprised him. Jeff's whole week had come tumbling out, and it had been pretty fucking traumatic—a whole shitload of pain that Jeff hadn't shared and Crick hadn't known about, and Crick had felt almost exactly like he'd felt for the entire last month.

Pretty fucking useless.

"He's got some serious shit going on, Deacon. His mom and going home and Kevin and Collin and...." Crick shuddered, that conversation in the barn replaying in his head.

"Hey, Jeffy, how're they hanging?"

Jeff hated the barn—everyone knew it. It was dirty and dusty, and his spiffy black shoes and impeccable clothes would get fucked up in the hay and the horseshit. But he'd taken off, and Collin had come in from the mudroom looking angry and miserable, and Deacon was fielding questions. Crick was the most likely candidate to go out and find out what was up.

"They're shriveled and hiding," Jeff said, his voice sounding small. Crick hit the light switch, and the series of fluorescent circles in the ceiling lit up in sequence. Jeff was sitting on a hay bale backed up against Lucy Star's stall, his knees up at his chest. "Wanna feel?"

Crick grimaced. "No, thanks. Deacon's got enough strain on his heart as it is."

"I'm sorry," Jeff said, his eyes focused on the stall in front of him. Bruiser, a horse Deacon was breaking for one of the Renaissance Faire riders, was in there. He was a monster-sized black gelding, but he had the disposition of a panda bear and was currently asleep on his feet.

"For cracking a bad joke? That's where we live, Jeff, don't tell me we can't go there now!" Crick was tired—he was limping. It felt good to just collapse in long-limbed laxness on the bale next to Jeff.

"For Deacon. For what's going on. You must be so scared."

Crick closed his eyes. Deacon said it every night when they climbed into bed. "Don't be scared, baby. It'll be okay." Fucking useless promise. Meant nothing. But Crick let Deacon soothe him because they didn't have any other choice. Crick needed to function, and Deacon needed Crick sane. End of story. So Crick let that angel's voice wash over him in the dark and reminded himself that it was enough that Deacon wanted it to be okay. He wanted to be there for Crick and Parry and Benny and the whole family. Deacon—who put his own welfare dead last—had, for once, made his health a priority, to do everything he possibly could to keep that promise.

"Yeah. I'm scared. I'm not brave like you, Jeff. I don't think I could survive what you did. It would break me."

Jeff's laughter in the quiet barn had been brittle and demented. "Is that what you think? That I'm strong? That I'm not broken? God, you're stupid."

Crick looked at him in surprise. "I know I'm stupid, Jeffy, but you're so strong. Man, you just hold people together, prop 'em up when they're down. You're one of the strongest people I know."

Jeff had abruptly wiped his cheeks on his sleeve and snorted. He was congested from sudden tears, and it wasn't a pretty sound. What followed then was incoherent, and Crick had needed to wrap his arm around his friend's shoulder and just sit and listen for a little bit, and by the time Jeff was done, even Crick was a little bit speechless.

"Wow. Jeff... Jesus, I'm sorry."

"Why? You're not the one who disowned me!"

"Never will," Crick said. He'd always known why it was so damned important to the guy to be invited to Sunday dinner—and welcome all the days in between—but for the first time, he was really able to look beyond Crick, and even beyond Deacon, into someone else's misery. It was a revelation.

"Thank you," Jeff sniffled. "What am I going to do with him?"

"With Collin? Keep him. He's a stand-up guy!"

The silence next was not encouraging.

"I can't do it, Crick," Jeff said after a flat silence. "You... looking at your face today... I remembered why I can't do this. Why I never even tried. I... I can't do that to this kid, you know? He... God. He still believes in ever after. I just want to be able to laugh a little before my meter runs out."

"Shut up," Crick snapped. "You're fine. Your white count is good—you told me yourself, because I actually bought a fucking calendar so I could keep track of when you go in and make you tell me."

Jeff patted his knee languidly. "Lookit you, Carrick. Quite the little nursemaid, aren't you?"

"I take Deacon's blood pressure four times a day," Crick said tightly. He did too. And he made Deacon nap when it was too high, and

they no longer drank anything with caffeine in it, and he timed Deacon's runs to make sure he didn't stay out too long, and.... Crick shuddered. It was all about control. That was something he'd learned from the military and then from Deacon himself—you controlled the things you could, and then the chaos of the world outside didn't feel quite so overwhelming.

Jeff nodded against his chest. "See. Here you are, taking care of everyone—you know what you could lose. You're afraid of losing it. So am I. But... you're in deep already. I don't have to be."

"God, you're full of it," Crick snapped. Caring about Jeff was easier than worrying about Deacon, but not by much. "Just stop pretending, okay? You can lie to me, and I think you've lied enough to Collin already, but you're going to have to tell yourself the truth eventually."

"Yeah, what's that? You've got all this newfound maturity and wisdom, go ahead, enlighten me!"

God. Like Jeff didn't already know. "You already care about him. Look at you—you can't hardly say his name, you're so afraid he'll hear you and show up, and you'll have to lean on him to make it better."

There was that emotionally flat silence again, and when Jeff spoke, Crick had to resist the urge to smack his head against the wall. "Well, Crick, the best lies are the ones you want to believe."

"Christ. It's like Mikhail all over again, you know that, don't you? Remember last year? You wouldn't shut up about how brain-damaged that 'little Rusky diva-bitch' was and how he needed to just 'get over his sorry self and give our poor cop a blow job and live happily ever after'— you remember that?"

"I can't believe you carried that, verbatim, around in your pointy little head."

"I can't believe after all that bullshit about Mikhail being dumber than a box of diapers, you're going to use Deacon as an excuse to make us do this with you all over again."

Jeff pulled away from him and stood up stiffly, stretching a little and shivering with the absence of Crick's body heat. He scrubbed his face with his hands and wiped his eyes again, making himself as presentable as he could in a barn, and then leaned over and kissed Crick's forehead.

"We all know that's not going to happen, Crick, because, unfortunately, this family has something better to do with its time right

now, doesn't it? Call me if there's any change with Deacon. Martin and I will be wandering by for dinner on Tuesday—I'll bring it, so don't bother cooking."

"Jeff, don't do this."

"Could you do me a favor and go tell Martin to meet me out by the car? It will be easier for everyone, right?"

"Jesus, Jeff! Don't make me do this!"

And Jeff's newly composed face wrestled with itself for a moment. "Please, Crick. Man, I know you're my friend and you want what's best for me. Right now, could you just stick with what I want instead of what you think I need?"

"Because tonight sucked so bad? Yeah. Tonight I'll let you off the hook. But because I'm your best friend, I'm on Collin's side on this, okay? He's a really good guy. You think you could give it a chance?"

"'Night, Crick. Give Martin a good half hour of family before you send him out to the car, okay?"

"Jeff...."

But he was already outside, moving with a long-legged, purposeful stride that didn't look like it belonged on his angular, expressive body.

Only Crick knew that he was going to his car to have himself a good cry and pull his shit together to face what amounted to instant parenthood. And Crick wasn't the guy who got to go make it all better.

"Fuck," Deacon said quietly. He'd taken off Crick's shoes and picked up Crick's fucking useless left hand and kissed it softly as the conversation had been related.

"Yeah." Crick's sigh was so loud it echoed, and Crick felt Deacon's body shake a little. "Don't laugh at me."

"I know, I know. It's just that when you were growing up, you used to sigh like that, like you had the world on your shoulders. Now that you really do, you'd think that sound would have changed."

Crick was forced to laugh a little too. And then all those fears that he'd kept so carefully masked at dinner, and during his conversation with Jeff, and over the last month as Deacon had been so hell-bent on pretending it was all okay, and there wasn't any real danger, and his father *hadn't* dropped dead out of the blue before he was fifty—all those fears possessed him at once, and he had to hold down hard on himself not to completely lose it. He moved his hand from Deacon's grasp and wrapped both arms around his shoulders and pulled his lover, his partner, his *everything* into his chest and tried to shelter that skinny body with his own wide-shouldered mass.

"You can't leave me," he whispered. "It's just that simple. No Deacon, no Crick. I'm not strong like Jeff. I can't just keep going for years and make everybody laugh and not take anything good for myself. I need you."

Deacon pulled back, and for the first time in a while, he looked angry. "This family needs you," he said sternly. "No bullshit, Carrick—it's not just us anymore. It hasn't been for a while. Start with Parry Angel and work your way out, and you'll find a shitload of people who need *you*, *here* at The Pulpit, to carry on if bad shit happens."

"Deacon, I'm not you—"

"No. You're better than I am. You *are* stronger. You *will* keep going. And you'll do a damned fine job of it. I just...." And for the first time since that fall off the horse, Deacon actually looked a little afraid. "I just hope you don't have to, that's all." His mouth—pouty lips, firm chin and all—started to quiver, and Crick held him tighter until he'd mastered himself.

"I was really looking forward to a long life with you, Carrick. I just was. I... I'd really like to see that through."

They were both shaking. Both of them. And Crick needed... he just needed.

He wasn't sure which one of them initiated the kiss, but it started soft and then went sweet and then went tender and then went tinder, and *then* went to out-of-control blaze.

And Crick wanted to be in control. Deacon, the oldest, the one everyone had come to depend on, the leader, the quiet center of their world—*he* usually led, but not tonight. Tonight Crick needed to be in charge, to control something about his lover, something about his *world*, even if it was only which tab went into which slot and the expression on Deacon's face as Crick oiled, stretched, penetrated him.

Deacon's head was tilted back, his back bowed to make it easier for Crick to enter, and his eyes were closed, his full lips slightly parted, and his hands were at his sides, digging into the comforter. Crick watched every moment as he slid inside that tight body until they were flush, and then waited until Deacon's breath came shorter and his hands started to pound at his sides on the bed.

"Shh... don't worry. I'll take care of you." Crick reached out to Deacon's hand and placed it on his cock. Together they wrapped fingers around it, tight and large, and started stroking, even as Deacon squirmed, impaled on Crick's flesh, and started to make little begging sounds for everything Crick had to offer.

"Carrick...." It was as close to whining as Deacon got.

"What?"

"You said you'd... you know?" Deacon's hand was shaking on his own cock, and Crick took a bead of pre-come from the tip with his thumb and raised it to his lips.

"What?"

"Take care of me?"

Crick pulled his hips back and slammed them forward. "Always."

"Auuughhhh...."

"Always!" Crick snarled, thrusting again. "Say it, Deacon!"

"Always!"

"Always!" Crick would *always* be there, he would *always* love Deacon, he would *always* take care of him.

They lost words then, and Crick slammed forward again and again and again, truly at home in Deacon's body for the first time, truly surrounded by this man who had promised to love him even further than death.

Crick's orgasm began to tighten his body, a purely physical thing. His balls grew heavy and tight, his spine began to tingle, his nipples, his cock, everything was bursting with the beautiful agony of climax, and he had to close his eyes, had to trust that Deacon was still stroking that magnificent body, trust that when he pulled back and slammed home— *Gaaaaawwwwddd*—that final time, that Deacon would be there, hot, tight, ready to receive him as he spilled everything, not just his come, into Deacon's receptive haven.

He collapsed, sweating, hot, shaking, on top of Deacon, forgetting for a moment that Deacon was sick and simply taking his open arms at face value. Deacon's stomach was slick with his own come, and Crick didn't care. Their skin would stick together, and it would be messy and probably pull the hair on his lower abdomen like mad, but he didn't care, because he was in Deacon's arms and he could always shower, but this moment, this moment here, when his lover was making shushing noises in his ear, that wasn't always guaranteed, now was it?

"Carrick James," Deacon murmured, and Crick took a deep breath, shuddering unstoppably, and tried to find his center.

"What?" Crick's voice was clogged. How did that happen?

Deacon took his face in both hands and pulled back against the pillow so they could look at each other. A hot droplet shuddered from Crick's chin to Deacon's cheek, and Crick closed his eyes. Oh shit. Oh shit, when had that happened? When had he gone from forceful lover to weeping willow? It was a good thing Deacon loved him, because he'd read the literature—this was supposed to be some sort of death sentence for a lover, wasn't it? Crying in bed made you a limp-dicked disaster. It was gospels of truth.

"Even if I leave you, I won't leave you, okay? Even if you carry the casket and have to say goodbye and find someone else to love, I'll still be with you, okay? I meant it. Always. You hear?"

Crick nodded. His cock softened, slid out of Deacon's body, and he missed the feeling of flesh merged with flesh. But the feeling of Deacon's muscle and bone underneath him, at the hips, at the chest—that remained. Deacon's green eyes were sober and wide, the dark fringe of lash around them casting a faint shadow against Deacon's cheek.

"Always," Crick echoed. "Always."

It was the one truth he knew.

Chapter *12*

Collin: Going Out

COLLIN knew he was hot. In high school, he'd been hit on constantly and he'd played it up. He wore his hair parted in the middle and hanging down the sides of his face because he knew it made the most of his bone structure, even when he pulled it back in a queue. He knew that some guys really liked the long hair thing, and he kept his healthy and shiny. He knew his eyes were unusually light—he wore lots of gold-brown and dark green, lots of navy blue, which made them look lighter. He had free weights at home and worked out when he wasn't playing rec-league and indoor soccer, and he took his soccer with brutal seriousness, so *that* kept him pretty fit too. He knew his frame was more rangy than big, although his shoulders were wide because of his height and the amount of time he used his arms and upper body in the shop.

Tonight, he did more than just *know* he was pretty. He blow-dried his hair back so that it was shiny and full away from his face. He used the slightest bit of eyeliner to make that fringe around his eyes dark and mysterious. And arrogant—mustn't forget arrogance. That was a turn-on. Hell, he even put a little bit of Vaseline on his lips to make them shiny.

His factory-faded black jeans were low on his hips and so tight someone looking hard could see that he was circumcised. His white belt was studded with silver, his black loafers (no socks, and fuck the fact that it was November and fucking cold outside) were spiffy shiny, his tan T-shirt spanned snugly across his chest, and his fashion-friendly, double-breasted cropped jacket was right out of GQ. Who gave a damn if it was the spring issue? Nobody in Sacramento really followed that crap, did they?

He looked fantastic.

He was the only one who had to know he felt like total and complete shit.

His loft room was pretty big—living above your mom's garage didn't have to be masturbating over Nintendo in a small, sweaty room. He'd done it up right with hardwood flooring, a nice area rug—sort of a cool one, done in olive, navy, tan, and brown, looking like shards of a mirror scattered over an earthen surface. He had furniture—a real couch/loveseat corner sectional, in olive and burgundy, and a little wooden dinette unit by his refrigerator and stove. His queen-sized bed was in the corner, made up, because when his sisters or their kids visited, it became furniture and/or a playground. It was a nice place and not, as his mother had openly worried, a den of sex and iniquity. Collin had brought a few men up there in the past three years, but none on the first date, or even the third or fourth.

He had, in fact, been living respectable, and he'd liked it.

But that didn't mean he didn't want to go out and fuck the shit out of something until it couldn't stand up anymore.

That's what he told himself, and every time he did, he hoped it would wash the disappointment of Sunday's family dinner away.

He'd been close—he'd felt it. He'd sat next to Jeff and saw those sly, almost *shy* looks that Jeff had given him from those sweetheart eyes. He'd bumped Jeff's knee under the table a couple of times just to watch the blood wash under that deceptively fair skin. He'd heard the apology in Jeff's voice when he'd tried to hint about Martin, and he'd seen that Martin had actually been happy when Jeff had run into Collin on the way into the door. Everything was going so well.

It was just Collin's luck that his second dinner at The Pulpit would be the night Crick and Deacon dropped an anvil on everyone's head.

Andrew had told him later about Deacon's poor health, about his surgery, about pulling the rug out from under everyone's feet when they'd learned to depend upon that man to center their world around him and Crick and the way they took care of the people around them. Collin hadn't known that when he'd dragged Jeff into the mudroom. If he had, maybe he would have just hugged the guy into submission, but he hadn't known, and so he'd taken the dumb-arse-wrong approach and given the guy a chance to run away.

But run was exactly what Jeff had done, and Collin had been left, in a room full of devastated strangers, until Mikhail had pulled him aside.

"You just let him go?" The man's accent was thick, and his face was working visibly to keep steady, but he seemed to be incredibly tough, because it was working.

"Crick followed him out."

"Yes, but *you* just let him go?"

Collin scowled. "I'm not some sort of stalker. I do have my pride."

Mikhail lifted one shoulder up in absolute disdain. "You have your pride, yes, but you do not have Jeff. I am not impressed."

"Well, what do you expect me to do, dammit!" Collin snapped, and Mikhail lifted that shoulder up again and this time curled his lip for good measure.

"At the moment, I expect you to do nothing, because that's what you have *been* doing. It is not for me to judge. All I know is that Jeff is damaged. I was damaged like that once."

"Yeah, and what did you do about it?" Collin sounded hostile. He knew it, but he couldn't seem to do a damned thing to fix it.

Mikhail shrugged again. "I did nothing. I was damaged. But my big stupid cop? He is too strong for pride. You are obviously not strong enough to hold a man of worth. Do not concern yourself. We will care for him."

Collin closed his eyes and counted to ten, and when he opened them, he saw that the little man he'd been about to deck was standing with his arm around his "big stupid cop" and a look on his face of such incredible tenderness, such besotted concern, that all of Collin's irritation seeped into the battered tile at his feet.

Too strong for pride? Was a look like that what being "too strong for pride" got you? It might be worth it, maybe, to lay his pride on the line and go outside and make the man with the big, hurt brown eyes look at him with that sudden shyness again, and maybe make him blush, and then, maybe, make him scream a little, in a good way, and worship Collin forever, just the way Mikhail seemed to be doing to Shane.

Then Collin saw the look that Shane bent on Mikhail, and his heart stopped in his chest.

Oh no. He couldn't do that. That look was as open as a child's. How long had it been since Collin had the sort of faith to look at another human being like that? The last time he'd looked at someone like they could carry the weight of the sun and the moon and the stars on his shoulders had been....

The morning his father was taking him to school, and he was happy because he got to bring snack.

Oh God. Collin's shirt was suddenly too hot, and his breath was coming too fast, and his eyes sought out someone, anyone in the room that wouldn't make him remember that moment.

Who he saw was Deacon, one arm around the guy who was his best friend, the other arm around the little girl, Crick's niece, as she balanced on his hip. Deacon looked happy, serene, content in all things, and from what Collin had heard before he walked in, this was a man who could very possibly leave the people he loved in the same abrupt, merciless way that Collin's father had, a thousand years ago at least, when Collin had been very young.

Crick strode inside from the front door then. Collin, who was actively sweating by now, saw him bend down and say something to a rather oblivious-looking Martin, who was watching television unnoticed by the other people in the room. Martin looked up, nodded amicably, and then Crick's eyes had, apparently against Crick's will, sought Collin out in the crowd. The look he'd given had been half sympathetic and half guilty, and Collin's face flushed hot-red, then white in anger.

Even Collin could tell he was about to get the brush-off.

Crick strode toward him, and Collin said, "Don't bother. I get the hint. I hope Deacon's okay, sincerely, but I'm going to call it a night."

He'd blown through the living room and grabbed his jacket with the car keys right before he slammed the door.

As he'd crunched his way to his car, he saw a dark figure in the front seat of Jeff's Mini Cooper, head resting on crossed arms on the steering wheel, and for a moment, he let his purpose flag. And then his pride came roaring out at him.

Screw it. Jeff wanted to handle this on his own? Well fucking let him.

And Collin peeled out of there in a spray of gravel and, yes, wounded pride.

THE next evening, he drove to the Galleria after work and bought the outfit. The day after that, he called one of his old club buddies and asked him if Gatsby's Nick was still gay and still happy. Club buddy said yes, but he and his husband didn't go anymore—they were too busy preparing the nursery for their soon-to-be adopted daughter, and that sort of thing had fallen by the wayside.

"You're twenty-nine, Desmond. What the hell are you thinking, trying to be a parent?"

"I'm thinking that I'm too old to go around getting banged in alleyways wishing Prince Charming would kiss my wing-tips. Aren't you?"

Collin hadn't answered, and he'd hung up shortly afterward. He really couldn't shake the idea that twenty-four or forty-four, what he was planning on doing was still really fucking childish, and he should know better by now.

Whatever part of him felt that way was still up and running by Friday night, because when he was walking down the outside stairs to open the garage, his mother saw him as she was pulling in from work with a bag of groceries in the car, and he found that he couldn't actually look her in the eye.

"A hot date?" she asked, with nothing more in her voice than pleasant inquiry.

"Clubbing," Collin mumbled, looking at his shiny loafers. Maybe he should have gone with the Burkes; those seemed so much more comfortable.

His mother's entire demeanor seemed to change, right? Where she was usually warm and welcoming, she was now cool and stiff—she had to be. Collin grimaced inwardly.

"I thought you had someone in mind," she asked carefully, and Collin's answering shrug felt hostile and defensive, and he couldn't seem to make that change.

"He didn't want me," Collin mumbled, and suddenly, Natalie's arm was balancing groceries on her hip and pulling him in for a hug with the other arm. Maybe he'd imagined the cool and stiff thing—maybe that had been his own condemnation smacking around in his head.

"I'm sure that's not true," his mother murmured. "Maybe, he just needed some space—and maybe he's going to need you to be the persistent, bull-headed pain in the ass that you're good at being, and you're going to need to run him down."

She backed up and looked him square in the face, and this time he *knew* he didn't imagine the reprimand.

"It's hard to look someone in the eyes, Collin, when you're feeling guilty as hell. Go out, have a good time tonight—you deserve it. But don't do anything you can't feel good about the next time you see him. That never works. I've seen you try it with other boyfriends, and it hasn't ended well, remember?"

But that had been different. He'd been trying to make it a clean break. He didn't tell his mother that, though—but he did nod, because if nothing else, she'd made her very painful, very sharp and shiny, point.

Three hours later, as the cab pulled up to the condos and Collin slopped his signature on the board after the guy had taken his card, he tried to remember what that point was.

"Thank you," he said somberly to the cab driver. "Thank you. You're a gentleman. You've been very kind."

"Kid, are you getting out here?"

"Yesh... yes. Absolutely. Twenty-five hundred Elknorm, Elfhorn, Elkhorn road, number thirty-seven." He'd memorized that from Jeff's paperwork. Oh shit—had that part come in yet? Nope. Nope, nope, nope, nope... because honestly? (And really, he was too drunk *not* to be honest.) Honestly? If that part had come in, and he'd been able to call Jeff and had an excuse to see him? He probably would not have walked into that club tonight.

He was halfway down the walk to Jeff's ground-floor condo when he realized he'd forgotten to say goodbye to his cab driver. Too bad, so sad, the guy had been a prick anyway.

"Jeffy?" he called while pounding on the door. "Jeffy? You in there?"

He heard Jeff swearing from the window where he thought there was a bedroom, and then a light came on, and then... he pictured Jeff running around in purple silk boxers, trying to find a bathrobe, and when he came to, Jeff was throwing open the door in a holy-God-are-you-shitting-me? Crimson silk dressing gown. His sweetheart brown eyes were wide and irritated, and his hair... oh holy shit... his hair was a *mess*. Oh my God—in his wildest dreams, Collin had not imagined that Jeff's hair was so unruly. It stuck out of his head like an uneven pincushion, without rhyme or reason....

It was awesome.

He grinned and ran his hand through it as Jeff was still standing in the doorway, looking completely dumbstruck.

"Hey, Jeffy. I like it. And it's all soft. It's not all stiff and hard, like your bitchy black heart. Maybe you should stop mousse-ing your heart."

Jeff's eyebrows rose about three, four hundred feet. "Oh. My. God. How much did you drink?"

Collin's smile was proud. "Only three shots. Two when I was going to get me a BJ in the bathroom, and the other one when I couldn't follow through."

Jeff tucked one hand under his arm and raised the other to his mouth, covering what looked to be a giggle. "Well... if this is what happens to you on three drinks...."

"My meds," Collin said with wounded dignity. "When I was in high school? I could frink like a dish! But now?" He shook his head sadly. "And he was pretty, too, Jeffy. You should have seen him. Blond. Blue-eyed. Damn near farm-fresh. And he wanted me. God, he practically groped me when I walked in the door, you know? Almost went down on me on the dance floor. Had the sweetest little mouth."

Collin sighed theatrically and noticed that Jeff wasn't giggling anymore. He wasn't hostile, either. He was... oh, shit. He was hurt.

Collin thought maybe he should explain a little more. He reached out to ruffle Jeff's hair, and when Jeff raised an arm to block, he leaned forward, stumbled, and somehow ended up pressing Jeff against the wall.

"His eyes were the wrong color, Jeff. That's what was wrong. They weren't brown. He was almost on his knees, and he looked at me, and his eyes weren't brown. I didn't want blue eyes. I didn't want twenty-two and farm-fresh. I wanted you. You weren't there. You just walked away and left me, and you weren't there, and he wasn't going to do it for me."

They were inches apart. Ohmigod, they were just inches apart, and Collin had just blathered on and on, not noticing that Jeff's eyes were big dark whirlpools in the light coming in from the soda lamp in the parking lot. Collin himself smelled like Scotch, but Jeff? Collin closed his mouth and then closed his eyes and took a breath. Jeff smelled *expensive*, like skin products and nice bath smells and things that probably made his skin soft over those stringy gym muscles, and maybe hairless, and *oh God, he felt so good.*

And all the hostility was gone too. "I'm sorry I left you," Jeff said breathlessly.

Collin nuzzled Jeff's cheek with his lips and then gently bumped noses with him. "Why'd you leave me, Jeffy?" Collin asked plaintively. "That wasn't nice. I just wanted to help."

Jeff's breath caught—Collin could feel it because they were just that close. His dark eyes seemed to search Collin's in the darkness. "You're a nice kid," Jeff said, and Collin was stunned by the sudden hotness in his eyes.

"Don't start that shit again," he muttered, resting his forehead against Jeff's. They were the same height—he liked that. He liked classic bottoms and being on top, but he liked the equality too. He liked that Jeff was older and Collin was bossier. It was push and pull and it could be... God. It could be so perfect.

"You're not thirty-two," Jeff said archly, and Collin blew a boozy raspberry.

"You're not either," he said, absolutely sure of it. "You're like a little kid with laugh lines. Where'd you get the laugh lines, Jeffy? How come you're strong enough to laugh but you got to run away to do anything else?"

It was almost like a steel wall, Jeff's scowl. It clanked down like a bank vault door, and all the softness Collin had seen was locked away behind it.

"See," Collin sighed. "Running away." He sagged into Jeff's arms again, because he was pretty sure Jeff would catch him, and he'd missed out on his chance for a random blow job from a random stranger. He wanted contact, and warmth, and if he had to be drunk to get it, well, lucky him. He was drunk already, right?

Jeff didn't disappoint him—not in this. Those angular arms were surprisingly strong. Probably all elbows and shoulder bones in bed, but strong now, and they supported Collin and wrapped around his shoulders and hauled him to the couch, which was fine, because the floor was being a bitchy mistress and trying to throw him over with every step.

They fell into the couch—a lush, white fabric thing, and Collin sighed. "If I wasn't drunk, I'd be greasy," he mumbled. He'd had to spend an hour on his cuticles and nails, trying not to look like a mechanic. "It's like not even your furniture wants me, Jeff."

"My furniture's too covered in cat hair to object," Jeff said dryly. "Collin, you didn't drive here, did you?" A sudden panic in that voice— it was sharp, and Collin felt cut to the quick.

"I'm resphonisple... responsible now," he said, with as much sobriety as he could manage. "I'm not stupid. I know why you run. I took a cab." Those things didn't really go together, did they? Shit. "I probably need some water," he muttered, feeling surprisingly lucid for a whole nanosecond. "And ibuprofen, so I can maybe move tomorrow. Christ. 'S'been a long time since I was driven to drink." He glared at Jeff, because he wanted the man to know damned sure who was responsible.

Jeff's mouth quirked up. "Yeah, yeah, Sparky. I get it. It's all my fault, right?"

"Damned straight," Collin agreed. Then he whimpered. "I hate this jacket, you know that? It looks good, but it's not comfortable. Should probably rip it up to work on the engines, you think?"

Jeff made a sound of disbelief. "Are you kidding me? This? This is *suede*. Double-breasted, cropped, ohmigod, Sparky—lookit you!" Jeff continued to make little tsking sounds as he unbuttoned the jacket and helped Collin out of it. He had to lower his head and slide his palms against Collin's stomach to do that, and Collin smiled a little, running his hands through that wild, wild, oh-so-soft hair. Jeff jerked up, the lapels of the jacket in his hands, and Collin's smile grew wide and lazy, because they were close again. He got to see Jeff's eyes widen and his mouth part softly, and Collin extended his tongue a little and licked his lips.

"You've been drinking," Jeff said, because maybe it wasn't obvious enough. He carefully slid Collin's jacket off his shoulders, and Collin, feeling like a tipsy cat, made sure to press his body up to the feeling of Jeff's hands on his shoulders.

"I've been *dancing*," Collin corrected him. "Did you ever go dancing?"

Jeff's eyes closed for a second, and an expression… oh God. Collin didn't know if he'd ever seen that kind of pain. "I was fabulous," was what Jeff said. His voice was crisp and arrogant and held just the right amount of trill to convince Collin that he absolutely didn't need to go again.

Collin was too drunk to buy it. "Aw, shit," he muttered. "One more thing, isn't it? How am I supposed to compete? It's not the age thing, or the mechanic thing, or the temper thing, is it? It's the dead boyfriend thing! How do I match that? I can't dance as well as he could or kiss or talk…. I'm just never going to get a chance to prove that I'm not second rate, am I?" Collin sighed mournfully and undid the snap of his damned tight jeans. "I should have taken that kid up on that blow job, shouldn't I?

"No," Jeff muttered, and then he was crouched in front of Collin and working the zipper to the jeans, and Collin was looking at him mutely.

"Are you offering?"

Jeff's narrowed eyes were practically a shouted "Oh *fuck* no!" but Collin couldn't figure out why he was down there.

"I've worn jeans that tight, Sparky. If you try to sleep in them, you're going to wake up with blue balls and the worst crotch rot of all time. Now lift up, and you can sleep in your underwear."

"'S'what *you* think," Collin told him perversely. "I'm not wearing any!"

Jeff backed up so quickly he fell over on his ass and made a clatter bonking his back on the coffee table. Collin started giggling and enjoyed it so much not even a deep voice—but still a young and puzzled one—cut through the nice foggy haze Collin had swirling in his brain.

"Jeff, man, what the hell is all that noise?"

Jeff's irritated scowl was actually starting to charm Collin—which was a good thing, since it didn't look like Collin would be seeing less of it.

"A friend of mine drank a little too much," Jeff muttered. "You remember Collin?"

"The boyfriend?" Martin asked dubiously, and Collin muttered, "Oh I *wish*," with a decided roll to his eyes.

"A friend," Jeff said firmly. "Martin, go back to bed. I'm going to get him some sleep pants, and he's going to crash on the couch for the night."

"Good," Martin mumbled, his voice receding. "Maybe that furry thing will sleep on *his* head tonight."

"Katy, you slut!" Jeff murmured, but he sounded indulgent—and tired. "Here, baby, let me go get you some PJs and you can sleep it off, okay?" He clambered up from his awkward position on the floor and stood, stretching. He went to tousle Collin's hair on his way out of the room, but Collin caught his hand.

"Don't," he said roughly, and maybe it was the dark, but Jeff pushed gently against Collin's hand and Collin felt a touch, down his cheekbone, down his jaw, then cupping his cheek. Collin captured him there, not wanting to let him go the way he had at Deacon's.

"I'm sorry I was a coward," Jeff said softly. "I didn't know how hard it would be on you. That's my fault."

"You're an awful lot of trouble, do you know that?" Collin asked, stroking the back of Jeff's hand. Jeff had been turning away, and the position was awkward, so Collin was relieved when Jeff conceded a little and turned back around and knelt again, so they were eye level.

"I keep telling you that, Sparky," he said, his voice low in the darkness. "I'm too much trouble, and you're too young, and too good a kid, to get caught up in all my bullshit."

"Your bullshit isn't the problem, Jeff," Collin muttered. "It's that you think the only way to do it is alone."

Jeff pulled his hand away, and Collin let him go. "I'll be back in a sec."

"Can we talk tomorrow?" he asked wistfully.

"I work tomorrow, Sparky—and so do you!"

It was true. Saturdays were busy days for a mechanic—people brought their cars in on weekends because that was when they had time. The shop was usually closed Sundays and Mondays. Collin hadn't thought about it, but he guessed Jeff was sort of in the medical profession, and those people didn't get a lot of regular time off either.

"Sunday, then?" he persisted, but Jeff was already down the hall and probably out of earshot, because there was no response.

Collin sighed, still very, very drunk. Not too drunk to have sex, he thought mournfully. No, that would have been convenient, but alas, not the case. His body was buzzing from Jeff's touch, and, yes, if he didn't take these damned pants off, he was going to be in some serious pain.

Of course, Standard Seduction 101 insisted that if he wanted Jeff to help him out of his pain, he should be naked and hard and looking confident of getting serviced when Jeff returned from the bedroom. But then, Standard Seduction 101 never mentioned a surly teenager in the house who was already pissed off about sleeping with the cat.

Collin might have fallen asleep a little when Jeff got back. He had some cotton pajama pants, a glass of water, and some ibuprofen with him, and enough concern to help Collin into the pants after he'd washed down the ibuprofen and finished off the water.

Wrestling with the jeans proved fun, and Jeff muttered something about, "Jesus, kid, these pants are the only reason a man like me would have pliers in his junk drawer."

When Collin snapped back, "*No* man should have pliers in his 'junk' drawer," Jeff had giggled for the rest of the awkward struggle out of the damned things.

"I'll give you that," he said at last, out of breath and, unfortunately, no longer face-to-face with Collin's "junk." Collin decided that laughter was a good start and that he wasn't going to push his luck. He pulled on the sleep-pants with only a little wobble and was about to sit down heavily on the couch when Jeff said, "No, no—stay standing for a sec."

He left again and came back with a damned fine sheet and a nice, thick blanket and a real pillow. Everything was in green and rose, and Collin was glad he was already gay, because even this guy's *linens* had gay cooties, but as he settled down into the incredibly soft sheet and *very* snuggly pillow, he was grateful beyond words.

"Thanks, Jeffy," Collin said. "You're a pain in the ass, but you're a really nice guy. You know, sometimes nice guys are worth it, don't you?"

He was rewarded with a kiss on the forehead and that fantastic, expensive smell. "I could say the same about you, Sparky. But next time, maybe skip the part where you almost get blown in a club bathroom, 'kay?"

"Worst almost-blow job of my life," Collin told him, savoring the kiss and the smell and the sheets and the safety. He heard Jeff's quiet laughter down the hall, and then the alcohol took over and he was asleep.

WHEN he woke up, the drapes were closed over another foggy, gray day, there was something warm, vibrating, and hairy on his chest, and it was mercifully dark in Jeff's living room.

Oh shit.

Jeff's living room. He was in Jeff's living room.

"Awwwwwwwwww...."

"It lives!" It wasn't Jeff's voice, and Collin squinted to see whose voice it was. For a minute, all he saw was a very dark face over a blinding white T-shirt, and then he put two and two together.

"Martin," he groaned. Oh good. Collin felt like shit, probably looked worse, and there he was. The elephant in the living room, eating what looked like a mixing bowl full of cold cereal with the force and verve of a backhoe at a landfill. "God. Don't you go somewhere in the day?"

"Uthullwy," Martin said through a mouthful of something colorful and sugary. He swallowed, and the sound echoed in the tympani chamber of Collin's skull. "Jeff told me if I stayed here to make sure you were okay, you'd get me to Promise House on your way out so he could pick me up there."

"Oh shit." Collin's skull pounded with the logistics of cabs and his car parked at the club and getting this teenager back to Levee Oaks when it was in the exact opposite direction, but he needed to go to work anyway....

"Oh *fuck!* Work!" He tried to sit up, and the monster on his chest clawed him casually. Collin screamed like a girl, wrapped an arm around the—oolf—cat (was that really a cat? Jesus. When did cats weigh that much?), and tried to sit up and think.

At that moment, the pants next to the couch started buzzing from the cell phone in the pocket, and he didn't even think about dodging Joshua's call, even though he was pretty sure he was in for the ass-chewing of all time. The cat wriggled out of his one-armed grasp and landed on the floor with an honest-to-God floorboard-bending thump, and he reached for the phone.

He had to hold the phone away from his ear for a minute before Joshua calmed down enough for him to reply, and he glanced at Martin in embarrassment as they both got an earful of, "… cars backed up from here to China, you dumb asshole, get your lazy fucking ass in here and stop worrying the shit out of me and your mother!"

That was Collin's cue. "I'm sorry," he said into the receiver, really feeling sorry. If Joshua had called his mother, they both knew he'd been out and probably remembered the dumbfuck kid he'd been and basically had a solid basis for thinking he'd done something amazingly stupid. He'd sworn he wasn't going to make people worry about him anymore, and this wasn't a very good way to keep that promise.

"You're sorry?" Joshua sounded disbelieving, and Collin sighed.

"Look, man, I'm sorry. I got drunk, took a cab to a… friend's house, and made an ass out of myself, okay? I've got to go back and get my car and get dressed—"

"And shower!" Martin interjected. "Man, you're rank—you smell like cigarettes, whiskey, and stale Axe."

"And shower," Collin muttered, rolling his eyes at Martin. "Anyway, an hour and a half on the outside. I'll stay late. Just take the cars, give a long estimate, and I'll get there and give you a break, okay?"

"You took a cab?" Joshua said suspiciously, and Collin had to laugh. They were still back at that.

"Yeah—took a cab."

"To a friend's?" Joshua's voice rose at "friend," and Collin would have smacked his forehead with his palm, but his whole head might have gone just rolling off his shoulders if he did that.

"To Jeff's," Collin confessed, wincing, and got ready to pull the phone away from his ear again.

Joshua surprised him, though. "And you're still there?"

"I got a pity crash on his couch," Collin confessed, and Martin made a snorting sound that seemed to spray milk and cereal back into that big-assed bowl.

"Promising," Joshua said after a moment's consideration. "His part's in—do you want to tell him that, or should we wait until Monday?"

Collin smiled a little. Monday was a day off. "We should wait until Monday," he said. "I think I could do something with that."

"Right, Boss!" Joshua said crisply. "Now get your ass in here so we can make some fucking money, okay?"

"I hear you." Collin ended the call (so much less satisfactory on the new iPhone than it used to be on his little flip phone) and slid back against the couch in pain.

"Jeff left you some water and aspirin," Martin garbled, gesturing to the coffee table, and Collin blessed them both as he washed down some more ibuprofen and finished off the ginormous glass of water that was sitting on the edge of the table. Which led to his second order of the day.

"Bathroom?" he had to ask, wondering if he could actually make it to the head with his bladder as engorged as it felt.

"Down the hall," Martin gestured. "Use the guest bathroom if you're smart. Jeff's bathroom smells like girl shit. It's all got boy's labels on it, right, but ain't none of it is Axe, so I'm staying the hell away."

Collin had to laugh, liking the kid in spite of himself. "Point taken. You, uhm, know that I sort of like the way Jeff smells, don't you?"

Martin grimaced. "Yeah, yeah, but I don't figure you want to smell that way yourself. Anyway, stop hopping from one foot to the next and hit the head. If you want to jump in the shower, I'll bring you some clothes. Jeff bought me a crap load of jeans and shit to wear when I'm working at The Pulpit—you can have some of that. But you can wear his boxers, right? I don't want any of your shit flopping around in my drawers, and I don't reckon that'll be a problem for him."

Collin's abdomen felt like it was going to explode. "Jesus, kid, stop making me laugh. Gay or no gay, we don't normally go commando in another man's fatigues, so the boxers are a nice touch. Thanks—I'm going to take you up on that shower now."

"You want I should make you some coffee?" the kid asked, still from his cross-legged squat on Jeff's stuffed chair.

Collin actually felt his knees go weak. "Kid, you do that, and I'll take you for breakfast any place in the universe, as long as it's drive-thru." If nothing else, he could use the coffee to wash down his meds, kept conscientiously in a little container in the pocket of his suede blazer.

Martin brightened. "Seriously? 'Cause I ain't been to Mickey D's in a hella long time! Can we go? I'm *dying* for a double quarter-pounder with cheese!"

Oh crap. Collin's stomach was making *bad* noises at the thought of greasy food, so he nodded greenly and escaped to the bathroom, where he peed so long he thought he might piss his balls out the chute, because hey! Everything else was going, why wouldn't they?

The shower was a blessing, except, apparently Martin was a fan of Old Spice, and Collin never had been. It was okay—smelling like Old Spice was a small price to pay for pants that were a little loose around the hips and Jeff's cotton boxers. (Collin was *so* keeping those! Not that Jeff would want them back, really, but still!)

A HALF an hour later, Collin was nursing one of Jeff's thermos mugs in the back of a cab, and Martin was with him. The boy looked *thrilled* to be in a cab, and Collin had to laugh.

"Kid, you took a Greyhound bus cross-country and it's a *cab* that's flipping your switch?"

Martin's brows drew in together, and those big milk-chocolate eyes looked a little wounded. "Well yeah, but I've taken the bus all over Atlanta—I ain't never been in a cab!"

Collin laughed again over some positively *sublime* coffee (he was still young enough to take his with lots of sugar and milk, but that didn't mean he didn't know the good stuff when he had it) and decided that his first impression hadn't been wrong—he did like this kid. Once the hostility and confusion were gone, what was left was… sweet. The kid was sweet, without any of the cynicism or self-annihilation or just plain old pissy-assed bullshit that Collin had carried around like a stale candy shell.

"Well, kid, if you think this ride is sweet, you're going to *love* what we're going to pick up."

AH, THERE she was, his baby, parked three blocks away from Gatsby's Nick in a little mom-and-pop store lot he'd remembered from the last time he'd been there. No parking meter, no parking ticket, and... look closely now, she *was* his baby... yup! No vandalism, either! Many thanks for small mercies, and canyagimmehalleluja, amen!

"Man, that's the one I saw at Deacon's!" Martin's eyes were huge. "She's amazing! Tell me about the engine—V8, four-twenty-seven supercharger, right? What's the horsepower? Top speed? Pickup? Are those trick rims, the ones that spin? I *love* those!" The kid's questions went on *forever*, but since he was talking Collin's favorite language, Collin had no problem answering them. She was, after all, his baby.

"She was the first car I got after I got my garage," he said with some pride. "It took me six months to get her running because most of the parts are out of stock or had to be made custom, and because it's not my specialty, it took me a year to get the body where I felt right about the paint job."

"You did the paint job, didn't you?" Martin said critically, running his hand over the door.

Collin sighed. Everybody had an opinion, didn't they? "Not my strength," he admitted candidly, and then Martin surprised him.

"You should have Crick do the touch up," Martin said as he got into the car and fastened the quick-release seat belt like a pro. "He did the freehand on Mikhail's van—he's really good."

Collin perked up and started the engine, glad of another reason to get in good with the people at The Pulpit; then he deflated a little. "Crick has other things to worry about," he said softly, and Martin's shoulders slumped.

"Yeah. Deacon's a good guy, you know? I hope he's going to be okay. It's weird, watching everyone get so upset about it. You forget, when your friends are talking shit about 'they' and 'them' and 'those, uhm, guys'—you forget that 'those... guys'—they've got people they love and shit. It's not just all about...." Suddenly Martin remembered who he was talking to and blushed, then threw his head back against the car seat with unnecessary vigor.

Collin felt a little bad for the kid as he pulled through the mostly empty streets of downtown Sacramento toward the freeway. "Yeah. The sex part squicks straight guys out," Collin conceded. "It'll do that when all you think about is tab A and slot B, right? Suddenly, you're thinking about slot C, and all you know about slot C is that Mom told you not to play with what came out of there because it's dirty, but you've totally missed the point."

Martin was staring at him with a mix of pure, unadulterated horror and fierce admiration. "Man, you are so totally grossing me out, but I hate to say it."

"You're dying for the point, aren't you?" Collin asked, grinning because the kid was giving him a chance.

"You gonna stop at that McDonald's? You buy me a hamburger, and I'll take it on the chin!"

"Jesus, kid, do you ever stop eating?"

"Do you see me eating *now*?"

"Point taken."

"Speaking of, don't you have one to get to?"

Collin was thoroughly enjoying this conversation. Hell, this kid was quick and completely unafraid. Collin thought that maybe losing his brother was the worst thing that had ever happened to him—until Martin lost Kevin all over again.

He pulled into the drive-thru and ordered the kid not one but two double quarter pounders with cheese, and then ordered himself a regular, because he still had a metabolism that wouldn't quit. He still had his coffee, but he got the kid a large shake, thinking that maybe that would keep him occupied until dinnertime, if it didn't make Martin throw up before then.

"So," Martin said through a mouthful of truly appalling caloric intake, "that point?"

Collin sighed and took the onramp to I-80, positioning himself for I-5 and the off ramp to Levee Oaks. "The point is that there's two kinds of sex, and it's not het or gay, all right?"

Martin swallowed and then inhaled another quarter of the burger. "I'm listening."

"There's poison-ivy sex—I have an itch, I want to scratch it, any orifice will do. You know what I'm talking about?"

Martin nodded and took a drink of his shake. He seemed to be doing okay.

"Then there's, 'I like to touch this *person*'. And that's the end-all and be-all of it. It's all about that *person*. I mean, sometimes, with that person, there's the whole poison-ivy thing, but you keep it in your pants then and still save it for that one person. Now, for you, I'm betting that person's going to be a girl. It's what's going on in your brain, it's what's making blood flow to your johnson, and that's all good, right?"

Martin nodded enthusiastically, and Collin took a big deep breath because maybe this point wouldn't hurt as much as Collin had feared. "Now I can't speak for all the gays at The Pulpit, right? I don't know them that well, and some guys, they swing both ways, and that's their business. But for me, and for Jeff, well, the only person we ever looked at when we wanted our poison ivy scratched was another guy. And when we wanted *that person* involved, well, that was a guy too. I mean, the same parts work, and where you put 'em is your business, but what makes things perk up and get excited? That's sort of, I don't know, predestined. One day, you, Martin, woke up and looked at girls and went, 'Hey—she's got *tits*, and they're *awesome!*' One day, I woke up and looked at a picture of David Beckham, the soccer star, and went, '*Ohmygod—I want me some!*'"

To Collin's immense relief, Martin didn't blow milkshake all over his leather interior.

"I think my brother had it bad for Viggo Mortensen," Martin said instead, after a thoughtful moment. "We must have watched *Lord of the Rings* about a thousand times, and you have to believe me when I tell you those are *not* a black man's movies. Not in Atlanta, they're not."

Collin digested this thoughtfully and took the I-5, grateful this was Saturday and not Friday, when traffic would be nucking futs. "I'll take your word for it. Just be glad it was that guy, and not one of the hobbits. That would have been...."

"Embarrassing," Martin filled in, a little of his original attitude trying to come back.

Collin nodded his head and helped it along. "Gandalf would have been okay, though. He's one of us."

Martin really did snort milkshake then, but he was laughing so hard that Collin handed him a napkin without comment and thought that maybe the car could take some milkshake in her upholstery if it meant Jeff's job was a little bit easier.

In the end, Martin turned out to be so much fun—and so much of a car nut—that Collin went the whole nine yards, got the kid an extra set of coveralls, and had him call up Shane and ask to stay and help out at the garage. There were safety protocols—Shane would have to come by with a checklist and some forms for Jeff to sign before Martin could do so much as change a tire—but in the meantime, he could deal with the customers, talk about the cars, and do some triage. He listened to a lot of squeaks, thunks, and women using big gestures and making really weird faces as they tried to mimic what their engines were doing. He got pretty good at saying things like, "Okay, ma'am, is it a Dodge Caravan? Then that's probably the belts." Collin was so proud.

The day was nuts—just plain nuts—and they were behind from the start, but the kid, looking respectable and happy in his coveralls and being unfailingly polite to the people who walked in, turned out to be a real asset, and Collin told him so after a couple of hours.

"You were really awesome, today, kid. I'm not sure we could have done this without you."

"You're just saying that because you want to get in Jeff's pants," Martin laughed, and Collin laughed back.

"Naw, man. I'm saying it because when I was fourteen, I was pretty sure I was too big a fuckup to help anybody out. You're doing great. I just wanted you to know it."

Right about the time Martin smiled a big hero-worship of a smile at Collin, Joshua walked up behind them and said, "Don't lie to the kid. You're still a fuckup, and we're still behind. Now get your ass in gear!"

Martin cracked up, which was as it should be, and Collin got back under a car, where he belonged. A couple of hours later, Martin walked into the garage with big bag full of paper containers with what looked to be more coffee and sandwiches.

"Some nice lady came over here with food for us all. She claimed to be your mother. I don't believe it—you're an asshole, and she's good people."

Collin stuck his head around the wheels of the truck up on the lift and blew a raspberry. "If you're not nice to me, I'll let *her* take you home and you can see how good she is when she's bitching at you to make your bed. Did you talk to Jeff yet, to see when he's coming to get you?"

"Two hours," Martin said. "I bet if you work your ass off, you can be respectable by then."

Collin shook his head. "You have no subtlety, kid. You don't ask a guy out the night after you took a pity-crash on his couch—that's bad form."

"Yeah? You got a plan?"

"I'm getting there. Now go away and let me work."

"It better be a good plan," Martin warned. "Jeff isn't stupid."

"Hey!" Collin gestured to himself a few times until Martin laughed and conceded that Collin wasn't stupid either. It was enough. Collin worked steadily, past the hangover, past the anxiety, past the embarrassment.

When Jeff pulled his car into the garage, all Collin could feel was the same familiar lift he'd felt for the last year whenever he'd seen the blue Mini Cooper parked at the diner. His sweetheart was here. It was time for Collin to claim him.

Chapter *13*

Jeff: Bending, Not Breaking

GOD, he was a pussy. All it took was one look at that big-dick Camaro, and Jeff's knees went a little weak. If he were any more of a woman, his panties would have flooded, but as it was, he had to settle for a grand-mal butterfly seizure in his stomach. And an erection.

It was the first time all day he stopped pretending that seeing Collin on his doorstep last night had been nothing more than an inconvenience.

His stomach had gone fluttery, his knees had gone weak, just like now, and when Collin had his drunken confession to *almost* getting a blow job in a club, he'd felt an absurd and unholy anger. And wasn't that ridiculous—who *almost* got a BJ in a club? It was almost an entrance requirement, like a stamp if you didn't want to pay the door fee twice.

But then….

Then Collin had been all bare and vulnerable, like one of those poor hairless cats. Poor baby. Jeff had always thought if he had one of those, he'd spend all his time knitting sweaters for the poor thing, and Collin being truthful was no exception.

I didn't want twenty-two and farm-fresh and blue eyes, Jeffy. I wanted you.

Considering the world of snark in which he and Collin seemed to swim, that was damned near poetry.

A boy could get a little weak in the knees for poetry, couldn't he? And Collin's age was starting to disappear. Jeff could remember that angry, hurt teenager and remember that he'd had an inkling it would come to this, that Collin would grow up into a very worthy man.

Any guy who would walk away from a club blow job to come see a guy who'd been as much a drama princess as Jeff had been was more worthy than Jeff knew what to do with. God... was it possible he could remember what to do with that?

The thought made his hands sweat on his leather steering wheel cover as he pulled up to the shop. Since the steering was still stiff, well, that made it particularly hard to drive, Jeff thought irritably. Maybe he should save all this gushy admiration to see if the guy could actually *fix his frickin' car!*

There were cars in every available parking space, but no customers, and Jeff thought that maybe Collin was going to be there all Sunday. As honest as he'd just been with himself, he absolutely *refused* to believe that it was a twinge of disappointment he felt in his stomach. Dead butterflies, maybe, but *not* disappointment.

Still, Collin came striding out of the little office in the front, and Jeff opened the door and got out and then stood there, the door in front of him like a shield, and wondered what he looked like as he greeted the pain in the ass that had haunted him through some of his worst moments in recent history.

Collin's hair was a little greasy and pulled back in a half-queue, and he looked tired, like maybe he'd been up all night drinking on a stomach that couldn't do that anymore, but he narrowed those tired eyes and smiled with purpose, and Jeff couldn't help the embarrassing little sound that came out of his mouth. Jesus, the kid was just so *pretty*, right?

"Heya, Jeffy," Collin said, his voice pitched low and familiar, and Jeff held onto that car door for dear life.

"Hi," Jeff said, swallowing hard. "Uhm, thanks for taking Martin today. He sounded happy on the phone—I'm glad he enjoyed himself."

Collin snorted and continued to work at his hands with the faded red cloth, which looked like it had recently been clean and was being used abominably. "Enjoyed himself? Jeff, we worked his *ass* off today, and he was *awesome*. Seriously, let me know if you're gonna keep this kid. I could use the slave labor any goddamned time."

"Don't I get a say?" Martin was coming out of the office, too, and he must have been wearing coveralls for most of the day, because his jeans and hooded sweatshirt were a little rumpled but practically pristine.

"No," Jeff said dryly. "That's why it's called slave labor. I understand you did good today, Martin—thank you."

"Thank you?" Martin looked affronted. "He promised to pay me!"

Collin nodded and pulled two twenties out of the front pocket of his coveralls. "All yours, junior. Don't spend it all in one place."

"Are you shitting me? Christmas is in a month and a week, and I spent all my money on my bus ticket!"

That brought them all up uncomfortably. Martin had run away from home—and his parents still wanted him back, on the caveat that talking about Kevin was not going to happen. Jeff had come to like the kid—like him a *lot*—but it wasn't fair, was it, to keep him there just so Jeff didn't have to face an empty condo and a handful of good memories?

"Well, by all means come back on Tuesday and Wednesday of next week," Collin said smoothly into the uncomfortable silence. "And if you want, Jeff can bring you Monday—Promise House should have cleared this place by then, and you can help me fix the steering in Jeff's car."

"Oh!" Jeff smiled genuinely and tabled the unhappy reality of losing Kevin all over again for just a minute. "You've got the part!"

Collin nodded. "I do—I figured, you bring the car in the morning, take mine for the day, and then come back, and maybe…." He blushed. That cocky little bastard actually *blushed*. But he finished the sentence. "Maybe, I take you and Martin out for dinner."

"You can leave me home," Martin said decisively, at about the same time Jeff's face fell to probably about his knees.

"That's game night, Martin, remember? You, me, Kimmy, Lucas—"

"Watching Lucas move on Kimmy and Kimmy shoot him down?" Martin interjected glumly, and Jeff nodded with sympathy. The last time hadn't been pretty, but the fifth or twelve-hundredth time Lucas had tried a compliment and Kimmy nuked him where he sat, she'd almost been in tears. He'd caught her hand and said, "It's all right, Kim, you're not beautiful. You're hideous, you have warts and green skin and a chick-beard. It's all good. Will you sit next to me and be my partner in Trivial Pursuit anyway?"

"Moron," Kimmy had scowled, but she'd squeezed Lucas's hand when she said it, and Jeff and Martin had rolled their eyes at each other and Jeff had felt a little hope.

"In that case," Martin said now, with the air of someone making a *horrible* sacrifice for the sake of his wingman, "you can have them pick me up on the way to your house, and you and Collin can go out to dinner. And then"—he perked up—"maybe I can have Kim bring Halo or something from Promise House, because I'm telling you, I've had about enough of video-golf!"

Jeff's electronics collection had wowed the socks off of Martin— but his actual selection of video *games* had un-wowed those socks right back on. Jeff was not a fan of games that made loud noises and showed shit exploding, and to Martin, that was the pinnacle of the craft.

"You didn't like Scrabble?" Jeff asked, just a little bit hurt.

"No, Jeff. I didn't like Scrabble," Martin replied with so much honesty that Collin cracked up completely and even Jeff had to smile.

"Okay," Jeff nodded, avoiding Collin's eyes. "I'll just call Kimmy and it's a…." His face flushed and then washed pale. Oh God. He wasn't sure he could say it.

Then Collin's honey-colored eyes caught his, and Collin said it for him. "It's a date, Jeff," Collin said, again with that low, knee-melting voice that brooked no argument and left no quarter.

"Yeah," Jeff muttered. "Uhm, a date."

"I forgot something," Martin said with no subtlety at all. He turned around abruptly before Jeff could even ask what, and Collin walked right up to Jeff's protective car door and put his hands on top of it, one of them on top Jeff's hand as he held it.

"Is that so horrible, Jeffy?" Collin asked, and his voice was still smoky, but now it was soft, and Jeff swallowed and conceded the truth.

"No," he said. "It's not horrible."

"Is it scary?" Collin raised his hand to just barely touch Jeff's cheek with his thumb. The hand smelled like hand-cleaner and engine grease, and Jeff didn't care. They were warm smells, honest smells, and Jeff was starting to like them.

"A little," Jeff muttered. "I don't even know what to wear."

"Wear whatever you want. We'll go wherever you want. I'd like to show you where I live—just to show you that it's a grown-up place and not a frat-boy pit, okay? And other than that? It's all your speed, Jeff. A Disney movie, a drag race, I just want to spend a little time with you. Is that so bad?"

His eyes were fabulous, really. That warm, light brown, and now they were smudged a little with weariness but still bright with hope. He still had hope. What business did Jeff have, crushing that hope? Couldn't he be strong enough to maybe hope a little too?

"No," Jeff breathed. "That's... that sounds... good."

Collin was drawing a little closer in the chill twilight, and Jeff's brain completely shorted out. Jeff Beachum, Sergeant of Snark, Wielder of Witticism, Dominator of the Double Entendre, completely ran out of things to say. He touched his lips with his tongue and watched as Collin gave a purely feline smile and then reached out with *his* tongue to trace Jeff's lips.

"Good," he whispered. "Then it's all—"

"Good," Jeff finished.

Collin's lips met his, so soft, so subtly, it wasn't hardly a kiss at all, and Jeff's mouth opened just a little, to take a breath and breathe Collin in, and then Collin's hand was cupping the back of his head and Jeff's whole world was suddenly Collin's breath, Collin's taste, Collin's tongue in his mouth. Jeff whimpered, and his knees wobbled, and he found himself clinging to Collin's coveralls and trying not to just sink into the front seat of his car.

Collin broke off the kiss and smiled, all smug like a lion, and finished it up with a peck on the lips. "Monday, right?"

Jeff nodded mutely.

"Good, right?"

"Mmm-hmm," Jeff said, sinking down into the front of the Cooper before he took his door with him.

"Good. I'll send Martin out and let him know he can find whatever he forgot."

"'Kay," Jeff muttered, still dazed.

Collin's hand reached down and ruffled his hair, and Jeff didn't even object. He just sat there, fingers to his lips, until Martin trotted out, gave Collin a low five, and clambered into the passenger seat demanding food.

Jeff was still so lost in the wonder of the kiss that he buckled on the nutrition thing and took Martin to McDonald's—the kid swore he hadn't been there in weeks.

JEFF left work early on Monday, roaring the Camaro out of the parking lot like he actually owned it. He'd been dubious when he left the Cooper and Martin at Collin's garage—he'd eyed that big-dick Camaro like a Siberian tiger, actually, sure it was going to strike at any moment.

"Don't worry, Jeffy. It's a car. You step on the gas, it goes. You step on the brakes, it stops. You have to take a dump, and you'd better pull over and find a bathroom because there's no electronic anything and you're going to have to do it yourself."

"Well, thank God for that." Jeff pulled up one side of his mouth skeptically. "You, uhm… I mean, I'm not going to step on the gas and find myself in the next county with a horse plastered on the grill, am I?"

Collin shook his head and pressed the keys firmly into Jeff's hand. "No, Jeffy. If you're as moderate on the gas with my baby here as you are in every other avenue of your life, you will not find yourself in the next county with a horse on the grill. But it's a good reminder of why I should always take a cab when I drink, so thanks for the mental image, by the way!"

"My privilege," Jeff replied sourly.

"The pleasure's mine," Collin said, and something about the sideways slant of his eyes made Jeff blush, and he barely remembered to say bye to Martin as he toddled off to work.

MARGIE was his patient today, and if her weight loss was subtle, her complete dismissal of the topic was not. "It doesn't count if the Lap-band's making me do it," she told him tersely, and he had a moment of irritation.

"The fuck it doesn't, sweetness," he snapped, truly upset. "Anything you can do to make your stay in this world longer and more productive, well, that's a win, okay? You're looking good."

He was holding the ultrasonic wand against her neck, so he saw her shoulders drop in resignation. "Thank you, Jeff. It's kind of you to say. Can I ask about you?"

Jeff was tempted to give her the party line, but he'd just gotten personal, and he guessed she was entitled. "I've got a date tonight," he told her, feeling foolish, but she wasn't put off in the least.

"Oh my God!" She broke away from the ultrasonic to give him an impressed look, and he grimaced.

"Stop it." He pushed on her shoulders to make her go back to where she needed to be.

"Who is he?"

"An auto mechanic," Jeff replied promptly, because the rest of it was too complicated.

Margie gave an actual ecstatic shudder. "Oooh… I love a man who works with his hands. And is straight."

Jeff wanted to hug her. "I love you more, sweetheart… now prepare yourself. This is gonna hurt…."

"FUCK, owie, owie, owie, fuck fucking owie!"

"Jesus, Crick, you are *such* a baby! I swear, I've got a school teacher in here who's tougher than you!"

"Is that the woman I passed on the way out? Because if I was in her class, she'd have me wetting my pants inside of ten minutes. That was one woman I would *not* want to fuck with."

Jeff sniffed to cover a sympathetic wince and then pushed back on Crick's damaged wrist, knowing it was going to hurt, but also knowing Crick needed it.

"As if she'd have you," was what he said. "That woman has better taste in men. Now squeeze my hand. Come on, boy, squeeze it…." Jeff barked at him some more and twisted him and finished with the ultrasonic deep tissue thing, because it was going to help with the soreness. When he was done, he handed Crick an ibuprofen, a cup of water, and a tissue.

Crick wiped his forehead and his eyes and glared wearily at him while Jeff tried not to feel guilty. It was his job, but he didn't always like it.

"You're not doing your exercises," Jeff said to counter the guilt. "You've lost mobility in that hand in the last week—what the hell have you been doing with yourself?"

Crick sighed and pitched the tissue into the trashcan with his good hand, then took the pain med and washed it down. "Deacon's doing worse," he said softly, picking up his shirt and trying to shrug into it.

"I know," Jeff said quietly. "I was there last night."

Deacon had tried hard not to let anyone see, but it was pretty clear that he'd been doing a good job of covering until the week before. His lips had been an unhealthy color, and he'd been unable to stand up and carry Parry Angel to her bath. Instead, he'd sat on the couch—an unusual thing for him—and let the little girl scramble into his lap.

Jeff didn't even want to think about the ruin of broken syllables his singing voice had become. Jon had left the house, hearing it, and Amy had gone after him, and Jeff had perched their daughter on Deacon's lap so she could join in with nonsense words.

Shane and Mikhail had worked impassively on the cleanup while Andrew had gone outside to tend the horses, and Crick had come in and spirited the little girls off to their bath. When Jon and Amy came back in, Amy announced that Parry Angel was going to spend the night with Lila, and when Crick had heard this, he had looked so... *relieved.*

"You're not taking care of yourself," Jeff said seriously now. "You're too busy taking care of everybody else. You need to knock that shit off right now, okay? If the worst happens, we need you, and we need the best you that you can be."

Crick nodded and worried his shirt buttons in one at a time. "I hear you. I used to wonder how Deacon could do it, you know? Work himself into the ground when we needed him so damned bad? Now I know. It's like, the people that are your heart? You can't take a deep breath if they're not well."

Jeff made some perfunctory notations in Crick's chart and gestured for him to sit down on the bed he usually had patients lay down on. He always reserved fifteen extra minutes for Crick—why have a GBFF if you weren't going to dish, right?

"When's Benny coming home?" he asked. It had been clear in the last week that even with Andrew, Crick needed help. Between the active little girl, the sick man, and the demands of the ranch, the two men were spread thin. If it hadn't been for the kids at Promise House coming over to work with the horses and Jon and Amy coming over to help with the cooking every so often, Jeff wasn't sure how the small business could have made it, even in the last month, and he found himself sweating bullets again for the tight-knit, sturdy family of Deacon Winters. God, money had been so close before. They had come so close to picking up and moving, and Jeff would have needed to move with them, because he'd already fabricated a family out of need and good wishes, and he didn't think he could fabricate another one.

"Wednesday," Crick said, apparent relief on his face. "If you and Martin wanted to come on Wednesday night instead of Tuesday, you can see her when she gets home—she's dying to meet Martin, and Collin, too, and since the house is going to be packed on Thursday, you'll get to talk to her a little."

Jeff found that his white lab coat was suddenly way too tight, too hot, and too sweaty. "Who told Her Royal Shortness about Collin?" he asked, suddenly a little afraid. Benny was… was *joyful* about the whole lot of them. She fussed like a little mother hen, and he was suddenly very much afraid of disappointing her. It was a date. One lousy date. Crick wouldn't tell Benny about one lousy date, would he?

"I told her," Crick said, the small smile on his face proclaiming that he enjoyed Jeff's discomfort very much.

"Oh, Jesus, Crick—what if it doesn't work out? I mean, God, I've already made a hash out of it once or twice, or I've lost track of how often, and I don't want her getting all excited for me when there's nothing to celebrate, you know?"

The smile faded, and Crick's face took on the stern lines of, had he known it, his boyhood hero and the love of his life. "Shut up, Jeffy. She left the only security she's ever had to go forge a future, and we had to call her back to tell her Deacon might not be here for long. She loves you—hell, she loves us *all*. If I've got even the tiniest bit of good news about somebody, whether it's planning the little 'ceremony' Mikhail is going to drag us to in the nut-shriveling cold after Christmas or the fact that she might not have to worry about her favorite uncle Jeffy—man, I'm gonna fucking tell her. My sister deserves any good thing we can give her, and all she's wanted since she moved into The Pulpit is for her baby to be taken care of and for us to be happy. I'm gonna give it to her. But you know what that means?"

"Christ." Jeff flopped down, ass first, on the bed next to Crick. "Yeah, I know what this means."

"It means you'd better not fuck this up," Crick said, but he looped a companionable arm around Jeff's shoulders, and Jeff leaned into his friend with sincere appreciation.

"And just because I love your little sister, I'll try not to," Jeff told him sincerely, and he was rewarded by Crick's sudden, unencumbered lopsided grin, the one that told him what Deacon had probably seen in Crick in the first place.

"The fact that you might actually get you some is not up for consideration at all, is it?"

Jeff shuddered, remembering the complete domination of those kisses. God, Collin knew how to make him feel small and vulnerable—and protected. Like he was surrounded by strength. Like someone was there to keep him safe when things got bad. Like nothing could ever hurt him again. "Well, you know me, Crick. I'm all about the short-term sex, right?"

Crick's arm tightened around his shoulders, and Crick dropped a kiss on the top of his head. Horrible brat—he *would* be six foot five inches tall. Crick had *grown* this last year, and Deacon had told Jeff repeatedly that it made him feel like a dirty old man. *I should have at least waited until the kid stopped growing before I married him.* God. Deacon had to be all right.

"I promise you, this one's going to stick around a while," Crick said fervently. "I feel it, Jeffy, he's in for the long haul."

"So's Deacon, Crick," Jeff told him with more confidence than he felt. "Deacon might just sort of fade away for himself, but we all know there's not much in the world he wouldn't do for you."

"God, I hope so. For both of us."

"Me too." There was a silence, which Jeff broke with a silly thought that had been bothering him all day. "What do you think I should wear?"

"The very fact that you even ask that is proof that you're not really trying here."

"But... I mean, I was going to go home after work and change, Crick—what should I wear?"

"Clothes."

"What kind?" Jeff fumed, crossing his arms in front of him obstinately.

"The kind you can take off, you dumb asshole. You may be thinking of this as a first date, but by my count, it makes three, and this guy deserves a happy ending."

"I'm *not* putting out for him."

"Prick tease."

"Fuck you."

"I'm not the one volunteering, here, Jeffy." Crick straightened and took away his comforting arm in exasperation.

"I'm just asking what I should wear!" God, couldn't anyone see it was a legitimate question?

"Wear some fucking optimism that it doesn't matter what you're going to wear," Crick muttered, shaking his head. "Now help me into my goddamned shoes, willya? Deacon's going to need to take his meds when I get home, and I don't want to be late."

So Jeff's day had been... *stressful*, was the word, by the time he roared out of the parking lot of the VA hospital, but it had also been... what was the word he was looking for?

Blessed.

Margie, Crick—it was like God was telling him to hope a little, to maybe give the kid a chance, maybe let him prove himself some.

Maybe Jeff wasn't doing anybody any favors by keeping the world out of his heart, was he?

This time, he let his heart jump up to his throat when he rounded the almost-desolate street of small businesses that featured the firehouse, the diner, and a DVD trading store all huddled together, with Collin's garage being the biggest lot on the block. He saw the Mini Cooper out in front, meaning that it was all done, and he saw Shane's GTO next to it, with Kimmy leaning against the door and Lucas leaning next to her. The pose looked casual, but Kimmy's face was taut and unhappy.

Jeff pulled up, feeling absurdly proud of driving that big, lusty muscle car, and went to see if maybe he could give Kimmy some of his optimism. God knew, now that one of them had it, it was time to share.

"All I'm saying," Kimmy protested as Jeff was walking up, "is that it would be stupid to leave a life in Georgia if you've got one."

"I don't," Lucas said mildly, without heat. Jeff had to grin. Lucas so far had proven to be, literally, the most cheerful person Jeff had ever met. When they'd played games at Jeff's house, the better to make Martin feel at home, Lucas had met every one of Kim's scowls with a smile and every bitchy word of cynicism out of her mouth with sunshine and chocolates. Jeff wasn't sure what sort of boys they raised in Georgia, but this one had balls of titanium good will, and Jeff just had to respect that.

The truth was, Lucas reminded Jeff of a slightly less weird version of Shane, and since he knew Kim would roll around in thumbtacks and lemon juice to protect Shane from *anything*, he had high hopes for the two of them, because, dammit, *someone* deserved to be happy, right?

"Heya, Kimmy," Jeff sallied, shutting the door of the Camaro gently but firmly—he had to be careful with it, after all. It was Collin's baby.

"Oh God, if it isn't Mr. Sunshine himself. What the fuck are you so happy about?"

Jeff tried for smugness—he used to be able to be smug about these things, didn't he? "I have a date," he said simply, and Kimmy's scowl melted away.

"Go, Jeffy! I'm proud of you."

Jeff blushed. "Yeah, well, it's been a while."

Suddenly Lucas, easygoing, titanium good will Lucas, looked sharp and disapproving. "How long?"

Jeff blushed even more and looked away. "Uhm...." Oh God, it was almost worse than being a thirty-two-year-old virgin, wasn't it?

"Aw, man!" Lucas turned around and kicked the GTO's back tire, and when he turned back around, his tanned, square-jawed, Georgia-boy face was almost grief stricken. "Kevin wouldn't have wanted that!" he snapped, and Jeff looked at him, as surprised as Kimmy.

"It's not—"

"You never called me. I told you to call me, I told you to keep in touch. I told you I'd be your friend after that, you know?"

"I—"

"I was supposed to look out for you, Jeff—you think I didn't get a letter too?"

Jeff and Kimmy looked at Lucas in confusion. He was crying. "Lucas… you didn't do anything wrong," Jeff told him earnestly. "You called and gave me bad news, you offered help—you did okay. You were injured too—it's not like you didn't have a whole entire life of your own to deal with, right?"

"But it's not okay! Not if you've been alone all this time!" Lucas turned around and kicked the tire again. "You just… when you didn't call back, I thought you had it all together. I should have made sure you had someone. I should have."

Jeff swallowed the absurd urge to laugh. "Sugarplum, as nice as it would have been to think I had my own personal dating fairy, it wasn't fair of Kevin to just land you with the job, okay? I…. If I've been alone this time, it's been by choice. Not because you failed Kevin, all right?"

"Fucking miserable choice, man," Lucas said, wiping his eyes, as vulnerable as a child. "That's not the way Kevin wanted you to be at all." He turned around and stalked off then, and Jeff looked at Kimmy helplessly.

"I'm not the one who's been flirting with him when he delivers the linens," Jeff told her, and Kimmy looked after him, her expression thoughtful.

"You know," she murmured, "maybe he really *is* in it for the long haul. What do you think?"

Jeff looked up and saw that Collin had spotted them—and that he'd apparently taken another garage-bay shower and was out of his coveralls. He was still cleaning his hands with a self-consciousness that was starting to charm Jeff, because Collin probably only cleaned his hands like that so he didn't get grease on Jeff's skin.

Jeff called himself back to Kimmy for a moment. "I think that if you don't go and make him happy, I'm not going to have a date tonight." It was an evasion, because he didn't need to say the truth. Lucas was just as sturdy and just as real as Shane was. She just needed to give him a chance.

"Yeah," Kimmy murmured. "Look, I'll go talk him down, okay? Stall a minute—he was looking forward to this. He likes Martin."

She went off to talk to Lucas, and Collin was suddenly striding toward Jeff, and Jeff's heart was thrumming in his ears like tiki drums. Collin's smile was heated, possessive, and promising, and when he got close enough, he ditched the grease rag in his jeans pocket and framed Jeff's face with his hands. "Miss me today?"

Jeff would have dropped his chin, dropped his eyes, hidden from the question, much the same way he'd tried to hide himself in Kevin's shoulder in that long-ago picture, but Collin's hands wouldn't let him. "I thought of you all day," he said honestly, and was rewarded for his candor when Collin took his mouth gently, tasting a little with his tongue, and Jeff was suddenly starving, not for just a taste, but for a full-course meal.

He groaned and opened his mouth and practically issued an engraved invitation, and Collin was there, taking over, being strong and soft and *hot* and those things that Jeff had learned he could be, in spite of his youth and his cockiness, and he tasted....

Oh sweet Jebus. He tasted like sex and sweetness. For crap's sake, he tasted better than chocolate mousse, chocolate fudge, or chocolate ice cream, and odds were good he wouldn't upset Jeff's stomach either. Jeff groaned and fisted his hand in that long hair, something he'd been *yearning* to do, and pulled Collin closer.

Collin made a surprised noise, and his hands dropped from Jeff's face and were suddenly planted directly on Jeff's ass, hauling him in flush and tight. *Oh. My. God.* His erection was swollen up through his jeans and against Jeff's thigh, and it was *huge*. Jeff might have thought the car was compensation for something, but apparently not. Apparently the big-dick car was just absolutely perfect for the man who.... *Oh God... oh God....* Collin thrust up against Jeff, and Jeff realized that all the blood that had been whooshing around his head with random thoughts of clothing had just rushed to his cock and the fervent, *burning* wish not to have any clothing on whatsoever.

He was, in about two seconds, as close to coming in Collin's arms, from Collin's kiss, as he usually was after half an hour of porn, a butt plug, and some serious wanking off. (Hey, a boy had to have his hobbies.) He pulled away almost roughly, took a big gulp of air, and put his hands on Collin's hips and pushed him back a cotton-picking-out-of-the-pubes inch, then leaned his forehead on Collin's shoulder and dragged air into his lungs like a drowning man.

"Hey," Collin soothed, moving those big, capable hands to Jeff's shoulders and rubbing circles. "Hey, damn… it's okay. I won't ravish you in the parking lot. It'll be all right."

Jeff nodded against that shoulder and continued to shudder, trying to get himself under control. The raw, painful urgency faded to a bearable ache, and he relaxed against Collin's body, for just this moment, sure that the other man could bear his weight.

Collin didn't let him down. Those arms…. God, this kid worked out or something, because those arms were so strong, and so capable, and they were around his shoulders, and Jeff felt like nothing could hurt him, nothing could hurt *them*, nothing in the world at all.

Maybe, just maybe, for a little while, tonight, maybe, Jeff could concede control of the world to the gods.

Chapter *14*

Collin: Sweetheart's Chance

COLLIN was glad Jeff had backed off, because he might really have revealed his age and dropped to his knees right there in the parking lot.

Oh *Christ*, Jeff tasted good. He tasted like... like coffee, and chocolate, and, holy mother of crap, *surrender*. He tasted like hope and like shyness, two powerful flavors Collin hadn't tasted before on Jeff's tongue, and there was no force on the planet that could make Collin not crave more.

"God, Jeff, what in the fuck was that?"

"I think it was hope," Jeff muttered, "but it's been so long I can't be sure." He took a deep breath and leaned back, and Collin let him.

"I like the outfit, Jeffy," Collin said, meaning it. Jeff was wearing jeans—not too tight—and a form-fitting ribbed sweater in sort of a power forest-green. It was understated, for Jeff, and casual, and Collin thought that he'd really love to take it off of him.

Jeff's laughter had the ring of hysteria in it. "Actually, it's not the one I'd planned to wear," he said, his shoulders still twitching. He resumed his lean against the GTO. (Kimmy and Lucas must have driven it, since Shane was nowhere to be seen.)

Collin followed him and moved forward, spreading his legs a little, so that he was straddling Jeff's thighs as he leaned.

Jeff shuddered and closed his eyes and jerked a little against him. But still, he kept talking, like clothes were really fucking important. "I had this whole ensemble thing, gray slacks, gray shoes, yellow shirt, sport coat—it was fucking gorgeous," he said, earnest as all get-out. "I was going to look just fucking fabulous, right? I spent all day planning it, right down to the socks and the scarf, and then I got home, and you know what?"

Collin's mouth quirked. "You decided I'd probably wear jeans, and you didn't want to look like the princess and the grease monkey when we went out and ate?"

Jeff rolled his eyes. "As if. No. The fucking cats used the whole outfit as a scratching post. I don't know why. Seriously. It's like the fuckers went psychic *and* psycho on me, because Katy even ralphed a hairball in the shoes." Jeff shook his head mournfully. "I thought we were friends!"

Collin remembered the furry mountain that had camped out on his chest and shook his head. "You can't make friends with a force of nature, Jeff. You just have to hope it doesn't go Class Five on you and yak up a hairball in your shoes."

Jeff smiled, and Collin saw that hesitant, almost shy hope in his eyes, and there was a sudden trembling in his chest.

"They usually cooperate," Jeff mumbled. "They like our life. They like the extra brushing and the kitty bits. I don't know why they'd decide that one outfit had to go."

Collin felt the trembling grow a little stronger. "Maybe they knew I'd like this one better," he teased, and Jeff's eyes got big.

"Yeah?"

"Yeah."

"I wanted to look good for you."

"You always look good for me."

"You've been so patient."

"I'm not patient tonight," he confessed.

"Me neither. Where's Martin?"

They both looked back toward the garage just as Martin emerged, doing that same thing with the grease rag that Collin did. He looked extremely pleased with himself. "Jeff, you're gonna love it. We did everything to total spec, and Collin spun it around the block, and she handles so sweet. He tuned up the front suspension and replaced the shocks and it's like a whole new car."

Collin wanted to smack his forehead with his palm and say, "D'oh!" What the hell kind of professional was he, anyway?

But Jeff was smiling at Martin like he was pleased to hear the details. He took a step away from Collin's body, and Collin backed up and let him for propriety's sake—and then he realized that, holy God, he was trying to be *civilized* in front of another human being and wished he could find the words to tell his mother. She might faint from the shock, but overall, he thought she might be pretty proud, and dammit, hadn't she earned *that*?

"So it's good to go?" Jeff was asking, and Martin nodded excitedly.

"Jeff, this was so awesome. I mean, I can deal with school, and I get good grades and everything, but this was... it was the coolest fucking thing in the world, you know? If I could do *this* every day, the grades might be worth it!"

Jeff blinked and looked at Collin for help. Collin did his best.

"The grades are always worth it, kid, and mine sucked, so that's saying something coming from me. I'd love to help you out, tell you about the classes and the stuff you've got to take to do this for a living. No matter where you end up, I'd be happy to teach you, okay?"

Martin didn't even pause at the reminder that this setup was temporary. He just smiled widely, his narrow, dark face absolutely alight with excitement. "That's awesome. I really want to take you up on that. Hey—where's Kim and Lucas? They need to take me to dinner, because I'm *starving*."

"They're coming," Jeff said, and Collin followed his eyes to the far end of the lot. Sure enough, they were deep in quiet conversation but walking toward the cars. They were holding hands.

JEFF was highly entertaining. He talked, he told stories, he gestured wide with those long arms of his—he was a consummate conversationalist, but then, Collin already knew that. He also knew the guy had heart and pain and a whole whirlwind of *other shit* to do besides entertain Collin. But that didn't stop Collin from appreciating the conversation.

Jeff subsided for a moment when their food came, and Collin watched him dig into a beef and feta cheese salad with some gusto.

"How do you do that?" Collin asked.

Jeff stopped, poised with a forkful of beef and lettuce aimed at his mouth. "Do what?" he asked before he took a bite.

Collin shook his head. "It's just... I mean... I *know* what these last couple weeks have been like for you, right? I was there for some of it. Some of it you haven't even let me see yet, and I *know* it's rolling around in your chest. I know it hurts, I know you feel it... but you just sat there and made me laugh my ass off at a story from some poor school teacher with the world's most insane staff room. How do you do that?"

Jeff shrugged. "I was in theatre in school," he said after he swallowed his food. "I mean, I loved swim team—it made me feel free, right? But drama? Acting? Those things, they made me feel like *me*." His voice dropped thoughtfully. "Like if I could be this person who made people laugh, that was... that was the Jeff who was supposed to be here." Jeff shrugged and tried again. "It's... my parents were great. I mean, it's hard to believe it now, but they were really great. I just guess I always knew that some of what they loved about me was the face I presented to the world. I... I liked the ability to present whatever face I wanted, I guess. I liked making people laugh. If people are laughing at something I said, for a minute, they...." He trailed off, looking really embarrassed.

"They love you," Collin said softly, and Jeff picked up his fork again, shoved in a mouthful of food, and mumbled to his salad. There was an awkward pause at the table then, and a part of Collin wanted to just grab Jeff's hand and say, "*I* love you," but he wasn't sure if that wouldn't end the conversation right quick. Jeff had left him in the middle of a date once—Collin didn't think he could deal with that happening again. But he was pretty sure that it was true.

The conversation started up again when Collin told stories about his nieces, and Jeff listened and laughed. There was a moment when Jeff stopped laughing and Collin felt their knees bump under the table. Collin trapped Jeff's legs with his ankles, grinning playfully across the empty plates and the paid check, and then Jeff got that shy look, the one where he looked from under his brows and smiled like a little kid.

Collin's whole body flushed.

"Let's get out of here," he muttered, and he didn't wait for an answer before standing up and grasping Jeff by the arm, ignoring the stares and the whispers, because even in Roseville, guys did not just sweep each other off their feet in public. Jeff went without an objection or even a little bit of tension in his wiry body, though, and when they got out to the car—they'd taken Collin's—Collin whirled him around, took that narrow face in his big hands and kissed him, balls out, while Jeff melted into the Camaro in complete submission.

Collin couldn't get enough of sweet, spicy, gentle Jeff. His hands came to Collin's biceps and gripped tightly, and he thrust his hips up against Collin's groin shamelessly, begging with everything from his pliancy to the little whimpers coming from his throat. They pulled back and Collin moved his hands up from Jeff's face to his hair, running fingers through the gel in it, massaging and rubbing and planting little fluttery kisses on Jeff's face, on his eyelids, on his cheeks, on the end of his nose, until Jeff was simply standing patiently, face up, his hair that amazing, unruly mess that Collin knew it could be, and his body was hard against Collin's in the right place and pliant in all of the right places too.

And Collin was still breathless, still trembling and urgent, when he placed a gentle kiss on Jeff's forehead and whispered, "Do you want to see my apartment now?"

"Do I have to do the walk of shame in front of your mother?"

"I have stairs—she'll never know you're there."

"God, that's kinky," Jeff half laughed, and Collin kissed him again until he was silent.

"I don't want kink," he said when the kiss was done. "I want you, Jeff, just you, honest and naked and in my bed. Can you handle that?"

Jeff looked away. "The honest thing isn't really…."

Collin nuzzled his cheek and then kissed softly down to the corner of his mouth, then captured his lower lip and pulled, suckling and teasing it with his tongue.

He let go and said, "You can do the honest thing, Jeff. I've got faith."

"Mmm… but—" and then Collin kissed him senseless again.

This time when he pulled away, Jeff said, "Yeah. Yes. Okay…." He bucked his hips against Collin's. "I'll do whatever you want, Sparky, just… don't leave me." He let that hang there for a moment and then realized what he'd said, and Collin watched his Adam's apple bob as he tried to fix it. "Like this," he muttered, thrusting his covered erection against Collin's thigh. "I meant—"

"I know exactly what you meant," Collin murmured. "Get in the car, Jeffy. I'm taking you home."

Things were quiet for the first few minutes in the car, and then Collin spoke up, feeling both young and old. "Jeffy, do you have your meds for tonight?"

"Yeah—don't you carry yours?"

It was true; Collin always had at least his next two doses in a little container in his pocket—for nights almost exactly like the one in which he ended up on Jeff's couch. The regimen didn't work well if it was interrupted, and the consequences of taking a double dose... he shuddered. "Good. Do you work tomorrow?"

"No. Hardly anyone comes in the two days before Thanksgiving anyway." Collin sensed Jeff's sideways look, as though he knew where Collin was going with this but wasn't going to volunteer.

"Do you want to call Kim and ask if she can stay the night with Martin?"

Jeff's flush was hot enough for Collin to feel, even in the seat next to him. "Uhm, we'll see."

Collin took a deep breath, knowing Jeff didn't mean to hurt. He reached across the seat and grabbed Jeff's hand. "Call her, Jeff. It will be good, I promise. You'll want to stay."

"You have so much faith," Jeff confessed shakily. "I don't remember what it's like to have that much faith."

Collin brought Jeff's hand to his mouth and brushed the knuckles with his lips. "I have faith in you, Jeff. That's all I need."

COLLIN tried to look at his garage apartment from Jeff's eyes, but he was just so proud of it, he couldn't. It had been his first project, after the shop had started paying off. He'd gotten the rezoning done for the extra plumbing and heating, and although he'd hired a construction crew, he'd also gotten in there and done some of the work himself. The stairs were steady and secure, and the room itself... well, he'd put it together with the idea that he wanted someplace that made him feel welcome. It had been only two years after high school, and the loss of all his friends still stung, and he'd wanted to walk into his own apartment and feel like he belonged.

Jeff smiled when he walked in. "The only thing it's missing is cats," he said with appreciation, and Collin groaned.

"No," he said decisively. "I'm perfectly happy lusting after men, but I'm *not* going to learn to knit and get me some cats. Those are your specialties, Jeff—you've got a corner on the market."

"Well, know your strengths." Jeff arched his brows wickedly as he ran his hands over the sofa and the love seat in the living space section of the apartment, and Collin chuckled.

"I've got some dessert, if you like," Collin said shyly. He'd bought some bananas and whipped cream. With a couple of mashed graham crackers, they had something tasty that would *not* rip up his stomach the way chocolate, his favorite, had been doing.

Jeff looked up hopefully. "Chocolate?"

Well, hell. "No, I'm sorry. It's been really fucking with my stomach lately."

"Yeah, mine too. I'll take what you've got," he said, and Collin realized that his face must have fallen, "but you know. I was just thinking that if I'm doing things that are bad for me, I might as well go all the way."

Collin was in the process of taking the bananas from the bowl on the counter and then reaching into the fridge for the heavy cream when the full import of what Jeff had just said seeped in. He looked up wryly. "You know, Jeff, maybe you'll have to settle for something that's both tasty *and* good for you, you think?"

Jeff's grin split his face. "God you're easy. Sure, I'll taste your banana!"

And Collin groaned, both from the pun, which he let Jeff see, and from relief, because Jeff wasn't looking anxious anymore.

He had the dessert going in short order, and Jeff came and leaned on the counter, watching him with a faint smile on his face.

"You're good in the kitchen, you know."

"You talk like someone who knows," Collin said easily, and Jeff shrugged.

"I like to cook—I like to make it fancy. It's not perfect, but it's not tater-tot casserole either."

Collin laughed and sprinkled some cinnamon on the little fruit sundae he'd just made, then put a fork on the plate and gave Jeff his. "Nothing wrong with tater-tot casserole," he said mildly. "My mom raised us on the stuff. Here, set this down, hang your jacket on the peg, and let's take this into the living room."

They sat on the couch, close enough that their thighs touched and their calves tangled, and ate the bananas slowly, savoring the details, and they talked. Maybe it was that it was just the two of them, and maybe it was the quiet intimacy of their position, but Collin noticed that Jeff's voice wasn't quite as loud, and he didn't trill quite as much. He kept his expressive hands contained, but he wielded his fork unconsciously like an extension of them, even when he was licking the whipped cream off with his eyes closed and little sighs in between bites.

There was a silence then, and Collin watched him finish the next to the last bite with quiet appreciation.

"Good?" he asked, belatedly, and Jeff nodded.

"You know, I try to enjoy small stuff. I forgot about bananas and whipped cream, but you forget sometimes. And then, you get your diagnosis, and you can't even sneeze over cat dander without that—"

"Fear," Collin said softly.

"Yeah. No reason for it at all—I mean, I'm a medical professional, right? But I can't get a hangnail without flashing over my entire course of treatment if it suddenly goes septic or something."

"It makes you feel in control," Collin murmured. He still wanted Jeff in his bed, maybe more than ever, but this subject, the big Plus Sign in their bodies—it needed to be addressed.

Jeff nodded. "Which is funny, because life is a big spiraling, out-of-control mess, right? Just look at Deacon."

"How's he doing?"

Collin actually felt Jeff shrink in a little on himself. "Not good," he said softly. "I know why he was putting off surgery, right? Because he wanted Benny to have a full semester at least, away at school, but I don't think he's going to be able to make that happen."

Collin very carefully took the plate out of Jeff's hand and set it on the coffee table with his own. Then he toed off his shoes and propped his feet up in his black socks, because it was his house and he wanted Jeff to know he could do that too.

Then he leaned back and put an arm around Jeff's shoulders that was all comfort and no demand, and Jeff relaxed back into it a fraction and sighed.

"I'm sorry about your family, Jeffy," Collin said softly, and kissed Jeff's temple. Jeff leaned into that too.

"Thank you, Collin. For such a fucked-up kid, you sure did win the grown-up race, you know that?"

"Yeah, well, I had some help," Collin told him honestly. "A really nice guy shared some time with me when I was at my low point, and I managed to pull through."

Jeff shook his head. "No, sweetheart. You had your mom going for you. You would have been okay."

Collin kissed his temple again and feathered his lips down to Jeff's cheekbone. Jeff tilted his head and let him.

"You were important," Collin insisted, and Jeff blew out a laugh— and then shivered a little as Collin traced soft lips over his jaw.

"I was so screwed up," Jeff confessed. "I'd been alone for so long, and I'd gotten *really* narcissistic, you know?"

Collin puffed a gentle laugh in Jeff's ear, enjoyed watching Jeff's knees fall apart a little and hearing the soft little sound that came from his throat. Ooooh... that sound really *was* sexy, and Collin's body went from "sleepily aroused" to "alert" very quickly.

"I never would have guessed," he said dryly, and then he touched his tongue to Jeff's earlobe.

Jeff shuddered and then kept talking, like maybe he had to talk about this before they progressed any further. "And then there was Kevin, and then the diagnosis, and Kevin's death and...." Jeff shuddered, and Collin's arm around his shoulders tightened.

"Why are you telling me all this, Jeffy?" Collin breathed, this time touching his lips to that fine column of Jeff's neck.

"Because," Jeff moaned, seeming to melt into the couch. "Because I'm not a hero, and I haven't done this in nearly six years."

Collin blinked and pulled back. "Six years?"

"Yeah, that gets people's attention," Jeff muttered, turning away.

Collin seized his chin and pulled him back around. "You were my hero because you took time off to talk to a scared kid," he said, meaning it. "You're still my hero because you're stronger than I think I could be, when the world really does seem to be out to get you. And I don't know what to say about the six years, except... *dayum.*" He was relieved when

Jeff smiled a little. "Don't you think you're due to hit that reset button, Jeff?"

Jeff's eyes were wide and dark, and his lean mouth was open, soft, and vulnerable. "Yeah, Sparky, you're right," he whispered. "I think it's time to hit that reset button." And then he leaned forward and initiated a kiss.

Collin was so surprised, he opened his mouth almost automatically, and Jeff's tongue darted in, tasting, experimenting, and mostly teasing Collin until he couldn't take it anymore and had to take over.

Jeff let him.

Oh God, he was *fabulous*. He was bananas and whipped cream and acerbic kindness, and *Jeff*. Collin couldn't stop kissing him, not for a minute, not for a million dollars, not for the world. Jeff moaned, tilted his head back, and pulled Collin closer, palming Collin's chest with his long-fingered hands.

And the kiss went on.

Collin didn't confine it to Jeff's mouth or the hesitant softness of his lips but kissed his stubborn chin and the sides of his narrow nose, his forehead, his temples, the lobes of his ears. If Jeff hadn't done this for years, Collin wanted this to be the kiss to end all kisses, wanted to tease his lips until they ached, wanted him to yearn so hard for Collin's hands on his body that he literally creamed in his jeans.

Collin wanted him to *want* this, hunger for it with everything in him. Collin wanted them so close that there wasn't room for clothes, or sweat, or dead boyfriends, or regrets.

He backed Jeff down into the softness of the sofa, and Jeff went, pliant and willing, and Collin had to pull away for a moment to breathe past the lump in his throat. Surrender meant surrender, apparently—if Jeff didn't trust him, Jeff wouldn't be here, in Collin's home, in his arms, or laying flat on the couch, gasping for air.

"Second thoughts, Sparky?" Jeff panted, and Collin shook his head, even while his face was buried in Jeff's neck.

"Never," he breathed. "Just appreciating the moment."

Jeff's hands were suddenly in his hair, pushing it back from his eyes and framing his face. Collin lifted up a little and met his eyes in the low light from the kitchen.

"I appreciate it too," Jeff murmured, and Collin decided that too much time had gone by without touching that lean mouth.

"Let's appreciate this in bed," Collin muttered between kisses. "Come on, baby."

Jeff pulled back and pouted a little. "Baby? I'm nine years your senior, Sparky—"

"You're my baby," Collin purred, and then he stood up and offered Jeff a hand off the couch, singing The Ronettes' song, "'Be my, be my baby... my one, and only baby... be my, be my baby....'."

Jeff scowled at him, and Collin grinned, still singing, before bending down and physically *taking* his hand, pulling him up off the couch with a grunt and taking his hands into a classic dance position. Still singing that song, he took the lead and began to waltz Jeff through his living space and back to the queen-size bed in the corner by the window.

Surprisingly enough, after some exasperated glances, Jeff's mouth quirked up, and he began to sing too. Step by step, they danced, backed around, until they bumped up against the bed. Jeff eyed it and licked his lips, and Collin knew what he was thinking.

There was a pause, fraught with tension, and Collin started to sing with a throaty baritone. "'Can't you hear me crying... can't you hear me crying...'."

Jeff smiled a little, but his face was still sober. "Can you?" he asked, and Collin closed his eyes for a minute.

"With every touch. Will you let me make it better?"

In answer, Jeff cupped his face and pulled him down for a kiss. Collin took over, being strong, being in charge—it was why he owned his own business; it was why his whole life had improved once he'd had the power to choose his course. It was how he'd dreamed of taking Jeff for years, showing the kind man who had given him hope how much of a man hope had made him.

Jeff groaned, and when Collin lowered his hands to Jeff's waistband, he didn't protest when Collin bunched the sweater in his fists and pulled it up under Jeff's armpits. Without being asked, Jeff raised his hands over his head, and Collin lifted the bunched material up his arms, pulled it over his head and off, capturing Jeff's fists and then holding those long, strong arms together for a moment before he ran his cupped hands down their length, firmly, so he didn't tickle the undersides, and then down the sides of Jeff's chest, teasing the pink (shell pink, as delicate as a girl's) nipples with his thumbs.

Jeff gasped and lowered his hands to Collin's shoulders to steady himself, and Collin captured the gasp with another kiss. His hands spanned Jeff's narrow waist, and he felt the tight abdominal muscles and the soft skin on the sides. Jeff sucked in that tight stomach when Collin reached the waistband of his jeans, and Collin slipped his thumbs down the front, following the slight trail of soft black hair.

Jeff's cock was poking up, and the waistband of the pants was more of a hip-band, and Collin dipped his thumbs deliberately under it.

The whimper Jeff made when Collin brushed his cock through silk underwear made Collin's knees a little weak.

Without another word, Collin undid the button-fly and shoved the jeans down Jeff's hips, leaving him to do the rest while he took off his own clothes. He pulled his own sweater off over his head and was arrested, then, by Jeff's hands on his belt.

He looked down and saw Jeff working his plain leather belt patiently. When Collin's pants were sliding down his thighs, he stopped for a moment and placed a reverent kiss on Collin's bare hipbone. Collin caught his breath, and Jeff planted another one, a little lower, and then another one toward the center, and another, and another, and then he was holding Collin's cock in one slightly chilled hand and rubbing his cheek on Collin's lower abdomen with a delicacy and a wistfulness that made Collin's chest hurt.

Collin rested his hands in Jeff's hair for a moment, massaging gently. It still stuck out in every direction, but with the gel all worked out of it, it was soooo soft. Jeff kept rubbing his cheek on the soft skin and silky hair of Collin's lower stomach. His shoulders trembled until Collin kicked off his jeans and socks and bent down over him, taking his mouth again, kissing away the quivers, the tentative moment of becoming lovers, and every doubt he was sure Jeff had about letting another person in.

Jeff fell back against the brown-orange comforter, closed his big sweetheart eyes, and gave in. Collin kept kissing him and started running his hands from his shoulders to his thighs, exploring, touching, arousing, inflaming, until Jeff's breath was coming in fast little gasps and he was arching uncontrollably into Collin's touch.

God, Collin wanted him. Wanted to take, thrust, fuck... but this wasn't really about what Collin wanted, was it?

Gently, even though Jeff's body was covered with stringy layers of gym muscle, Collin lowered his body until they were pressed together, full-on chest to hip, thighs against thighs, and simply touched him, enveloping as much skin as he possibly could. Six years... six years, Jeff had been without the full-body contact of a lover. The responsibility was almost terrifying, but Collin had never backed down from a challenge.

Jeff sighed and shuddered and wrapped his arms around Collin's shoulders and pressed closer. Their groins were rubbing together, their cocks touching randomly because that wasn't the focus of their rhythm, but after Jeff whimpered—so sexy!—and bucked against him, Collin knew that things were getting urgent. Six years—it wasn't going to take much, not the first time, and Collin wanted it to be all about the touch.

He reached to his end table and pulled out the lubricant and a poly glove, but left the condom inside. There wasn't going to be any penetration here, no exposed tissues, just orgasm and whole skin, and for a moment, they could mark each other like any other lovers, could forget the *no*s and give into the *yes*es, enjoy the bananas and whipped cream when the chocolate could hurt them.

Jeff whimpered again, gasped his name, tried to wrap a leg around his hip and force their bodies to grind, but Collin didn't let him. He covered his battered, scraped knuckles and dumped lubricant on the glove instead and slid between their bodies, pivoting his hip to one side and grasping both of their cocks in his wide-palmed, long-fingered hand. Jeff let out a long, keening gasp, and Collin could feel Jeff's prick, the soft-skinned, hard length, up against his, intimate, pleasurable, and so, so good. He stroked firmly and let Jeff thrust to keep the timing right, and stroked and stroked, feeling the flare of Jeff's cockhead catch against the flare of his own.

Jeff started to gibber, "Collin, God, can't... can't... oh God... please, God, Collin... gotta...."

Collin kissed his temple, the corner of his mouth, his chin, and still kept thrusting, still kept stroking, using Jeff's pre-come as more lubricant, remembering to skate his thumb on the flat skin of their heads. "Come on, Jeffy, come on...."

Jeff's eyes closed tightly, and his whole body jerked under Collin's, and his come splashed, scalding, between them. It was hot in Collin's fist as he stroked, still holding their bodies together as Jeff's balls emptied, and it coated him, slicked him, and he buried his face in Jeff's neck, howling as he climaxed.

Jeff stroked his hair as he drifted down from his climax, and Collin laughed in exultation, their bodies rocking together, marking each other with lovemaking. He felt Jeff's kiss on his ear, his cheek, and he turned his head enough to capture his mouth in a sweet kiss.

"God!" Jeff muttered after the kiss had ended and they rested, forehead to forehead. "How could I possibly have lived without that?"

"Easy," Collin said, still laughing. "You were waiting for me."

"It was worth it."

Collin had to kiss him again. He had to, more than breathing, he had to kiss him again.

"Yeah, Jeffy. So totally was."

THEY never did get to the condoms, but they did have to shower, one at a time, in Collin's little cubicle, twice.

Collin loved penetrative sex, and he loved making someone come with his mouth—he did—but right now, this first time, he didn't want anything between them, not even the thing that would keep them both safe from another strain of HIV. It was almost like being back in middle school, before he knew what the hell his pecker was supposed to be doing. In a way, that had been some of the best sex of his life—it had been breathless, sensitized, exciting sex, even if it had just been his hand down Mark Kittredge's pants and Mark moaning, "Ohmigod, ohmigod, ohmigod" over and over again.

That was the same thing with Jeff, except it was Collin, thinking "Ohmigod, ohmigod, ohmigod, ohmigod, ohmigod," right up until they came.

And in the end, the final best part was the part that Collin hadn't even cared about until he'd grown and learned to appreciate it.

In the end, the part he loved the most was after their second shower, when Jeff went to put his pants on. Collin let him put his silk boxers on because Collin had put his cotton boxers on (having your junk flop around could be really uncomfortable sometimes), but he stopped Jeff from putting his jeans on.

"Kimmy's got it all under control," he said softly, reaching out his hand to stop Jeff from getting dressed. "Stay."

Jeff took a few breaths, just looking at him. Jeff's neck was red, and so were his lips, from being kissed and nibbled and sucked on. His cheeks were flushed, and his eyes were bright and lazily hooded, as though he was relaxed, truly relaxed, for the first time since Collin had ever known him.

"Stay?"

"Yeah, Jeff. Come on." Collin slid under the comforter and opened it up, inviting Jeff to come in and spoon. "Stay."

And Jeff did. Collin reached above him and turned off the lamp at the headboard, and Jeff slid in next to him, smooth, silky from the shower, and softly skinned and warm with hairy legs and a smooth chest and sweet, sweet trust that Collin would wrap a strong arm around his chest and keep him safe from everything, everything bad in the world.

Collin did his best.

Chapter *15*

Deacon: Homecomings, Heartbreaks, and Hospitals

JEFF brought Martin with him on Wednesday night, when he brought dinner. Deacon was supremely grateful for the dinners—he'd told people so, and it had been hard for him, because it felt like such a compromise in pride not to be able to do something simple like cook for his family, especially when Crick and Andrew (and the kids from Promise House) were doing all of the real work.

It was just so hard to move.

Every five steps involved a big gasp of air; every time he lifted himself up to walk, he had to get up carefully because of the ache in his shoulder; every trip to the bathroom was like an Olympic event. His most practical use was to entertain Parry Angel, but walking outside to play with her took a tab of nitro and a nap. He'd once thought failure was his worst nightmare, but he was starting to rethink that. Alcoholism was horrible, and it had taken more will power than he cared to admit to decide to never drink again, but this? This was completely outside his control. This was his body betraying him, in the prime of his fucking life, and it wasn't fair.

God, Crick deserved someone who could make love to him every night.

The doctors were making promises, though, and Deacon had learned to live on hope back when Crick had been in Iraq. Hope was what he talked to Crick, hope was what he fed Benny over the computer, and hope was what he sang to Parry Angel every night. His family fed them food and Deacon fed them hope—it was all he had.

So when Jeff came to sit by him and Jon as Amy took over the kitchen for the night before Thanksgiving (which he was starting to understand was equally as important as the big day itself) he wanted to give Jeff some of his favorite dish.

It helped that Amy had recovered from her worry and her grief somewhat, since the night he'd made his announcement and was her spunky little self again.

"So, Jeff, you bring me all this food and then think you can take over the kitchen?"

"Amy, darling, Martin and I just—"

"Yeah, yeah, yeah... I don't care. Your stuff will get served in about an hour, and I'm going to decide what to do with the rest of this, because I think we may need to use Shane's refrigerator *and* my refrigerator to house all of this! My God, boyfriend, how many people do you think are going to be here? I cooked too!"

"Fourteen," Jeff said dryly. "Fourteen people are going to be here."

"What about Collin?" she asked sharply, and the disappointment in Jeff's voice was obvious.

"He's got his own family."

"Did you invite him over for dessert?"

"No, but—"

"But what in the hell, Jeff. Get on the phone!"

"Amy, he's got—"

"Now!"

"Okay, okay, okay!"

Deacon smiled a little as he continued to read Parry Angel her story. All was quiet for a minute while Jeff went into the mudroom with his cell phone and then came out scowling—but looking excited anyway.

"He's coming—"

"Over the phone? You're good!"

"You are so not funny!"

"I'm fu-ricking hysterical. Now get the hell out of my kitchen!"

Deacon chuckled for real then, even though it meant he had to stop and catch his breath, and Jeff flounced in and sat on the far end of the couch with his arms crossed and his eyes in the attitude position.

"So he'll be here for dessert," Deacon ventured when Parry's story was finished. "Parry, you want to go get your baby dolls out here? Uncle Jeffy will help you bring the furniture, and you can play."

Uncle Jeffy smiled immediately and disappeared, coming back with an armload of assorted dolls and rocking chairs and tables and things, and the little girl commenced a secret ritual of her own in the setting-up.

"Is Lila still asleep?" Deacon asked, and Jeff nodded, toeing off his loafers and turning in the corner of the couch so he sat facing Deacon, his knees up to his chest.

"Yeah, I never would have known she was there," Jeff said with a sigh. "We'll have to wake her up before dinner."

"Better waking Lila than pissing off Amy. Jesus, Jeff—you cooked like you don't have any faith in the woman."

Jeff blushed. "Sorry, Deacon. It's just that Martin was sort of homesick, so we started looking into recipes and how many things we could make that were like the cooking in Georgia." Jeff sighed then and looked a little guiltily at Deacon. "Amy needed to cook anyway, Deacon. You can't eat half the shit we brought—it'll kill you at first bite."

And for some reason *that* seemed funny too.

"Maybe offer to take it to Promise House. Shane's family is going to eat there at one and then be here by three. A little home-cooked and some leftovers wouldn't hurt."

Jeff perked up. "Good idea—Martin will like that too."

"So," breath "how's that going?"

Jeff stopped and looked at him, really looked at him. "It's going great, actually. The kid's been raised right, just like Kevin. He... he just wanted to know about his brother, you know?"

Deacon shifted on the couch to give his ribcage more room to expand. "So what have you told him?"

Jeff shook his head. "Nothing. He just... just keeps asking me questions about... well, really, being gay. 'Do all gay men wave their hands so much? How come Collin doesn't use herbal shampoo? If

Deacon and Jon are such good friends, why didn't Deacon turn Jon gay?'."

Deacon made a sound on that last one that he was sure wasn't good for him, and Jeff made the same sound.

"Yeah, I know—he's tactless and he's invasive, but… it's like he doesn't mean any harm by it, you know?"

"It's just his way," breathe "to figure out if his brother was still his brother," Deacon told him. "He figures if he can get a handle on what 'gay' is, he'll have a handle on Kevin."

"I know, I know." Jeff's face fell a little, and it wasn't hard for Deacon to read between the lines.

"You wanted to talk about Kevin," he said softly, and Jeff nodded.

"Having Martin in the house is as close as I'll ever get," he said softly.

"Well," Deacon said, trying hard to make the pause sound like deliberation, "what do you know now that you didn't know before?"

Jeff laughed a little. "I know arrogance is a family trait, that's what I know!"

Deacon smiled too. "And…?"

"And I know that they were raised to be good Christian boys. They went to church every Sunday, just like I did, and as soon as Martin starts getting hit on, he's going to be screwing everything with an X-chromosome, same as Kevin did with the Ys."

Deacon did laugh then, and it was a breathy, thin sound.

"I learned that I was lucky," Jeff finished softly. "Really, really lucky."

"But not dead yet," Deacon interjected, and Jeff blushed. Crick entered the doorway at that moment, and Deacon looked up and smiled at him. Crick didn't smile back, not even to make Deacon feel better.

"Who told?" Jeff was asking, and Deacon turned his attention back to maybe the most lost person in his little family. If Jeff was opening up, that was a reason to focus.

"Who didn't?"

"Yeah, yeah—I asked Kimmy to babysit, I might as well have taken an ad out in the paper or had a banner run across the news."

"Hey," Crick said, finally walking into the room and joining the conversation, "if the news actually ran a banner screaming 'Jeffy got laid!' I might finally watch the damned news!"

"It would do you good," Jeff snorted. "Where's Benny?"

Crick had gone to pick her up from the airport, and now he rolled his eyes and smiled wickedly. "Andrew was right there to help her with her bags. Want to see?"

Jeff made big eyes. "Oooh… other people's love lives—that's even better than television!" and hopped up to go out on the porch.

Crick came over to Deacon and offered his good hand to help him up. Deacon took a deep breath and gave his hand up, allowing Crick to help him from the stuffed chair, for sweet heaven's sake. Crick was about to put his hand under Deacon's elbow, but a fulminating glance from Deacon stopped him.

"I'm not dead yet," he ground out, and Crick shook his head.

"Your lips are blue. When was the last time you took your nitro?"

"An hour ago," Deacon admitted, and Crick hissed out a breath. He wasn't supposed to take the nitro more than once every two hours.

"Man, your color is the south side of shitty. How you doing?"

"Not so bad I don't want to see Benny and Andrew," Deacon evaded mildly, and Crick grimaced at him, not fooled for a minute.

It didn't matter—they were all on the porch now, even Parry Angel, who had toddled out with Jeff, and lined up just in time to see Benny set her luggage down as Andrew clicked the trunk of Crick's sedan shut.

"You miss me at all, Drew?" Benny asked, her teasing voice floating up to them under an early evening sky of velvet-black. All the men on the porch caught their breath. Miss her? Of course he'd missed her. Every time he'd come up the porch steps, they'd seen his face fall when he remembered she wouldn't be there. Every time he'd played with her daughter, they'd caught the wistfulness when he saw the shape of Parry's nose or of her eyes and realized she was the spitting image of her mother. He'd hidden it well—he'd chatted on the phone with her about everyday things like horses and what Parry Angel had said that day, and probably thought none of the people who came to The Pulpit noticed, but Andrew missed Crick's little sister with the same heartache and intensity with which Deacon had missed Crick.

The only difference was Benny's life hadn't been at risk. That, and Andrew had the family to talk to, every minute of every day.

"Did I miss you?" Andrew asked, rubbing his hand absently on the wiry black curls buzzed close to his scalp. "Not so's you'd notice."

The three men at the banister all held in a collective smirk, and Deacon hoped Andrew would get this kiss going before Parry noticed that her mama was out there, or his chance would be gone for good.

"No?" Benny said, hiding a smirk of her own. "That's too bad. I missed you every fucking minute of every fucking—mmmm…."

They waited for the shock to wear off as Andrew took her chin in his hand and met her lips with his, and then they waited until she wrapped her arms around his shoulders and started to respond breathlessly. Then they watched as Jeff waved his fingers in the air with a one, and a two, and a three—

"Awwwwwww," they all said collectively, and then burst out laughing when the only change in the attitude of Benny and Andrew's first kiss was Benny's carefully extended middle finger. Deacon's jaw, which had been tight and sore while he was waiting for Benny to get home, relaxed fractionally, and the pain that radiated down through his arm eased up.

The kiss lasted, of course, until Parry Angel suddenly realized who was being kissed by her favorite Drew.

"*Mommeeeeeee!*" she squealed, and Benny broke away from Drew so fast he was left stumbling forward so she could run up the porch and sweep her ecstatic little girl in her arms.

DEACON felt better after that—maybe it was the night air, or the happiness at seeing Benny again. Benny was, well, Benny. She filled the house with joy because she lived there, and her knitting immediately took up a bag in the corner, and her voice, her quick, lively chatter, her profanity—which she tried to tame now, so Parry Angel didn't pick up on it—and the way she cared about everybody, openly and officiously and without apology. For much of her life she'd endured in a single bedroom with her sisters, a brutal alcoholic for a father, a weak enabler for a mother, and a brother who worked his ass off to give her anything he could manage.

Once she came to live with Deacon and the people around her loved her unconditionally, she responded with so much affection that she lit the world.

Benny and Crick were the reasons Deacon had faith in people.

Crick helped Deacon back to his chair and got Benny's luggage situated, coming back into the living room from the hallway in full holler. "Benny, isn't that all the shit we sent with you, minus the furniture?"

"Yeah, genius—I've set it up with my professors that I only have to go back for finals. I figure maybe I can hit up Mikhail to use his van, since the performance season is over, and drive down one day to take my finals and get the furniture, and then I'm done. Off that campus and the hell out of LA for the rest of my natural life."

Benny came in with her baby on her hip and a soda in the other hand and enough casual attitude to remind Deacon that she'd grown up a lot in the three and a half years since he'd taken her in as a runaway.

"Benny," Deacon muttered, "that's not what we discussed!"

"Yeah," Benny said, coming to sit on the couch near him. "I know it's not what we discussed. But it's what I want."

He realized that he'd been holding an impromptu court all day, because everyone from Jon to Benny had come to sit by him instead of making him go to them. He was grateful—damned grateful—but at the same time he was suddenly so furious that he felt his cheeks grow red and his jaw ached from clenching. Dammit. God-fucking-dammit. He hadn't meant to make them all work like this. He was the strong one—even when he'd been his weakest, he'd been the one taking care of Benny, of Parry, sending care packages to Crick. He was the one who beat up Kimmy's scumbag ex-boyfriend and talked a skittish Mikhail in from the cold. It was his only way to give back to them, and now… now he was reduced to an old man in the corner, struggling to find breath for words.

"Benny, you were only supposed to come home early this semester—"

"And I hate it there, Deacon. I know you want what's best for me, right?"

Deacon sighed. "Always, Shorty."

"What's best for me is here. I miss my baby, pure and simple, but it's more than that. All those big dreams I had, all that confidence to go and just knock the world on its ass?"

"Yeah?"

"I got that from here. And I just spent three and a half months thinking that I needed all that family to be that girl, okay?"

God, he was so weak. "We wanted you—"

"Yeah. So did I. But I just got this family, Deacon, and now you're sick, and now I know how damned easy it is to have my family yanked away from me. Don't make me leave it now, please?"

Her hair was brown. Her real, actual, color, just like Crick's color but lighter, brown, and not blond or orange or pink. It was cut short and frowzy around her eyes, making her small, heart-shaped face look gamine and appealing and her blue eyes look enormous, and he had to swallow against how much they had all missed her.

"Parry missed you so bad," he said, and it was true. The little girl was still snuggled up into her mother's arms, her hands clenched tight and her little face buried in Benny's neck.

"What about you, Deacon?" she asked gently, and he had to look away.

"Well, Shortness, you do sort of brighten up the place," he said, not wanting to tear up, because *God*, had he missed her.

Benny was suddenly on her knees in front of him with her head on his lap, and he was stroking her pixie-cut hair back from her face like he had when they'd first become roommates, two lost souls running away from their fear for Crick and their loneliness in general.

"I knew you missed me," she said into his thigh, and he laughed a little.

"Yeah, well, I get attached easily," he said playfully, and she turned a tear-stained face up to him, because she cried at the drop of a hat, and smiled, even as she clutched Parry to her.

"I'm so glad you do," she said earnestly. "God, Deacon, you look like shit. You were supposed to stay healthy for us, you know that?"

"What can I say?" he asked rhetorically, trying to swallow past his tight jaw. "I'm contrary that way."

As it turned out, the night before Thanksgiving was actually livelier than the real thing usually was. Shane and Mikhail stopped by to pick up the extra food that Jeff had brought, and they stayed to eat some early pie and some of the dinner too. Kimmy and Lucas were still at Promise House, but Martin asked Shane a sly question about his sister, and Shane replied with a smug smile.

"No, no, no sleepovers yet, you nosy little snot, but, well, she's giving him the time of day, and that's an improvement."

Deacon was glad—he was glad for all of them, because even Jeff, who had seemed so damned lost, looked like he might actually be found, and that was an improvement. He popped his sore jaw and smiled. He wanted his family to be happy.

Crick and Andrew had needed to go out and feed the horses while everyone was gathered, and Deacon missed Crick as soon as he walked out. Crick must have said something to Jon, though, because Jon walked him over a slice of pie, away from the crowd in the kitchen. It was then that Deacon realized that he hadn't even made it to the table this night. It was crowded and chaotic, and usually he made everyone sit down, but his arm hurt, and his breath was short, and he was so very sleepy.

"Deacon, you want some?"

Deacon shook his head. He had, in fact, been a little bit queasy all day. "No, not hungry. But sit down for a minute—you look worried."

"I'm worried about you, you dumbass. Man, I know you were waiting for Benny to get home before you had that procedure, but she's home. She's home to stay. You think you can call the doc tonight and ask to move up the date a little?"

"Crick ask you to ask me that?" Deacon put two and two together, and Jon nodded.

"He was having a hard time not freaking out, and he didn't want to freak you out—seems that's a bad thing to do when someone's got a heart condition."

"Crick"—breathe, swallow, will that jaw to loosen—"worries too much."

"Yeah, well now you've got the rest of us worried too. So how about we call that doctor now, so you can talk to him, and maybe we don't have to call an ambulance later when you can't."

Deacon nodded dumbly, realizing that was probably exactly what needed to be done. "Yeah," he said softly, and Jon gave a strangled little sob and collapsed on the couch, like everyone had been doing.

"Thank God. I'll take you to the other room, but I want you to call him now."

Deacon scowled at Jon. "Man, don't you have to cook? We've got a house full of people who—"

"Look—you comforted Benny, checked in on Jeff, but I'm watching you, man. You can hardly meet Crick's eyes, and that means you're feeling guilty about something, and something is usually your health. He's going quietly insane, can't you see it? Look, I'll just walk you into the bedroom and dial the phone, okay? Can we do that? Please? Deacon, if twenty-five years of friendship means any fucking thing to you, can we do that for me?"

"Yeah," Deacon said, feeling like his voice was from far away, "but Jon, could you do me a favor and help me up? Nothing seems to be working right."

He ended up calling the doctor from the flat of his back, lying on the bed that he and Crick had been sharing for coming up on two years. He reckoned that about everything he loved was in this room, from the colors Crick had chosen, to the picture Crick had drawn them for their picnic-cum-wedding and the framed prints of the art Crick had painted in Europe, to, most times, Crick himself.

The doctor—and Lord, how Deacon wished he could go to Crick and Jeff's doctor, because Doc Herbert, as Jeff called him, seemed so accessible compared to this yahoo—listened to Deacon try to gasp out an explanation and then said the first sensible thing Deacon had heard all day.

"Mr. Winters, I need you to do me a favor and give the phone to someone else, okay?"

"Yeah, whatever. Jon, he wants to talk to you, or maybe Crick, but probably you, since Crick's out feeding the horses."

Jon ran his hand through his pretty, pretty movie-star hair and picked up the phone, shaking in agitation. "Yeah, Doctor Mackey, I'm his friend. No, not his husband, his friend—what do you need to know?"

Suddenly Jon was touching Deacon's neck and looking at his watch and then spouting a number into the phone, and then he was saying, "Yeah, Doc—I'll get him packed and get Crick ready. Crick's going to be a total basket case."

"Yeah," Deacon mumbled. "He gets excited about shit. What did the doctor say?"

Jon swore and wiped his eyes with the back of his hand. "The doctor said you've been having a heart attack all day, you dumbass. He's sending an ambulance, and Crick's riding with you, and the rest of us will hold down the fort and then come to the hospital and worry. You're doing this procedure as soon as you're stabilized, and then, when you're all nice and recovered, I'm gonna rip you a sweet and shiny new asshole, because this is the second time in our lives you've scared the shit out of me, and I don't forgive easy!"

While he was talking, he grabbed a duffel bag from under the bed and started shoving drawers open and throwing pajamas and underwear and Deacon's shaving kit into it without a lot of consideration for the objects themselves. When he was done, he suddenly loomed up over Deacon, and he looked so miserable.

"Pretty speech," Deacon said. "Did you practice that?"

"Shut up, asshole," Jon sniffed. "I'm going to go scare the shit out of Crick now. You go anywhere while I'm gone, and I'll fucking kill you."

He disappeared for a minute, and then Crick was there, sitting next to the bed, holding his hand, and Deacon smiled. Crick. All he'd ever wanted since that one magical day in April had been Crick.

"You look like hell, Carrick James."

"You're the one going in the big bus, Deacon."

"You're coming with me, right?" His voice trembled, warbled, and he was embarrassed. He wasn't really as scared as he sounded.

Crick's wide, capable hand surrounded his, and Crick leaned over and kissed his cheek. "There's not a place on the planet I'd rather be," he said softly.

Things got confused after that, but he remembered Crick was there, even as the ache that had started in his shoulder swelled more and more insistently to his chest, and his head ached fiercely and words wouldn't come.

He was conscious of Crick there—all he knew was that Carrick wasn't going to leave him again.

When the whole thing was over, they told him that he was in full-on cardiac arrest by the time the ambulance got to the hospital.

Chapter *16*

Jeff: Containing the Explosion in Your Head

JEFF wasn't exactly sure how he and Martin ended up the hospital—or rather, he was pretty sure he didn't know how Martin had ended up there with him.

He was the family's resident health care professional, so after Deacon's discussion two weeks earlier, he'd done some research into Sick Sinus Syndrome (and what a fucking quirky little name for it) and had thought he had a handle on things. He was worried, but not consumed—it was treatable, right?

God, he'd underestimated Deacon's considerable will.

Thinking back about the day, about Deacon sitting still, swallowing convulsively (against the tell-tale tightness in his jaw, Jeff thought now in disgust), it seemed as though he'd been getting all his ducks in a row. All his family was happy, and he could finally relax enough to go into A-fib.

Awesome, Deacon. Happy Thanksgiving to you, too, you self-martyring bastard.

It wasn't fair—it wasn't. Jeff knew that. But he'd taken such steps, such precautions to not be angry at Kevin. Kevin was a hero. Kevin had loved him. Kevin had gone off to war.

Even after the letter, the painful dethroning of Jeff's dreams, he'd somehow managed to keep that vision of Kevin absolutely pure. It had been a moment of chance, a moment of depression. If Jeff had been there, Kevin wouldn't have felt so low that taking enemy fire had been the only way—he knew it. It was circumstance, a moment of weakness. All heroes had them.

He hadn't scaffolded his heart for Deacon that way, hadn't built the struts to support the lie. He thought of Deacon as the patriarch of his little family, the one he'd thrown his lot in with, just sitting there, practically dying in front of them, and he *needed* to hit something. He needed to scream, to detonate that little bubble of self-containment and narcissism that he'd been so attached to until it exploded outward and laid waste to anyone unlucky enough to be near.

Collin would be the first to go.

He knew this. He had the ability to be coldly rational; it was why he could hurt people for their own good. In that coldly rational part of his brain, he knew that if Collin were here, Jeff would take all of this pain out on him—and then Crick. And then Martin. And then anyone else nearby.

So he would keep himself cold, cold and rational. If he could hurt other people for their own good, he could keep his own pain contained for the same reasons. He would be Jeff the helper, Jeff the comedian—he knew that role. He was comfortable in it. It would keep his bubble intact, and then he could be true for his friends.

"I should have left you at The Pulpit," he said to Martin apologetically. "Benny and Andrew and the babies are there—it would have been happier there. I'm sorry. I didn't think."

Martin looked up from his corner with his video game and shrugged. "It's no worries. It's not like you planned this, right?"

Jeff shuddered and then grimaced. "I was just hoping... you know. I... I met your brother in the summer. It's the closest thing to a holiday with him I was ever going to get."

Way to go, Jeffy—keep it light!

Martin looked suddenly old. "You just take care of your people, man. They sure do take care of you, right?"

"Right," Jeff muttered, and then wandered off to see if he could take care of Jon and Amy.

Jon and Crick were sitting on the couch with Amy in between them. Amy was knitting furiously on something that looked easy and mindless, and Jeff was acutely jealous.

"Bitch," he muttered. "I didn't even have my emergency sock in the damned car."

Amy looked up and smiled a little, then burrowed in the bag at her feat. "I've got sock needles and a spare skein," she said, and Jeff had to laugh. Maybe it was the mother thing that made her come prepared—even with extra knitting.

"I may take you up on that, sweets," he promised, thinking he really would. The sock yarn was a subtle blend of fall colors, and Jeff fell in love a little. How wonderful would it be to just touch that and get lost in a stitch at a time for a while? He actually felt his heart rate even out a little, and then he was angry again.

Great. While Deacon was sitting in the living room, going into A-fib, maybe he should have been knitting a fucking sweater, and wouldn't that have helped?

"But first, do you want some water or a soda or something?" he asked, afraid that anger was going to get the best of him, and everybody shook their heads.

"Later," Amy murmured. "Maybe ask Shane or Mikhail. And tell Kimmy to come over here—if you won't knit, she can have it."

"She might chew your face off," Jeff warned. Kimmy had all the temper her brother did not.

"Good!" Amy looked excited. "Something to occupy my time! Where's Lucas?"

Jeff had heard Kimmy talking as they'd left. "He's over at Promise House—the kids are going to be disappointed when those three don't show up for Thanksgiving. Lucas's gonna be the papa-in-charge, I guess." Poor guy. See? That was what happened when you smiled at a pretty face. Your whole life went to hell, and the next thing you knew, you were caught up in a shitload of drama that was not your own and wondering if this was the price of getting laid. "I'll go get Kimmy."

It was silly, really, but no one wanted to get into too big a group. Jeff had seen it before. Big groups meant big talking, and nobody partied in the waiting room of the OR. So Jeff was on his way over to talk to Kimmy, passing in front of Martin again to get to her, when suddenly Mikhail broke away from his little group of three.

"Go on, cow-woman. Ask Amy for her emergency sock. Like that woman would deny you anything."

Jeff had to laugh. "Are the fiber few that predictable?" he asked, trying to entertain.

"Shut up, Jeff. You look like hell."

"Fuck you too," Jeff replied, annoyed.

Mikhail scowled at him. "Martin, why are you not at The Pulpit, or Promise House? It is happier there."

Martin looked up and rolled his eyes. "It's like you're trying to get rid of me or something. Man, can't I just be here for Jeff?"

Jeff looked at him, pinching the bridge of his nose. That wasn't the answer Martin had given *him*. But it was… oh God. It was everything.

"I'm so grateful," he said, his voice, which he'd tried to keep light and comforting, suddenly breaking.

Martin shrugged. "Like I said. No worries."

Mikhail shook his head and shuddered. "Martin, I hate hospitals. Last year, my mother was dying, it felt like I lived here. And when she was no longer coming for chemo, my big, stupid cop—he decided to try dying once or twice, and generally, the charm is gone for me. I think you and me, we should go outside and get a football or a Frisbee or something, what do you think?"

"I think you're trying to get me out of the way so Shane can talk to Jeff and do that super-mojo counseling thing he's so good at."

Mikhail smiled. "You are very smart, much smarter than I was at your age, you know that?"

"Mikhail, it's one in the morning, and this neighborhood ain't that great. How stupid *were* you?"

Mikhail met Jeff's eyes, and Mikhail's gaze was ineffably sad. "You have no idea, you great-hearted boy. But let us go. If we are lucky, we can find ice cream. It is the one good thing about these places, you shall have to trust me."

"Mikhail!" Jeff said, about to watch two of his diversions walk out the door, Martin's arm slung companionably around the little Russian's shoulders. They looked about as mismatched as two people could be.

"Call your boyfriend, you stupid man!" Mikhail snapped, giving Jeff a decidedly rude salute over his shoulder without even looking back.

"He's right, you know," Shane said quietly. "Where's Collin?"

Jeff practically jumped, because Shane had moved into his personal space while Mikhail and Martin disappeared around the corner.

"Collin has his own family," Jeff mumbled. "I was going to call him in the morning and tell him maybe showing up for dessert was out, you know?"

"Bullshit," Shane said, and his voice was edgy and upset, and Jeff looked at him sharply. Shane looked as bad as everyone said Jeff did.

God, this really *was* family. This really *did* hurt as bad as family could. Jeff was suddenly so very, very cold, he almost severed his tongue with his chattering teeth. "Is not bullshit! Collin *does* have his own family!"

Shane's hand was warm as it covered Jeff's, and for a minute Jeff was tempted to jerk his hand back in so Shane wouldn't notice that it was icy with sweat. "Yeah, but that's not where he wants to be right now," Shane said softly, and Jeff shook his head and looked away—but he didn't retrieve his hand.

"How in the hell would you know that?" he muttered, trying to get his shock under control. That's what it was—he was going into shock. Suddenly his black fury at Deacon eased—he was going into shock out of sheer emotional overload, and he kept trying to deny it. Maybe Deacon had done the same thing with the heart attack—he'd kept thinking, *I'm smarter than this. This can't be happening to me.*

"Because if Mickey hadn't let me be there when his mom was sick, it would have felt like a kick in the balls."

"But he broke up with you after she died!" Jeff protested. He wasn't delusional; he remembered that part!

"So I would know," Shane replied with gentle humor, and Jeff's tremors eased. How did he do that? God, he was such a great big solid mound of muscle and quiet strength, how did he just soothe people's nerves with that sweet smile of his?

"It was one night," Jeff said, and the smile disappeared.

"Man, Jeff—you're something else, you know that? The sarcasm, I get. Full-voltage gay, that's who you are. But all of that—the spiffy clothes, the trill in the voice, gestures—and not once did I figure you for a coward. My bad. Next time, I'll have a better idea who I'm dealing with."

"Tough words for someone who's still holding my hand," Jeff shot back, mostly because it was true.

"That's because I don't believe them," Shane said softly. "C'mere, Jeffy." He extended an arm and tucked Jeff underneath it as if he were a baby bird. "I'm not the guy you need, but I'll do until you call him. Now call him."

Somehow, Shane had managed to pick his pocket when Jeff wasn't paying attention, but Shane's body was warm and comforting and almost sexless, and Jeff wasn't going to give him shit and risk having that comfort removed. Jeff sighed. Shane wasn't his. They'd never make it— ever, even a little—as a couple. Shane might as well be a big, burly woman as far as that went. If Jeff was willing to take this sort of comfort from Shane, who had Mikhail to go home to, maybe that meant the big, hairy man-mountain was right. Maybe it was time he let himself need.

Jeff felt his own cell phone being pressed into his hand, and he sighed, sort of longing for the old days, when you weren't allowed to use the damned things.

He hit Collin's number, listed under "Sparky," and listened through the message.

"Uhm, Sparky? Yeah, uhm, Deacon's sort of in the hospital, so, uhm, probably no dessert at The Pulpit tomorrow. Uhm...." Shane squeezed his shoulders and Jeff closed his eyes. "I'm at Davis Med Center, and I don't know how long this is going to be, because they've got to stabilize him and then they're going to operate, and, well. I know you've got plans tomorrow, but, I don't know. If you feel like—"

Beeeeeeeeeeeep.

"Fuck."

"It's all good, Jeff. I think he gets the picture." Shane chuckled warmly, and Jeff burrowed into his friend's comfort without shame.

"You're a really good friend, Shane," he said, with simple faith.

THE wait went on.

About a half an hour after Mikhail and Martin left in search of ice cream, Deacon's doctor came into the OR with news. Crick stood up to go talk to him, and Jeff didn't need Shane's subtle push on the shoulders to go join him. Jeff was the GBFF—he was up.

"Deacon is stabilized," Doctor Mackey was saying as Jeff came up alongside Crick. The hand that sought out Jeff's was as icy as Jeff's had been not half an hour before.

"Glad to hear it," Crick said, his voice wobbly and cracking. "Can we see him?"

"You can, Carrick—you've got his living will, and Jon's listed as his legal counsel, so you're the designated visitors. But you've got to make it quick. We're putting him under in about five minutes. I don't want to wait another second before we cauterize those nerve endings in the atrium, or we're going to have to go through the last five hours all over again, and quite frankly, I don't know if he'll make it."

Crick nodded, and Jeff pushed at his shoulders. "Tell him we love him," he said, and Amy told Jon the same thing. It was funny—Crick and Jon disappeared after the doctor, and Amy and Jeff simply filled in their places and held chilly hands while they waited.

In about two, maybe three and a half million years, the two of them returned, both looking as gray-faced as Deacon had when the ambulance arrived. Amy rushed into her husband's arms, and Jeff let her go.

Crick took a sort of lost look around the waiting room with bleary, brown eyes and ran a hand through his stringy hair. "I've got to get the fuck out of here," he said after a second, and as he pushed through the door to the waiting room, past a returning Mikhail and Martin, Jeff sensed the eyes of everyone else on him, and he nodded. It was still his up.

He caught up with Crick at a vending machine in the corridor— Crick was attempting to buy a soda, and the *wheemp-whomp* of the machine as it rejected his dollar bill repeatedly echoed loudly. His injured hand was shaking too badly to straighten the bill when he put it in the slot.

Jeff nudged him aside and straightened the crumpled bill, then sent it smoothly through the feeder, and then the other one, when Crick held it out for him. Crick made his selection, and the thump the plastic bottle made was loud enough in the silence of the corridor to make the two of them jump.

Crick leaned back against the wall, downed half a bottle of soda, and belched so loudly that Jeff could swear the soda machine rattled. Then he spoke randomly into the waiting silence. "I don't know how you do it. You just… you're so strong."

"You're doing a lot better than I would be," Jeff told him truthfully, but he wasn't surprised when Crick shook his head.

"It's like… I don't see in color anymore, you know? I look at something and I think I know what it looks like, and then I think about what the world would look like without Deacon, and it goes to black and white."

Crick was an artist. He didn't draw and paint as much as he would have liked to, but then, Jeff was pretty sure he wouldn't have traded his life with the horses and Deacon for any other life on the planet. For Carrick James to see things in black and white—that was saying that the sun was silver and the moon was dark as pitch.

"He'll be all right," Jeff said, believing it. "That man's got a one-track mind—he wants to wake up and see you."

"And ride horses," Crick said with a semi-hysterical laugh.

"But mostly see you."

"It's like I spent all that time," Crick went on, not hearing any comfort because he couldn't, "watching his diet, checking to make sure the things he ate, or did, or the way he lived would make him stay with me for as long as possible, and none of it mattered. I mean, I get what happened to me"—he held up his damaged arm for emphasis. "I get it. I was dumb as pus, I had no fucking business being in Iraq, and that's what fucking happens in a war zone. But Deacon… man, he…." Crick threw his head back against the wall so hard it cracked, but he didn't wince.

Jeff stood up from his crouch at the soda machine and put his hand behind Crick's head, making shushing noises.

"Easy, there, chief," he murmured, but Crick didn't even bend his knees to make it easier to comfort him.

"He told me to go home and get some sleep," Crick muttered. "He said, 'Get some sleep, Carrick James, you can't make yourself sick. Folks will need you.' God. God, I'm just so mad at him!"

"Why? He didn't choose this! It's not like he *wanted* to be sick, right?" *This makes sense, Jeff, you know that.* "Nobody *wants* to be sick. Nobody *asks* to be sick. He didn't even do anything dumb, you know? He didn't engage in anything he knew was risky, he didn't step in front of a fucking grenade… he's totally fucking innocent—you don't get to be angry at him!" *Don't yell at the suffering spouse, Jeff, you dickhead—what the hell's the matter with you?*

Crick was looking at Jeff with a sort of blank revelation on his face, and Jeff was powerless to stop talking.

"I mean, if he has one wish on earth, it's to spend more time with you, right?" His hands were stiff against his sides, and his jaw was locked, and he felt a wave of red fury just sweeping his body. "He wants to be together. He was taking steps to do that, healthy or sick, and you were helping, and this isn't his fault!" *This is about Crick, Jeff, you know that, right?*

"I know that, Jeff," Crick said, and Jeff should have seen the weary acceptance on his face, but he couldn't.

"It's not like he yanked the rug out from underneath you, or just yanked your entire world out from under your feet because you proved to be a fuckup that he didn't understand, right?" *Deacon wasn't the one who did that, was he?*

"Yeah, Jeffy, I know."

"I mean, you guys had your entire lives together, right? Why in the fuck would he want to leave you?" Jeff ran a shaking hand over his face and wondered why he couldn't shut up. "There's no reason for it—he didn't do it on purpose, he didn't want this, and what kind of asshole would just… just fucking leave you or kick you out? Deacon wouldn't do that. He wouldn't do that to you."

No, but someone did that to you, didn't he?

"Jeff, Jeff, you're really freaking out here, okay?"

"I'm fine. I'm fine. And you're going to be fine too. Because he wouldn't do that to us. Deacon wants to stay. He's *dying* to stay, and I'm so jealous, Crick, so fucking jealous because even if he can't, even if God's the vicious liver-eating, balls-ripping motherfucker we all think He is and takes Deacon away, he wanted to stay, and no one's wanted to stay, not in my entire life, and at least he—*oh God*!"

Jeff would have fallen to his knees then, because his entire body just gave out on him as his brittle glass bubble exploded outward, leveling anyone in its path, but two strong arms caught him from behind as he fell, and suddenly he was being turned around and held, just held as he disintegrated, crushed like a flamboyant Christmas tree ornament under the heel of a pagan god.

"I'm sorry," he managed, enveloped in the comforting smells of engine grease and soap and sleepy man. "Collin, tell Crick I'm sorry, please tell him I'm sorry."

Crick's face appeared between Collin's shoulder and Jeff's line of sight, and Crick reached out and ruffled Jeff's hair. "It's okay," Crick said softly. "You can't be strong all the time, Jeffy. I'll be okay."

"No you won't," Jeff mumbled, absolutely sure of this. "You won't be okay. You can say you're okay, and you can think you're okay, and suddenly you're having a meltdown when someone needs you the most."

Crick dashed his cheeks with the back of his hand. "Don't worry—don't worry about me, okay, Jeff? I'll go in with everyone else. Jon'll be happy to have me fall apart on him. You've earned a break from being everyone's fairy-Jeff-father, you hear me?"

Collin's arms tightened around his shoulders, and Crick disappeared, and it was suddenly Jeff, alone with the man—not the kid, the man—who had come through for him when he didn't know he needed it.

"God, Sparky, I'm so glad you're here."

"Jesus, Jeff, I'm so glad you called."

Jeff sniffled and wiped his face on Collin's shoulder, wishing maybe for the first time in his life that he was just about two inches shorter. "Yeah, well, if you don't tell someone you care about that you need them, it's sort of like a kick in the balls, isn't it?"

"Yeah, baby. It would be. Thank God you didn't do that."

Jeff didn't have any more words then. He just stood there, shivering in Collin's arms, wondering if God would listen to him pray after he'd just called the Big Guy all those awful names.

Eventually Collin guided him back to see his family. Crick was sitting between Jon and Amy again, except this time, he was laying his head on Jon's chest and crying quietly with simple stress. Jon, who had known Crick since he was nine, had an arm around his shoulders like the big brother he truly was, and Amy was cuddling into Crick's arms in sort of a family sandwich.

Jon looked up when they walked in, with nothing in his eyes but simple concern. Jeff smiled sheepishly, and Jon cocked his head—it was the same look he'd given Deacon the year before, when they used to make him get on the scale to make sure he was taking care of himself, and Jeff's smile went watery. Jon nodded, like that was the way it should be, and Collin situated them on another couch. To Jeff's surprise, Martin came and sat next to Jeff there and patted his shoulder.

"You hug me, and I'm outta here," the kid grumbled, and Jeff nodded.

"Understood."

"Jeff, what time is it?"

"Around 2 a.m. You want I should send you back to The Pulpit? There's food and a bed, or at least a decent couch."

Martin nodded. "Next time someone else goes, I will. Look, I hate to ask—you're paying for my cell phone plan—but is there any way I could... you know. Tomorrow. Call my parents?"

Jeff swallowed. "Too much drama for you?"

Martin shook his head. "Naw. Man, I just want to... you know? I'm still pissed at them, but I sort of want to talk to them anyway."

Kevin's kid brother was an all right human being, wasn't he? "No worries. Talk as long as you want."

Martin nodded, and then, shocking the hell out of Jeff, he turned his back and leaned up against Jeff's shoulder, settling in for a wait. It was the sort of thing a kid would do with a friend or a brother—and Jeff settled in on Collin accordingly.

"You realize," he said softly, looking up at Collin with such total weariness he knew he'd be asleep in moments, "that you're supporting a whole lot of drama on those double-wide shoulders, don't you?"

Collin grinned, shaking his brown-gold hair out of his lean face, and Jeff felt it, right under his sternum, in the dead pit of his gut, how pretty he was. "It's easy," Collin said. "Youth has its perks."

Jeff's shoulders shook right up until his eyes closed abruptly, and the pain and the fear and the stress were all swallowed by the pleasant dark. For an hour or so, not even the uncomfortable couch or the hospital noises intruded on his peace.

Chapter *17*

Collin: I'm Just a Baby Duck

THE last time Collin had been in a hospital (and not the CARES clinic) had been when his niece, Kelsey, was born.

The Labor and Delivery unit was *so* much happier than the OR waiting room.

Collin had been asleep when he'd heard his cell phone buzzing, and Jeff's voice in the message had sounded… *strained.* Desperate. In pain.

But that had been *nothing* compared to what Collin had heard as he'd rounded the corridor and found Jeff in a shrapnel-studded cyclonic meltdown on the guy he was supposed to be comforting. Oh Jesus. Poor Jeff, who loved so much to be there for everyone else. *God, baby, how could you let the pain get this bad?*

Collin tightened his arm around Jeff's shoulders. When Jeff murmured "Collin" into his chest, Collin felt something huge release from around his ankles, and he felt like he could swim in air for the first time since they'd both woken up early Tuesday morning and dressed hastily and without romance to hurry off to their jobs.

He'd said "Collin"—*not* Kevin. It was one thing to know the guy had waited six years to break his celibacy over his dead lover. It was another to be absolutely certain that Collin was *not* a substitute for dead hero boyfriend.

It was Collin's name Jeff had called out when they were making love, and it was Collin who was comforting him now. These truths made the being awake in the OR in the gawdawful crotch of a slutty dawn absolutely worth it.

"It's good you came," Martin said suddenly, still facing the back wall. He was resting his head on the back of the couch, and the fact that he was leaning on Jeff seemed at once very young and very dear.

"Yeah?"

"Yeah. He needed someone. Maybe has for a long time."

"Doesn't bother you who anymore?"

Collin felt rather than saw the shake of the head. "My folks, they've got their shortcomings, you know? But they always taught us to recognize good people. Jeff, you, all these folks here—good people. Maybe, I talk with my folks, they'll see that Kevin never stopped being who they thought he was. It might make them happier to know."

Collin risked waking Jeff up to reach over and rub the back of Martin's head—Martin didn't say anything, but Collin heard his accepting grunt and figured they were good.

THE wait went on.

About half an hour after Martin fell asleep, Crick got up and came over.

"I'm so glad you've got his back," he said softly.

"He's going to feel awful," Collin told him, stroking the dark hair back from that fair skin for a moment. "He... he really loves you guys. All he wants is to be part of the family."

Crick's grin was crooked and watery, strained almost beyond recognition, but right there, Collin saw the boy he'd idolized in high school and realized that the man was so much finer than the boy had even promised to be. Maybe, maybe, Collin was like that too.

"Maybe if you're *really* a part of a family, you can make it all about you, and they'll forgive you," Crick said, and Collin managed a wicked grin back.

"I'll tell him you said so," he said dryly. Then, because it needed to be said, "God, Crick—I sure do hope Deacon's okay."

Crick nodded. "Yeah, well Jeff had a point when he was swimming in the crazy pool—if Deacon leaves me, it's not because he wants to."

Crick nodded firmly, like he was trying to prop himself up. "And if anyone's stubborn enough to live for that, it's Deacon."

Collin reached out and squeezed Crick's shoulder, and Crick closed his eyes.

"You've got a big family, don't you?" Crick asked.

"Four sisters, three nieces, a nephew and a mother who knows everything."

"Well, your family is welcome to ours anytime. Just ask Mikhail—we're hard to shake."

Collin grinned. "Thanks. My mom would figure you need more women in your family anyway."

Crick's grin was a little more real this time. "My little sister would probably agree with you." He breathed out then, a true, worried, pained sigh, and then he did what Collin figured was the grown-up thing, and Collin hoped that he could measure up the same way.

"Benny and Amy are trading places around 6 a.m. Maybe ask Martin if he wants to go back to The Pulpit by then. We should know something, good or bad. They're putting in a pacemaker, and the doc says that after the surgery, recovery goes pretty fast. We should know something by then."

Collin nodded. "So if this goes well, he should be all right, then?"

Crick shrugged. "Jesus… I don't want to tempt the gods, but… but yeah. Yeah. If we can make it through the next few hours and the two weeks of recovery, the doc says it will be like he was never sick." Crick shook his head in amazement. "Wouldn't it be great, if someday this was just a really shitty memory?"

Collin thought about that, thought about the memories of people who *hadn't* made it, and knew that Crick was probably thinking the same thing. "Yeah, Crick. I'll be rooting for that until we get news."

Crick wandered off, Jon joining him to make sure he wasn't alone, and Collin dozed for a bit. He woke up when Jeff stretched and yawned, then got up quietly, careful to make sure Martin had adjusted and wasn't going to go flopping backward when he stood up.

"Gotta use the john, Sparky. Back in a moment."

He was, and after he wiggled back in against Collin and behind the sleeping teenager, he was awake enough to talk. "Sorry about the meltdown," he murmured. "I don't know if I'll ever be able to look Crick in the eyes again."

"Crick gets it," Collin told him honestly. "You know, he was a real hellraiser in high school. It's funny to see him so sober and responsible and grown-up and shit."

Jeff's laugh was like sandpaper on a badly tooled engine part. "You should talk, Sparky. You're not that long out of high school yourself."

Collin groaned. "Aw, Jesus, not that shit again!"

Jeff sighed—but his relaxed, intimate pose didn't change. "It's going to bother me, Collin," he admitted. "I mean... you were what? Eighteen? I feel like I cheated to get you. I imprinted on you early, like a baby duck—"

"A baby duck!"

"And you just kept following me."

"And what? I was too cute to give back?"

Jeff's smile was crooked. "Yeah, baby. You're just too damned beautiful to throw back. So I'm going to try and keep you. It may not be the most noble thing I've ever done, but... but you came. I needed somebody, and you came. I can't just give you back after that. I'm sorry. That's me—weak gay man. Make me a T-shirt, but it had better be athletic fit with that window-pane material that's so very, very in fashion, you know?"

"Off-white," Collin said with a little bit of a smile. "It should be off-white, because gray wouldn't do justice to your eyes."

"You're playing my song, Sparky."

"I'm not a baby duck, Jeff."

"I know."

"I'm a grown-up—I got all the kid out of my system a long time ago. I know how to sac up and take care of things."

"I can see that."

"That includes you."

Sigh. Shiver. "Lots of damage that you didn't have a fucking thing to do with, Collin. God... I don't want to dump it on your shoulders."

"Give me a chance, Jeff. Your damage on my shoulders might feel as good as you feel in my arms."

Jeff raised his face—swollen red eyes, washed out, pale skin, vulnerable quiver to his mouth and all—and said, "Good answer. I'll take you up on it."

Collin lowered his mouth and kissed him, and they both shuddered with sudden need. Jeff pulled back first—there was a teenager lying on him, and "need" was going to have to get tabled to "want" for a little while, if they were both going to be as grown up as they'd just pledged to be.

They talked quietly then, about not much in particular—what Jeff and Martin had made for Thanksgiving dinner, how Collin thought his mother might actually really love Jeff.

She hadn't really approved of his other boyfriends, he admitted. "But I think she really likes you."

"She's seen me once!" Jeff protested as spare, gray light made its way through the waiting room window.

"Yeah, but you were being a good guy then. She thinks I'm a bad boy—I need a good boy to keep me honest."

Jeff looked slyly at him through long, dark lashes. "I'm not *that* much of a good boy."

"Thank God."

AT 6 A.M., Amy left, taking Martin with her and promising to let him sack out on the couch before she put him to work in the kitchen. "We need to feed everybody, dammit!" she moaned, a little hysterically.

"Yeah, but I've been cooking for two days!"

"Well, I'll give you a break to watch the parade," she said practically, and Jon was behind her making "night-night" faces to Martin and then crossing his heart in promise. That alone was probably the only reason Martin actually agreed to go.

A little slip of a girl arrived just as the sky was brightening to real day, and she was immediately rushed by everyone from Crick to Mikhail and Jeff as they all fought for a hug.

"I don't see anyone doing this to Kimmy!" the girl complained, obviously trying to keep things light in spite of the terrible strain of worry at her eyes. The shape of her eyes was pretty familiar, and Collin took a couple of looks between the girl and Crick to realize that they were somehow related.

Kimmy looked up from the sock she was halfway through and smiled blearily. "I've got sharp pointy things in my hand, Benny. They tend to keep men at a distance."

"Don't even think about it, little sister," Crick warned, his voice sounding like powdered cement. "I know how to use those things too."

Benny rolled her eyes. "Yeah. You're an amateur. Here, sit down with me, and I'll show you how it's done."

Benny settled down with her knitting and gave her brother a project she'd obviously brought for him in her bag. Collin started to wonder if he'd have to learn or something—was it a membership requirement? Was there yarn that didn't soak up engine grease? And before he could ask the questions aloud, the doctor walked in, and everyone stood up in a jangle of electric nerves.

It's funny, how relief can hit like a wave, either buoying your body up in a surge or knocking your knees right out from under you.

At the doctor's quiet smile, Crick rolled to his feet and leapt, shouting, "*Whooooo!* He's okay? He's okay! *He's okay!* We can see him, right? When can we see him? Oh God, can I see him now?" Benny leapt at her brother, practically climbing him like a tree, and Crick held her tight, whirling her around for a minute while they chanted, "He's okay, he's okay, he's okay...."

The doctor waited for a moment, still smiling, while Crick and Benny leapt and everyone else fell back down quietly into their seats. Eventually Crick had to put his little sister down and listen to the doctor's instructions. The "sick sinus rhythm" had been eradicated, and a normal rhythm had been restored, with a pacemaker to keep things functioning well. Of course Deacon would have to have regular checkups, and the next two weeks would be critical in terms of keeping Deacon still ("Oh Lord!" Benny moaned) and making sure he didn't stress himself out ("Oh Lord," Crick muttered), and he could come home in two days.

Collin couldn't remember being hugged or hugging other people so much in so short a span of time, and his skin drank it in like *really* good coffee—it was rich, it was life-sustaining, and it made him feel alive, but at last the coffee buzz failed, and everyone felt, deep in their bones, the weariness that came from worrying for a friend until the night turned.

Of course Crick and Benny would stay there until Deacon woke up, and everyone else was advised to go home and get some sleep.

"But dinner, at The Pulpit, at six o'clock," Benny said, looking a lot older than eighteen. "We all made food, I'll be damned if it's going to waste, and you know, I think we've got something to celebrate."

Everyone nodded wearily but happily. Jeff moved closer to talk to Benny, and she looked up as she packed her knitting away. "Amy texted me. She said Martin is *out* in my bed right now, so go ahead and leave him there, okay?"

Jeff nodded. "Yeah, that's fine. He'll be happier if he wakes up at The Pulpit and has something to do, anyway. Thanks for letting him stay."

Suddenly Benny's arms were around Jeff's neck super-tight, and he was hugging her back. Collin looked at the two of them and thought of his sister, Charlene, the one he hated, and wondered if maybe he should do something about that. He tended to take his sisters for granted—too many girls and only one boy. But Jeff was hugging the girl like he'd die just to make her happy, and Collin was struck again by the truth. This was his family. They came with Jeff, hell, high water, or hysteria in the hallway. It was a good thing, but Jeff hadn't been kidding about a lot of drama. Of course, Collin hadn't been kidding when he said he could take it, either.

Eventually they were out in the parking lot, and Collin said, "I'll follow you home, okay?"

Jeff blushed, looking flustered since the first time he came apart in Collin's arms. "Uhm, okay. I thought you were going to go hang with your family or something, Collin."

Collin scowled, tired and not ready to put up with this shit again. "Careful, Jeffy, you're a few degrees and a good swing away from getting me square in the nads."

Jeff blushed again. "That would be a shame," he murmured. "Your balls are two of your best qualities."

Collin let himself smirk. "Glad you agree. Now get in your car, and I'll be there about ten minutes after you."

"Ten minutes?"

"I'm starving. I'll bring home breakfast."

Jeff's shoulders bent a little, and a wistful smile crossed his face. "Coffee? Real coffee. With caramel, since chocolate's killing me right now. Can that be part of breakfast?"

"If you want it to be," Collin said mildly, arching his eyebrows to make that more suggestive than Jeff probably meant it.

But Jeff didn't let him down. "I'll let you know what else I want with my sausage, Sparky. Just bring me the coffee—you'll be surprised what I can rustle up."

Collin managed a laugh on the way to Starbucks for coffee and croissants.

When he got to Jeff's house, Jeff was in a red, silk dressing gown, still wet from the shower, and he answered the door on the phone. He grimaced, ushered Collin inside, and looked with lust at the coffee in the cup tray. "Thank you!" he mouthed, and Collin nodded and made his way to the kitchen/dining room while Jeff made a series of complicated expressions into the phone.

"Yeah, yeah, Archie, I appreciate the fact that you're calling me up on ten o'clock Thanksgiving morning and all, but I'm sorry, I can't make it."

Collin raised his eyebrows. "Your dad?" he mouthed, and Jeff's sour grimace was all the answer he needed.

"No, I'm not calling you 'Dad'—not right now. No, I'm not going to sit in my apartment and sulk. I told you I have a family—in fact, most years, I've got two."

Jeff listened to the other line, but not patiently. Collin took off the lid to his latte and blew on it, watching in amusement as Jeff swiveled his hips and made little talking motions with his hands as his father spoke on the other end. Jeff didn't really need to worry about the age difference—apparently, he was emotionally stunted enough to put them both on equal ground.

"No. No, you don't take precedence. I know you just had some lovely epiphany about the fact that just because I'm gay doesn't mean I'm the devil, and I'm real fucking glad for you, Archie, but you know what? The family that cares about my narcissistic ass even when I'm being one? *That* family really needs me right now. I just shared twelve hours in an OR waiting room with my kin, and we're going to celebrate a happy ending to that, okay? You want me to come around Christmas, you let me know—but I warn you, Christmas is usually taken up by three little girls and a whole bunch of gay men falling over themselves to spoil them rotten. I might see Mom a few days after—you let me know if you want to be there."

Jeff clicked his phone shut with a sigh that didn't seem at all exaggerated and then put his face in his hands. Collin handed him a caramel latte, and Jeff blew on it through the cup lid, sighing appreciatively when he finally took a sip. He took another, took a bite of the offered croissant, and sighed again.

"I probably seem like a real bastard, don't I?" he asked, sounding depressed, and Collin shook his head.

"Ten years? Eleven years? No. I don't care if you were in college—he abandoned you. It takes more than a shitty day and a phone call to make you want to drop your real life and go run into his arms." Collin took another sip of his coffee and said maybe his tenth prayer of thanks that day for his mother and even, although he'd left way too early, for his father. Collin had been loved—and it hadn't just been picture love. His mother had loved him—desperately, worriedly, but with her whole heart. His father had been a kind man. His sisters all said so, his mother talked about it constantly—all of Collin's memories were of his kindness. As an adult, he'd asked his mother once if his father would have been disappointed that Collin was gay, and his mother had rolled her eyes.

"He would have been disappointed that you didn't manage to get the bicycle over the roof of the garage that last time you tried, but the gay thing? No worries, Collin—your dad would have been proud that you lived to see some settling down. He was nice that way."

"I know," Jeff muttered. "I mean, I feel all righteously dignified, you know? But at the same time, I feel like I'm setting a really shitty example for Martin. I mean, he was going to call his parents today— what kind of... I don't know, big brother? Adult? Whatever the hell I am to him—what kind of whatever am I if I can't forgive my own parents for...."

"For exactly what his parents did to him," Collin said grimly. "Jeff, I'm not saying that the two of you should *never* forgive them, but, you know. Hatred isn't a small thing. It's not a 'wave your hand and poof! It goes away!' sort of thing. I mean, it would be great if we could just rush up to every bigot we know and say, 'I'm so sorry I'm gay! I forgive you for hating me even though I never did anything personally wrong to you!' but I'm not wired that way. I don't expect you to be either." Collin took another drink of his mocha, and Jeff smiled at him wearily.

"You're really wise, Sparky. Can I be like you when I grow up?"

Collin gave a cheese-eating grin and the world's shittiest sensei impersonation. "Absolutely, grasshopper—but first you must take me to bed and allow me to drool on your pillow!"

Jeff laughed a little and scrubbed his face. "Yeah. Sleep is a good idea. But I warn you, you're going to be sharing that pillow."

"You mean that fur hurricane that tried to cave in my chest? No worries. I think it likes me."

Jeff snorted. "That's what you think. If they like you they try to sand your face off. You want to shower?"

Collin smiled. "Only if I can wear your boxers to sleep in."

WHEN Collin got out of the shower, Jeff was already in bed, mostly asleep. He was wearing red striped pajamas, the kind with the wide notched collar and the satin piping, and he was clutching one of the fur mountains—the long-haired calico one—to his chest. Collin had heard the thing's purring from the bathroom door.

True to Jeff's word, there was a pair of white cotton boxers on the wine-colored comforter, and a plain, white T-shirt with a rainbow ring around the arms and the neck.

"Asshole," Collin muttered affectionately, putting both of them on.

"Mmm?" Jeff murmured, and Collin slid behind him, tangling his bare, hairy shins with what felt to be about a thousand acres of flannel under the umpteen-thread count cotton sheets.

"Jeff, don't you have to be a Victorian virgin to wear something like this?"

"Shut up or I won't push the cat off the bed."

Collin reached around Jeff's chest and shoved with all his formidable upper body strength. There was a thump big enough to shake the windows and an indignant yowl, and then Collin wrapped his arm securely around Jeff's chest and pulled him back, so their bodies were tightly flush with each other. He raised his other arm over his head and used the new and improved closeness to nuzzle Jeff's neck.

"I'd be careful when I put my shoes on," Jeff murmured. "Katy holds grudges."

"Katy is just going to have to get used to a new order," Collin insisted. Jeff *mmm*-ed and pushed his hips sleepily back against Collin's groin. Collin was almost instantly hard.

Jeff's body was suddenly not quite so pliant in Collin's arms. "Oh *hel*-lo!" he said, his voice much more alert than it had been a minute ago.

Collin lifted his head and braved that unruly dark hair to trace the outer edge of Jeff's ear with his tongue. "This surprises you?"

"Sex? In this bed? With another person? What's not to be surprised?" Jeff's voice had taken on a strained note, and Collin could feel that his next thrust backward with his bottom was almost against the guy's will.

"It'll be good for us, Jeffy," Collin murmured. "It'll help us work off some tension, make our nap better...."

"Those are horrible reasons for sex," Jeff muttered, and to his horror, Collin realized Jeff was pulling away. Jesus—was there anything short of complete emotional honesty that would impress this guy?

"How about I want you," Collin said candidly. "We just sat in a waiting room to make sure your friends wouldn't have to say goodbye way, way the fuck too soon. Both of us are walking testaments to the fact that sometimes just living here on the planet takes will power and some of the greatest chemical advancements of the twenty-first century. Can't we just make love because we care about each other, and we're alive, and we're happy about that?"

"I *am* happy about that," Jeff murmured, and to Collin, it sounded like he was in a state of wonder. "I *am* happy about that." He turned in Collin's arms and surprised Collin by meshing their mouths together in a full-on, brain-seizing, knee-melting, cock-stiffening kiss. Collin spent a minute simply being ravished, enjoying being taken, before he had to assert himself. He rolled Jeff, ridiculous maiden-auntie pajamas and all, under his body in one smooth motion and laid him out, kissing him silly, kissing him until his eyes closed and he simply bucked up against Collin, begging to be touched, begging to be taken.

Collin pulled away and scrunched that pajama top up, unbuttoning the top button and pushing the thing up over Jeff's head, then kissing down his jaw and along his neck and down the front of his chest. He was waxed, and his muscles were taut and defined and still that curious, fair color, in spite of the paint of the tanning bed.

Collin loved it—God, he was so tight and pretty and polished and sweet and delicious, just for Collin to eat whole. He suckled on a nipple, wondering about some amazing skin cream that tasted like mint, and then kissed his way down Jeff's stomach, which was tight with sit-ups but with skin that was so soft and so vulnerable that it quivered by the time Collin was done kissing it. Jeff groaned and knotted his hands in Collin's hair, which was still clean and wet from the shower.

Collin looked up wickedly. "You want that, Jeffy? You want it all?"

Jeff nodded and whimpered. "God, Sparky, yes. I want... I want everything."

Collin grasped Jeff's cock through his pajamas and gave it a hard, certain squeeze, and Jeff all but thrashed around him, doubling up, clutching Collin's hand to his groin and turning a gasp into a breathless howl.

"You come this soon I'm gonna throttle you!" Collin laughed, and then clambered over Jeff's shuddering body to his end table, where all good boys kept their lubricant.

"Oh. My. God." Thick, thin, long, short; graduated balls; wide, triangular bases; ginormous realistically skinned and *humongulous* and unrealistically sized; purple, pink, blue, white, clear; stainless steel, hard plastic, polyurethane, glass, and holy God and set that dildo on speed dial, there was even one made out of stone. "Cheese and fucking crackers, Jeff—would you look at this collection?"

"A boy's got to have his... *hooobbbbieesss....*"

Collin looked at him, giddy and exasperated. "Get your hand off, Jeffy." He reached over and grabbed Jeff's arm, pulling his hand forcibly out of his pants.

"Well hurry up with the glove and the lube, dammit!"

"God, you're a fast starter—do you have a preference?" Collin ruffled through the drawer until he found a box of, praise God, unexpired condoms.

"Yeah, alive and breathing! Get your ass in gear!"

"You talk a good game," Collin said, still looking at that big ol' drawer full o' sex toys, "but if you're so hard up, why the new condoms?"

Jeff kicked off his pajama bottoms and sat up on his knees, shoving Collin's boxers down as he turned on his knees across from Jeff. "They make clean-up a breeze." Jeff extended his hand. "Now gimme."

Collin handed him two condoms, and Jeff took Collin's engorged cock in his hand and then let out sort of a sigh, his urgency melting away as he closed his eyes and stroked.

"You feel so good," he said with a sigh. "So warm. God, I forgot what that was like, having that in my hand." He leaned forward and dragged his tongue up the length, around the head, back down again. Collin sucked air through his teeth and clenched Jeff's hair in his hand, giving a little tug up.

"Jeff, you're not the only one who's close, okay? Get a move on!"

Jeff's fingers actually trembled while dragging the thing down, and Collin was squirming in honest-to-Christ agony by the time the condom was in place. Jeff tore the second package open and went to do himself, but Collin took it from him and nuzzled his cheek and the side of his mouth quickly.

"I don't trust you," he teased truthfully. "You're going to come if I let you touch yourself." He kept his movements quick and clinical and then finished up by leaning over and taking Jeff's length in his mouth, deep-throating once, from base to tip, and enjoying the strangled, "Nnnnggghhhh!" sound that Jeff made when Collin got to the bottom. Collin could have lingered—and he planned to. He planned on doing this a *lot* in the future, but not right now.

"Now scoot back," he ordered, and in that moment, Jeff's total compliance didn't surprise him at all. It was, in fact, everything he'd read in Jeff's movements, his hunger, the way he'd responded to Collin's first touch. Jeff wanted to be cared for, and Collin wanted to take care of him. They were perfect.

In the past couple of years, Collin had learned to truly enjoy preparing a lover. He slipped a condom over his finger and dripped lubricant over the poly, then scooted between Jeff's spread knees and placed a hand on Jeff's thigh, stroking as he went.

"You gonna tell me how you like it, Jeffy?" he murmured, and Jeff begged.

"New," he said, thrusting his hips up, widening his knees, pleading for invasion with every shaking muscle in his body. "Real. You."

Collin breached him quickly then, taken with urgency, taken with the need not to tease, not to linger. Jeff's entire body shook with a sigh of relief, and Collin tucked another finger in the condom and rubbed again.

Jeff started to gibber.

Collin added another finger, just to make sure he was ready, and when Jeff started pleading, he spread his fingers, stretching, stretching—

"Goddammit, Sparky, get up here and fuck me!"

Collin chuckled and slid—slowly, enjoying the slide of skin—up Jeff's body, until they were face to face. Jeff's fair skin was flushed, his hair was *wild*, and his lips were swollen with kisses and with biting them while Collin was teasing him into a frenzy. God... God, he was beautiful.

"Say my name," Collin commanded gently, and Jeff closed his eyes and groaned, long, drawn out, desperate.

"Collin... Jesus, Collin, please?"

Collin smiled, ground up into the crease of his thigh, all slick and lubed and everything. "I don't know, Jeffy," he teased. "I've seen the, uhm, stiff competition. I don't know how I'm going to measure up."

Jeff's eyes opened then, and he was still desperate and still hot but suddenly very, very serious. "Live," he said. "Breathe. Be warm. Want me."

Collin swallowed, for a moment—the first and only moment—very aware of the age difference. Collin had a couple of broken hearts left in him. He could love and lose a time or two and maybe, *maybe*, still come out okay.

Jeff couldn't. Jeff had spent his entire great, generous, soft heart in one gamble. If he loved again, if he threw his everything into it, he had this time and this time only. Collin had better know for fuck sure what he was doing.

"I promise," he whispered, as deadly serious as Jeff. "I promise. I'll live. I'll be warm. I'll want just you." And then he dipped his head and kissed Jeff with everything, throwing himself into this gamble with his whole heart, content in his faith to, just this once, concede his fate to the gods. Jeff raised his head and met him, and they kissed tenderly, then frantically. Then Jeff started making those keening groans again, and Collin absolutely had to possess him. He positioned himself and thrust gently, stopping when Jeff's body sprang closed around his shaft.

"*Oh damn!*" he breathed. So tight. So welcoming. Jeff groaned again, and Collin thrust forward and stayed for a moment, breathing hard, while Jeff clenched and relaxed around him. Jeff started to buck, trying to make him thrust, and Collin was too, oh God, too close to tease anymore.

"Please, Collin," Jeff begged. "Please. Fast and hard. God, baby, I need it so bad."

Collin pulled back his hips and snapped forward, and again, and again, and again, and Jeff wrapped those long legs around Collin's hips and urged him on, pressing insistent heels against Collin's thighs.

"C'mon, baby," Jeff started to chant. "C'mon, c'mon, c'mon...."

Collin kept coming on... thrusting, thrusting... it didn't take long. He pushed himself up and reached between them, grabbing Jeff's cock and squeezing, milking him as furiously as he could without being cruel, and Jeff threw his head back against the pillow and simply *allowed*. *Allowed* Collin to fuck him, *allowed* Collin to stroke him, *allowed* Collin to pleasure him, and that complete, total surrender turned Collin on like nothing else.

Jeff suddenly convulsed, his entire body lost, frenzied, clenching in the throes of climax, and Collin closed his eyes and returned the favor and allowed himself to come.

Collin couldn't stop kissing his face, though, as they came down. He kissed his sweaty forehead and his flushed cheeks, placed little butterfly kisses down his sharply lined jaw and his angular chin. It was when he placed little breathy kisses in the shell of Jeff's ear that Jeff's labored breathing caught up with him, and he started nuzzling back.

Eventually, the two of them stilled, content just to stay quiet and let their breathing return to normal.

Collin stood up and went to get a warm washcloth, and the two of them cleaned up the condoms and themselves, and then he put on his boxers and glared at Jeff, who was trying to fix that ridiculously virginal pajama ensemble.

"Boxers," he grunted, and Jeff managed a passable sneer.

"Oh, look who's all grown up and issuing orders!"

"I'm not joking, Jeff. You, me, skin to skin. I'll let you wear the pajamas when Martin's here, but when it's just me?"

Jeff sighed at the mention of Martin's name and then wadded up the pajamas and made a passable pitch at the hamper. "They're actually really comfortable," he groused, and Collin slid into bed to snuggle, just like they'd been doing before all of the lovely sex.

"So am I. How much time do we have before we should wake up and get ready?"

"About four hours."

Collin sighed happily. He could live on four hours. "Excellent." He wrapped his arms around Jeff's chest, loving that Jeff's body was still warm from the sexual exertion. "You set the alarm?"

"Yeah, Sparky, I *can* take care of myself, you know."

"Mmmm...." Collin's nose was buried in the back of Jeff's neck, and he was sweaty and warm and smelled vaguely of mint and something else that should have been manly, but on Jeff was just... just sweet and a little bit sharp. "You know what, Jeffy?"

"What?" Jeff sounded pretty close to sleep himself.

"You are *so* worth the wait."

Jeff's chuckle was almost inaudible. "So were you, Sparky—and that's saying something."

Collin didn't have any words for that, so he just concentrated on licking his neck instead, until the both of them were dead to the world.

Chapter 18

Crick: Not a Gambling Man

SEVENTEEN years earlier, Deacon Winters had been the prettiest boy a young Carrick James Francis had ever seen in his life—so pretty, in fact, that he'd even eclipsed the beautiful horse he'd been working in the dusty ring that hot summer day.

He'd been golden, like a god, and patient, and soft spoken. Carrick had never guessed at the almost paralyzing shyness behind that quiet exterior, or the painful vulnerability. He'd never thought his golden god would succumb to alcohol—or have the strength to claw himself out of that pit for love and love alone.

He didn't know that his golden god was recovering from mono at the time, and that his body was still weak and not quite functioning at optimal level. He didn't know that his god's father had a weak heart, and that the loss of Parrish Winters would wound his vulnerable son deeply. He didn't know that the alcohol and the stress, the weight loss and the everyday cold-palm sweat that was Deacon's life talking to strangers, and even to the friends that made up their family, would take their toll.

The one thing he'd loved about Deacon, would always love about Deacon, was his strong, great, generous, golden god's heart.

The one thing that had betrayed them both was the simple fragility of the weakened human organ that powered the living cage of his soul.

The idea that Crick's golden god, who had loved him so simply and so faithfully even as boys and young men, was mortal, that the living cage might someday disintegrate and the soul that Crick was bound to would expand to brighten the larger universe was....

It was a thousand thousand bound, excoriated, flayed, dismembered, bloody, bloody, bloody hells.

And Crick was not okay.

He'd gone home to shower and to take care of the horses and then, supposedly, to sleep. But the horses had been taken care of by the time he got there, and by the time he got out of the shower, his house was full of family. Martin was asleep in Benny's bed, and Benny and Andrew were asleep in his and Deacon's bed (Benny under the covers, hugging Deacon's pillow, Drew tucked chastely under an afghan, which would probably amuse Deacon to no end), and Amy was in the kitchen, working off all of her worry while Jon played with the babies.

Crick showered, looked helplessly around the only house he'd ever really considered his home, and said, to no one in particular, "I can't stay here when he's not here. I'll be back in time for dinner," and then he bailed, bailed on their family, on his responsibility to keep them together, on everything Deacon had told him to live for and to keep going for. Crick bailed on all of it, not even waiting for an answer to see if any of the people he loved would understand.

He ended up at the hospital, staring with longing at the heart of his home.

Deacon was asleep, but his Crick-sense must have been tingling, because he opened his pretty green eyes and smiled faintly at Crick hovering at the doorway.

"Don't you have a house full of people?" he slurred, and Crick grimaced. That was Deacon—responsibility to the bone.

"Yeah, but there's only one I really wanted to see."

Deacon closed his eyes, but his smile deepened. "I'm glad."

Crick pulled a chair up to Deacon's bed and dropped in it, suddenly feeling the thirty-six hours without sleep and the fifteen hours of bone-draining worry. "I don't have words right now," he apologized. "I...."

Deacon's hand made a restless movement, and Crick captured it. "'S'okay," Deacon mumbled, and Crick pulled the hand—careful of the IV trickling in and the heart monitor wires that he bumped as he moved Deacon's arm—and held it up to his face.

"Yeah, you stubborn asshole," he muttered. "You're going to be okay. You keep telling me that. The doctor's even told me that. But... God, Deacon. I don't think I'll be okay. You almost died, and I don't think I'll be okay ever again." His tears made glossy tracks on that calloused, roughened, workaday hand, and Deacon's fingers tightened on his.

"Maybe our thirties will be better," he mumbled, and Crick felt a hysterical laugh welling up in his chest.

"First you've got to make it to thirty," he giggled, and Deacon's chest made a little rise and fall, even though his eyes were still closed. Deacon's birthday was in two weeks. He'd be twenty-nine.

"Better chance now," Deacon said. "The pacemaker's got at least five years on it."

Crick looked up to the bandage site on Deacon's bare chest. It had been shaved and disinfected and was so small. Crick could see the swelling where the tiny device had been implanted, and if it wouldn't have hurt like hell, he would have kissed it reverently. Oh, blessed, blessed technology that gave Deacon more time on the planet.

"I want to go on another vacation," Crick said out of the blue. "I want to take you to the ocean and let you see whales. I want to go somewhere you've never seen before and watch your face light up as you see it. I want… I want to watch you coach Parry Angel's soccer team when she's five, and I want you to be the one to walk Benny down the aisle. I want to see you in the ring at least once a day this summer, because you're so beautiful when you work horses, it's like watching magic happen, right there in front of my eyes. God, Deacon… there's so much I want for us… I just need you to not ever do this again, okay?"

Deacon's chest rose and fell deliberately. "Is sex included in any of that?" he asked plaintively, and Crick got used to the hysterical sound of his own laughter.

"Every goddamned day. You have a moral obligation to make sure I walk funny for the rest of our lives, okay?"

"Awesome." He took another deliberate breath, and Crick realized it had been a hell of a day.

"I should leave."

That hand tightened. "Don't go."

Crick felt the tears come back, when he thought they'd about dried up. "After everything you did to stay with me, it's the least I can do."

"Talk to me," Deacon mumbled. "I may not talk a lot back, but I want to hear."

So Crick talked. He told Deacon about Benny and Andrew, so tentative, so unassuming, and how the whole family was holding its breath with hope for them. He talked about Amy and Benny, making sure they all gathered around the table to give thanks for each other, and how Jon had been watching cartoons with the little girls as he'd left.

He talked about Jeff.

"I can't imagine," he said after a moment. "I can't imagine how hard today was on him. And then... he just... he came unglued. And he was furious. And at first I thought he was furious at you, because I was furious at you, and then...." Crick couldn't look at Deacon for this part. He laid his head on the bed and kept stroking that quiescent, work-roughened hand.

"It was all about Kevin, you know? And I realized that what Kevin did... how he died... you lived with that fear for two years. I almost did that to you. And Jeff... he'd lived through our worst fears. I couldn't take it, Deacon. I know I promised I'd hold together, I'd keep the family together, but I can't do it. I can't be you, I can't be Jeff. If you didn't pull through, I would have fallen apart, and I would have let you down...."

It wasn't just tears this time. Crick couldn't remember sobbing so hard since his best friend had died in high school. God. Just... oh... Jesus. For that moment, as he unburdened himself on a man who'd just had heart surgery, he felt so small, so weak, and so alone.

And then he felt Deacon's hand in his hair, stroking softly. "Don't cry, baby. You'll be okay."

"I love you, Deacon."

"I love you too."

"I'm not joking about forever." His voice cracked, cracked horribly on that last note. He didn't care. Jeff had waited five years to fall apart, but Crick had never been great at delayed gratification. He needed to let it all out now, or he might never talk to Deacon again with a whole heart. "You're my one shot. I will *never* love anyone as much as I love you."

"Me too."

Crick sniffled, thinking that he didn't sound grown at all. "As long as that's clear."

Deacon's eyes were partially open, sleepy and wandering, but he squeezed Crick's hand, and Crick turned his head and saw that he'd focused on Crick.

"It's a load off my mind, Carrick James. Now put your head back down and go to sleep for a bit. I'm not going anywhere."

Crick nodded, reassured. For a moment, as the heart monitor beeped and the purified air chilled his skin, they were kids again. Deacon was the golden god, and all things sat on his shoulders, and Crick would follow wherever he went.

At home, they had people looking to him, and he'd need to return eventually. But as long his hand was in Deacon's, he would always follow where Deacon needed to go.

Chapter 19

Mikhail: Big Stupid Feelings

SHANE, Kimmy, and Mikhail stopped off at Promise House on the way home from the hospital, the better to tell their four runaways that Deacon was going to be okay.

The kids were happy, jumping and hugging, and even their little meth recovery boy managed to put off his cigarette for fifteen minutes while everyone celebrated over Jeff's extra food in the kitchen. (That really had been thoughtful. Mikhail made a mental note to have the kids write him a note of thanks. Shane had two fortunes to spend on this place, but after seeing how much these children ate, Mikhail thought he might need more.)

The two boys and two girls who were Promise House's population at the moment (Shane had in mind something bigger by the time it was finished) had been really fond of Deacon—Shane had known that. He enjoyed the moment in the brand new, spanking clean industrial kitchen, watching the kids standing up and eating out of plastic containers while the cooking smells of turkey and potatoes heated the tiles and the friendly yellow walls.

What Shane did not know, but Mikhail did, was that the kids were just as happy to see Shane there that morning as they were to hear that Deacon was going to be okay.

Shane would not have fit in with these kids when he was a kid himself, Mikhail thought critically. He would have felt awkward, looming over them with his height and his wide shoulders and his roundabout way of speaking. But as a grown-up, Shane had become comfortable enough in his own skin to love them unconditionally and to acknowledge his own differences cheerfully, in a way that made the kids comfortable with themselves as well as with Mikhail's gigantic-hearted lover.

Mikhail watched as Shane gave the girl who had been working the streets not two months ago a hug, like she was any other fourteen-year-old, and then ruffle the pickpocket's hair—and then checked his pocket theatrically while everyone giggled. The kids all faced Mikhail's big cop like little magnets would face true north, and Shane simply looked out at them and accepted them for who they were.

Mikhail tried to ignore the shake of his hands when he turned away from that tableau to rinse his re-used plastic butter-bowl out in the sink. Kimmy was suddenly there, shoulder to shoulder—the irritating heifer was actually *taller* than he was—and her voice, quiet in his ear, was surprisingly soothing.

"It's okay, you know," she said quietly.

"What's okay, cow-woman? The fact that someone cooked for you this morning so you can sleep? I have to admit, that is a blessing. You should thank Lucas accordingly, in a way he would not appreciate from me."

"Stop being an asshole, Mikhail," she said, but her voice wasn't sharp at all. "It's okay if you're suddenly afraid. You're worried what life would be like without him. What if he hadn't decided to quit the force? What if—"

"What if that was him on a hospital bed? Again? Because I saw it, heifer. I was there. I watched him dying, and I had to leave him there, without knowing...." Mikhail tried to master his own voice. Failed. "And I had to live with that fear—and it was only months, you may think. I only had to worry about him in that job that tried to kill him for months. But... but Jeff only knew his lover for months, and that job *did* kill him, and...."

It was all muddled, wasn't it? That was what you got when you stayed up all night, talking to a teenager about his beloved older brother, who actually *had* succeeded in killing himself with his own fucking valor. That was what you got when you wandered around in a hospital, chased relentlessly by ghosts who all moaned terrible messages about being alone, forever alone, locked in a box, submerged in your own bitterness.

"Yeah," Kimmy said softly, her arm coming around his shoulders. "Yeah. It's okay if that's what you're thinking. No one's going to call you selfish if a lot of your worry is for Shane and not Deacon. Especially me." Kimmy's voice wobbled, and Mikhail sighed, trying to get his runaway emotions under control. He was done with being the little lion man, the one who was a world unto himself. He had a family—Shane had given him a family—and part of that was giving cow-woman the benefit of believing she'd been hurt too.

"He is fine," Mikhail said, lifting his shoulder in his usual shrug. "He is fine, and you and I are not sentimentalists, and so we shall be too."

Kimmy buried her face in his neck and laugh-sobbed for a moment. "Of course we are."

"You will see. We will leave and go home, and there will be no caterwauling about our feelings. We will pick up dog shit, that's what we'll do. We will pick up dog shit and feed the shameless pussies and take a shower because he smells like a bull and I smell like hospital cafeteria, and then we will go to bed and this"—his hands came out and encompassed the two of them, shaking shoulders, clogged voices, and all—"this will go away."

Kimmy nodded. "Everything except the dog shit, Mikhail. I had Lucas go over to your house and pick up this morning so you wouldn't have to deal with it."

"Lucas?" Mikhail said blankly. "My God, woman, is that some sort of horrible test? The one man in years I find even passable for you, and you make him pick up your brother's dog shit?"

Kimmy's giggle had fewer tears in it this time. "Yeah. That probably means I should really put out for him, you think?"

Mikhail turned around and wiped his hands on a nearby towel and then gave the sister of his heart a very deliberate hug. "Maybe keep the suspense, Kimberly. This one might actually deserve you. Thank you. It will be nice to not wallow in real shit this day."

With that, he looked up and caught his big cop's eye. Shane smiled amicably, and Mikhail could see the weariness he'd held back with his cheerful banter.

"Enough is enough, children," Mikhail said crisply. "We have been up all night, and he will not be nearly this entertaining if he is falling asleep in his shoes."

"Killjoy!" muttered one boy, their street hustler, the one who had found a box of kittens and stayed awake for his first three weeks nursing them all until they could eat for themselves. Shane had found homes for all but one of them, or Promise House would be in the same straits as their own home, pick-up wise.

"But of course I am," Mikhail said with pride. "It is the Russian in me—I cannot help it."

Shane rolled eyes in his direction, and the kids laughed, which was fine. "He's right, guys—I'm bone-tired. We'll be back later tonight for pie, so make sure you save us some."

To the children's credit, not one of them suggested that maybe Shane could stand to skip pie. Which was fine, because Mikhail's cop was not fat.

And he was not stupid either. They didn't say much during the five-minute drive from Promise House to their own home until they pulled up to the gate and Mikhail mentioned that Lucas had picked up for them while they'd been gone.

"Awww," Shane groaned good-naturedly. "That's awfully sweet of him, but not particularly nice of Kim!"

Mikhail smiled. "I don't think it was that way," he said, hopping out of the GTO and opening the gate. When Shane had driven through, he didn't close the gate and go running across the clever balance beam Shane had constructed for him so that he might not have to deal with the six dogs. Instead, he braved them, waving tails, insatiable affection and all, to walk to Shane's side.

He wrapped a fierce arm around Shane's waist, thinking that when Deacon had stopped running, Shane and Jon had pushed themselves farther and faster on their runs out of grief, and Shane's waist wasn't as solid as it should be.

"Hey, Mickey," Shane murmured, dropping a kiss on Mikhail's head. "Long fucking day, you know?"

Mikhail nodded, feeling his chin quiver, and after they got up to the porch and into the house, Shane stopped and turned Mikhail's shoulders so Shane could see his face instead of having Mikhail staring down at his tennis shoes.

"You step in something?" Shane asked, indicating he knew very well their shoes were both clean.

"Just your damned mortality, all over again," Mikhail replied irritably. He slid his eyes sideways, knowing his face was going to crumple and not wanting his big, brave cop to see it.

Shane didn't have to. In a moment, Mikhail was mashed up against his broad, solid chest, and he wasn't even ashamed when the first sob shook him.

"God, I hate your job," he muttered, his voice broken and clogged, a general mess all around.

"Baby, I haven't worked that job since June."

"I don't give a shit." And that was all he had in way of words. His shoulders shook, and he couldn't seem to stop crying. Shane bent down and dotted his face with little kisses at the corner of his eyes, on his forehead, on his cheeks, whispering soothing bullshit words that seemed to work anyway. What really worked was when Mikhail stood on his toes and took Shane's dear face between his hands, feeling the dark stubble against his palms, and took Shane's mouth furiously, so full of fear that the only way to empty it was into the physical act of taking.

Shane took him instead. First he took him into the shower, and then he took him *in* the shower, and then he took Mikhail to bed and made love to him so tenderly, with such quiet passion, that Mikhail's climax was more of a shattering than anything else.

In the aftermath, when they both fell limply against the mattress, Shane touched his face, his chest, his hands, with such gentleness that finally, *finally*, Mikhail felt put back together.

And only then, in the arms of his big, stupid, perfect, beloved miracle, could he sleep.

Chapter 20

Jeff: Hope and Pie

THANKSGIVING at The Pulpit was *exactly* what everybody needed.

Crick was there, looking tired but at peace, and Jeff was mightily impressed with his inner strength, even when Benny told Jeff privately that it was because Crick had gone back to the hospital because he couldn't sleep when Deacon wasn't in the house. Still, he was up, around, talking, albeit distractedly, to the family, and, yes, looking very, very grateful.

The talk was quiet, but they kept making each other laugh, so it truly was joyful, and the food was *awesome.* Of course, Amy, Benny, *and* Jeff had all been cooking their hearts out with worry—even after much of what Jeff and Martin had brought had been donated to Promise House, there was still enough to last The Pulpit until Monday on ham and turkey, stuffing, and sweet potato dishes alone.

Martin had greeted Jeff with an enthusiastic hug—and then sort of a sly, guilty look, and Jeff's heart sank.

He pulled the boy aside and said, "When are you going home?"

Martin shook his head. "Not yet." And then he smiled, genuinely and with his whole heart, when Jeff's shoulders sagged with relief. "You're going to miss me?"

Jeff nodded. "Well, yeah, kid. You brush the cats, you live on cold cereal, and you come to all my family gatherings. Best. Roommate. Ever."

Martin looked at his feet bashfully. "You're not bad either," he said to his size thirteen toes. "I don't want to leave yet. I... don't feel like we've said everything yet."

Jeff swallowed hastily and nodded. "You're a really smart kid, you know that? Kevin used to say you were going places he'd only work security for. I... I'm so glad you came." Jeff laughed at himself a little. "Does that make me a selfish bitch?"

Martin grinned, a little cocky now that he'd actually lived with Jeff for two weeks and not "caught the gay," as it were. "Naw... not selfish. Maybe still a bitch, but that's just how you roll."

Jeff's laugh was absolutely delighted. "Happy Thanksgiving to you, too, you obnoxious little shit. Go get me a soda."

Martin trotted off, and Collin came up behind him—they'd driven separately, and Jeff had arrived a few minutes earlier—and put strong, warm hands on Jeff's shoulders. Jeff melted into his touch, surprised by the complete level of trust inside. Maybe he just didn't have room for anything else.

"When's he leaving?" Collin asked, like he was shoring himself up for the worst.

"Not yet," Jeff told him, and it wasn't his imagination. Collin blew out a sigh of relief and wrapped long arms around his chest in a welcome hug.

"Good. I'd miss him—he's good people."

Good people. Jeff turned around in Collin's hug and searched those pretty golden eyes. "His brother was the same," Jeff said quietly. "You're just like them."

Collin looked stunned for a moment, and before he could take it the wrong way or get too serious when Jeff was finally feeling good about them, Jeff cracked a grin. "Except for the short haircuts and the real deep tan, of course."

Collin's smile was crooked, and Jeff kissed the droopy side of it. His family was happy and at peace, and he wanted Collin to be the same way. Sex (making love) that morning had been... amazing. Perfect. Transcendent. As far as sex (making love) with a real, breathing human tended to go.

Jeff would crack a joke or something about how good sex shouldn't break Collin's smile, except....

Except he couldn't lie to the kid like that.

"You're one of the best men I know," Jeff said seriously. "And you've seen the company I keep, so you know that's saying something. Now go get me a plate of appetizers before I get all gooey or something, because I'll never forgive you for that."

Collin wandered off to trade elbows—and talk about cars—with Shane at the counter, which was filled with appetizers, and Crick wandered over to plop down on the couch nearby and pat the seat.

"Sit, Jeffy."

Jeff executed an intricate bow. "Whatever you say, my liege."

Crick's sound wasn't quite a laugh, but Jeff would take what he could get. "Oh my God… guess what Jeffy did during his nap."

Jeff was suddenly too hot inside his cashmere sweater. "It wasn't my fault," he said, trying for insouciance. "I was giddy with relief. My judgment—"

"Is awesome, Jeff. It's about time you gave him a chance."

Jeff sniffed. "Well, for the record, his original chance came on Monday night, you know that, right?"

Crick laughed tiredly. "Yeah, Martin may have said something to that effect. Why?"

Jeff's shrug tried for light, but it felt like he was shrugging with the world on his shoulders. "Because you can't really talk about my judgment being impaired when I went out on a date, didn't get drunk, and stayed the night, can you?"

"Is that a bad thing?" Crick asked quietly, and Jeff gave him a weak smile.

"It will be if I break his heart."

Crick let out a weary sound. "Don't do that, Jeffy. I've done it. The results sucked."

"It would be for his own good," Jeff protested almost inaudibly. Collin and Shane were really getting excited about something. Shane was waving his arms around—he was even a little taller than Collin—and making engine noises, and Collin was nodding approvingly. Even Martin was getting into the act. Jeff couldn't read lips, but he got the idea that they were making something go fast. Very, very fast.

"Bullshit," Crick snapped, looking in the direction Jeff was. "It would be for your good, because you're terrified. Any idiot can see it. And I don't blame you, okay? But I think better of you than that. Collin's not Kevin. For one thing, he's got 'don't scare easy' written all over his face."

"Kevin wasn't a coward," Jeff defended, but he found his tongue tangling over the words as he said them.

Crick sat up then, since Jeff hadn't leaned back, and rested his forearms on his knees. "Look, Jeff—I'll say it again. Don't make a liar out of me. You are so much braver than I am, and you're so much braver than Kevin was too. You just need to realize it, that's all. Now grab your balls in one hand, your heart in the other, and own up to the fact that you could really love this guy—and that he's worth it. Okay?"

Jeff looked up at Crick and realized that he was exhausted and querulous and that Jeff had maybe tread on his last nerve after a truly horrific day.

"Of course, sweetness. It's your day. For you, I'll be General Patton himself."

Crick bobbed his head. "Thank you. 'Preciate it. Now since no one's bringing us any food, let's get this barbecue started!"

They sat down at the table, and for a moment, nobody moved. They looked at each other helplessly—everyone from the men, all of them, dressed in their best jeans and good button-down shirts (Jeff was the only one in slacks), to the women, who were dressed nicely and had put makeup on (Benny was even wearing an actual dress, with flowers on the skirt and everything), to the little girls, who were both dressed in those frothy, rustly princess-type dresses made of pink taffeta and lace— and realized for a moment exactly why they were there.

Benny spoke first. "God, we don't pray, uhm, at all. Ever. But we're all thankful. You brought Deacon through, and you gave us each other if... well, you know. We won't talk about that. Thank you. We're grateful. Please don't ever scare the crap out of us like this again. Amen."

Jeff smiled as he said, "Amen." Only Benny.

They were midway through dinner when Collin, who was sitting at his left, suddenly jumped a little and swore.

"Problems, Sparky?"

"I forgot to call my mother," Collin groaned. He excused himself from the table for a moment and then came back looking apologetic.

"Did she forgive you?" Jeff asked quietly, under the quiet hum of talking family.

"Sort of."

"Sort of?"

"She sort of has a request."

"And…?" Jeff made a gesture, and he and Martin met puzzled eyes.

"She requests our presence for pie, if we have to eat it at eleven o'clock at night. But she'd prefer nine."

"Pie?" Martin looked up, happy. "I like pie!"

"You already ate a pie!" Benny said from across the table. "And you're going to eat more for dessert. Isn't that enough pie for you?"

"Apparently not," Jeff told her. "He wants to eat pie at Collin's house too."

"Well you have to go!" Shane said, surprising everyone. "It's his mother!" He looked around for support and was met by bemused and puzzled faces. Jeff realized, almost sadly, that a lot of the mothers at this table were either deceased or MIA. That alone would have made up his mind for him, but then:

"Only you, beloved," Mikhail said softly, a surprisingly sweet smile crossing his face. "Only you would have such reverence for your boyfriend's mother. Let Jeff go where he wants for dessert. As long as he gives us all details over Sunday dinner."

Jeff grinned at the little man. "With you, Princess? I might even take pictures."

Mikhail's grin was all evil, as if to make up for the sweetness. "They had better be of Collin's mother. There are some things you cannot un-see."

Martin, Andrew, and Jon all put their hands over their eyes, almost at the same time, and Martin's cry of, "Ow! Ow! Ow! Ow!" made Jon and Amy's daughter look at him with curiosity and pity.

"Ouchie?" she asked her mother, and that made the table break into laughter. And pretty much decided the matter as well. Which was how Jeff got to see Collin's house again, and this time enter the house proper through the front door instead of sneaking up the back garage stairs to get laid in Collin's apartment. (Somehow meeting Collin's mother in the house itself made that entire act feel a lot more like Jeff's college years, a thing that didn't particularly please him at all.)

That feeling wasn't mitigated in the least when Collin entered without knocking, as though he knew the door would be open. Natalie Waters was sitting on a recliner with her knees drawn up underneath her, looking much like she had that day in the diner when Martin had arrived. Her hair was dyed a dark red-brown, and her fine, brown eyes shifted from the television to the doorway as they walked in.

She had a cat on her lap—a huge old long-haired ginger tom—and that made Jeff like her almost immediately. The cat took one look at Jeff, hopped down, and ran over to nose-hump his shoes, and for the first time since, maybe, pre-adolescence, Jeff was embarrassed in front of a friend's mother.

"Uhm," he said into the amused silence. The cat's purring was making the floorboards vibrate, he was absolutely sure.

Collin's mother laughed delightedly, put her hands on Jeff's shoulders, and reached up to kiss his cheek. "You've got cats!" she said, and Jeff smiled shyly and nodded.

"They're not cats," Martin said in disgust. He bent down and picked up the ginger tom, flipping it on its back and cradling it like a child. That cat loved it, going so far as to let its head flop backward and drool, just like Katy did when Martin tried the same tack on her. "Jeff's animals are like... like fur mountains or hurricanes, or... fuzzy acts of nature—"

"Or purring boulders," Collin took up, in complete agreement with Martin. "Or fur-covered lard factories or witness protection programs for fleas—"

"They do not have fleas!" Jeff made his voice indignant, but he knew what they were doing, and he loved them both in that moment, just like family, because he was no longer nervous, and he now had something in common with Collin's mother, and maybe, just maybe, it was going to be okay.

Over pie (and he'd passed up Benny's chocolate cream pie for Natalie's apparently famous pumpkin mousse, so he was glad it measured up), he thought that maybe he should give Collin's mother a medal for making it okay.

"He tried to fly over the garage?" Jeff repeated blankly, looking at a rather embarrassed Collin, who was probably on his third piece of pie. (There was also banana cream and apple—Collin seemed to be eating one piece of each. Martin seemed to be eating everything that was left.)

"More than once," said Natalie dryly. She reached over and ruffled her son's hair, and Collin pulled away from her, sounding young for the first time since Jeff had seen him in the diner, the day Martin had arrived. "Jeez, Mom! Do you mind? With the hair?"

Sure enough, Collin's glossy hair was now in a fuzzy halo near the part in the middle, and Collin was trying to smooth it down.

Martin smirked. "You can do that to me, Ms. Waters." He rubbed his palm over his short-cut hair, which had what looked to be a crop circle carved into it this week. "See? Doesn't ruffle."

Natalie grinned at him with full-wattage warmth, and Jeff watched as Collin just seemed to melt a little. God, how could you resist a boy who loved his mother?

Jeff offered to do cleanup, and he didn't need a libretto to read the mom-to-son eyeball contact that sent Collin into his old bedroom to show Martin all of his old model cars. Here it came. The grilling.

What he got was a hug instead. "I'm so glad you came," Natalie murmured, and Jeff smiled at her weakly.

"Starving teenager and all?"

Natalie's cheeks became hard and shiny apples when she smiled completely. Jeff had noticed that Collin's did the same, and he just wanted to kiss that appled cheek right now with all of the sentimentality he swore he never possessed.

"What he eats, I won't. Collin's sisters will probably write him thank-you notes tomorrow after we go shopping."

Jeff shuddered. "Black Friday? Really? Brave women!"

"We survived Collin's childhood!" she said lightly, and Jeff had to agree.

"You've done a good job raising him," Jeff said, feeling awkward. "He's… he's a good boy."

He was discomfited by her suddenly shrewd look. "He's a good man," she said pointedly, and Jeff flushed.

"Yeah. Yeah, he is."

"See, the thing is"—she picked up a dishcloth and started to dry dishes and put them away as she spoke—"Collin was there when his father died."

"Oh my God!" Collin hadn't mentioned that.

"Yeah, it was, uhm, a massive coronary. Gray just went over while he was driving Collin to school. It was strange," Natalie continued, like her voice wasn't a little shaky, even so long after the fact, "Collin—the way he reacted to it. I remember, when I told him that his father had died and that he'd tried very hard to make sure the car stopped so Collin wasn't hurt. Collin just looked at me and said, 'That can just *happen?* People can just *die?*' And it was like he spent the whole rest of his childhood *inviting* death, just because he was so angry at how random it was, you know?"

Jeff swallowed, thinking about Collin's cockiness, his confidence, his bold humor. He'd gained that challenging the biggest baddie of them all, hadn't he? He'd taken Death on the chin, and when Death had said, "I know where you live, little man!" Collin had backed down.

"Yeah," he murmured, suddenly wanting to be alone with Collin more than anything. *Death knows where we all live, baby. About all we can do is hold hands until he comes knocking. If you're game, I am, 'kay?*

"Sorry," Natalie murmured. "I didn't mean to make you uncomfortable."

Jeff shook his head. "No," he said, then, more positively, "no—not at all. It's always a good thing to know where Collin is coming from."

"And where's that?" Natalie asked kindly.

"Same place I am," Jeff admitted, feeling unaccountably vulnerable in front of this nice woman. "Blind fucking fear. He's just braver than I am at facing it."

"Well, sweetheart, he was five. Maybe he's just had longer to plan his battle strategy, you know?"

Jeff offered a warm but shaky smile. "I think you managed to survive his childhood, and you're a very wise woman. I should probably listen to you."

Natalie surprised him then with a kiss on the cheek—and then a careful wiping off of her lipstick. "I think you should come to Friday night videos next week. My daughters need to meet you so they know I talk sense."

Jeff smiled and ducked his head, understanding this for the honor it was. "Martin and I will be there," he said, and it was a date.

At that moment, Collin stuck his head into the kitchen. "Mom, I'm gonna steal Jeff for a minute and take him out for my one-a-day, alright?"

Natalie grimaced. "Eww, Collin! Are you *still* doing that?"

"Well, yeah. But only once a day!" Collin grinned cheekily, and Jeff excused himself and followed Collin out the back door of the little ranch house. He wanted to see Collin's old room, which was apparently completely devoted to model cars and trains in the hopes that one day Natalie's grandson would want to play there, as well as the room that had been painted for the granddaughters, and even the room that Collin affectionately called "Mom's crap room" because it was full of fabric, yarn, and scrap book supplies that never got used.

Jeff snagged his leather jacket because it was cold enough to make his breath white, and followed Collin to a small little alcove between the outside brick portion of the chimney and the garage.

"I haven't bought any cigarettes in almost a month," Jeff told him as Collin retreated in the shadows. "Didn't want to show Martin any bad hab—"

Jeff felt two fists in his jacket lapels dragging him against a hard young body, and Collin's mouth was hot and hard on his.

"I didn't come out here to smoke," Collin muttered, kissing the corner of Jeff's mouth and then his temple and then his throat. His hands were everywhere, down Jeff's pants, cupping his ass, under his shirt, stroking his back, and Jeff thought bemusedly that this was maybe one of the dangers of having a younger lover, because he'd thought they were done with this for the day, but Collin was kissing him like they were just getting started.

Collin gave Jeff's ass a squeeze, his finger slipping down into the crease, almost grazing Jeff's entrance, and his knees threatened to give out. "No, baby," he muttered, trying to think rationally. Collin's hand slid to the front of his pants, and Jeff's eyes threatened to roll back in his head. Dammit, dammit, dammit, he didn't have a change of clothes or a come-cloth or a condom—although he wouldn't put it past Collin to have two of them, lubed and ribbed and ready to roll in his pocket—and they had maybe ten minutes, so they had to improvise.

He told himself he remembered how to do this in less than three and slid his hand down Collin's pants and squeezed.

Collin ceased his own groping, buried his face in Jeff's shoulder, and groaned.

Jeff laughed softly, pulled his hand out, and fumbled with the fly of Collin's jeans, then moved to his side. Deliberately he shoved one hand down the front of Collin's pants and pulled out Collin's (quite large and impressive) cock and started to stroke. Collin whimpered, so obviously in need, and Jeff wrapped his other arm around Collin's shoulders and stroked Collin's far cheek.

"Suck on my fingers," he whispered, and Collin turned his head and did, in rhythm with Jeff's stroking on his cock, and Jeff nuzzled his ear and his neck as he did. "That's it, baby, make them nice and wet. You know where they're going, don't you?"

Collin groaned, releasing Jeff's two fingers from his mouth with a pop, and Jeff whispered, "Spread your knees, Collin. Spread 'em...."

Jeff's fingers and cuticles were perfect, smooth, no tiny cuts, not even so much as a dry patch of skin. They were soft and clean after being in the dishwater, and Jeff had no qualms about sliding his fingers down the crease of Collin's pale, bare ass and probing gently.

Collin groaned when Jeff found his entrance, and Jeff leaned over, capturing the groan with his mouth as he thrust the first finger in. Collin's knees almost buckled. He had one arm wrapped around Jeff's waist, and for the first time, Jeff felt like he was supporting them, supporting them both, his beautiful warrior who would face down Death for the hell of it but who backed out of the fight because he chose to love life instead. Collin thrust hard against Jeff's hand and spurted some pre-come, making his glide slippery and hot-cold with come and the chill of the clear night.

Jeff added another finger and spread them.

Collin screamed into the haven of Jeff's mouth and shot come over the dark space of lawn beyond their little patch of cement.

Jeff ignored his own bursting hard-on to nurse Collin through the aftershocks, holding him tight and fastening his pants with tender, trembling fingers.

When Collin was dressed and his shirt was pulled down around the waistband of his jeans and he was leaning against Jeff, shivering, he managed to speak. "God, man, I had no idea you were built for that kind of speed."

Jeff laughed a little, wondering how long his own erection was going to last. "Men don't usually brag about that, sweets. Just a few techniques left over from my clubbing days."

"If you don't get him off in three minutes, it wasn't worth leaving the club?" Collin asked dryly, and Jeff blushed a little and nodded.

"It's *always* worth leaving the club," he said, knowing his voice was smug and not really caring.

Collin laughed and groaned and suddenly caught Jeff up in a fierce hug, the kind that made Jeff want to lay his head against that hard, broad chest and concede everything to the gods.

He managed to lay his head on Collin's shoulder, and, after wiping his hands discreetly on the inside of Collin's shirt (since Collin could go inside and change right after Jeff left) he traced a high, sharp cheekbone with his knuckle as they stood and recovered themselves in the chill of the night.

"Collin?"

"Yeah?"

"This is going to be a long-term thing, isn't it?"

Collin's eyes were dark in this light and unfathomable. "I'm planning on it."

"I'll plan on it too," Jeff said. If Collin could plan on "long term" when he knew damned well and firsthand that there were no guarantees, then Jeff could too.

"I...." *I love you. I think I do. I think maybe I loved you a month ago. I think five years ago, I loved who you would become. I love you, but I'm terrified, and I think right now I'll just take this, my head on your shoulder, your breath in my ear, and tell myself that this is all I can hope for, it's more than I deserve, it's more than some people get in a lifetime. I love you, but I'm going to tuck it up in my chest for a little while more, until I'm stronger, until I'm braver, until I'm sure I won't hurt you with the jagged parts of myself that are still catching on my own heart and ripping little holes in it.*

"You what, Jeffy?"

"I should probably be thrown in the nuthouse for even thinking about this," Jeff muttered. "But...."

"But?"

"But I'm glad. I'm glad it's not going away tomorrow. I'm glad you were here. Happy Thanksgiving, Collin."

Collin captured his mouth with gentleness on his breath and kissed him so softly it was like they barely touched. "Happy Thanksgiving, Jeff. When can I see you again?"

Next week, next month, next year.....

"Tomorrow night," Jeff begged, and Collin kissed him again.

"I'll come over at seven. I'll bring a movie—*Transformers* or something. Martin will love it."

"Sounds awesome, Sparky. I can't wait."

"Jeff?"

"Yeah?"

"I really like it when you call me 'Collin'."

"Well when I really like you, that's what I'll call you," Jeff retorted primly, and was gratified by Collin's laugh.

"Bitch."

"Fetus."

"Shut up and kiss me."

"Bossy fetus… mmmmmm…."

Hope tasted even better than pie.

Chapter 21

Collin: A Tickle of Panic

DEACON came home the Sunday after Thanksgiving. Collin was in the quiet welcome-home party that lasted just long enough for the man of honor to fall asleep. After that, Collin was amused, and then impressed, as Jeff, Shane, and Benny worked out a schedule in which some of the kids from Promise House came out and helped with the horses and other members of the family would cook. Mikhail got miffed, at one point, when he was not allowed to help as often as he would have liked, and turned around and huffed off in Collin's direction.

Collin regarded him with a smile over his soda, and Mikhail crossed his arms and sulked. "I'm sure someone else will cook just fine," Collin said helpfully, and was regarded by Mikhail's scowl.

"You do not understand," he muttered. "Last year, these people— after my mother died, they… they rode to my rescue. You cannot do enough for these people. I cannot do enough."

Collin raised his eyebrows, impressed yet again. "I'm sure you'll get your chance," he consoled, feeling trite, and was rewarded by a bored roll of Mikhail's eyes in his direction.

"Just you wait, engine-man. They will help you, someday, and you will be at a loss. You have family now—lucky you. But this family, they will stand for you, and you will be lost as to how to pay that back, and I would laugh at you, but here I am. Only allowed to cook chili."

Mikhail stalked off after that, and Collin was left looking at him in surprise. An exasperating little diva? Yes. But a beloved member of this little family? There could be no doubt.

Crick came in from doing the horses and looked at the finished schedule with a face that'd he seemed to have set on "stoic." "You guys... this is awesome," he mumbled. "This... this will help so much...."

He smiled a little, kissed Benny on the cheek, and ducked his head as he walked off to check on Deacon.

Benny shook her head. "Oh my God! He gets any more terse, and he's going to be just like Deacon!"

Jeff looked after him thoughtfully. "I think," he said quietly, "that Deacon just did what Iraq didn't."

"Fuck," Benny muttered, forgetting about Parry Angel's big ears for a minute. "Man, even I know that's a shitty way to grow up."

Jeff looked up and locked eyes with Collin for a moment, his own dark and brooding thoughtfully. "You're telling me."

Collin didn't have to ponder what he was talking about, and for all of a week or so, he wondered if Jeff wasn't going to try, once again, to convince him to find another crush. That would have been impossible, of course, because this thing had gone *way* beyond "crush" and right into "I'll live in your pansy-assed condo with its-embarrassing white carpeting if only I can sleep next to you every night and watch your insanely long beauty routine every goddamned morning."

It was getting perilously, insanely, awesomely close to love.

So everything was roses, right? (Roses—Collin made a mental note to send Jeff roses. Jeff would appreciate roses, and it wasn't a thing Collin had *ever* gotten to do with another boyfriend. Most of his other boyfriends were wiry little men who would rather have a gift certificate to Sharper Image.)

That was until two weeks after Thanksgiving.

The week after Thanksgiving, which was also, coincidentally, almost three weeks before Christmas, Collin felt a tickle in his throat.

This was a bad thing.

The week itself had been wonderful, in fact. Spectacular. Awesome.

The Monday after Thanksgiving—the night after Deacon came home—Colin went over with a movie, and they'd had a boys' movie night. It was complete with microwave popcorn, which Con, the fuzzy gray mountain with the bugged-out eyes, liked to steal off of their laps one kernel at a time and bat around the lovely Berber carpet until it was dead. They drank too much soda, and there were boos at the screen from all parties involved. Collin loved watching bad action flicks—he'd always considered them interactive entertainment.

The second movie had been a romantic comedy, and while Martin had sat cross-legged on the recliner, Jeff and Collin were sitting next to each other on the couch. In the dark. By the end of the movie—and bedtime for all—Jeff was leaning back in Collin's arms, and they'd both been dozing enough to snap to attention when Martin stood and turned the lights on.

"Oh gag me!" Martin muttered, rolling his eyes as they startled and remembered where they were. "You guys are just so damned sweet it's giving me sugar-shock."

Collin blinked sleepy eyes and then grinned when he realized that the "gag me" hadn't been about the gay—it had simply been about the sweet.

"Go, Martin," he mumbled. "Way to let the love in." God, he was tired. He and Jeff had both worked the day after Thanksgiving, and Thanksgiving had been sort of a helluva day.

"Yeah, yeah, yeah. You want me to *really* let the love in? I'll tell you what. You spend the night in Jeff's room instead of on the couch, so I don't have to see your skanky ass when I'm up trying to watch cartoons in the morning, I'll take it as a personal favor."

Collin had been planning to drive home, but he wasn't going to look a gift night in Jeff's bed in the mouth. Or the ass. Or whatever. "Aren't you a little old for cartoons?"

"Just the fact that you have no idea how awesome cartoons are at my age proves that you are too old to try to relate to me. Get to bed, old man."

"Hey!" Jeff protested, standing up with Katy in his arms, which was difficult when you were tired. It must have been—Jeff had to stop and sway for a minute in order to get his balance. "If he's old, what the hell am I?"

"You hella old. Now go to bed. I know you both have to work tomorrow, and I want you dressed before you come out of that room, or I really may have to vomit."

Martin stalked off to bed muttering about too many men in their underwear, and Collin and Jeff stood and blinked bemused eyes at each other.

"Was I dreaming, or do we get to actually sleep in the same bed tonight, Sparky?"

"I don't know. Let's go fall into bed where we can dream about it some more."

They did, tired enough that really all they did was run slow hands over each other's bodies and tease each other into a languid hardness before they fell asleep, but they were together, healthy and happy, and it was enough. Collin had forgotten how lovely it was to just *sleep* with a man, and he decided he should do more of it.

THAT Wednesday, the day he had the tickle in his throat he didn't want to talk about, Collin, Shane, and some of the kids from Promise House made short work of Collin's workload. It was a lot more fun than he'd anticipated—Collin got to teach the trade that he'd spent most of his life learning from grease monkeys just like him. It felt pretty damned good, and Collin got to spend more time with Shane, which was nice. The big man didn't always talk in a straight line, and sarcasm seemed to hit a big cotton-walled dead-spot in his general vicinity, but he was kind, calm, and knew a hell of a lot about cars.

He also doted shamelessly on Mikhail, without being nauseating about it. The kids knew it, and they gave him gentle grief about being 'nad-snapped, and Shane just smiled and shined it all on.

Collin could see why Jeff adored him—and called him things like Hairy Hoover at the same time.

That night, he was able to quit early, and after a stop at his place to shower, he made his way to Jeff's. Martin was with him, and rooted through his video game collection while Collin showered. He'd been at the garage all day, too, and Collin figured he'd earned the right to pick something out that involved blood, guts, and copious amounts of violence. Eventually, they made their way to Jeff's snazzy condo with some takeout and a new video game.

The video game was a hit, but they were done playing by nine o'clock, and Martin looked at them and sighed.

"Not that I don't really love the hell out of you two, but I gotta say, I'm missing me some homework."

Collin wrinkled his nose—"Ouch!"—but Jeff looked sympathetic.

"Getting close to decision time, isn't it?" he asked kindly, and Martin shrugged.

"You know," Jeff said, looking nervous, "you could always enroll in the school district here. We've got your records for independent study packets, and the district I live in is a lot more diverse than Levee Oaks."

Martin managed a grin. "You mean there's more black people?"

Jeff grinned back. "And brown people and yellow people and peach people…."

Martin shook his head. "You know, I can*not* get used to that. Lucas was, like, the only white person in our neighborhood." He sighed thoughtfully. "But then, Kevin was probably the only gay person in our neighborhood, too, so well, maybe, you know…."

"It makes sense," Collin said, glad to have something to contribute. "Maybe that's why they were such good friends—because they knew what it felt like to be on the outside." He thought painfully of his little group of friends in high school. They'd been so tight, almost incestuous. They were hip, they were gay, they were fucking invincible.

Until they'd all been taken down by fucking.

He wondered about those kids who hadn't gotten tested, and how they were doing. God, the past was hard to look at sometimes.

Martin apparently thought the same thing. His arms were wrapped around his knees, and as impossibly tall as he seemed to be, it was an awkward, defensive position. "No way to hide being white, though," he said quietly. "Maybe that's why Lucas worked so hard to help Kevin hide being gay."

"That is a really good point." Jeff looked at Collin then, and Collin was thinking that Jeff never would have been able to hide it, even if he'd tried. How *had* his family managed not to know? "It helps to have friends that understand you. Martin, do you know *anyone* back at home who might understand that Kevin was still Kevin?"

Martin thought about it, hard, and then shrugged. "I've got a cousin…." He looked sideways at Jeff, embarrassed. "I've been giving him a hard time since we were little. But I think he might be, for reals."

Jeff breathed out hard through his nose. "Okay. Well. That's a start. No pressure, okay? You really are welcome as long as you like. But…." Jeff's unhappy glance landed on Collin again. "Look, Martin, I haven't been able to visit my family for… it's going on twelve years now. And it hurts. I have a new family now, you know that, and… and I love them, maybe even more because I don't think I ever have to worry about them yanking the rug out from under my feet. But...."

And Collin had a light bulb moment about why Martin was still there. This was hard. Pulling on the thread of how this unlikely teenager had ended up in this unlikely household led to the unraveling of wool dyed in pain like strong tea. Jeff's family, Jeff's pain, Martin's family, Martin's pain... God, even Collin's unholy mess in high school, it was all somehow connected, wasn't it?

Even a fourteen-year-old could see it, because Martin kept his arms tight around his knees for comfort when he said, "You don't want that for me."

"I didn't want it for Kevin, either," Jeff said heavily, and Collin tightened his arm around Jeff's shoulders. God. Just ouch. "That's why you didn't hear about me until you found that letter."

Martin nodded, then stood up, like this conversation had nowhere else to go. "Man, I'm gonna go read for a while. You keep buying me these dead white people books, I may as well read them."

There was a soft breeze of relief through the room. They'd get there—eventually the conversation would get there, probably without Collin's presence, but these things *would* be talked about. Just not tonight.

"Which dead white man are you reading now?" Collin asked curiously. He'd never been a fan, himself.

"Charles Dickens. Dude, if I'da lived during the French Revolution, I woulda gone straight out and killed some of those fools."

Collin managed to hold his chuckle in until Martin disappeared into his bedroom, but then he leaned in and giggled into Jeff's neck, wrapping his arm around Jeff's chest until the giggles stopped.

And then Jeff looked at him from tired, kind eyes and lowered his mouth for a kiss.

It was maybe the first time Jeff had taken control of a kiss, had held Collin's face between his hands, had initiated touch, had plundered Collin's mouth, insinuated his hands to touch Collin's chest, had, quite simply, seduced Collin until he'd muttered, "Is Martin going to be able to handle noise this time?"

Jeff grunted. "I hope so, but I'll try not to make you scream too loud."

Collin had chuckled against his mouth, thinking Jeff was kidding, and then they'd scampered to Jeff's room like naughty children. That was when Jeff undressed him, slowly, kissing collarbones ("So sharp, Sparky!"), biceps ("Are you really ticklish?"), and the tender, furry skin below Collin's belly button ("I love that your carpets match your drapes!"). He kissed, he commented, and he generally simply desired, until Collin's hands moved feverishly, knotting in Jeff's hair when Jeff sank down to his knees and stripped off Collin's jeans and underwear.

"Jeff, I'm close...." His voice had a hint of warning, but Jeff murmured, "Don't worry, Sparky, I'm totally prepared."

With that he produced one of those ultra-thin poly condoms from his pocket and rolled it on Collin's swollen, aching erection. Then he lowered his head and engulfed Collin's cock with his entire mouth, tightening his lips and pushing his head all the way down to the base and sucking so hard Collin was surprised his eyes didn't roll back, disappear, and pop out the end.

Jesus, could Jeff give a blow job.

It was exquisite, hard on the shaft, delicate and teasing around the head, his mouth warm and moist, even through the condom. Collin had to shove the heel of his hand into his mouth and bite down hard to keep from just screaming his release to the heavens, and even when he had spurted, the condom filling wet and hot around him (which had always been sort of a turn-on), he was hard-put to keep from groaning loud enough to wake the tenants in the next condo.

He fell to the bed sideways, panting and still struggling out of his jeans, and looked at Jeff, who was pulling himself off of his knees, still completely dressed.

"Damn."

"Is that all you got?"

"Day-*um*. Jeff...."

Jeff shimmied out of his yoga lounge pants and put one knee on the bed in his T-shirt and purple (!) silk boxers.

Collin scowled. "T-shirt off too," he said, and Jeff complied, that easily.

"I don't know, Sparky, I think maybe you should read some puckered, angry white men too—you need to work on your vocabulary."

Collin grunted and scooted until his head was on the pillow; then he set about the business of removing the condom and wiping off with the wet-wipes Jeff had started keeping by the bed, before pulling up his boxers, which were still wrapped around his ankles.

"You want I should finish you?" Collin asked, and Jeff shook his head.

"Not... I just wanted to give," he said, blushing. He couldn't meet Collin's eyes until Collin caught his chin and *forced* Jeff's dark brown eyes to meet his own.

"What?"

Jeff shook his head violently and then wriggled under the covers.

Collin followed suit and then turned off the light. "It's dark, now, Jeff. You can talk to me."

"Very funny, Sparky."

"I'm totally serious. Now turn over so I can spoon you." Jeff did, and Collin plastered himself to Jeff's back, pulling that long, sharp body against him and settling his arm between the bony ribs and the hipbone that wouldn't quit. His arm fit good that way, and since they were the same height, it meant he could bend his head slightly and touch his lips to the back of Jeff's neck. He did that for a few moments, and then, when Jeff hadn't said anything, he pushed insistently with his forehead.

"What?" Jeff asked, sounding a little groggy.

"You were supposed to talk to me."

Jeff was quiet for a moment, stroking quiet patterns on Collin's arm. Collin shifted and captured his hand, almost surprised when Jeff's voice came out of the darkness. "It was just your turn to get something for nothing, that's all."

"Come again?"

"I didn't come the first time."

"That wasn't my idea!"

Jeff's fingers came over his stomach to lace tightly with Collin's fingers. "Well, no shit, Sparky. It was my idea. Haven't you ever... just cared about someone so much, you wanted them to be happy, and your own bullshit was just not in the picture?"

Collin closed his eyes until he saw stars and breathed carefully. "Every time we're together," he said at last.

"Yeah, well." Jeff tried to shrug, but Collin was wrapped too firmly around him to let his shoulders move. "Just wanted to show it for once, that's all."

Collin felt like laughing and crying at the same time. "What brought that on?"

"Brain damage. Now go to sleep."

Collin moved his hand lower, wrapped it around Jeff's semi-erect cock through his boxers, and squeezed, just a little.

Jeff captured his hand again. "Stop it, Sparky. You need your sleep. You've been spending the night here and going to work in the morning—you look tired."

"Yes, mommy."

Jeff's entire body stiffened. "Uhm... *ewwww*!"

Collin chuckled for a minute and then said something absolutely sober. "If I ask you something, do you promise not to make that little-girl-icky sound again?"

"Yeah, Sparky. Pinky promise."

"You're hilarious. Ha-fucking-ha." Collin blushed in the dark. He'd never asked a lover this before—HIV or non-HIV—but it was a small thing, a simple intimacy that he missed. He tried not to dwell on it, but sometimes, when his throat was tickling and he was too tired too soon, it popped up in his mind, and he just wanted to share this one small loss.

"So spill," Jeff murmured, kissing his hand absently in the dark.

Maybe it was the kiss that did it. It was, after all, about the simple closeness. "That's what I'm asking. Do you ever miss the... spill. The taste? Actual come? It's why... it's why I like having you come *on* me sometimes, instead of coming while I'm *in* you." Collin's whole body was blushing now, and he was sorry he'd brought it up. "I miss the taste... do...did...."

Jeff swallowed. Collin could hear it in the dark. "Did I want to taste you?" he asked, his voice small. "You mean, did I want to have sex with you without the big brain-condom of being careful between us? Is that what you're asking?"

Collin closed his eyes. Now he was embarrassed not because it was sex, but because it was painful all over again. "Yeah."

"Sparky, if you... you have no idea how badly I want to be that close to you. I want to taste you and feel you skin to skin, inside me, nothing held back. But you want to know what I want even more than that?"

It was Collin's turn to swallow. "Hit me with it."

"I want us both to be around a good long time, long enough that our... our—God this is corny—but our goddamned hearts are closer than that one little sex act can be. Is that so wrong?"

Oh God. Collin felt weak—Christ, he never got teary. Not over movies, not over books, not over lovers. Maybe it was the tickle in his throat, and maybe it was the tiredness, or maybe it was just... just Jeff. A month ago, he's been a crush with some gratitude thrown in. Now, he was... he was complex. Prickly. Kind. Generous. In pain, and so brave.

And Jeff wanted them to be around for a while. He wanted their hearts closer than their bodies, as much as it pained him to say something so sincere.

"It's not wrong," Collin whispered. "It's not wrong. I want it too. Jesus, Jeff—I want it so bad, I can't even tell you."

Jeff rolled over in his arms then and captured his mouth in another one of those drugging kisses. This one was long, deep, and slow, and when it came to an end, they were both breathing hard, but not with passion.

Jeff pressed his lips to a spot on his cheek, and Collin felt his tongue come out and taste the embarrassing little track of a tear.

"That," he said, pulling back and licking his lip a little in the street light coming through the window. "Tasting your tears beats tasting your come any day, Sparky, you hear me?"

Collin nodded and kissed Jeff's forehead. "I hear you, Jeffy. I love you too."

Jeff didn't say it back, but Collin hadn't expected him to. It was like the tears—the words just came, because he felt them. Collin didn't want to belabor them, but some day, he thought, he might want to casually mention that he'd never said them to another man.

So the next morning he was unprepared and pissed off to find that the little throat tickle, that faint bit of tiredness that had made him not just jump Jeff's body until they made embarrassing noises deep into the night, had turned into a full-blown sore throat, headache, and the flu.

Oh shit.

It wasn't entirely true that every bearer of HIV felt like he or she was one sneeze away from the hospice. What *was* true was that taking care of one's health was abso-fucking-lutely imperative. Don't let yourself get rundown, don't let yourself get too tired, wear a hat and gloves in the cold, take your vitamins and eat your vegetables like it was an Olympic sport—those were practically the exact words of Collin's doc at the CARES clinic. He'd lived by them—it was yet another reason to keep the garage apartment by his mother: she could make broccoli taste good.

So waking up with a sore throat and a thick head—that was not a good thing. Waking up and having your lover put his hand on your forehead and say, "Jesus, Sparky. You're burning up. I'll call Joshua and tell him you're not coming in today," was *really* not a good thing.

"Goddammit!" Collin groused (whined), trying hard to open his eyes. "We're up to our ass in alligators today. I can't be sick."

Jeff looked at him over Collin's cell phone, which he'd snagged from the jeans that had simply lay where they fell the night before. "Sorry, Sparky, you *are* sick. In fact, you've got a fever. Tell you what— I'll call Shane and the kids from Promise House. They'll help Joshua take up the slack, and I'll drop Martin off before I take you to the doc's."

"The whole world gets the flu," Collin said plaintively, although he knew that wasn't true. He'd gotten his non-viable-virus flu shot like all the other good HIV patients, and if he had a cold and a fever now, his white count must be low, and that would mean....

"Aww, fuck," he groaned, seriously put out. "I really don't want to fuck with my meds!"

No one wanted to fuck with his meds. The side effects of the huge chemical antiviral medications that he and Jeff took to stay healthy ranged from psoriasis to nausea to diarrhea and its nasty cousin, constipation, to a permanently limp dick. Once the meds were established just so, balanced so a guy could eat decent and his skin didn't turn green and his dick didn't fall off, he didn't want to mess with a good thing. God knew what tomorrow would bring if he had to fuck with his goddamned meds.

When all was said and done, it was a damned good thing Jeff was there to help him find out.

Chapter 22

Jeff: Don't Worry, Baby

JEFF knew.

He'd felt Collin sleeping restlessly next to him that night, hot, sweaty, and uncomfortable, and when he woke up, instead of being sprawled possessively over the bed and over Jeff, Collin was in a tight little shivering ball.

Oh for the love of sainted crap.

For a moment, just a moment, Jeff, who was usually as dry and as practical about health issues as he was about everything else, actually spiraled into dizzy void of panic. Collin… oh Jesus. The boy who'd given him hope, who'd made him safe and taken his endless load of emotional shit, and oh, Christ on a cracker, who had allowed him to *feel*, as in, lay down your life on the railroad tracks for this person *feel*, for the first time in six years….

He was sick. And in Jeff and Collin's world, sick was a scary fucking thing.

It was all Jeff could do not to call Doc Herbert and drag Collin screaming in his underwear to Jeff's one source of medical comfort for the last six years. In fact, he deliberately walked into the bathroom, brushed his teeth, and wet-combed his hair before he walked back into the bedroom, took a deep breath, and woke Collin up with a hand on his forehead.

He didn't tell Collin that he'd already taken his temp using the quick-acting ear thermometer that he'd bought when he'd first been diagnosed and was paranoid as hell.

It was 102.3.

He called Joshua, keeping his voice as mild as possible, but the older man wasn't fooled a little bit. "You want I should tell his mom? She's got his doc on speed dial."

Jeff swallowed. "So does Collin," he said softly. "I'll call her when we've got a plan and a diagnosis. They may need to switch up his meds."

"Blargh," Joshua said succinctly, and Jeff found that he could smile.

"You're telling me."

Jeff found the number for Collin's doctor on speed dial, and suddenly his health care professional possessed his body and calmed him the fuck down.

"Yeah, I'll bring him in immediately. IV antibiotics—the whole thing. I am aware. Yeah—after you check his viral load we'll see about a new anti-viral. Yeah—I'll be taking care of him through this, no worries. I can call his mother. Don't worry—I've got it all under control."

He clicked Collin's phone shut and turned around to find Collin looking at him blearily. "Jesus, Jeffy, do you ever."

"Yeah, well, Sparky, age has its perks. There ain't many, but they're there."

Jeff looked at him, as he lay there in the almost-delicate queen-size bed. His body was still tan, and he looked wrong, somehow. God, that body—it was so lean and tight and active and vital—it wasn't right to see it limp and helpless. It wasn't right to see that lean, tanned face all pale, with high spots of color in his cheeks. Collin was so strong, such a grown-up, such a young man to have all his shit together so tightly. No one should see him like this.

He rolled over and groaned, burrowing into the big, fluffy pillows that Jeff indulged in. His hair was a royal mess, and Jeff appreciated what it must take to grow it long and keep it clean and shiny. Collin, with all his man-quirks, had the occasional secret pocket of queen, and that bad-boy long hair was part of it.

God, he was dear.

"Collin, baby, I don't want you to worry about a thing, okay? I've got this all covered. No worries. I'm going to take care of you."

Jeff moved closer to the bed and placed a solid kiss on Collin's temple, and Collin, who had been nothing if not a grown-up and a real man since he'd first made his move on Jeff, actually whimpered as he moved into Jeff's touch.

"I promise," Jeff whispered, kissing his cheek, "I'm going to take care of you."

There were so many things—but Jeff had been a meticulous planner, a creature of detail, for the last six years of his life, and even before that. You didn't get into med school without organization and thinking ahead and being able to make a goddamned list and keep a sane head.

Step 1: Call doctor. Check.

Step 2: Call work and have them cancel your appointments. For two weeks. Check.

Step 3: Call Collin's mother. Tell her you're taking him to Kaiser and that you'll call her later. Stay as calm as she is, like this is all routine. Pretend your hands aren't sweating and you're not thinking about how, dammit, you've fallen for this man, so hard, so deep, it's like falling off a building and punching a hole through the tarmac to the hidden black caverns of trust, pain, and fear beneath. Check.

Step 4: Call Shane, bless him, and try not to remind him that you spent two weeks last February finding ways to convince his skittish diva-bitch boyfriend that the family at The Pulpit was worth a gamble. Get complete cooperation from Shane about getting the kids from Promise House to come in and keep Collin's business running without him, and a surprise volunteer from Mikhail to come get Martin, which eliminated Steps 4 and 5, where you were going to try and find a way to convince Kimmy or Benny to come get Martin anyway and drop him off at the garage. Check.

Step 5, revised: Try not to let the quiver in your voice get away from you as you tell him thank you, forever and ever, and he says in that calm way of his, "No worries, Jeff. Take care of him. We'll be thinking good thoughts, okay." Check.

Step 6, revised: Thank Martin in complete surprise when he shows up in the kitchen with a small overnight bag already packed and tells you that Collin is dressed and ready to go and that Martin would wait for Mikhail by himself. Check.

Step 7, revised: Accept his hug, and his comfort, and his whispered, "He's going to be all right, Jeff. He's going to be all right. Man, I've got faith, okay? You're both going to be all right," with complete and total surrender. Abandon stupid list because your dead boyfriend's kid brother is letting you cry a little on his shoulder, and you feel like a big grateful, sentimental, worried wiener before you pull yourself together and remember that you've got a strong pink backbone and a set of hairy balls, and that someone you love (oh, holy shit, you really do) is counting on you to come through.

Check.

COLLIN was a little better in the car—the ibuprofen helped bring the fever down just a notch, so he was a little more comfortable.

"I'm sorry," he mumbled as Jeff tucked him under a warm flannel blanket for the trip. "You have to go to the hospital again."

"Remember I work in one, Sparky," Jeff said lightly, taking a sip from his coffee mug before he set it in the holder and got ready pull out of the condo parking lot. Martin had made him coffee while he'd been on the phone and trying not to panic. The thought of that kid's kindness and his solid, life-saving hug that morning made Jeff want to cry. *Oh, Kevin, you have no worries. Your little brother is already a fine man.*

"I forget that sometimes," Collin said dreamily. "I forget how good you are at taking care of people, because you never seem to take care of yourself."

Jeff let out a weak laugh and took another sip of that wonderful coffee. Jesus, with all his other talents, Martin could put the baristas at Starbucks to shame. What the fuck was that all about? "I don't know if you've noticed, baby, but I'm all *about* taking care of myself, and I have the grooming product bills to prove it." He set the coffee down and was surprised to find his hand in Collin's hot and sweaty one, even as he negotiated the car across Truxel to Garden Highway. Kaiser on Cottage, that was what Collin's mother had told him.

"That's not what I'm talking about," Collin mumbled, and Jeff tightened his grip on Collin's hand.

"I know what you're talking about, Collin," he murmured, suddenly too worried to be anything but completely sincere. "You're talking about what you've been doing for me for the last month. Don't think I don't know. But don't make me get all gooey about it right now, okay, baby? I'm going to take care of you, take care of this, and I can't do it if I'm thinking about all the fucking ways that you're wonderful and that you take care of me, because then I'd just be a blubbering ball of sobbing queen at your feet, and that's not what you need right now. You need Jeffy the strong, okay?"

"You're always Jeffy the strong," Collin whined. "When do I get to see Jeffy the weak?"

Jeff swallowed hard and kept his eyes on the road. "Jeffy the weak is the guy who would have bailed on you to cry in his room while your mother took you to the hospital. As God is my witness, Collin Waters, you are *never* going to meet Jeffy the weak."

Collin chuckled. As sick as he was, it was an awesome, carthy, groin-pounding sort of sound. "Aha. My insidious plan of following you around like a puppy and then sweating all over you is working."

"God, Sparky," Jeff half laughed, "you pretty much had me at 'I can fix your car'."

Collin swallowed and pulled his hand out of Jeff's to massage his throat and then his temple. Jeff saw that, realized the poor guy probably felt crappier than he had that morning, and pulled around a ninety-year-old woman reliving her golden years at the Del Paso intersection. This wasn't the greatest area in the world—Jeff was glad to speed through it.

"That's good to know," Collin said weakly. "It could have spared me a whole lot of trouble."

Jeff stopped at the light rail signal and turned to Collin, smoothing his hair back from his sweaty forehead. "Yeah, but now you've earned blow jobs for life," he murmured, and Collin's grin promised. Promised health. Promised the long haul. Promised, if Jeff thought about it, everything that Kevin's live-for-the-moment grins had not.

"There is that," Collin agreed with dignity, but he was closing his eyes, and Jeff was glad.

"Take ten, Sparky," he whispered. "We'll be at the hospital soon enough, and you know those people. They're exhausting."

"You sure are," Collin mumbled back, and Jeff had to smile. Irritating brat, getting in the last word like that. He had better be all right, and that was all Jeff had to say about the matter.

A few hours later, they were back in Jeff's apartment, and Collin was hooked up to an in-home IV complete with fluids, antibiotics, and everything a health care professional needed to take care of the man he loved.

"Why are we here again?" Collin asked groggily. The antibiotics were working, his fever was down, but he wasn't out of the woods yet.

"You're here because there was an outbreak of the mutant vaccine-resistant flu," Jeff muttered, double-checking his bag and using the ear thermometer again with the handy little disposable cones. "One hundred. Good. Some Tylenol, some rest, two more days of antibiotics, and we might not have to spend another fucking minute in a goddamned hospital."

It wasn't until Collin had been set up on a cot in the hallway, with the IV running, that it had hit Jeff and hit him hard how much time he'd spent in hospitals waiting for friends in the past year. Shane, Deacon, Collin—he was done with the institutions in general and the inside of them in specific. It wasn't like work anymore. Hospitals had abruptly become very, very personal places, and he hated them. His blood congealed in his chest, just froze up solid, at the thought of seeing Collin there for the next week, hoping his viral load hadn't suddenly spiked to the heavens, hoping acute HIV was not one blood test away.

And for a moment, he remembered all the hope he'd had when Kevin had shipped out, and he almost despaired. He almost stalked out of the hospital and gave up, left Collin alone to die the way Kevin had seemed to want to do, just so he didn't have to be there to watch the inevitable occur.

And then he'd asked himself how many times a guy needed to tell himself to sac up before that advice stuck. Seriously. Crick was twenty-five goddamned years old, and he'd been injured in Iraq, come home to face dispossession from the home he'd loved, and had just looked his lover's death in the face and come out on the other side.

Jeff, for all his high talk of being older and wiser, couldn't deal with one lousy goddamned fever? Oh *fuck* that. Seriously, *fuck that*!

Jeff had looked around, feeling his irritation at himself, his worry, his need to *do something* to prove he was up to it for the pale, sleeping man on the cot next to him, and realized that, ohmigod, there were an awful lot of people in cots in this goddamned hallway.

And that was when Jeff had taken charge.

On any other given day, he might have said the hospital was the best place for a sick man, but not Collin, and not this day.

First, he'd waylaid the first nurse he could find and begged, cajoled, and then just plain bullied her in the name of working there once a month as a float, goddammit! Into giving him a look at Collin's charts. His vision had blacked and his knees had gone watery in relief then, because Collin's viral load was only slightly elevated, and apparently this really was a case of a weak vaccine and a really wretched bug, and they could work with that, Jeff thought optimistically. They could definitely work with that.

But not here.

Jeff looked around the hospital again, grimacing.

Collin's immune system may have been doing its job, but the fact was, it *was* compromised, and now he was surrounded with sick people. Jeff could care for him just as efficiently as the nurses in his own home, and there wouldn't be any one's germs but Jeff's and Martin's, and, well, Jeff at least had been swapping spit with Collin for over a month, and their white cells were probably vibrating in tune.

He started making some more calls to Shane and to Amy and Jon, and then to Doc Herbert, and finally to Collin's mother, and by the time the doctor got there, Jeff had a plan.

The plan was to go home. Go home to Jeff's nice, neat little condo, with the two cats who could sleep in Martin's room for a while, and the television and the clean sheets and the sound system and the lack of germ-ridden sick people who could fuck up Collin's compromised immune system even more.

Home to where Amy would bring food for the three of them and help with the clean-up, and where Jon would come pick up Martin in the morning and drop him off in the evening, and where Natalie would come by for a couple of hours while Jeff used the gym and got out of the apartment and the sight of Collin's sleeping body and the worry so he could sac up and go back and do it all again.

Home to where Jeff could take care of his lover, could bitch at him, bully him, and beg him to eat, home to where Jeff gloved up and put his Physician's Assistant certificate to work and took him to the bathroom and kept him clean and generally didn't let him get sad, or morose, or depressed about being sick, and about it being a big deal, and about being afraid that his reward for surviving the killer of all flus would be an elevated viral load and a fusion inhibitor added to his cocktail after all.

Home.

Their home, wherever they were, wherever Jeff could go to sleep and know that Collin was breathing in, breathing out, and going to be okay.

On the third day, Crick came over before Martin got home, and Jeff blinked at him in confusion. "Don't you have your own man to take care of?"

"Jesus fucking Christ, Jeff, you think you could have called me and told me Collin was sick?"

Jeff pulled up a corner of his lip in thought. "Really? I told everybody else!"

Crick rolled his eyes and laughed and shouldered his way in with a Crock-Pot of something that smelled yummy. "Benny sends her regards."

"That's sweet—but I repeat, doesn't your family have enough to do?"

Crick set the Crock-Pot down on the counter and plugged it in. It looked to be chicken and tomatoes and something wonderful, and Jeff closed his eyes.

"God... that smells a-maz-ing!"

Crick grimaced. "Does it? Because Benny has been working out her worry and stress by cooking health food, and honestly? I'm full. I'm full, and you want to know the kicker?"

Jeff found himself giggling. "You're craving steak?"

"And chocolate. Goddammit, Jeff, I might as well be pregnant!"

Jeff couldn't help it. It was the reason he'd glommed onto Carrick Francis in the first place. Crick could make him laugh about the damnedest things.

He burst into giggles. He giggled until his knees went out, and he found himself sitting flat on the floor, laugh-sobbing into his knees, and he was only dimly aware that Crick had sat himself down on the ground, game leg and all, right next to him and had wrapped an arm around his shoulders until the hysteria had passed.

"It's hard," Jeff murmured, and Crick gave his own short bark of laughter.

"You're telling me."

"But you know what would be harder?"

They both knew. Firsthand, the both knew.

"Not being able to do it at all."

A few minutes later, Jeff had hauled Crick creakily to his feet and they were both seated on the couch and talking about the things in their lives that mattered most.

"He's going to be fine," Jeff said positively. "He is. He probably won't even need a fusion inhibitor—"

"Are those bad?"

Jeff shrugged. "Another med is always bad, baby. The more meds, the more of a chance for a reaction, and then they have to adjust the cocktail and then... it's just a hassle, and it's scary and... and it can be a really scary thing."

Crick swallowed and pulled his fingers through his longish, straight hair. "You never talk about it," he said softly, and Jeff shrugged.

"What's to say? It's like... it's like Deacon. He may only have been sick in the last two months, but... well, if you two hadn't been watching for it, things would have been a lot worse."

"Heart disease runs in his blood," Crick confirmed, and Jeff's smile was ironic.

"Well, HIV runs in mine. Me and Collin—we have to be careful, just like Deacon. We have to eat right, take care of ourselves, take our meds. The flu isn't just the flu, ever—it's a trip to the doctor's and antibiotics and...." Jeff's hands waved and encompassed his home, temporarily turned into a hospital so his boyfriend could sleep restlessly, larger than life, in Jeff's bed, instead of being vulnerable and diminished somewhere else.

Crick nodded and took a bite of Benny's chicken soup. "It's better," he said quietly. "It's better at home. I thought that when I was injured, and I think that now that Deacon's home. He has something to look forward to when he wakes up. He keeps walking into the stables. We won't let him work out yet, but the horses... he's just happy around them. I'd be going crazy this last week if he hadn't been there. It's like... like waking up next to him is—"

"The only way you know you're home," Jeff said quietly, thinking about the sound of Collin's breathing.

Crick nodded and smiled, and Jeff looked soberly back.

"Can I tell you something?" he asked, thinking that Crick might understand this like no one else on the planet.

"Fire away."

"When I opened that letter and saw what Kevin had done to me, on purpose, for a second… just a second, you know, I thought maybe he had the right idea—"

"Jeff!"

"No, no." Jeff waved his hands irritably. "Hear me out. Not that I've never been tempted, but… but just that without his family, maybe I wouldn't have been able to take care of him, you know? I mean"—Jeff smiled weakly—"Crick, I was alone for a lot of years without family before I met Kevin. By the time you came along…." He shuddered. "I mean, Doc Herbert—he was good to me, and I love him and his wife to death, but… that feeling. That feeling where you fit. Where your brother can show up with a pot of soup that his sister made you and hear about your deepest fucking fears, right? I hadn't had that in so, so long. And when Kevin died, I was just so afraid—so afraid that part of me that could take care of other people would have failed him anyway. And I've been seeing it, these last two years with you and Deacon, but I swear…." Jeff put his half-eaten soup on the table and pulled his awkward knees up to his chest, wondering if it was a habit he'd caught from Martin or if it was just the sort of mood he was in.

"Until I was in the hospital and saw him there, looking helpless and vulnerable, when he's so… you know!" Jeff gave a strangled half-laugh. "You know what it's like, to see someone who was born to be strong, and their bodies just betray them in the worst way. And then it's up to us to take up the slack. And I thought, 'Jesus, I can't let him down. I couldn't look myself in the fucking mirror if I let him down.' Right?"

Crick couldn't look at him. "I let Deacon down," he said, his voice so quiet Katy's snores from the stuffed chair almost drowned him out. "He told me to take care of the family, but look at you—you couldn't even call me when things got crappy. I'm sorry, Jeff, I'm…."

"If you don't shut up, sweetness, I really will have to kick you in the shins, you know." Jeff dragged a hand across his cheeks and thought that he really had landed on his feet when he met Crick. It had been a long time in freefall before that, but Crick, Deacon—if he hadn't felt safe enough with them, he might never have felt safe enough to let Collin in.

"Wow, Jesus, you're a pal," Crick said dryly, but the threat had worked. He wasn't apologizing anymore.

"Yeah, well, I do my best."

"Jeff?"

"Yeah?"

"You shouldn't have ever doubted. You're the best fairy-Jeff-father on the planet. You'll take care of him when he needs it, and you know what?"

Jeff smiled a little, and for the first time since he'd picked up the phone and Lucas had answered, he felt like it was all sweetness in his heart when he did that.

"He'll take care of me."

"Damned straight. Don't give him any shit for getting sick, okay? It's like… like me taking care of Deacon. It's what we were born to do."

CRICK left soon after that, and Jeff cleaned up their dishes, wishing that Jon would get there while Collin slept. Deacon's best friend was funny and charming and talked smooth as a movie star, and after that five-fathoms-deep confession to Crick, Jeff wanted some of that chatter. He could see how someone as serious as Deacon always was would be tight with a man who never stopped trying to make people laugh, and he was glad Jon seemed to take a liking to him. Jon wasn't as sarcastic as Jeff was, but he sure did appreciate it when Jeff let the snark out of the box.

But Collin woke up instead, and Jeff went back to sit with him. He was clean—Jeff had given him a sponge bath that morning, enjoying the fine shaping to Collin's muscles without shame. Collin had made a crack about him being a pervert, and he'd simply grinned and said, "Hey, you'd already seen my sex toy collection when you said you loved me. You have no excuses for not knowing what to expect."

Collin had tried for an evil horny chuckle, and Jeff had told him that as soon as the IV was gone and Collin was stronger, he'd make Collin keep that promise. Collin had fallen asleep soon after, smelling like Jeff's favorite aromatherapy body gel without complaining once about the scent.

Jeff enjoyed it now, closing his eyes and tasting the combination of dark wood and Collin's skin, even as he and Collin kept up desultory conversation.

Suddenly Collin was tugging on his hand. "Come lay down with me, Jeffy. You look exhausted."

Jeff smiled at him a little and put his hand on Collin's forehead. It was cooler now—not the 98.6 brass ring yet, but getting there. "Well, this guy I know got sick and…."

"And you've had to take care of him," Collin said soberly, seizing that hand and kissing it. "I know. I'm sorry, Jeff—I never wanted you to feel like you had to—"

Jeff cut him off right there. "Naw, baby. You don't get it." He remembered his conversation with Crick, and he felt it, to the bone, how much he needed Collin to know what was in his heart, without any window dressing or snarkasm icing—just him. Naked Jeff. Let the world hide its eyes.

Jeff leaned forward pulled Collin's hand into his lap, careful of the IV. The backs of Collin's fingers were still tan over the scars, and the faintest odor of motor oil still remained and probably always would. It smelled even better on him than the dark wood shower gel, and that was a fact.

"See," Jeff said quietly, "the thing is, taking care of you is… it's not like payback for all the times you took care of me when I was a flaming hot mess, not even close. It's not… it's not like an obligation. It's not something that comes with the package—I mean it is, but that's not how it feels. I mean, I take care of people, Collin. They let me into their lives and let me work their bodies and let me hear their problems, and I'm honored to do it, because I *like* helping people. I used to think I was too selfish, too weak to do it—I'd been alone for a while, I was used to thinking of myself only. When Kevin died, it was like… like God telling me I wasn't good enough or couldn't love good enough to help people. Like taking care of Kevin if we were both sick—that was just beyond me. And then… then it felt like Kevin felt the same way, you know?"

Collin's hand tightened over Jeff's, and Jeff just kept kissing it and pretending that he wasn't getting tired, gooey tears all over the back.

"You're fully capable of taking care of another human being," Collin said, his voice dry, like he was trying to get Jeff to stop crying without stating the obvious—that he *was* crying, and he wouldn't stop anytime either of them could foresee.

"But with you, Sparky," Jeff rasped, "it's an honor. It's a privilege. It's a gift. You're letting me take care of you. You're trusting that I'll do it right. I mean, I had to call in the cavalry to help, but…."

"But they owe you, so it was no big," Collin put in, and Jeff nodded.

"Because that's what families do. And families let you take care of them, and forgive you if you're too fucked up to do it right the first time, and… basically… you're my family, Sparky. You're the boyfriend who wouldn't go away. I mean, I pray… *beg* the powers that be that you won't go away. I… I really… God, Collin. You're such a big part of my heart, you know? You're such a big part of my heart right now, if something bad happened to you, there wouldn't be anything left. Everyone's always afraid of the virus, but it's not the virus that will kill me. It's losing you."

Collin lifted an arm then, the one with the IV attached, and Jeff crawled into the bed next to him and cried quietly, because Collin was going to be fine, just fine, and so was Jeff, and it really wasn't too much to hope anymore, oh no it really wasn't, that they could be just fine, and just happy, and just in love, together.

JEFF fell asleep then and was embarrassed to wake up and realize that Martin was there, talking to Collin about cars and about working in the shop and how much fun it had been, but how much everybody missed him.

Collin threw his head back against the pillows and groaned. "Oh, God—Martin, I can't thank everyone enough, you know? I mean… Jesus, you took care of my shop for me. If I was Jeff, I'd cry about that."

"Fuck you, Sparky," Jeff mumbled, and Collin's arm tightened around his shoulders, followed by a kiss in his hair.

"I knew you were awake," he said with a grin, and Jeff put his hand automatically on Collin's forehead.

"Good. Because I'm awake, you're better, now go clean the cat boxes and make me dinner."

"Ew!" Martin interjected. "But make sure you wash your hands first, okay?"

Collin chuckled and shook his head, and Jeff pulled back far enough to read his embarrassed expression. "How about tomorrow, Martin? Right now, I think I'm still going to need help to go take a leak."

Martin grunted. "Deadbeat."

Jeff struggled to sit up. "Do you need that leak thing now, or was that just an example?"

Collin started to answer and then was taken over by a gigantic yawn. "That was an example, Jeffy. But I do need"—yawn again—"to sleep."

Jeff struggled to his feet and was surprised by how firm Collin's grip was around his wrist. "Kiss me nai' nai', Jeffy. Please?"

Jeff yielded, placing a gentle kiss on Collin's forehead, aware that Collin had closed his eyes as Jeff leaned over. Jeff slid out of bed then and stood and stretched, carefully not looking at Martin for a moment.

"You ready for some dinner, kid? Crick brought over some chicken something that's pretty damned good."

Martin perked up at the mention of food. Jeff kissed Collin's cheek one more time as he turned out the light on Collin's side of the bed, and then he closed the door and ushered Martin out. Collin was already mostly asleep.

In a few minutes, Jeff had Martin set up at the table—Amy had apparently known that Benny was cooking this night, but she'd sent over some fresh-baked bread that pretty much put a capper on the chicken stew (what was it called with chicken and tomatoes? Jeff had no idea), and the two of them ate quietly.

Martin tucked into his second bowl before Jeff started the conversation—and even he was surprised by what came out of his mouth.

"Your brother was a good man," he said quietly, and Martin actually stopped eating, his spoon poised between bowl and mouth, to hear him.

"Yeah?"

"Yeah." Jeff nodded adamantly. "He was the best. He fought for his country, and he was as honorable as he absolutely could be. You know that's what killed him, right?"

"His honor?" Martin sounded really confused, and Jeff wondered how badly he could fuck this up.

"His fear, really, that people wouldn't see the honor because of the gay."

Martin set his spoon down back in the soup bowl, and Jeff thought that could be the first time in nearly six weeks that he'd seen the kid actually stop eating.

"I'd say that was stupid," Martin murmured thoughtfully, "but I might have been one of the people responsible for that."

Jeff took a risk and reached out and put his hand over Martin's. "You're a good kid, Martin. You're responsible and very hip and a lot older than your chronological age, but you were nine. Everything you knew when you were nine, you were taught. That's not your fault, you know?"

Martin nodded and then looked back at Jeff with such an obviously torn expression on his dark, oval-shaped face that Jeff could practically read his mind.

"You can still miss them," he said softly. "Even if you think they're wrong, you can still miss them."

Martin swallowed and nodded. "Watching Collin get sick and knowing... man, something that small might put him down—I'm so scared. Isn't that stupid?"

It was Jeff's turn to swallow. "No."

"And when I'm at home, when I'm scared, my mom makes me biscuits with butter and sugar and tells me it's going to be okay, and it's so weird, because all I want is my mom to tell me it's going to be okay, because Collin, he's like a kick-ass friend, right, and I'm worried about him, but whenever I think about that, I realize that my mom's... she'd think Collin would probably have this coming, and then... I don't even know how to think anymore."

Martin wiped his eyes with the heel of his hand, just like Jeff did, or Collin, or Crick—just like Kevin had, the day he'd shipped out. Jeff stood up then and bent over Martin as he sat down and hugged him, just like Martin had hugged Jeff that morning Collin had first gotten sick. Martin tucked his face into Jeff's shoulder and took a long, shuddering breath and then pulled away.

"You know what to think," Jeff said, his voice wobbling terribly. "You know that your brother was a good man, and he got scared. You know that he loved you. You know everything you loved about him was true, except for who he liked to kiss, but you were nine, and it wasn't any of your business anyway."

Martin nodded. "But how am I supposed to go home... and just not talk about that?"

Jeff took a deep breath. "Stay right here," he murmured, and then he ran back into Martin's bedroom.

He'd put the picture away when he'd moved into the condo—he'd had to. Thinking about Kevin all day, every day, had been killing him. But he'd kept it in a box of stuff he'd actually taken from home—swimming trophies, his high school diploma, yearbooks—and he kept those on the top shelf of the closet in Martin's room.

He came out, embarrassed by the dust but triumphant, holding the framed picture to his chest.

"I was going to make a copy of this," he said, feeling suddenly shy. "It was going to be your Christmas present, because, you know, I thought if I gave it to you for Christmas, you'd be too polite to throw it back at me. But I think you might want it now. I'll make a copy for myself later, but right now, I think it might... I don't know. It might let you go home."

Martin looked at him, still wiping his eyes, and such a complete attitude of trust in his expression that Jeff prayed he wasn't wrong.

He turned the picture around then, so that the two of them, Kevin smiling into the camera and Jeff peeking out shyly from his shoulder, were easily visible, and handed it to Kevin's little brother.

"Oh God," Martin whispered, smiling a little. "Look at him. He's so happy."

"Well, I don't mean to brag," Jeff joked weakly, and Martin tried a soggy grin at him.

"You look happy too."

"We were."

Martin looked at it again and nodded, and then he wiped his eyes again. "You could have been happy together," he said. "If he'd have come back, you would have taken care of him."

"Damned straight." Jeff nodded. He could have. He knew that now like he hadn't six years ago. It was part of who he was.

"I'm really glad he knew you," Martin said, nodding again. "Jesus, Jeff, I'm so glad he got to be happy."

He put the picture down and stood up and cried in Jeff's arms then, Kevin's little brother, and Jeff cried with him even though he'd thought he was about done with crying for the day. This was different, though. These were good tears. These were saying goodbye tears. This was Kevin giving his blessing, because Jeff had done right by him, and now Jeff could move on.

His future was waiting in the bedroom, and he'd be up and around and ready to make trouble soon enough.

Chapter 23

Collin: A Clean Bill of Health

MARTIN'S father showed up on Jeff's doorstep to collect his son on Collin's last day of rest (Jeff mandated and doctor approved) before he went back to work. It was five days before Christmas.

Collin was padding around the apartment restlessly in the fleece-lined leather moccasins that Jeff had bought him, wondering if there was a video game in the condo that he hadn't played until he'd mastered the top level and hoping that noise he'd just heard in the living room was *not* Katherine the Great-Assed Cat Bitch trying to climb the Christmas tree. Again. (Katy didn't seem to realize that she weighed in at twenty-two pounds and that if she got so much as two feet up the trunk, the tree was going down. It was a good thing all of Jeff's ornaments were new and made of painted tin instead of glass.)

He was thinking about maybe cooking.

It wasn't that the three of them had been starving or anything—in fact, far from it. Amy cooked, Benny cooked, Collin's mother cooked. People dropped by—his mother, his sister, pretty much every damned person he'd met at The Pulpit at one time or another. Shane had been a nice visit, mostly because he talked shop the whole time, and that was one of Collin's favorite languages. That and watching Mikhail sit on the floor and make delighted lurve to the cats had been worth the price of admission.

It was just that Collin was ready to be... a family. Even with Martin there, he'd enjoyed the closeness, the intimacy in their little household. He loved the nights when Jeff sat in the corner, reading a crime thriller (Collin could never get the connection between the guy who used three different smells of shampoo and the guy who read about blood, guts, and entrails, but he liked it), and Collin and Martin played video games or watched television. He knew family—he hadn't been trying to kill himself his entire childhood; there had been quiet times, too, times when he'd just laid his head on his mother's shoulder and watched TV and let the destruction of the world commence without him.

Those moments in Jeff's house felt like that. He liked them.

He realized that he hadn't been to his own apartment in two weeks—and it didn't really bother him. It was a nice place; he sort of missed his own couches under his ass, or the color of his bed spread, but it didn't have Jeff in it, it didn't have Con-the-cat-mountain, and it didn't feel like those moments, putting his head on Mom's shoulder, except with someone infinitely more exciting than Mom.

So there he was, puttering around the apartment, wondering if there was anything new on Netflix or if maybe he should read another chapter or two out of Jeff's book (because he was starting to see the appeal of the things with paper) when the doorbell rang.

He answered it to a six-foot-six-inch black man with a chest like an ale barrel and only a little bit of thickening in the middle to indicate late middle age.

He blinked, feeling very pale and every minute of the last two weeks in convalescence. "Martin's father?"

The man looked surprised and then really, really uncomfortable. Collin did a mental inventory and decided that, no, he didn't look all that gay today—loose jeans and a gray hooded sweatshirt with his niece's soccer team's logo on it were butch enough, right?

"Jeff Beachum?" the man asked, squinting, and Collin blushed. Yeah. He was a little young to be Jeff, that was true.

"I'm Collin, Jeff's friend." For once in his life, Collin kept his gay to himself. This was Martin's father, and it was not time to piss people off. He didn't even hesitate or emphasize or put quotation marks around the word "friend." "Jeff's at work. We... we, uhm, weren't expecting you."

Actually, they had talked it over with Martin and made plans to put him on a plane after Christmas. Lucas was staying in Levee Oaks (and Collin was now invested enough in Jeff's life to want more details from Kimmy about why, exactly, that was), and they couldn't bear to put the kid on a bus. Martin had told them that he'd talked to his parents—they were ready to take him back, and he said that was all he'd ask of them for now. He also said he wanted to come back during the summers to work in the shop with Collin, and Collin had been, well, pleased. That had felt good, like a victory except better, because the kid was good company, and because Jeff loved him too.

So they were expecting to say goodbye to Martin, but they thought… oh shit. Jeff was going to be crushed. They thought they'd at least have Christmas, first.

"Well, Martin's mother wanted him home for Christmas," Mr. Turner said, as if that was enough to change the course of the entire fucking world.

"Well," Collin said hesitantly, "we were going to put him on a plane the day after. We've got reservations and everything. He's, uhm, sort of looking forward to Christmas with our family."

God, he really was. Shane, Mikhail, Kimmy—hell, Benny, Andrew, Crick, Deacon, and the little girls. Martin had been going Christmas shopping with Jeff (very often on the Internet, it was true) for everybody, and he'd been enthusiastic and excited. He'd called them "his white-people family," and Jeff never failed to remind him that Andrew would probably take exception to that.

"Well, he belongs with us," Mr. Turner said, his ferocious brow furrowing. He ran a hand over his gleaming bald head, and Collin smiled at him weakly. Oh, he was so not in a position to make this argument, but Martin and Jeff weren't here.

"Look," Collin said with a grim smile, "Jeff's not here. He'll be home around six—"

"I only need Martin," Martin's father said grimly, and Collin felt his bitch coming on.

"Yeah, well first you've got to prove you're related," he snapped. "'Cause Martin's a good kid, and he wouldn't leave people who've been good to him without saying goodbye. I don't know where *you* were raised, but I'm seriously doubting he knows you."

Mr. Turner blinked slowly, his thick curling lashes making him look almost as young as his son for a moment. "I'm sorry?"

"I'm not. Look, if you give me your contact information, I'll let them know you stopped by, okay?" He'd also let Shane, Mikhail, Crick, Deacon, Jon, and Andrew know. And hell, why not the women and his mother for good measure? Martin's father could come face Jeff's whole famn damily if he was going to try to jerk that boy out of this home against his will.

"Where the hell is he?" Mr. Turner asked gruffly. "I thought he was living here!"

Collin scowled. "He *does* live here. But he's interning over at my garage right now—"

"The garage you work at?"

"The garage I own."

"Well what in the hell are you doing here?"

"Recovering from the flu."

"So my boy's working your sweatshop for you?"

Collin sighed and chewed aggressively on his bottom lip as he tried to figure a way out of this conversation. "Your son is with an entire group of runaways, currently learning a trade from my employee and the guy who runs the runaway shelter nearby. The difference is, he stays here, because he's family."

Martin's father snorted. "Not *your* family!" and Collin resisted the urge to kick him in the shins.

"He is now," Collin said quietly instead. "And I'm not letting my family get hauled anywhere he doesn't want to go." He held up a hand. "Look, you can make this a legal thing, but I've got to tell you, the police force is sort of on our side in this neck of the woods. Besides, you take him by force, and he will hate you for life. Trust me, I used to be a headstrong teenager, and I'm telling you that the only reason I'm still talking to my mom right now is because she never tried to force me to be anyone I didn't want to be. So you can make this big and ugly and lose your son in the most important way, or you can take a breath, go find a hotel, and settle in for a day. Everybody"—and he did mean everybody if he could do anything about it—"will be here tonight. Come back and talk to Jeff and Martin then."

Martin Turner's father made a "humph" sound and backed up a step, and Collin wondered if he looked as pissed off as he felt. He felt like a bantam chicken against this man, but Jesus—come to Jeff's house, insult Jeff, insult *Martin*, and then try to lay down the law.

"I'll be back," he threatened, and Collin tried very hard not to look relieved.

"Show up around seven—we'll have dinner," he said, and that, of all things, seemed to surprise the man.

"Dinner?"

"Yeah. Dinner. Like people who have a common interest."

"I don't have no common interest with you, you little—"

Collin held up a hand. "Think about your sons, Mr. Turner, and maybe stop right there?"

To his surprise, Martin's dad actually stopped talking and looked *really* uncomfortable. "Martin's not a faggot," he said gruffly, and Collin wondered if there was some sort of medal they awarded to boyfriends who dealt with this sort of thing voluntarily.

"No, sir, but I am, and Martin really likes me. Try not to piss me off, okay? Dinner at seven. We'll see you then."

And with that he shut the door closed with exaggerated gentleness, then leaned back against it and wondered if it was leftovers from the flu or the sudden adrenaline that left him feeling weak.

Then he went and got himself a soda, and the remote control, and Jeff's house phone. All the numbers were in the phone, and Collin needed them all.

By the time he was done calling, his soda was done, he really needed to pee, and he would have liked a nap. He did the first thing but passed up on the second—there was company coming, and he wanted to do Jeff proud.

Jeff was unsurprisingly meticulous, and he even had a "girl" (aged forty-something) come in and do things like scrub the tile in the bathroom and dust the tchotchkes on the mantle, so Collin didn't have a whole lot to do, but he did it anyway, so Jeff wouldn't have one of those strange freak-out moments that he seemed prone to about the way things were supposed to be. Collin didn't think much about his father these days, but when he did, he realized that Grayson Waters had always been about warmth and heart, and not appearance—and his mother, as much as she loved a nice presentation, was the same. He wondered now about Jeff's life as a child. Jeff often said it was "picture perfect," and as Collin put absolutely everything in its place, he found himself wondering if maybe Jeff's quest to be a caretaker, to work in the health-care field, to be a reliable friend, wasn't somehow related to that.

Jeff wanted to be the real, and not the picture.

That morning before he'd left for work, Jeff had read off a list of things Collin was absolutely not supposed to do: no cleaning the house, no stressing, no going outside in his bare feet, no opening the door to plague-ridden zombies, no drinking all the soda Jeff had bought for Martin, no playing in the toy drawer....

"What do you mean no playing in the toy drawer?" Collin was surprised, because... well... because he was there alone, with nothing to do but lie in bed. Why wouldn't he want to play in the toy drawer?

Jeff had raised his eyebrows and pursed his lips. "Sparky, we have real live people to play with now. Save yourself for that, okay?"

Collin had given a lazy grin. "You mean, after five or six years, you don't want me to waste myself on the fantasy?"

Jeff nodded adamantly. "Honey, now that I've got the real thing, he'd better be up to the job."

Now, vacuuming the last of the pine needles (for the moment) out from under the tree, Collin thought that maybe Jeff had been tired of the fantasy all along.

He certainly showed signs of wanting to make it real with Collin.

"You like the cats, don't you?"

Collin raised an eyebrow at him from his prone position on the couch and tried not to grunt as Con kneaded one final round on his abdomen. The cat placed himself carefully and looked at Collin with the imperious glare of an emperor from his big, buggy eyes. Collin started the requisite stroking from the top of the cat's head down to the base of its tail, wrapping it up with a tight scratch there where it made the big lump of fur hump against his hand like a horny club kid.

"'Like' is a mild sort of word for what Con and I have," Collin replied, leaning forward to touch noses with the big doofus. Constantine half-closed his eyes and twitched his whiskers back. "I'd go with the deeply twisted interpersonal relationship that a hero has for his nemesis, sort of a Batman/Joker thing, if the Joker suddenly started going down on Batman like a porn-star on Viagra."

Jeff looked at him in alarm. "Jesus, Sparky, stop touching my cat!"

Collin laughed at him. "Not on your life. He's my cat now—you can have Katy, the slut. She'll go down on anyone, but Con will only go down on me." Collin looked up at Jeff then, an evil glitter in his eye. "Sort of like his owner."

Jeff got up and flounced off—it was bedtime anyway, and Martin had been asleep for an hour. "Yeah, you want to see some of that action, and you'd better put your horny Joker on the floor and come to bed."

Collin did just that and caught up with Jeff in the hallway, pulling Jeff's body of sharp angles back against his, marveling at how soft that body became when it was flush against Collin's and nestled right in his arms. "Why does it matter that I'm bonding with the furball, Jeffy?" he asked, nuzzling Jeff's ear. He knew the answer, of course, but he wanted to hear Jeff say it.

Jeff sighed and melted completely. "That cat's been with me for six years, Sparky, you do the math."

"I will if you say my name."

Another sigh, and his surrender was trembling against Collin's skin. "I want you to be around longer than the damned cat, Collin. Would you like a diagram?"

"All I need is three little words."

"I love you. Now let's get out of the hallway, before we wake Martin up and find out he really does vomit on command."

Of course, he'd said it since, more and more often, but that first time had been so unexpected, so... so *given*, as though Collin should have known. But then, Jeff really did love those cats—maybe Collin *should* have known.

Collin finished vacuuming and then went to take a shower—and then, seriously, that nap. He *did* know, he thought in the shower, and later, sliding between Jeff's fine thread count sheets and a comforter that Jeff had changed right after Thanksgiving to match the season. (Who *did* that? Really?)

How could Collin not know that Jeff loved him? Even without the words, there was the kindness, and the passion, and the caring. The way his eyes gleamed in the dark as they kissed each other, the sound he made when he stretched out in Collin's arms.

It was real. It had *never* been just a crush, it had *never* been about the hero worship. It had *always* been what Collin knew they could have, the terrible flames when they made love, the spitting sparks when they bickered, the constant, enduring warmth when they touched in stillness.

It was love. It was forever. And, for as long as he had any control over the situation at all, Collin wasn't going anywhere.

Which was good, because after his nap, he'd have about fifteen minutes to get dressed and look solid before the entire world showed up at their door to see them as a couple.

DEACON and Crick arrived first, and Collin was pleased to see them. It had seemed silly, somehow, convalescing at the same time Deacon was, both of them bored out of their skulls but not allowed to even be in the same room. Of course, the bug that had leveled Collin would also level Deacon, because his immune system had been compromised by the surgery, so they'd had to resort to phone calls, which was a laugh, because Collin did all the talking and Deacon sort of grunted encouragingly into the phone. Collin had remarked to Jeff that he was pretty sure Deacon approved of him, but he couldn't tell for certain.

"Oh, honey, Deacon adores you."

"How in the hell would you know that?"

"Crick told me so. He speaks fluent Deacon—him and Jon are about the only two people on the planet who can!"

That reassurance was what Collin had needed to make The Pulpit the first of his calls that afternoon, and now, he could hear Deacon as he got out of the truck and started walking down the pathway that led between the condo buildings.

"I'm not wearing that!" he snapped, and Collin peered out the window over the sink to see him stalking away from the truck. Crick had been holding a breathing mask out the window, but at Deacon's words he snatched it back and said something that Collin couldn't make out.

Deacon turned around and scowled. "I'm fine, Carrick James. Now park the goddamned truck around back before Jeff's neighbors call the cops with a redneck alert!"

"Can you be a gay redneck?" Collin asked, opening the door, and Deacon grinned. God, was he pretty. Collin got how Jeff could totally ogle the guy without ever really falling for him. He was pretty like angels were pretty—all of that glory was meant for his god, and Deacon's god was Jeff's rangy, smart-assed best friend.

"I hope so," Deacon replied as he walked in and wiped his boots on the entry rug. "Otherwise I'm going to have to grow my hair longer or use a whole lot more sun block."

He looked good, Collin thought critically. A little like Collin in that he was thin and pale, but he moved with vigor, and there wasn't even the slightest sign of the breathing trouble or the blueness around the lips or the fingernails. Collin was glad—so glad—that Jeff's friend was going to make it. It seemed like a good omen, like a symbol that all the worst shit was behind them and the best shit waited in the wings.

Collin laughed and invited him in, and was shortly overwhelmed by *everybody* arriving at once, most of them with food.

"So," Benny said, setting up two casserole dishes and turning on the stove for Amy's biscuits, "you invited him for dinner, but you didn't tell him that the house would be full of gay people?"

Collin grinned diabolically. "And their sisters and best friends and nieces."

Benny turned and grinned back. "God, you're good. You're going to fit right in. So, what does Jeff think about all this?"

"We'll find out when he gets here—let's hope Shane and Mikhail get here with Martin first."

They did, and it was a good thing Collin had straightened up, because people were sitting on the floor and on the counters and on the beds. It was a madhouse, but it was also a Christmas party, and people were talking gaily and chatting like they did at The Pulpit or at his mother's house. Joanna and Amy seemed to be getting along swimmingly, and Collin's mother immediately went into the bedroom to watch a video on Jeff's smaller television with all five of the little girls—it really was like home.

Martin walked in, Shane and Mikhail at his heels, obviously surprised by the masses. "What in the hell?"

Collin squirmed, hoping for the first time that Martin enjoyed being the center of this much attention. "Your, uhm, dad stopped by this afternoon. He wanted to take you home. I, uhm, told him you were going home after Christmas, you know?"

Martin's smile was blinding. "And you wanted to show him that he's not the only one with the family card, right?"

Collin flushed. "I'm not a good grown-up role model," he assured the kid. "You really shouldn't copy your behavior after me at all."

Martin cackled. "No, no—I think you're doing fine! Holy God—is that *food*?" And that was the end of the conversation—he shot into the kitchen like a bullet and started laying waste to all before him, but just like Thanksgiving, there was more than enough.

Mikhail watched him with a rather bemused expression. "You could feed my entire apartment complex in St. Petersburg for a week with what that boy eats in one day. Where does all of that food go?"

Collin thought about it. "You would not be*lieve* how much toilet paper we go through in a week."

Mikhail's eyes grew to the size of soccer balls, and over his shoulder Shane turned red and fell back against Jeff's wall in the effort not to laugh.

"Stop it, you irritating man!" Mikhail snapped, blinking, but Shane was too busy laughing.

"Oh Christ, Mickey, he's just like Jeff!"

Mikhail eyed Collin sourly. "Yes, except Jeff is funny," he sniffed, and then flounced off.

Shane grinned at Collin. "You just took him down a peg or two, that's all. Don't worry, he likes you fine."

"I hope so," Collin replied, somewhat absentmindedly. He'd just seen Jeff's car flash by through the kitchen window. "I'm going to be around for a while."

Suddenly Mikhail's big boyfriend caught his attention with a hand on the shoulder. "You have no idea how glad we are to hear that," he said quietly. "You're so good for him."

Collin grimaced. "Let's see how good he thinks I am when he sees I invited his entire family without telling him."

"Why in the hell would you do that?"

Collin started to shift from foot to foot before he reminded himself that the whole point here was that he was a damned grown-up. "He really needs this," he said quietly. "This time with Martin, it's been... it's like resolution, stitches and bandaging for this big open wound he's been carrying around, pretending it doesn't exist. He deserves that healing, Shane, you know? I don't want him to give it up before he's ready."

He thought he sounded lame, but Shane nodded his head like Collin was really speaking his language. "I hear you. Well, sometimes healing is ripping off the bandage—and here comes the patient now."

Jeff looked entirely bemused as he walked in his own front door. "Where are the cats?" he asked, ever practical, and Collin was glad he had an answer for that one.

"Locked in your bathroom. What's that in your hand?" Collin made a grab for the festive bag of what looked to be sweets in Jeff's hand.

"Soy-fudge from Margie," Jeff muttered, looking dazed as he realized that his entire family was in his smallish apartment. The living space at Deacon and Crick's house was really much larger.

"Awesome, how's she doing?" Collin had heard a lot about Margie since he and Jeff had started dating, and now he grabbed the bag and reached inside, pulling out a piece of sheer perfection and popping it in his mouth before Jeff could lecture him on eating healthy. They'd already pretty much both given up smoking completely—a guy got some soy-fudge. "Mmmmm..." he sighed. "God, it's almost better than real fudge. I didn't think that was possible!"

"She'll never be a supermodel, but she's healthy," Jeff said, answering his first question and looking around his apartment in a complete daze. "Collin, why is the entire fucking free world in my living room?"

"Mmm... God!" Collin closed his eyes and experienced another chocolate-gasm. "I think I love her in a totally sexual way that has nothing to do with her as a person and everything to do with this fudge!"

"You're stalling!"

"Yeah... mmm...." Collin shuddered in true sensual delight. "But not because I want to."

"Seriously!" Jeff hissed, probably because Mikhail had just walked by twice and rolled his eyes, and Collin knew it was time to get serious.

"Okay, seriously, Kevin's father is coming to get Martin, and I didn't want to let him go until after Christmas."

Jeff blinked, obviously stunned. "He's coming to get—"

"He already came, actually. He's huge. Jesus, I thought Martin was big—you can't see it in the picture, but Kevin must have been built like a... a—"

"A Panzer tank, yeah," Jeff supplied. His voice was calm, but his hands kept going from his hips, to crossed in front of his chest, to carving invisible shapes in the air between the two of them. "So why is the world in my living room again?"

They were still in the dark of the hall, and Collin took advantage of it by leaning into Jeff until he backed up against the wall. Then he took Jeff's bag of heaven in one hand and put the other one on Jeff's bony, skinny hip. Gently, he bumped his nose up against Jeff's cheek until Jeff turned into his kiss. Jeff's lips parted reluctantly, but Collin moved his hand up, framing Jeff's face and holding him steady as Collin dove in and plundered the resistance and the attitude right out of him. He didn't come up for breath until he felt Jeff relax, and that was when Collin relaxed into him, straddling his feet and pushing his lower body in contact—not for the sexual arousal, per se, but mostly for the full touch between the two of them.

"They're here for the same reason I am," Collin told him firmly. "Because we love you, and we want you to have this Christmas with Martin so you can say goodbye to Kevin, and you can move into a stunningly happy new life with your insatiable young lover who will never let you down."

Jeff opened his mouth to say something snarky—Collin could see it in his eyes—but then he stopped himself and sobered, swallowed, and took everything Collin was offering at face value. His smile changed then, from wicked to soft, and he nodded.

"That sounds like the best plan ever," he said softly. "But I need to go change and take a leak and pet the babies first, okay?"

"You need to go sniffle in the bathroom like the big emotional queen I know and love and then pull your shit together for the family," Collin interpreted, and Jeff rolled his (dewy) eyes and wiped them with the back of his hand.

"Yeah, yeah, yeah… you say po-tay-to—"

"I say go get changed and entertain these people."

"Well get off me, Sparky, because there's a Panzer tank who's about to plow down my door in T-minus-five minutes!" Jeff planted both hands on Collin's chest then and shoved, and Collin let him go.

He moved into the living room and sat down next to Deacon, satisfied that the party/rescue mission could go on without him for a moment. Deacon was eyeing the plate of steamed spinach and lemon chicken in front of him with a resigned air.

"You know what I *really* want for Christmas?" he muttered to himself.

"What?" Collin asked cheekily, and Deacon grimaced and slanted his eyes sideways.

"A steak dinner. How's Jeff?"

"Quietly panicking in the bathroom," Collin said confidently, and Deacon nodded sagely.

"Excellent. Why aren't you in there with him?"

Collin looked at him in horror. "Freaking out like this is something Jeff really would rather do alone. Once he's found his backbone and done what he needs to, that's when I get to pick up the pieces."

Deacon *hmm*-ed appreciatively. "Sounds like a good system. I couldn't do it, but good for you."

"You couldn't let Crick freak out on his own?"

Deacon shook his head. "Nope. We did plenty of freaking out alone when he was in Iraq. I'd just as soon freak out together if we've got the chance." He took a tentative bite of the chicken and looked at his plate a little more favorably. "But then, Crick doesn't really freak out a lot."

That's because you didn't see him while you were in surgery. Collin thought it but didn't say it. Besides, even then, Crick seemed to have had most of his emotions under control, and Collin thought, not for the first time, how much Carrick Francis had grown from the kid Collin had admired in high school. And then it occurred to him that he had grown, too, and he was just feeling damned proud of himself when there was a solid knock at the door.

He'd gotten comfortable and had to struggle to his feet, and that was unfortunate, because Mikhail was the one who answered.

The living room grew absolutely quiet as the thundering voice of Martin's father filled the room. "Are you Jeff Beachum?"

"No. Holy God, are you Martin's father?"

"Yes, and I'm here to get my son!"

Collin was just rounding the corner at that point, and he watched Mikhail's eyes get really large. Without even bothering to answer the man, he turned on his heels and went running toward the kitchen, shouting, "Shane! Shane! You must keep the boy from eating any more! You have no idea what will happen!"

Collin was face to face with Martin's father then, and they both heard Martin say, "You stay away from my eats, little man, or I will *end* you!"

"You need to put that down, Martin, or you will *never* fit through another door!"

Martin's laugh was strained, and Collin looked over his shoulder through the door that connected the kitchen to the entryway in time to see Martin pat Mikhail on the outraged head. "That's just my pops, Mikhail—no worries. He won't be here long." Martin put his plate on the counter then and came into the hallway through the kitchen.

"Will you, Dad?" he asked seriously.

"Martin, enough of this bullshit. Go get your bags and we can go."

"No." Martin took a deep breath and was obviously going to follow that up with something, but his father interrupted him.

"No? What do you mean 'no'? Boy, haven't you caused enough goddamned trouble as it is? Now go get your stuff and get your ass out to the car so I can get you home to your mother. She is worried sick!"

"She didn't have no cause to be!" Martin replied, obviously upset. "I called you both, I told you where I was, I told you why I was here, and I even told you when I was coming home. You just don't want me here because you don't like the people I'm with—"

"You're damned right I don't!"

"Mr. Turner?" Both men, the older and the younger, turned toward the hallway going back to the bedroom. There was motion from the other side of the hallway. Collin, who was feeling damned superfluous by this point, turned to see Jeff, wearing high-end sweats and a long-sleeved fuzzy shirt, padding down the hall in his own moccasins.

Kevin Turner's father turned his head and widened his eyes. "Who in the hell are you?"

Jeff swallowed, and Collin would have run to him and sheltered him and shored him up, except Collin knew he didn't need it. He'd seen Jeff in action, and he knew Jeff would do just fine.

"Mr. Turner, I'm Jeff Beachum. I knew Kevin."

Chapter 24

Jeff: Living Promises

JEFF actually knew his first name—Ambrose—but it felt like this was a surname sort of situation. Kevin had loved him and feared him in equal parts, but then Kevin had been the oldest and had shouldered the responsibility of being a good example and the caretaker of the younger kids. Kevin had once told him that he might have come out in an act of adolescent rebellion—if he hadn't worried about Martin and his brothers and sisters and how hard that would make life for *them.*

And also, he had admitted that he'd miss them like hell once his parents kicked him out of the house.

So Jeff thought he was prepared for meeting Ambrose Turner, colossal size and all.

He was wrong.

The big man narrowed his eyes and said, "Who?"

Jeff swallowed. "Kevin Turner. Your son."

Ambrose Turner shook his head slowly and thrust his lower lip out. "I don't know who that is."

Jeff sucked in a breath, because it felt like he'd been gut shot. *Oh, Kevin. I know who you were. Martin remembers you. Don't worry, baby. We've got your back.*

"Dad...."

Ambrose turned toward his youngest son with a snarl. "I told you to go get your stuff!"

"He's not going until he's ready," Jeff said, and went to move between them.

"Who in the hell are you to tell me what my son is or is not going to do? You are nothing to him—"

"We're his family!" Collin snapped, moving up next to Jeff.

Jeff was so grateful he reached for Collin's hand and was reassured to feel those long fingers wrapping around his. *Thank you, Collin, for helping me carry my baggage. It's not nearly as heavy anymore.*

"*I'm* his family."

"And so are we," Jeff said firmly. "Martin came here to find out about his brother. His brother would have wanted me to take care of him, and I have. *We* have. That makes him family. Please respect that we've got his best interests at heart too."

Ambrose Turner's upper lip curled, and his fists shook at his sides. "I don't have to respect anything about you. You're the little faggot that fucked with...." He swallowed. "You made Kevin wrong. And now I don't have a son. And I'm not going to let you do that to Martin."

"Oh no, Dad!" Martin said excitedly, with the heartbreaking teenage certainty that once *he* saw the truth, the world would have to see it with him. "That's a myth. It's totally not true—I'm just as straight as I was two months ago, I swear!"

"*I said get your shit, Martin, and let's go!*" Ambrose Turner's panicked roar cut through the background chatter and rattled the tiny apartment. There was a sudden wail from Jeff's bedroom, where Parry and Lila had been playing with Collin's nieces under his mother's supervision, and the entire atmosphere went from tentative to hostile in one breath.

And that was when Deacon invaded the little space in the hall and took the hell over. "Mr. Turner, you need to step outside with me and Jeff here, and maybe Collin, Shane, and Crick too."

"I'm not—"

"You just made my niece cry, Mr. Turner. You've got to the count of three before you step outside and have this conversation, or Shane here is going to call his old partner on the force, and there's going to be a squad car here where you just scared the hell out of a room full of children. How ugly do you want this, Mr. Turner? Because you just took it from uncomfortable to scary, and that means you need to get the hell out of Jeff's home for the rest, you hear me?"

Jeff looked up and saw that Crick had put his hand on Deacon's shoulder, and Deacon covered it with his own. He was up to this—he hated to talk to people, but dammit, no one made Parry Angel cry.

"Deacon…." Martin sounded really unhappy, and Deacon turned to him and winked.

"No worries, Martin. I hate to go talk about your future without you, but I'm thinking maybe your father needs to listen to someone he's not pissed at right now, okay?"

"Dad, so help me, you lay one finger on these people and you couldn't keep me home in an iron cage, you hear me?" With that, Martin stalked back down the hallway, presumably to help calm down the girls, and his father opened the door behind him and backed out, glaring warily at Deacon, and then at Jeff, Collin, Shane, Crick, and—*Benny?*

"What are you doing here?" Jeff hissed under his breath, and Benny grinned.

"Well, he needs to know it's not all gay men, right?"

"Jon? Andrew? Guys who could hold their own?"

Benny rolled her eyes. "He's not a woman-beater, Jeff. He's not going to start throwing punches with me here. And I think Andrew would just piss him off."

"What makes you say that?"

"The fact that I had to physically restrain him when Parry started crying. Getting slugged in the face really would piss Mr. Turner off."

Jeff had to laugh a little, but then Deacon started talking, and the urge to laugh passed.

"Don't *ever* threaten my family again, Mr. Turner." Now that they were outside, Deacon was in his element. His spine was straight, and the scowl he'd leveled at Kevin Turner's father was unwavering. "We can resolve this here like adults, but don't raise your voice unless you mean it. No one speaks that way to my people."

"Who in the hell are you?" Mr. Turner sounded outraged—and also puzzled.

"Family," Deacon said evenly. "And I think you know something about it. Now Martin wants to stay, and Shane here knows more about runaway rights and CPS than you can possibly imagine, and, like I said, we can do this ugly. But I will tell you this, and I say it with everything I know in my heart. You make a scene, you throw a punch, you drag your son out of here kicking and screaming, and you will have lost him. He may end up coming back to you today, but once that kid gets out of your house, you will never see him again. You let Jeff here have him for Christmas, let them remember Kevin together, and you may get a chance to know him as a man, and maybe know your grandkids to boot. But a lot of that hinges on this thing right here. You take him out now, and he will never respect you. You give him this, and he might forgive you just a little for shitting on Kevin's memory."

Ambrose Turner looked positively dumbstruck. "Who *are* you? I don't know any of you from Adam, and now you're telling me not to threaten your *family*? I just want my son!"

Jeff took a deep breath. "We don't want to keep him from you," he said, feeling brave. God, it seemed so easy for Deacon—he stood up, he spoke from the heart, and people listened. Jeff was good at getting people's attention when he cracked a joke, wiggled his ass, and flopped his wrist—but this stuff, the important stuff... God. It seemed that the only way to get them to listen was to come unglued.

"Then what in the hell do you call this?" Ambrose waved his hands at the crowd of people standing around, glaring at him, and Jeff got frustrated enough to step forward and wave his hands.

"Family! Goddammit, aren't you listening? Kevin and I were *family*, and you can deny it all you want, but the fact was, we were everything but married!"

"Bullshit, you faggot motherfucker!" The words rang and hung there, in the frosty, damp night, and Jeff fought the temptation to roll his eyes. Like he hadn't heard *that* before.

"You can call me all the names you want, Ambrose, but that's not going to change the fact that you lost one son because he was afraid of you doing just what you're doing now, and you're about to lose another son, and eventually, even you are going to run out of children to piss off, so you may want to learn a thing or two!"

There was a terrible moment then—a dangerous moment. Ambrose Turner had never been abusive; Kevin had told him that. But every man had his limits, and it looked like that idea—the idea that he might lose his son—that was his limit. He struggled with tears for a moment; then his face twisted with anger and he took one violent step forward—and that was all it took. Suddenly there were four big men in front of Jeff looking angry, and then, to everyone's surprise, one tiny college student standing in front of them.

"Get out of my way, little girl!" He sounded angry, but he was clearly bewildered, and some of the violence seeped out of his shoulders, his expression, and the situation became just a fraction less violent.

Benny felt it—she must have. "Oh I don't think so, asshole!" she snapped. She sounded irritated, like a sister or a friend, and not like a fighter. Jeff thought he might throttle her later, but now he was grateful. Decking Jeff? A real possibility—Jeff was a man, and one who'd hurt him deeply. Decking Benny? Not Kevin's father. And Benny was capitalizing on his hesitation, without a doubt.

"These guys look all big and mean and tough," she told him conversationally, "and I'm sure they'd take you down, but I'm the one who's had to sit in hospitals or be on the phone about hospitals or worry about hospitals for all of them, and I'm not going to do it!"

"Benny...." Deacon said, obviously trying not to let any humor seep into his voice.

"Don't you patronize me, Deacon Winters!" Benny snapped, turning around to him and glaring at him with her hands on her hips. "I'm done, do you hear me? I'm fucking done. You come out here and posture all you want, but a single one of you gets hurt or loses a nostril hair or catches a cold—that's you, Collin, you *asshole*, did you even bother to put on a coat?—and I will end you. I will quit cooking for a month, or... or send Parry Angel to boarding school in Japan... or... I don't know, go down to Georgia to meet Drew's folks and not come back. Are you listening to me? Any of you? Because right now, the only one here *not* on my let's-scare-Benny-pissless shitlist is *Jeff*, but we've all been worried about him since we met him, so he doesn't count!"

Benny whirled back to Ambrose, and all of the other men, Jeff included, shifted restlessly and met sheepish eyes. It occurred to Jeff, and probably to everyone there, that maybe they might have wanted to bring Andrew, Jon, Mikhail, and Lucas after all. Hell, even old Joshua would have been a better bet than Deacon and Collin at this point, not that either of them would have admitted it.

"And you, Mr. Turner," Benny resumed, "you should be ashamed of yourself. Your son is *proud* of his family—why in the hell do you think he's here? He's proud of Kevin, and he wants to make sure Kevin's memory is done right, and you're here shaming him in front of Kevin's family!"

"I *was* Kevin's family!"

Benny took a step back—they all did—but they didn't retaliate. They couldn't. How could you retaliate when someone that angry let that much pain slip through? Jeff pushed his way through his honor guard, letting his hand linger on Collin's hip as he went, and then stood next to Benny, holding her hand.

"Thanks, sweetheart," he whispered in her ear, and she wrapped her arm around his waist and shivered. None of them had bothered to put on jackets, and Jeff figured he was about half a minute from shooing Collin and Deacon back into the apartment on general principle.

"Mr. Turner?" he asked quietly, when the silence of letting the big man pull himself together had gone on long enough. "Mr. Turner, we all really love Martin. We don't want to keep him from you, I swear. We just want to borrow him from you for a little while, and he wants to stay here and see what kind of person his brother was when he could be himself."

"I was his *family*!" Ambrose Turner whispered, looking at Jeff with an agonized plea for understanding, and Jeff nodded and hoped that maybe, at last, they had some common ground.

"So was I," he said softly.

"How in the hell can you even *say* that?" The words were angry, but the volume, at least, had softened.

Jeff looked around and shrugged. "Don't you see? That's why there was a letter for me at all." And God. Just saying that out loud put paid to a lot of pain, didn't it? "Because I was someone Kevin wanted to say goodbye to. I was someone he would have trusted Martin to—that's what that letter meant to me, do you understand? And this here, and all those people in the apartment—they are *my* family. You want to know how we all fit together, that's fine. Come inside, have some dinner, and meet everybody."

He dropped his voice because he wanted this next part to be sincere. "We'll be civil to you, I swear. But when you've met and talked to everyone, and you know that we're mothers and sons and fathers and brothers and we're not all degenerate and we *don't* all want to convert Martin for our evil purposes and share the gay, I *really* hope you let him stay. Please? Kevin always said you were tough but fair. You've got to know I haven't seen any of the fair yet. Please don't make a liar out of him."

There was a weighted silence, and Kevin's father stood up and glowered at them all—but he was moved, Jeff could tell. Jeff took the attention off of him for a moment by saying firmly, "Deacon and Collin, get your skinny asses inside. Neither of you are in a position to stand out here in the cold, do you hear me? Benny—do your thing, sweetheart. I'm behind you!"

Collin looked at him with a little bit of hurt. "Jeff...."

Jeff's stern expression softened. "Go inside, baby. Don't make me worry about you, okay, Sir Galahad? Shane and Crick'll take care of me, right? I mean *look* at them. Shane's like the Terminator—he'll take a beating and just keep coming back."

"And what does that make me?" Crick asked, a little offended.

"Too gay to hit with a clear conscience," Jeff said dryly, and Crick returned with an outraged, "*I fought in the war, dammit!*"

Deacon was the one who turned around and said, "You were wounded in the war, Crick—you're the one who told me that the fighting thing was sort of an overstatement."

"Get your ass inside, geezer," Crick snapped, and Deacon looked over at Kevin's father and made sure they had eye contact.

"Mr. Turner," he said levelly, indicating respect—and a solid stand. He waited for a minute, until Kevin's father caught his eyes and nodded. Then he did what Crick and Benny had asked and went inside with Collin, and Jeff loved them both more for it.

After that, there were fewer of them, and Kevin's father, and a whole lot of bewilderment.

Ambrose Turner looked at them and swallowed, wiped his cheek on the inside of his sweatshirt, and swallowed again. "You were in the war?" he asked out of nowhere.

Crick shrugged, held up his twisted hand. "Medic," he said briefly. "That's where I met Drew—he's inside, and from Georgia too."

Ambrose chuffed out a breath. "Who's Drew?"

"The only other black man in the room besides your son," Crick said dryly. "Benny and Drew, they've sort of got... an understanding. He's definitely family."

Well, good, Jeff thought. Maybe that would put paid to the race thing—or at least not make it quite the elephant that it could be. More like a water buffalo, maybe?

Ambrose nodded, as though conceding the same thing, then looked at Jeff. "That kid," he said after another thoughtful, awkward minute, "the one you called Sir Galahad?"

Jeff tried not to stiffen. "Yeah?"

"Isn't he a little young for you?"

Jeff fought against a giggle, turned it into a chuckle, and then set it free. "Yeah, yeah he is. But so was Kevin. That didn't stop either of them from being bossy little shits, you know?"

Ambrose gave a frustrated sigh. "Do I know about bossy little shits? I'm out here because Martin refuses to take orders—what in the hell do you think?"

Jeff swallowed. "I think you'd be surprised at how mature Martin's become these last months." Good. They were talking about Martin now—right where the conversation needed to be. "He practically kept Collin's garage running for the last two weeks when Collin was sick." That was somewhat of an overstatement—Joshua had done most of it, with a lot of help from Shane, but Martin had been there, too, and it seemed like a stellar conversational gambit. It must have worked, too, because Ambrose perked up a little.

"He has? Well... I *would* like to hear about that."

Jeff heard Shane and Crick both give little sighs next to him, and he felt some of the steel seep out of his spine as well. "Come inside, Mr. Turner. Have some dinner. You've been on a plane most of the day—sit down on my couch and meet some nice people. The apartment's crowded to the gills with folks who would like to tell you about Martin. Won't you please come and listen?"

Ambrose Turner grunted and shrugged—and then let Jeff lead the way. As soon as they cleared the door, Martin greeted his father with a hug, a fierce one, that was returned quietly, and in kind.

Then Martin took his father's hand and said, "Come on in, Pops—meet everyone. I'll get you a plate of food. They're really nice here, I swear."

THEY didn't all hold hands and sing Kumbaya by the end of the night. Ambrose Turner didn't suddenly become a card-carrying, rainbow-flag-waving member of PFLAG. Jeff didn't sit down and find a replacement father figure for the man who had been trying to contact him from Coloma for the past three weeks. In fact, Ambrose spent most of his time talking to Lucas and Kimmy, or Andrew and Benny, then Jon and Amy, and finally, Joshua, Natalie, and Collin's oldest sister, Joanna: in short, anyone who wasn't gay by any way, shape, form, or stretch of the imagination, and who couldn't push the comfort zone of a Baptist virgin, much less a happily married father of five.

He must have bitten off the words "faggot," "queer," or "homo" eight to twelve times a piece. It would be *years*, if *ever*, before he and Jeff had the same kind of talk about Kevin that Jeff and Martin managed.

He almost choked on his tongue when he walked around a corner and found Shane dropping a kiss in Mikhail's hair after Mikhail made sure that Shane wasn't involved in a fight. He almost choked on it again when he caught Collin whispering in Jeff's ear. He didn't catch Deacon or Crick, because they were so good at holding themselves like cowboys that they managed not to scandalize anyone in public, but when Jon and Amy started talking about the two weddings at Promise Rock, he had to excuse himself. The little girls found him a few minutes later, hiding in the bathroom and petting the cats and sneezing up a storm.

But he didn't yell at anyone to stop it. And he didn't grab Martin by the arm and haul him out. And he did listen to the stories about Martin learning a trade. And he did actually *hear* that his son had been helpful and kind during a time of great trouble.

And he did show approval as Martin talked excitedly about horses, and cars, and the people at Promise House, and why he was grateful for his family.

And he looked quietly, without anger, at the picture of Jeff and his dead son, looking very, very happy for maybe the last time in Kevin's life.

And in the end he did shake Jeff's hand as he left and thank him for the dinner.

And in the end, he did let Martin stay for Christmas.

It was more than Jeff had hoped for, but not too much to ask.

CHRISTMAS was simply lovely. The family was healthy. There was food and gifts, and even hidden chances for Collin and Jeff to sneak off and have bang-out monkey sex a couple of times. The best part of that was that they always managed to turn it into making love instead.

Two nights before Christmas, Martin, Collin, and Jeff sat around Jeff's kitchen table and wrapped gifts for all of their family, including the Doc and Mrs. Herberts, who were thrilled to meet Martin the next day, and talked.

They talked about Christmases past and the wonderful things their parents had done to please them as children. They talked about favorite gifts and things they had wanted more than anything in the world but didn't seem as important now as the fact that someone loved them enough to give them that gift on Christmas morning.

They talked about Kevin.

Martin talked about how his older brother used to take his own money and buy each of his brothers and sisters something that he knew they wanted, but that his parents disapproved of. When Martin was nine, Kevin bought them all their first video game system—it was the last Christmas gift Kevin ever sent.

"I think," Martin said quietly, dangling a piece of fancy ribbon for Katy to bat at, "that he was trying to tell us that maybe what my folks approved of wasn't everything in the world, you know?"

Jeff smiled a little. He should have guessed about the secret subversive in Kevin. The fact that the man hit on Jeff while pretending to "teach him a lesson" should have made *that* obvious enough. So in turn, he told about how they first met, and Collin chortled (and admired Kevin's move), and Martin laughed until he dropped Katy's ribbon (she was ignoring it anyway) and put his head in his arms and just let it go.

When he was done laughing, he sat up and wiped a little at his eyes and said, "What happened when he came back?"

Jeff blushed. "Oh, kid, I don't think you'll *ever* be comfortable enough to hear that part of it, you think?"

"I thought you walked around and talked for a while," Collin said thoughtfully, and Jeff blushed even further.

"Well, yeah. But the night still ended up in my apartment!" Martin made a "woot!" sound, and Jeff grinned, still blushing, and said, "Thank you. I'm glad you approve."

Martin looked embarrassed. "I do," he mumbled, picking up his next gift from the pile. "I approve of all the good you could give him, right? Is there any more of Margie's fudge left—hey! Get off of me!"

"It's a hug, kid—no strings attached."

Martin returned it, briefly, because he was fourteen, and then stood up, rolled his eyes, and went looking for the last of the soy-fudge.

Collin reached around the table and grabbed Jeff's hand and kissed it, and Jeff moved into him and bent down and kissed *him*.

"What's that for?" Collin asked, his lean mouth quirked up a little at the sides and his brown eyes soft.

"A different sort of approval."

Collin's grin was blinding. "So I made the grade?"

"Every damned day. Twice on Christmas."

"Excellent. I worked hard on that!"

"I hope I was worth the effort," Jeff said soberly, and Collin planted his big, wide-palmed hand on the back of Jeff's head and pulled him in for a kiss.

THE day after Christmas they put Martin on a plane with hugs and a few tears and an admonition to text and e-mail often (which he did, after New Year's) and a promise to fly him out during the summer, with his parents' permission, so he could intern for Collin because he loved it.

Lucas stayed in Levee Oaks, which was nice, because when Jeff, Crick, Mikhail, and Kimmy met to knit the next day, Jeff and Kimmy no longer got to sound like the dried-up old spinsters that they had been two months earlier, and Kimmy's smiles were just a little bit softer as well.

The day after that, Jeff and Collin went up to Coloma to visit Jeff's mother for Christmas. She didn't remember Collin, but enjoyed her See's candy and hand-knit socks very, very much. Jeff's father was in the room and, much like Ambrose, managed to keep his mean-assed opinions to himself. Jeff caught up on the Porters and the Masons and the Beachums and told his father to give them all his regards. His father learned for the first time that his son had HIV. He looked really, really sad when he heard that, and he put his hand on Jeff's shoulder for just a moment as Jeff talked to his mother about the fact that he was doing fine. Jeff allowed the touch, acknowledged it with a pat of his hand, and then kissed his mother's cheek goodbye. Then he turned, shook Archie Beachum's hand, and left.

Much like Martin's father, it wasn't holding hands and singing Kumbaya, but it was seeing his mother once a month and maybe making it to dinner with his father next time, and it was a start.

Collin held his hand on the way out, and when they got to that fabulously gaudy, big-dick Camaro in the sedate old-people's parking lot, he turned Jeff around and hauled him in for a hug that made Jeff yearn.

"Oh, God, it's an hour and a half back down the hill," Jeff groaned, resting his forehead against Collin's and panting.

"Yeah, Jeffy, but you know what, right?"

Jeff pointed his chin sideways and smiled shyly up at Collin from under his eyelashes. "We have the apartment to ourselves?"

Collin's grin was diabolical. "I'm going to have so much fun making you scream."

They both had fun—and Jeff *did* scream. And then they kissed, naked, alone and together, and Jeff thought that family was nice, but *this* sort of family was even better.

"God, Sparky, I'm glad you didn't quit," he said when he pulled up for air.

"God, Jeff, I'm glad you gave me a chance," Collin echoed, rolling his eyes a little while he twined his naked, hairy legs with Jeff's.

"So, when are you moving in?" Jeff asked casually, like his heart wasn't in his mouth. It wasn't as though Collin had been back to his apartment more than a handful of times since he'd recovered, but this was more than that, and by Collin's slow, leonine blink, he knew it.

"When we find a place together in Levee Oaks," Collin responded after a short pause.

Jeff looked around. "You don't like the condo? It's got a pool and a weight room!"

"We can afford our own pool, Jeff, and our own weight room, and another bedroom so we can have three cats, maybe, or even a dog, and enough space between us and the neighbors that I can *really* make you scream."

Jeff blushed, felt his cock swell where it was trapped between his groin and Collin's lean hip. "You think I'm holding back for the neighbors?"

Collin's grin was evil. "I'd sure like to find out."

"So, a house?"

"Yeah."

"In Levee Oaks, the anti-gay capitol of the Northern California bible belt."

"Yeah." Collin smirked but held firm.

"That's quite a promise."

"Hey—I loved you through the flu, baby. You owe me."

"Isn't that the other way around?" Not that Collin had been a bad patient, ever, but still.

"I was delirious—I could have confused you with David Beckham—you ever think of that?"

"Oh shut up." Jeff half-laughed his way through his anxiety. "Yeah, well, maybe living is our biggest promise anyway. Sure, let's find a house. It'll be fun. Con and Katy won't know what to do with themselves. We may have to get another cat just to give them something to whomp on."

"Yeah?" Collin said, his entire body vibrating with excitement. "You know, for gay people in California, buying a house is like a wedding ceremony, right?"

Jeff rolled his eyes. "Sparky, you think *that's* a wedding ceremony, then what Shane and Mikhail are doing in February is *really* going to float your boat."

"Yeah? What's happening in February?"

Jeff just laughed and kissed him, because he was dear and perfect, and they were buying a house together, and planning for February would come soon enough.

THE gods must have been smiling on Shane and Mikhail that day, because after pissing down rain for a week, there was actually sunshine the day before and the day of their sweet little wedding ceremony out on Promise Rock.

It had been nearly a year since Jeff had been to Promise Rock, and there had been some changes made in that time since Shane had taken over the adjoining property to Deacon's for Promise House. The first thing Shane had done was clear out all of the overgrowth and make sure the snake population was managed. Unlike Deacon, who had favored potbellied pigs as a first defense and a shotgun as a last resort, Shane had simply had a local wildlife society come and get them all. (He had no idea what they did with them, as long as it was legal, humane, and Mikhail didn't have to see a single scale, rattle, or flickering tongue.)

The other thing he'd done was have the service road that Deacon used as a kid all scraped and graveled. When guests came to Shane and Mikhail's wedding, they drove down a nice, maintained gravel road instead of a ruthless piercer of tires and gobbler of axles, and Jeff told Collin that this alone was a great improvement.

The guests parked on Shane's side of the little swimming hole and walked through a cattle gate, now propped open, and across a rise before venturing down to the little corner of the world that used to belong to Deacon and his father alone.

Kimmy was there to greet them, her lithe dancer's body sheathed in a long, ruby-red dress with a white wool coat and her long, brown-blonde hair recently streaked and hanging down her shoulders and back in big, full spirals. Lucas was with her, wearing a dark wool suit with a crimson tie to match the woman he so obviously adored.

Jeff greeted her by taking both hands in his and kissing her cheek, because she was lovely, and because the occasion called for it.

"How you doin', heifer? You look scrumptious."

Kimmy gave him a watery smile. "I'm fine," she said, her voice a little throatier than usual. "Aw, fuck. I'm going to be a mess when Jon's talking. Shane's just worked so hard, you know? He so totally deserves this, and so does Mickey—"

"You get to call him Mickey?" Collin asked from behind Jeff's shoulder.

"Sister-in-law privileges," Kimmy said seriously. "I asked. Wow, Collin, you clean up pretty!"

Jeff had helped Collin pick out his brown pinstriped suit. It had wide lapels and a tawny gold tie, and the kid looked sharp as hell. Jeff had gone with classic black, because the two of them didn't do the twin thing, but that didn't stop them from holding hands as they were escorted down the rise and over the narrow part of the feeder stream that had been converted to irrigation farther away from the levee.

The curve of the stream formed a wide, deep spot that had been used as a swimming hole for years. At the edge of the swimming hole, forming a sort of hollow, was a big granite boulder surrounded by its smaller brothers, interspersed with a stand of oak trees. In the summer, the hollow was nice because the shade by the stream was about fifteen degrees cooler than the surrounding grasslands, which were usually scorched and brown starting around May.

In the winter, the grasses were green and had been freshly cut, both on The Pulpit side and the Promise House side. It would have been unbearably cold, except Deacon had thought to rent some gas-powered heaters—the tall kind that looked like lamps—to stand in a semi-circle around the biggest boulder.

Jeff understood that this was the third wedding that had taken place at Promise Rock, and that near the boulder was where people stood.

"They decorated," Jeff said with a smile.

He had been to the second wedding that had been held there, and it had been lovely. When Deacon and Crick had been married—much to Deacon's surprise—the family had stood around the couple in a loose circle while the newly ordained Jon-the-Unitarian-minister had conducted the ceremony. Shane and Mikhail had modeled their wedding after that one a little, with some added touches that were exclusively them.

Besides the standing heaters, which were very appreciated in the shade, where the ground was still frosty even at one in the afternoon, there were red-and-white standing bouquets and big, red, indoor/outdoor carpet spread on the ground. The fold-up chairs by the document signing tables were the same, but the rich white-and-red flowers were there too. (So was a random assortment of blankets, neatly folded, that Jeff was pretty sure the guests would appreciate after the ceremony.) The kids from Promise House stood attentively at the documents and a guest book, most of them armed with disposable cameras as well. Shane had obviously bought them new clothes—and given them duties. They looked pleased and proud and very conscious of their dignity, and Jeff loved the big man all over again for giving kids like Martin a chance to be kind and good and proud.

Propped up on one of the tables, near the blankets, was a picture of an arresting-looking woman holding a surly-looking teenage boy by the hand. Mikhail's mother, Jeff thought sadly, and her son, not long after they'd arrived in the country. Well, it was fitting—she had died last year around this time. Instead of remembering her in grief, they were remembering her by giving her the one thing she'd always wanted: a secure future and a loving home for her son.

There was music, powered by a generator in the back of a pick-up truck that had been driven to the other side of the stream, a rather eclectic mix of old and new rock and roll.

"I like this song," Collin murmured, as Bruce Springsteen's "Gypsy Biker" played in the background. "But it doesn't sound like ballet music," he added thoughtfully, and Jeff smirked.

"It's Shane's music," Jeff said with certainty, and Kimmy took his arm and smiled.

"Mine too. And Lucas too—we're all fans."

"What kind of music does Mikhail like?" Collin asked curiously.

"All kinds," Mikhail said, coming along side of them. "But today is not a day for me and my ballet. Today is a day so everyone can see my perfect cop and know I make him happy."

"I never doubted it," Jeff said sincerely, and Mikhail rolled his eyes.

"Well, I did. And that is why we have this day, so everyone knows that I doubt it no longer. And as for the paperwork?" Mikhail's shrug was one-hundred-percent Russian peasant. "That is for the government people. Fuck them. It is no matter to me if they think we are married. As long as our friends know."

With that, Mikhail trotted off, looking to greet other guests, and Kimmy gave an exasperated smile after him.

"That really stuck in his craw, didn't it?" Lucas asked with a quiet smile.

"The whole 'California marriage' thing?" Kimmy said with a shrug. "Well, yeah—but pretty much mostly for Shane's sake. He's got this whole idea about government and the police force and how Shane's not getting his just due." Kimmy grimaced at her brother-in-law fondly. "So, per usual, it's all about Shane. God, I can live with someone making his life all about Shane."

"How about all about you?" Lucas asked slyly, and Kimmy's blush was lovely to see.

"Lucas, you make your life all about her, and I personally will cook you dinner once a month."

"Yeah!" Collin said at his side. "Family game night. I miss it. You guys on for that again?"

"Yeah, Sparky," Kimmy said, taking them down to the little circle of friends that was exactly like Deacon and Crick's, only a little larger. "But first we have a wedding to go to."

"Did you just let her call me 'Sparky'?" Collin asked with a little bit of indignation, and Jeff laughed.

"Sister-in-law privileges: she has 'em."

"Fine—but I'm inviting Joanna and her husband to the next game night. She'll clean you out."

"In what game?"

"Doesn't matter. Joanna pretty much kicks whatever ass she wants."

"I'm going to kick *both* your asses if you don't quiet down! Jon's here!"

Jon had presided at Deacon and Crick's wedding in his one suit, and he wore that same suit now. His streaky blond hair had just been cut and styled, and his wife was standing next to him on her tiptoes, adjusting his blood-red tie. Amy was dressed like Kimmy and Benny, in a long red sheathe dress with a white coat. Benny stood across from Collin and Jeff in the loose circle, holding her daughter by one hand and Drew's arm with the other. Jeff had a moment to snort at the ways of women, and then Amy stepped away and walked to the edge of the circle, where Shane and Mikhail were waiting patiently for Jon to be ready. With an impish smile, Amy grabbed both of the men by hand and dragged them to where her husband stood.

"Nice going, hon. We don't know which one of them would have bolted."

"Neither of them," Amy replied sweetly. "I just wanted to see how nervous they were."

"How nervous are they?" Crick asked from behind Deacon. He was tall enough to peer around his beloved's shoulder while keeping his arms wrapped around Deacon's shoulders protectively.

"Not nearly as nervous as you were, Crick," Amy replied smartly, holding up what were obviously dry hands, and Deacon responded with a smile.

"He was only nervous because he snuck up and married me when I wasn't looking. I don't think that's a problem here, is it, Shane?"

"No, sir," Shane said calmly. His usually riotous, brown, curly hair was cut nicely and styled so it stayed put—and Jeff was glad, because he was the one who'd referred Shane to a stylist to make sure he looked his best.

"How're you doing, Mikhail?" Deacon asked, and the little man bounced on his toes.

"*I* am doing fine, Deacon," Mikhail said with determination. "However, we only have three hours before these heaters quit and I freeze my tiny little ass off, so I suggest we start."

"Why does he get to be called 'Deacon'?" Collin asked softly to Jeff, but it was Kimmy who replied, "Because Deacon is Deacon, Sparky, now hush!"

"You heard them, Jon," Deacon said with a smile. "Get your ass in gear!"

Jon executed a full bow in Deacon's direction, and abruptly all the side chatter—like Collin's question to Jeff—stopped.

"We all know Shane and Mikhail," Jon said with a smile, "and most of us are familiar with traditional wedding vows. But Shane and Mikhail already love and honor each other, and both of them have left the idea of obeying right out of their dictionaries, and so we're left with the only tradition that I'm comfortable with at weddings, and that's the tradition of Promise Rock.

"Now, I'm not sure if even Carrick James knows this, but when I was five years old I thought I was the loneliest kid on the planet. I was crying in the bathroom—you know, little kids' bathrooms with the toilets that barely touch your ankles? And this boy who hadn't spoken in two weeks of Kindergarten comes up to me, and he tells me that if I stop crying, his dad will take us to Promise Rock. Now, I had no idea what Promise Rock was, and those may have been the last words Deacon spoke in public school for at least four more years, but that weekend Deacon's father brought the two of us right here and played with us for hours.

"It was my best day ever, right up until Parrish brought us again. And again. And then Deacon and I came out here, and then Deacon and Amy and Crick. And this place we're standing in has come to mean something huge—a lot bigger than it probably looks to those of you who are new.

"This place, Promise Rock, is where you get to go if you keep your promises to the people who love you. It's a reward for trusting another soul enough that you let them make you happy. It's this family's place, our private place, where we go to tell the world, and God if he's listening, that we are family because we choose to be. It's where we make the things in our heart real.

"My wife and I were married here, and I had the privilege of performing the ceremony for the brother of my heart to the man he's always loved, right here."

Jon paused a little, swallowing hard and blinking at Deacon, who gave his best friend, the brother of his heart, a crooked grin. Jon nodded, like he could keep going now that Deacon had seen that this place was the family's holy place, and that Deacon had made it so.

"So being married here, that means you're our family. That means we're not letting you go, because you can't have too much family. And I can't think of two better people to stand here and announce their intentions to be family than Shane and Mikhail. This place is not about what the rest of the world thinks—which is good, guys, because I've got to tell you, the rest of the world would *not* get you at all."

There was laughter then, and Shane's smile grew wider, if that was possible, and Mikhail's look up at his lover was all adoration. Mikhail got Shane, and that was all that mattered—it was so simple and so obvious, and Jeff felt a hand at the lapel of his dark wool suit with the nipped in waist, and suddenly the red linen kerchief that he'd put in his pocket for looks was held up to his face, and he took it from Collin gratefully.

God, he was such a queen—but just look at them. Who cared if he was crying? The whole world should cry at their wedding—it should be a law.

"But we get them," Jon said seriously. "We get that their life is all about making promises to listen and to understand. It's all about kindness, especially when it's unexpected, and it's about loyalty, which is always, always deserved. It's about hearts that are lost without each other, and about never letting go when they're found. It's about the unlikeliest of people fitting each other like lock and key.

"That's you two. You two together—you're everything that love should be. And I'm madly in love with my wife, and I should know." More laughter, which was good, because Jeff wasn't sure if there was a dry eye in the house. He looked sideways and saw Collin frowning fiercely and swallowing hard. After handing Jeff his handkerchief, he'd locked his hand with Jeff's at their sides and was currently strangling it with the effort not to join the crowd.

Forget it, Sparky. Wait until you watch our little diva bitch come completely unglued. We're doomed. It's three days before Valentine's Day—give it up, baby, we're a whole family of sobbing queens.

"So now it's your turn to talk—make your promises here on Promise Rock. Family like you is exactly what this place is for."

They spoke then, the little Russian dancer and the big, good-willed cop, and although their words played and twined like ribbons at a Maypole, they never stopped looking at each other with their souls in their eyes. They were about as pure and purely in love as Jeff had ever seen two people in his life, maybe even purer than he was, when he was with Kevin, because they'd lived for each other when the rest of the world had tried to kill them off. (In Shane's case, multiple times, and Mikhail had endured some near-misses as a lost teenager himself.)

Jeff wouldn't compare, though—not anymore. He had loved and lost, and wonder of all wonders, he'd lived. And he'd keep living, not because he had to, not because of memories, but because he had a family who loved him, and a lover who was family.

He listened as Shane said something about Mikhail being with him as long as he drew breath, and Mikhail said, "You had better keep breathing, you big, stupid cop, because my life is now so tangled with yours that there is no separating them. You carry my heart in your chest wherever you go—just make sure it is not ever too far from my side."

That right there was where Collin lost it, and the entire clearing could hear the big shudder of breath he pulled in through quivering lips and the shaky exhale. Jeff wrapped an arm around his waist then, relieved to feel Collin's steel strong grip over his shoulders.

"Scared, yet, Sparky?" he whispered.

Collin shook his head and ignored the tears caught in his brown lashes. "Happy," he whispered back. "Now I know what to say when it's our turn."

Jeff caught his breath then and tilted his head a little, so it touched Collin's shoulder. They had found a house—they hadn't had time to move in, but they'd joined their finances and the bid was in escrow, and it was going to be all official in no time at all.

But there, right there, in this holy place of promises, Jeff had felt it. He'd felt the rightness of living with his lover in front of God and everyone, and he felt all of the promise the future could bring.

Mikhail stopped talking then, and the two men kissed sweetly, a slanting bit of sunshine carving through the oak trees to bless them both with gold.

Their gathered family stopped sniffling long enough to applaud, and then Jeff felt himself drawn roughly into Collin's arms, and a tender kiss of his very own was his to return.

They pulled back, both tasting salt, and Jeff said, "Ours will be in the fall."

Collin nodded. "Right here, right?"

"Absolutely."

"Good. Good. We'll make promises. Like, I promise I don't need to wait until then to love you."

Jeff nodded. "You'd better keep that promise, baby." He sniffled and used his handkerchief. "It's what I live for."

They pulled apart then to go congratulate their friends and to celebrate. Days like this one on Promise Rock were what made living sweet and being in love sweeter, and they were both old enough and wise enough to never, ever take that for granted.

And as long as they were hand in hand, they never would.

AMY LANE is a mother of four and a compulsive knitter who writes because she can't silence the voices in her head. She adores cats, knitting socks, and hawt menz, and she dislikes moths, cat boxes, and knuckle-headed macspazzmatrons. She is rarely found cooking, cleaning, or doing domestic chores, but she has been known to knit up an emergency hat/blanket/pair of socks for any occasion whatsoever or sometimes for no reason at all. She writes in the shower, while commuting, while taxiing children to soccer/dance/karate/oh my! and has learned from necessity to type like the wind. She lives in a spider-infested, crumbling house in a shoddy suburb and counts on her beloved Mate, Mack, to keep her tethered to reality—which he does while keeping her cell phone charged as a bonus. She's been married for twenty-plus years and still believes in Twu Wuv, with a capital Twu and a capital Wuv, and she doesn't see any reason at all for that to change.

Visit Amy's web site at http://www.greenshill.com. You can e-mail her at amylane@greenshill.com.

Also by AMY LANE

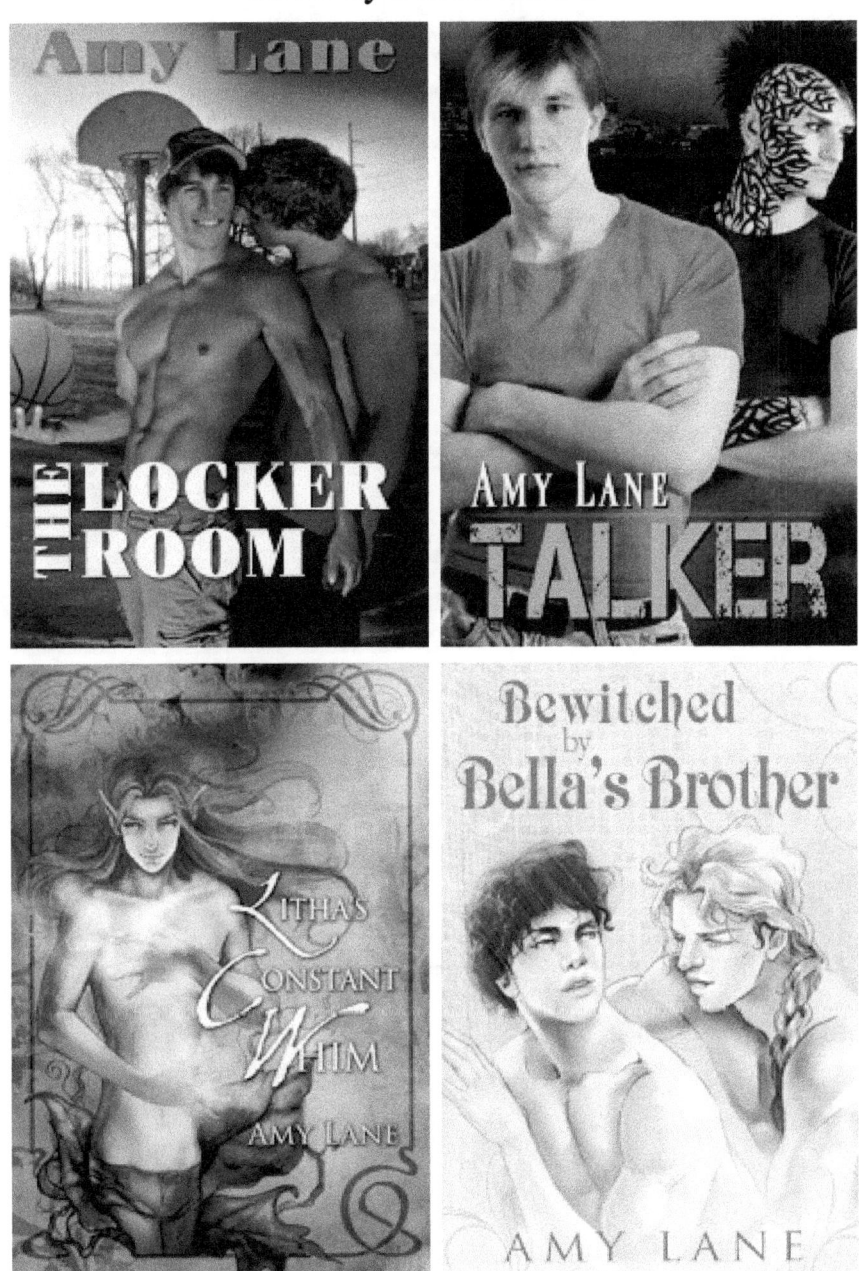